BUILDING VICTORIA

M. D. Cooper

Cover Art by Tom Edwards

ISBN-13: 978-1533367136
ISBN-10: 1533367132

DEDICATION

This one is for the fans. Thanks for the emails, messages, and encouragement.

ACKNOWLEDGEMENTS

As always, I owe my faithful beta readers (especially Jill) for their thoughtful comments and great ideas.

I also would like to thank Anglada-Escudé et al for taking a long look at Kapteyn's Star and finding two super earths there. The story was better for your discovery.

Lastly, thanks to Kapteyn's Star; your peculiar point of light in the sky that will pass us by, likely never to be seen again.

THE WORLD OF AEON 14

For the seasoned science fiction reader, there will be little here which they have not seen in another story, be it planetary rings, nano technology, AI, or mind-to-mind communication.

However, for those who may not know what a HUD is, understand the properties of deuterium, or be able to name the stars within the Sirius system, I encourage you to reference the appendices as you read.

You may also visit www.aeon14.com to read the primer, glossary, and timelines there.

PROLOGUE: SILENCE BETWEEN THE STARS

STELLAR DATE: 3243433 / 02.13.4168 (Adjusted Gregorian)
LOCATION: *ISS Intrepid*
REGION: Interstellar space, near Estrella de la Muerte

It was dark again.

The ship coasted through the void, the relative warmth and light of LHS 1565 long behind it. Ahead, the dim, red disk of Kapteyn's Star was barely visible.

Bob monitored the thickness of the interstellar medium, keeping watch against dense pockets of plasma and molecular clouds. With the scoop barely operable, the ship was all but naked as it drifted through space.

Though it was only moving seventeen-thousand kilometers per-second, a cluster of atoms, or stray plasma could do significant damage.

As if to emphasis his thoughts, sensors registered a hit on the dorsal arch, and he detected silicate residue in the meter-wide dent on the hull.

If an AI could worry, Bob worried.

He re-ran fuel consumption simulations, looking for any energy savings he could manage to increase power to the scoop and shields. He decided on which sacrifices to make and shut down more sections of the ship until only the habitation cylinders were lit and warm.

Bots herded animals from the ship's other parks to the cylinders, where they were introduced to the ecosystem in the least destructive ways Bob could manage.

He knew the humans would appreciate the effort to save their plants and animals—though the sentiment was largely lost on him.

Other parts of his mind continued to focus on the internal component analysis he was performing.

Bob watched the ship through every sensor he possessed; checking and cross-checking every piece of data gathered, testing it for accuracy and corruption every way he knew how.

The humans blamed themselves for the calamity in the LHS 1565 system—or Estrella de la Muerte, as his avatars had named it. However, he found more fault in himself. He was faster, smarter, and more powerful than a million of them; yet he failed to detect the sabotage done to the ship.

It was an event which would not repeat. He and Earnest worked long and hard to discern a method for detecting any sabotage and component corruption. There would be no further modification of his body.

The knowledge didn't stop the recrimination to which he subjected himself.

It also didn't stop him from perseverating over new ways the mission could be jeopardized. There was still the issue of Jessica Keller, and how she had made it onto the ship. If she was here, he had to plan for the presence of Myrrdan—or anyone else in known space, for that matter.

Even he could not discern why Myrrdan was so successful—if that word could apply. Analysis of his mass murders, acts of terrorism, and ability to evade all attempts to catch him showed he was highly augmented—easily four times more mentally enhanced than a class 2 human.

That level of augmentation shouldn't be possible without noticeable physical alterations, but either Myrrdan was the greatest charlatan of all time, or he was as smart as the data suggested.

If Myrrdan was on the *Intrepid,* it was to acquire picotech, the atomic-size technology which would elevate the New Eden colony to the center of human commerce and power.

Though, if stealing the picotech were his endgame, his methodology was questionable. Why let the ship leave the Sol system at all? More importantly, why point it at a star and sabotage its drive systems?

Bob had far too many questions, for which there were no answers.

To reduce variables, he'd insisted that all humans go into stasis. It made his primary task of physically inspecting, and reprogramming every piece of hardware on the ship much simpler.

There was one human he would permit to wake, in fact, he required her to wake.

Tanis Richards was nearly as large an enigma as the possible presence of Myrrdan on the ship. Granted, an enigma that mostly worked in his favor.

She nearly made Bob believe in the luck experiments.

From time to time strange notions came about in the human sphere. One of them was breeding for luck. Initially proposed several thousand years earlier, the premise was that certain humans had exceptionally lucky events happen in their lives: events such as winning the lottery twice, or evading death multiple times. These humans were bred together in an attempt to produce offspring more prone to luck.

No measurable results were ever observed.

Tanis seemed to defy reality with her luck. Bob had checked her lineage, to see if she was the result of any luck experiments, but had been unable to find a link. Still, she survived when she should not, and had done things that she should not have been able to do—things like Linking with the fighters in battle, as the *Intrepid* exited the Sol system.

Bob knew others had run the math, and had all come to the same conclusion he had—the outcome of her actions had been impossible.

Whether or not she did have luck, things often went better with her around—she had saved his life more than once. Bob intended to have Tanis out of stasis as much as possible, to make use of whatever special rift in space-time and probability her presence created.

He decided that this was as good a time as any to wake her. Maybe he would be able to gather more insight into what made her tick.

RUDE AWAKENING

STELLAR DATE: 3243433 / 02.13.4168 (Adjusted Gregorian)
LOCATION: *ISS Intrepid*
REGION: Interstellar space, near Estrella de la Muerte

"So you're just going to wake me randomly?" Tanis asked, unable to hide the annoyance in her voice. "How often do you intend to do this?"

<*I don't know, it'll be random,*> Bob replied.

Tanis let out a long sigh. "You know that's not an answer. You must have some idea how often it will be, and how long you expect me to stay up. I do intend to actually see New Eden you know…preferably before I'm falling apart from too many re-juvs."

<*Perhaps a few dozen times, given the length of our journey. For no more than a month at a time.*>

"A month! Alone on the ship!" Tanis surprised herself with the strength of her own outburst. "I'll go insane! I need some sort of companionship."

<*I feel obligated to make some sort of comment at this point,*> Angela's droll tone joined the conversation.

Tanis rubbed her eyes and sat on the edge of the stasis pod. "I'm sorry Ang…I don't mean to be rude, but I think you know what I mean—I'm no social butterfly, but even I need some human interaction."

<*The captain suspected you may feel this way,*> Bob said. <*He authorized me to bring Joseph out of stasis as well, if you really desire it.*>

Tanis rose up from the edge of the stasis pod. "You're damn right I desire it. Let's go get him up." She was in the passageway before the words left her mouth.

<*You may have wanted to grab a shipsuit,*> Angela chuckled, as Tanis raced through the freezing corridors in nothing but her thin stasis suit.

"Why is it so cold?" Tanis asked through clenched teeth.

<*I'm saving power,*> Bob replied. <*I was about to advise you to change, but then it was too late.*>

The chamber where Joe lay in stasis wasn't far. Critical personnel couldn't occupy the same chamber, but Tanis made certain he was close as possible.

The door slid open, and she raced through, arms wrapped tight around herself.

"Stars! How cold was it out there?"

<*Only thirty degrees below freezing,*> Angela said. <*Nothing a modded military girl like you can't handle.*>

<*I'm warming the surrounding area,*> Bob said. <*It'll be above freezing shortly.*>

Joe was exactly where she had left him, first pod on the right. She signaled the unit over the Link, and after a moment the stasis field snapped off and the pod's cover slid open.

"Wha…what's the emergency?" Joe mumbled as he struggled out of his pod, "are we disintegrating?"

"Nothing so serious," Tanis's lips twisted in a wry smile. "We're babysitting a nervous AI."

<*I resent that,*> Bob said.

"I just call it like I see it," Tanis replied

Joe stood, and Tanis wrapped him in an embrace. "It's nice to wake and see you…without some emergency."

The embrace lasted only a second before Joe pulled back.

"Holy crap!" Joe exclaimed. "Why are you so cold?"

<*She couldn't wait to see you. Even sub-zero corridors couldn't delay her,*> Angela's avatar wore a thick jacket in their minds.

"You could have taken the time to get some clothes. They are stasis pods, after all…I wasn't going anywhere."

Tanis felt herself flush. "Sorry, I just got caught up in the moment."

Joe smiled and leaned in for a kiss. "This is about all of ice-cold Tanis I can handle right now."

Tanis laughed softly. "I'm starved, let's get some food. I think a BLT would really hit the spot right now."

Joe pulled a pair of shipsuits from storage. "I could use a bite too, but let's get dressed first. I don't want to lose any bits on the way to the officer's lounge."

"Is that really what's up, Bob?" Joe asked as they walked through the slowly warming passageways. "You a bit worried about being alone?"

<*Do you blame me?*> The AI's mental tone betrayed no self-doubt, only conviction. <*Every time you're not around, something goes wrong.*>

Joe laughed and nudged Tanis. "You're his lucky charm."

"I think *I* resent that."

Half an hour later, the pair sat at a small table in the officer's lounge, working their way through a light lunch.

"So let me get this straight," Joe said after taking a gulp of his coffee. "You plan to wake Tanis every so often—randomly—to have her check things over and make you feel better, and, because she can't live without me now, I get woken in the deal too?"

<*That about sums it up. I need you to check whatever things you instinctively think you have to, and see what doesn't look right.*>

"Are we going to be the only humans up this entire time?" Tanis asked. "The captain won't be woken at all?"

<*I won't say that I won't wake him—but at present I don't plan to. I've never been embedded in a human—it's not possible for me to be—but my time with Amanda and Priscilla has taught me the concept of trust, and I trust you.*>

"Awww…he's like a city-sized puppy," Joe chuckled.

"You seem to think this is amusing," Tanis gave him a sour look. "You're forgetting that this essentially works out to years and years of extra work."

"You're looking at it glass-half-empty," Joe replied.

<*Unless the glass is in a hard vacuum, it is always full,*> Bob interjected. <*And even then, you could argue that it is still full of the base energy of the universe.*>

Joe paused for a moment. "Damn… never thought of that. There goes logic—ruining another perfectly good figure of speech."

"You were saying?" Tanis asked.

"Right. Anyway, we're going to have long walks in the park, and by the beach—if we wanted to, we could have decades to spend with just one another. Maybe I could even teach you to fly."

"Yeah. And maybe. I could teach you to tell a joke." Tanis stuck her tongue out at Joe, then paused. "So Bob, you really just want us to do whatever we think we need to do? Just check the ship over, hang out for a few days or a week and then go back under?"

<*That's about it.*>

"How often do you want us to do this?"

<*I think about two or three hundred times will do.*>

Tanis nearly choked on her BLT while Joe dissolved into hysterical laughter.

<*What happened to a few dozen?*> Angela asked.

<*I was softening the blow. Do you think it helped?*>

"We should walk the ship—the whole ship," Joe said later as he and Tanis relaxed in the officer's common area. "It's just the sort of thing that could give us a fresh perspective. and something to do."

"It may take more than a day or two," Tanis mused.

"I'll bring a snack, and I bet there are lots of quarters along the way we could crash in."

"What the hell," Tanis sat up. "But first, let's get armored and armed, at least lightly."

"No argument here. I imagine I'm going to hear rogue bots around every corner, for the first day at least. Not to mention, armor has built-in heaters."

An hour later, they sat aboard a maglev train, riding to the bow of the *Intrepid* in silence. Both Joe and Tanis sported light armor, several sidearms and multi-function rifles. Packs rested on the floor beside them, containing food and supplies.

<*I feel like you think I'm some sort of untamed wilderness,*> Bob's voice came over the Link.

"Sorry Bob," Joe said, "Memories of dark corridors with no power and no comm are still too fresh. To us that was just a couple months ago."

<*Not to mention that you're only ten percent through your component check,*> Angela added.

Tanis turned to look out the window. She watched as the train entered a vast, dark chamber. Emergency lighting in the distance showed the space to be hundreds of meters wide, and many more long.

A light slid into view far below the train, and Tanis saw a bank of superconductor batteries in its dim green glow. Several other similar lights winked on and off in the distance, as the train raced on.

She looked up the cavern on the ship's schematics, and saw that it was the power storage and regulation chamber for the particle accelerator. The sparsity of green lights revealed that most of the batteries still were offline; a result of the damage to the primary ramscoop.

"I can't believe I've never been here before," she said to Joe.

He nodded. "Me either. Though it's not that surprising, I guess. I just checked, and apparently I've only set foot in about five percent of the ship."

Tanis checked the places she had been. "I've got you beat. I've been in six percent of the ship."

"Always have to be one-upping," Joe laughed.

"I don't see how stating a fact is one-upping."

"Um, Tanis, you even said, *I've got you beat.*"

Tanis grinned. "I have no recollection of the events to which you are referring."

A minute later the maglev slowed and stopped at a small station; the end of the line, or the beginning, depending on how you looked at it.

Joe led the way to their destination, a small observation deck above the main scoop emitter, and the furthest forward they could get on the bow, without crawling into maintenance tunnels.

They stepped through the entrance, and both stopped, looking at one another in surprise. The observation deck was dimly lit, soft music played over a physical sound system and a servitor stood beside a bar with a selection of food and wine.

Joe pulled off his helmet and let out a low whistle. "One heck of a posh lounge, I was expecting a maintenance viewport, or something."

"These couches feel like real leather," Tanis sat and leaned back, clasping her hands behind her head.

<The scoop techs managed to syphon a bit of budget into ensuring some of the finer things were available to them,> Bob commented.

"Quite the view," Tanis said as she gazed out the large bay window that wrapped over half way around the lounge.

"Can almost see behind us," Joe laughed, as he handed Tanis a glass of wine.

"I can't quite make out The Kap."

"I can't either, but there's Canopus to the right," Joe pointed at the white-blue star.

"And Sirius up there to the left. Just a bit further around and we'd be able to see Sol over there," Tanis pointed at the rear wall of the observation deck.

"Huh…I just checked, and we're actually farther from Sirius now than we were back home at Sol—thought it looked brighter."

"And we're traveling further from New Eden every minute—seems counter-intuitive," Tanis sighed.

Joe nodded and sat beside Tanis. They enjoyed the silence for some time, simply staring out into space, arms around each other's shoulders. Eventually Tanis looked at Joe, "We'll have to do this often during our thaws."

"Absolutely."

After finishing the glasses of wine, they discussed the route to the stern of the ship. While serving on the *Intrepid,* they had spent the majority of their time in the dorsal arch. Rather than travelling through familiar territory, they opted to work their way down through several dozen decks below them, and travel through the sections of the ship directly above the particle accelerator.

Outside the observation lounge, the utilitarian corridors felt even more stark than on the way in.

Their HUD overlays led them to a wide vertical shaft, which dropped over thirty meters, and rose several hundred more above them. It was lined with various pipes, waveguides, and conduit. Several bots flitted up and down, a few swerving out of the way, as a lift rose up the shaft.

Tanis and Joe stepped on the lift, and she punched the button for the lowest level. The lift waited a moment, then dropped down the shaft. With the low gravity—due to the particle accelerator running on empty—there was a moment her feet lifted off the platform.

"That was a bit disconcerting," Joe said.

"You're telling me," Tanis said as she looked over the railing. "It's quite the drop."

The bottom of the shaft pierced the ceiling of yet another vast chamber, one which appeared to be at least a hundred meters wide, and several hundred long. Above them, the roof of the chamber was punctuated by several other shafts, like the one they had just entered through. Bots flitted in and out of them, appearing to be working on the large object below.

"This must be the main scoop's field generator," Tanis said, as the realization dawned on her.

"I've never seen one that looked like this before," Joe commented, as the lift settled next to a catwalk.

"You've never seen one that can emit a field over ten thousand kilometers wide."

"Touché."

They stood a moment longer, looking at one of the *Intrepid*'s many hearts.

"Well, let's roll," Tanis said, as she picked up her bag. "We have a long way to go."

The rest of the day was spent passing through endless kilometers of corridor, bay, and chamber. The posh lounge, looking out over the ramscoop emitter should have prepared them, but they were still surprised by what lay in the nooks and crannies of the ship.

Rounding a corner, near one of the hydroponics chambers, they stumbled upon a statue in the middle of an intersection. It appeared to be a life-sized goat made of solid crystal. Upon closer inspection, they realized that the crystal was data storage, containing the DNA and all knowledge associated with every known bacteria going back to the twentieth century, cross-referenced with every time each bacterium had been found in a goat.

There also appeared to be a personal 2D vid collection of goats stored in the crystal. Many of them depicted people yelling at goats, which seemed to cause the goats to seize up and fall over.

"Wow, someone really likes goats," Joe commented.

"Maybe a bit too much," Tanis chuckled.

Not long after, they entered another corridor that was a clear tube surrounded by what appeared to be a brownish substance. Tanis leaned close and let out a small cry.

"It's just dirt!"

Joe frowned and peered closer. "What? What for?"

"I think it's a giant ant farm."

Joe walked down the tube, running his hand along the plas. "Huh, so it is. The sign down here says it's the personal property of some guy named Pete, and, that no one's to mess with it."

Tanis laughed, "well, I guess we'd best be on our way."

After several more kilometers of ship, Joe yawned and stretched. "I know we've only been at it for a few hours, but I'd worked a full day before stasis, and I'm bushed. What say we find some place to crash?"

"Sure," Tanis agreed. "Ironically, we're not far from my quarters, just sixty-two decks down."

"That would take all the fun out of the adventure!" Joe looked shocked. "We need to bivouac somewhere exciting."

"There's a security duty station, not far from here, that had some bunks for folks pulling back-to-back shifts," Tanis offered. "Does that satisfy your sense of adventure?"

"Humph…I guess it'll have to do."

The next day brought them to the ship's transverse cargo corridor. A memory of that first trip, through the kilometer-wide portal came to Tanis. She remembered first meeting a younger, somehow softer Amy Lee. All the while trying not to gawk at a cargo hatch many of the star cruisers she'd served on could fly through.

"I remember when they were building this thing," Joe said, apparently on the same train of thought. "I flew a fighter in here, and buzzed a bunch of haulers that some MOS guys were driving. They were a bit upset, to say the least."

Tanis laughed. "No wonder they knew you weren't up to running security and brought me in."

"You act as though that wasn't my master plan."

<*That's because it wasn't,*> Angela inserted into their conversation.

"Angela, girl!" Joe said. "I was beginning to wonder if you were still with us."

<*Where else would I go? I've been having chats with Bob about the nature of the universe, and our place in it. His math's a bit beyond me, but I think I'm starting to get it.*>

"Which 'us'?" Tanis asked. "Organics or AI?"

<*Both,*> Bob replied. <*We're all AI, don't you know that?*>

"Uh…forget I asked," Tanis laughed.

From the transverse corridor they debated whether to go through one of the cylinders, or to take the maglev that ran along the particle accelerator to Engine.

In the end, they opted to take the maglev, because they could stop at Earnest's observation lounge, which would give them a great view of Sol, and a last glimpse of Estrella de la Muerte, before its dim red point of light disappeared from view.

Arriving in the lounge a half hour later, Tanis remembered how much she loved seeing the *Intrepid* from here. It was only a dozen decks above the SOC, and she had come often to collect her thoughts.

Below, the two habitation cylinders rotated, reflecting starlight onto the dorsal rail, cargo cubes and lattice of struts that wrapped the rear half of the ship.

Just over sixteen kilometers away, the engines rose up beyond the cylinders, one side still blackened and twisted. The main engines were inactive; without the main scoop, there was insufficient fuel to light them up, and without the port side A1 fusion engine, a balanced thrust was impossible.

Instead, the two smaller engines were running at low power, pushing the ship ever faster toward The Kap.

"Looks a little worse for wear," Joe said.

Tanis nodded. "We've pinned a lot of hope to this ark, drifting alone in the black."

"Not really an ark," Joe mused. "It's not as though Sol is drowning."

"Are you so sure?" Tanis asked. "I'm here because I'm fed up with the TSF and Sol politics, but many believe all of Sol is doomed."

"I know some people think that, but I didn't know you did—at least not in so many words," Joe replied.

"Thing is; Sol doesn't really need humans anymore—but there are trillions of them. Pretty soon, they'll all be able to live forever, but heavy elements are getting rare enough to cause concern."

She paused contemplatively. "Unless something changes, they're going to have some very big conflicts, and soon."

Joe nodded. "You're not wrong. But there have always been shortages and conflicts. They'll survive."

"Some will," Tanis agreed. "But that's makes this an ark. We're taking the best of the best, and the tools to build a new Sol."

<*What do you think it will be like?*> Angela asked over the Link.

"What New Eden will be like?" Joe replied.

<*I was thinking of The Kap, what we'll make there,*> Angela paused. <*The idea of building a throwaway colony is hard to accept.*>

Tanis nodded slowly. "You wonder if we'll end up staying; if Terrance and the Reddings will crack open the picotech."

<*Along those lines, yes.*>

Joe leaned against the window, and ran a hand down his cheek. "Do you think they would? They'd risk letting the whole crew and colony know."

"Hard to say," Tanis replied. "It may be that repairing the scoop emitter and the annihilator would be a lot easier with pico. I imagine the annihilator would be. I'm more concerned about building around a red dwarf."

<*They do tend to be temperamental,*> Angela agreed.

"The Kap is an old, old girl, I doubt she has much kick left in her," Joe said.

Tanis reached an arm around Joe. "Let's hope she takes it easy for the next couple of centuries."

"Centuries?" Joe gave Tanis a startled look. "I thought we were only going to be there for fifty years or so."

"It'll still take seventy to get there," Tanis replied. "Either way, let's hope a temperamental red dwarf is the worst of our problems."

<*I cannot believe you just said that.*>

A HOME WITHIN A HOME

STELLAR DATE: 3245116 / 09.22.4172 (Adjusted Gregorian)
LOCATION: *ISS Intrepid*
REGION: Interstellar space, en route to Kapteyn's Star

"I'm dying for some greenery," Joe said. "What say we hit one of the cylinders this time? Lil' Sue or Old Sam?"

It was their eleventh random wakeup; Tanis and Joe were doing their fourth full-ship walkabout. While they had visited several smaller parks, it was not the same as the wide-open spaces within a cylinder.

"Sounds good, let's visit Old Sam this time. I vote we take a maglev and skip the boring parts," Tanis replied.

Joe nodded his agreement and Tanis flashed him a smile.

"Last one to the train's a…whatever!" She said and broke into a run.

"Seriously?" Joe called out as he chased after her. "A *whatever?*"

Old Sam was roughly as Tanis remembered; lakes, trees, plains—over one hundred and fifty square kilometers of it. Small bots flitted through the air, maintaining the cylinder's systems and ensuring the wildlife remained in balance.

"We could spend weeks in here just wandering around," Tanis said as they picked their way down an overgrown path.

Old Sam was in its summer cycle and the long sun which ran down the cylinder's center beat down on them mercilessly. Tanis looked back at Joe and smiled at his red cheeks.

"First the race and now this," Joe grimaced. "You're dying for an adventure, aren't you?"

Tanis laughed, relishing the fact that she didn't hear her voice echo back from bulkheads. "The danger quotient in my blood *is* alarmingly low."

"Well, there's that low escarpment a few miles from here; it would make a fun climbing exercise." Joe replied.

"In full gravity? After months of low-*g* on the ship? Not sure how the docs would feel if I woke them up to fix my broken neck."

"Tanis Richards turning down a challenge?" It was Joe's turn to laugh. "I'll have to save this conversation to use on you later."

"You asked for it!" Tanis broke into a lope that brought her up to ten kilometers per-hour, not her top speed, but more than Joe could pull off.

"Not fair," Joe called out from behind her. "Augments are cheating."

<*Cheater,*> Angela laughed in Tanis's mind.

<*You know it's…*> Tanis stopped mid thought and mid stride.

To her right was a stretch of young trees with a lake visible between their trunks. To her left was a patch of bramble that contained a mixture of plants, which indicated a garden had been the genesis of the growth.

What really had her attention was the cabin beyond the overgrown garden.

It was a single story structure with a small veranda on the front. A pair of homey windows looked out, though one was broken, with a branch growing through it—likely belonging to the tree that had broken through the roof and was now over ten meters high.

Joe stopped beside her, his breathing heavy. He put a steadying hand on Tanis's shoulder.

"What's up?"

Tanis took a moment to reply. "I think this is Ouri's cabin."

<*You are correct. It is.*> Angela supplied.

A slow smile crept over Tanis's face and she turned to look at Joe. "I have an idea…"

DOG STAR

STELLAR DATE: 3246187 / 08.29.4175 (Adjusted Gregorian)
LOCATION: Brilliance Station
REGION: Lucent, Luminescent Space, Sirian Hegemony

The shuttle began its final docking procedure with Brilliance Station. Slight vibrations rippled through the deck as thrusters fired periodically to match velocity and attitude with the station.

Markus stretched his long spacers' legs out into the aisle, trying to work out a kink in his right knee that had been building for the last hour. Beside him, Simon shifted uncomfortably, his three-meter frame pressed up against the windowless bulkhead, head cocked to the side in the small space.

Markus felt a little bad that his younger companion had the worse of the two seats, but he had spent many long trips against the bulkhead of Luminescent shuttles in his youth. The next generation could pay their dues too.

"You going to make it?" he asked Simon.

"Hard to say, I may never stand up straight again."

Markus chuckled.

This was the final leg of the multi-week journey from their mining platform to Brilliance Station. Most of the trip had been spent aboard an in-system Noctus ore hauler, and while it wasn't spacious—there was room to move. Somehow, the five-hour journey, while sitting in the Noctus section of this shuttle, felt considerably longer.

A little food would have helped, but the Lumins didn't think it was a worthwhile investment to give the Noctus passengers food when they could simply not.

Markus hardly noticed anymore. He had been in Luminescent Space enough that he was no longer fazed by the opulence and decadence of the people—which they denied to the Noctus at every opportunity. For Simon, this was his first visit. The short glimpse he'd gotten of the first class cabin when they had entered the shuttle made the young man slack-jawed.

An attendant opened the door into the rear cabin and cast an eye across the lower-class passengers, making certain they were all seated and orderly for the docking. The two metal studs gleaming on the bridge of her nose marked her as a member of one of the lesser families. High ranking families in Luminescent Society had metal studs from their nose up into their hairline.

Her survey only lasted moments and then the door was closed with a sharp snap

"Damn shorts," Simon muttered. "Would it kill them to show us common courtesy?"

"Boy," Markus snapped. "Watch your mouth; you never know who might overhear you, and what they might say. You will not utter that word in Luminescent Space."

Simon sighed, but didn't say anything else disparaging about the Lumins. Something so innocuous as calling them "shorts" could put you in front of a judge, getting fined, or even a jail sentence.

The Lumins really had no sense of proportion, or humor for that matter.

A clang echoed through the ship, and the pull of gravity tugged at the passengers. The station's grappling mechanism pulled the shuttle into the dock, and centripetal force began to take effect. Within a minute, Luminescent-normal gravity of 1.0*g* was in effect.

"Agh, I feel like I can't breathe," Simon felt his chest and swallowed. "How do they survive like this?" he asked.

"It's not the most pleasant thing, but keep your discomfort to yourself, it doesn't do to let them see you stooping or pulling at your clothes."

A second clang heralded the umbilical latching onto the ship.

Markus stood before the 'remain seated' lights switched off. Beside him, Simon leaned across both seats, stretching as much as the space would allow.

"We've now completed our docking procedure," the captain's voice came across the ship's auditory systems. "First class passengers may begin debarkation. Other passengers please wait until our first class guests have finished clearing the shuttle."

The captain was most certainly a short. He didn't speak with their accent, which meant he came from one of the outer habitats at the edge of Luminescent Space. The way he emphasized the word "other" spoke volumes. Moreover, there was only one first-class passenger; Markus had seen her in the debarkation area on Glorious Station.

The boarding area back on Glorious Station was sparsely appointed. Few Lumins had been present, but she stood out because she was quite tall for one of them, perhaps just over two meters—more with the heels she wore. Her hair was a brilliant red and it reminded Markus of Angie before she had died in an asteroid accident.

The Lumins loved talking about light, and it was apparent in everything, from the naming of their stations to the clothes they wore. The latest trend in Lumin fashion was a skin-tight covering of some glowing iridescent material. Some were brilliantly white, almost hard to look at, but this woman's was muted to a dull pewter.

Simon had stared at her for at least a solid minute before Markus elbowed him. With studs nearly to the top of her forehead, she was likely one of the first upper-class Lumins the boy had ever seen. Not to mention that Simon had never seen a woman exude so much sexual power while simply standing still.

Markus had to admit she was quite striking and would have liked to soak in her beauty for some time as well, but doing so would have earned a visit from a security drone.

The light above the exit changed from red to green and the remaining passengers shuffled out. Markus caught sight of the captain and was surprised to see that he *was* Noctus. The disdain on his face was plain to see as he tried to distance himself from his own people.

Fool, Markus thought. *Just because you despise us doesn't mean the Lumins think any more of you—they don't think of you at all.*

The corridor outside the shuttle had a clear wall and the light of brilliant Sirius and its dimmer brother, Lucent, shone through. Though Brilliance station orbited the Lucent at a distance of only 0.5AU, Sirius A—currently 15AU distant—was still significantly brighter, providing something close to the amount of light Earth received from Sol.

Very little filtering blocked the radiance as it washed across the passengers, many of whom squinted in the glare, as they shuffled along in the heavy gravity.

Noctus stations rarely had any windows. To them Sirius was a harsh and cruel master, not a life-giving light filled with beauty. Looking at it meant blindness; being exposed to its light directly would certainly be followed by genetic damage; it was the destroyer, the bane of all life.

"It's amazing to be able to look at it with my own eyes," Simon said. "It's beautiful."

Markus nodded his agreement. "It's easy to see why they constantly talk of light and brilliance and luminosity. Looking at the two sisters with your own eyes is quite the sight."

He rested a hand on Simon's shoulder, "you'll have plenty of time to dawdle later. With the stars so close together they'll have every portal open, you'll see them dozens of times while we're here."

As they walked through the tunnel Markus caught a glimpse of the red-headed woman ahead of them. She was moving slowly, probably lost in a conversation on the Link. He found it interesting that she had altered her outfit. It was now much lighter in hue, flashing and glowing with wild abandon. It still had the gray tint and a perhaps hint of burgundy as well, though that might have been her hair reflecting off it.

"Now who's staring?" Simon laughed.

"She's striking," Markus shrugged. "I've never seen one of their women so tall."

The docking tunnel emptied into a large atrium so bright that Markus and Simon had to shield their eyes. Simon looked up and let out a cry. He grabbed the railing which ran around the upper-level balcony.

Markus looked up and smiled. He may dislike—or more accurately, despise—the Lumins, but they did have some amazing architecture.

Along the walls wide steel pillars rose up, arching toward each other, but tapering to fine points before reaching the center of the ceiling. The actual ceiling was completely transparent. Markus assumed there must be some sort of glass or plas above their heads, but it was completely indiscernible.

For all intents and purposes, it appeared as though the ceiling had never been put on and the pillars were attempting to capture Lucent which was always directly above.

Markus knew how Simon felt. Excepting shuttle bays, this was probably the largest room the young man had ever been in. Shuttle bays were always fully enclosed, and filled with ships and cargo. This space was clean and empty—excepting the shifting crowds entering and exiting the corridors which led to waiting ships.

Pulling his eyes from the architectural spectacle, not to mention the many Lumins in their gleaming outfits, Markus pulled out a small tablet. He waited a moment for it to auth with the station's systems and then retrieved Brilliance Station's layout, looking up the location of their meeting.

The Lumin overseers at the company didn't really need Markus to come in person and present his plan for the upgrade of the SK87 mining platform, which he ran, but he suspected they did it to remind him of his place in the grand scheme of things.

Luther, the general manager and overseer of the mining platform, should have been there as well, but he was vacationing on the garden world Radius. He had instructed Markus to deliver all the summaries and reports to the supervising board alone. Even when Luther was present Markus did most of the talking, as Luther barely knew what was happening on his own station.

The wireless network protocols granted him limited access on Brilliance Station, but it was enough to load directions to their meeting. He had to all but pull Simon while the young man slowed to stare at everything. Markus couldn't fault his young companion overmuch. He remembered his first trip to Brilliance, some thirty years ago when he had been a young man. The gleaming corridors and holo ads selling things he had never even heard of had boggled his mind.

Now, the cornucopia of products available was more insulting than fascinating. He barely had enough money to buy lunch on Brilliance, let alone any of the fancy toys that Luminescent Society wasted its money on.

He pushed his dislike of Luminescent opulence out of his mind and focused on his presentation.

The platform he worked and lived on, SK87, was performing well and Luther wanted to expand it. Markus had been sent to present the plans to the assessors for approval. Convincing the Lumin oversight board that it was the right plan would not be hard; a thousand years of delegating any hard work or menial labor meant they didn't have much experience with assessing work schedules and ROI projections.

Markus was distracted by a particularly useless Lumin specimen they passed. He couldn't be certain if it was male or female, but its arms and legs ended in wheels and it was spinning and rolling through the corridor, giggling as it went.

"I can't believe we work our entire lives so they can turn themselves into useless…I don't know what's…just useless," Simon muttered.

Markus chuckled. "It wasn't entirely useless; I imagine you could put some sort of bucket on it and turn it into a hauler."

"I can imagine what the yard foreman would say about that," Simon laughed softly

"We have about three hours before our meeting," Markus said. "I know a place near here where we can get some food and relax for a bit."

Simon nodded his assent and Markus led him through the wide boulevards to a less trafficked area. The overt gaudiness of the station was somewhat diminished, but it was still far more opulent than SK87.

Before long they reached their destination, a small restaurant that would serve Noctus—though only with automated servitors. After the robot had brought their food, Simon spent some time eyeing it suspiciously.

"Try it," Markus prodded him. "It's not often you get to eat something that wasn't grown in a vat."

Simon looked horrified. "You mean this was alive?"

"Of course, Lumins only eat real food. No vats or mush for them."

Simon sat staring at his food for several minutes and eventually screwed up the courage to take a bite.

"Mmmm…I didn't know food could taste so good! How do you go back to eating the crap on the platform after this?"

"With great sadness—though sometimes the thought of eating plants and animals unnerves me," Markus commented.

The pair enjoyed the rest of their meal in silence, looking out the portals at the star-side view of Lucent and the world of Incandus below.

"Have you ever been to a planet?" Simon asked Markus.

"No, I have to admit that the thought scares me a bit. Once you're down there you're stuck, and everything wants to fall on you. I think it would terrify me."

"I've seen pictures," Simon's voice grew wistful. "Parks larger than SK87, larger than anything we've seen—can you imagine?"

Markus nodded. If he hadn't seen pictures himself, he would never have imagined anything like that even existed. The Lumins lived lives the Noctus could only dream of.

A few hours later, Markus and Simon sat in one of the company's many conference rooms, waiting for the Lumins who would review their proposal. The room was spare, but elegant in its appointment. The table was a shimmering plas and the chairs appeared to hover on invisible plinths.

Markus had never been in this particular tower before, but was unsurprised by the luxurious appointments. He kept his focus on ensuring the presentation went well. Once done they could get off Brilliance—hopefully before he went blind from all the bright lights and reflective surfaces, which were already giving him a headache.

Simon had carefully distributed hyfilm around the table for the committee to take after the meeting—the Lumins seemed to react better to physical media than pure holo presentations. He now sat fumbling with his notepad, prepared to jot down any pertinent thoughts. The device could not record here, as the Lumins disallowed Noctus to record anything in Luminescent Space; physical notes were the only way to record decisions.

It also allowed the Lumins to revert nearly any decision by simply claiming the Noctus had incorrect records.

After only several minutes of waiting, the company team filed in. There were three men and two women. Markus was surprised to see that one of the women was the Lumin he had followed off the shuttle.

"Markus, good to see you," Yusuf, the President of Resources and Extraction, said.

He did not offer to shake hands.

"It is good to see you, sir," Markus nodded his head in deference. He did not expect to see Yusuf here. It wasn't a good sign—the president of R&E only made appearances to Markus's detriment.

Yusuf did not acknowledge the gesture. "You know Thomas, Vlad and Sarah. Our newest member is Katrina; she manages transport and logistics for platform services."

"It is good to meet you," Markus nodded again. "I have one of my young team leads, Simon, with me. He knows the internals of our platform inside and out."

None of the Lumins acknowledged Simon. Markus barely rated their attention and he had spent decades garnering the meager level of respect he now had.

The discussions were largely perfunctory. Most of the details of the platform's expansion had been reviewed by the non-sentient AI Lumins employed for such tasks. It was Markus's belief that the Lumins only brought him here to remind him who was the final authority in his life.

When they came to living quarters enhancements Yusuf scowled at the display.

"This expansion does not seem to be in proportion with the rest of the platform. It brings your living quarter allotment from 10% of platform space to 12%."

Markus nodded. "Yes, sir, it does. 12% of platform space for living quarters is standard when platforms exceed twenty-eight cubic kilometers."

"On *new* platforms that is the case, but this is an expansion of an existing platform, those concessions do not apply." Yusuf spoke offhand as though he had given this little thought, but Markus knew the man. He was doing this on purpose to keep Markus in his place and not let him garner too much favor with his own people.

"Surely—." Markus began, but was cut off by the wave of Yusuf's hand.

All of the Lumins looked entirely implacable with the exception of Katrina whose lips twitched for just a moment, her expression belying a moment of consternation.

"Seriously?" Simon erupted beside Markus. "You're going to increase our population by 120% to facilitate the additional throughput, but only increase our living space by 90%? We're already crammed in cheek to cheek!"

"Simon!" Markus put a hand on his young companion's shoulder in an attempt to quell his outburst.

"No, Markus, no! You're as much a part of the problem as they are. I've seen it for myself, you bow and scrape and take whatever they give," Simon stood to his full three meters as he yelled. Towering over the table, he reached into his jacket and began to pull something out.

"For the true Sirians and our independence!"

Markus fell back, aghast that Simon would do something so rash.

The Lumins looked alarmed at the outburst, with the exception of Yusuf. A smile played at the edges of his mouth and a stasis cone snapped down around Simon. A high pitched whine pierced the room and a decoupling field tore apart all matter in the cone.

The field broke Simon's body down into a fine mist in moments. Markus listened for an explosion, or something that would indicate the young man had reached for a weapon.

Nothing.

Yusuf waved his hand and a holo appeared over the table showing Simon's last moments in slow motion. He turned and zoomed; they could all see what he was pulling from his coat

"Hmm... a flag," Yusuf sighed. "A lot of theatrics for a piece of cloth." He looked to Markus. "Let's hope your next assistant has more brains—and you have the intelligence to not make a mistake like that again. You run your people well. If not for that, I would kill you too."

Markus couldn't believe the calm in Yusuf's voice. He had seen Lumins kill Noctus before, but never like this, never so casually.

Yusuf looked to his committee. "Unless there are any objections I approve this expansion proposal, excepting the disproportionate increase in living quarters." He waited a moment to see if anyone spoke up; when none did, the President of Resources and Extraction stood and left the room.

Markus stood, silently watching them file out, unwilling to look at the seat where Simon should have been. Only the new woman, Katrina, looked him in the eye. Her expression showed a flash of sympathy and then she too was gone.

Markus barely noticed. The only thing on his mind was the thought of telling Simon's mother.

He barely remembered getting back to the shuttle.

As he sat silently in his small quarters on the trip back to Sirius, a plan to started to form in Markus's mind.

There had always been talk of rebellion among the Noctus. It had been present for his entire life, waxing and waning over the years. At present, there were more whispers in dark corners than usual, especially among the youth who had not been alive for the previous generation's failed attempts—and the Lumins' retribution.

The dissidents traded seditious documents and data, and held their small rallies in hidden areas of the platform. Markus had always tolerated them while ensuring they didn't get too vocal and cause problems.

He had thought he was doing the right thing by protecting his people, keeping things in balance. But something about how casually Yusuf had killed Simon triggered a change in Markus. Maybe he had just had enough and had gone past his tipping point, but one thing was for certain: he saw things in a new light.

Markus knew why the other rebellions had failed. It was not because of lack of conviction, or even a failure to take a given platform or station.

Past rebellions had almost always succeeded at taking their initial objectives, but holding them was the problem. The Lumin space force arrived and either the rebels surrendered or were destroyed.

The way to succeed was to leave Sirius.

REVOLUTION

STELLAR DATE: 3246204 / 09.15.4175 (Adjusted Gregorian)
LOCATION: Mining Platform SK87
REGION: Noctilucent Space, Sirius Hegemony

Markus could still hear the sobbing cries of Simon's mother in his ears. She had been so eager to hear how well her son had done in his new role. To go from that, to news of his callous death at the hands of the Lumins, may well be more than she could bear—especially after losing her husband in an accident several years earlier.

Markus made a note to check in on her in the days to come. The community on the platform was tight-knit and neighbors would console her and help her through this time—but it never hurt to be sure she didn't need additional counseling.

Around him the corridors of the platform, ever bleak, seemed even more so. Endless kilometers of obedience, centuries of acquiescence.

Markus's tall frame was hunched; his years weighed more heavily upon him than ever before. He barely noticed others as he passed them by, be they the Noctus workers—his people—or the sparse Lumin guards of the station's garrison.

Although his frame implied defeat, his mind was churning with a fire he had not felt in many years. He had a plan and was about to take the first step in launching it.

He made his way past the platform's two-hundred-year-old refinery—one of the areas he had proposed upgrades for that fateful day on Brilliance Station; past the bio vats in hydroponics; and into the waste reclamation area.

There was no doubt in his mind that they were meeting. He knew the players, knew how they thought, and what drove them. It drove him now as well.

It was a good place to meet, security patrols rarely came down to reclamation. The smell was enough to keep even the most brutish of them from making much more than a cursory examination every few weeks.

Markus, on the other hand, knew every corridor, every hatch, portal and conduit on the platform. Even without intel from people loyal to him he knew where this meeting would be held.

The door was unmarked; there was nothing to separate it from any other hatch in reclamation. It was a thick, gray plas, but through it he could hear the sound of voices raised in anger.

Markus took a deep breath and steeled himself for the storm he was about to endure.

He opened the door.

The first thing he noticed was that the room had many more occupants than he would have expected. Over forty men and women stood amongst the tanks and pipes, expressions ranging from rage to sorrow drawn across their faces.

The second was the figure of Sarah standing on a large vat, yelling at the crowd, whipping them into a frenzy.

"You see how they so callously kill one of our best sons, in cold blood, with no regard for us. We are worse than slaves; we are the children of slaves, and the parents of slaves. We raise new slaves and secure generations of our children as thralls of the shorts."

The crowd replied with groans and cheers at the appropriate times, but perhaps not as enthusiastically as Sarah had hoped. After being pushed down for so long it was hard to even know what standing should feel like.

Markus had always liked Sarah, even though he knew she despised him. She saw him as nothing more than a puppet of their masters. Little did she know how often he had worked tirelessly to protect his people from far worse than they knew.

He knew that she felt, very keenly, for her friends and family, the people of the platform; she wanted more for them, but her pain manifested as anger and she was toxic to those around her. Because of this, her meetings were usually attended by only a dozen, at best.

"You!" She spotted Markus and leveled an accusing finger at him. "You have some gall coming here after what you did."

There were nods and murmurs from the crowd as she spoke. The stares of his people bore into him, and he had to force his shame down, lest it make him turn and flee.

Sarah continued with her barrage before he was able to formulate a response.

"How long did it take to wash Simon's blood off your hands? How much did you have to bow and scrape for their forgiveness after his death? After you stood by and watched them murder him?"

Several others called out, their anger a palpable thing to Markus. He didn't expect them to be so visceral and a kernel of fear began to form in the pit of his stomach.

He held up his hands, his expression mirroring the sadness that filled him.

"I am at your mercy," he said just loudly enough to be heard across the space.

The room fell silent at his words. They were so ready for his anger to meet theirs, to give them a reason to hate and harm.

"Is that all you have to say for yourself?" Timmur, a tug operator called out. "Simon's father was a friend of mine, is this the respect you pay him, getting his son killed?"

"It is not all I have to say for myself," Markus replied, his voice gaining strength. "I have been wrong all of these years. I have tried to find the perfect compromise between us and the shorts. I thought…I thought that if I could keep us under the radar, I could make a better place for us.

"I was wrong."

No one spoke, even Sarah, usually ready to call out a biting retort to any statement, wore a shocked expression.

A voice broke the silence, Markus couldn't see who spoke, but the words reverberated through the chamber.

"What will you do?"

"I have a plan to save us, to save each and every one of us," Markus replied. "I plan to make your children's children never know the yoke of slavery."

Sarah's eyes were bright as she asked, "do you plan revolution? Are we going to overthrow the Lumins?"

Markus shook his head. "No, we are going to do what our ancestors did when they came here. Cross between the stars in search of a new home."

PLANS

STELLAR DATE: 3246713 / 02.05.4177 (Adjusted Gregorian)
LOCATION: Mining Platform SK87
REGION: Noctilucent Space, Sirian Hegemony

"Tell him to put it where I said," Markus all but yelled into the comm. "If he puts it there, how will we mount the new set of batteries next month?"

The platform administrator was silent for a moment.

"Good, make sure he does it then."

Markus switched off the comm and looked back at Luther. "Sorry about that, there's a lot of wrangling to do."

The overseer steepled his fingers, looking over the tips at his administrator. "Will there be a problem completing on schedule? There is a lot riding on this for me."

Markus knew that all too well. Not only because Luther reminded him of it almost daily, but because he understood how political capital was spent in Luminescent Society.

Despite not attending the meeting that infamous day on Brilliance Station, Luther had laid a much of the groundwork for the station's upgrades. He was a lazy ass, but he was a lazy ass with connections.

It could be worse, Markus mused, he could have an overseer who was a micromanager. At least Luther couldn't be bothered to actually check up on any details. So long as the quotas were met and profits were where they should be he was happy.

"We're on schedule and we haven't missed any deliverables during the buildout," Markus replied. "If we keep it up we'll set a new record for efficiency during a platform upgrade."

Luther smiled. Markus knew the man loved to brag about successes when his district quorum assembled. Successes that Markus and his people bled to earn for the useless Lumins.

"Very well. I'm returning to Luminescent Space tomorrow, but Steven will be remaining behind to ensure that things keep moving smoothly," Luther said as he stood. "Be sure to keep him apprised of your progress."

Markus nodded as the overseer left his office.

Now Steven was a problem.

In every way that Luther was distracted and unconcerned with details, Steven was obsessed with minutia and strict adherence to procedure.

The overseer's assistant was new to the position, and obviously working to prove his worth. Unfortunately, he did that through pointing out Markus's failures and questioning all of the platform administrator's decisions.

He wasn't the first sycophant Markus had endured, but he would very likely be the last.

Once he heard Luther pass through the outer office he called James on the comm.

"Boss?"

"Sorry for hollering at you," Markus said. "Luther was doing that thing he does when he wants to act like he cares about what goes on here. Usually, if I yell at someone it makes him feel like stuff is being done. You happened to be handy."

James chuckled on the other end of the line. "I've done that myself, when he does one of his bi-annual visits to the yards."

"So long as you don't try to pull it on me, we'll be fine."

"You? Never." Markus could all but see James's grin on the other end of the comm.

Markus chuckled. "Of course not. Speaking of visits, I'll be by later this afternoon to review the shipments with you."

"You bet, I'll probably be out in the east yard."

Markus closed the connection. James had given the signal that an anticipated shipment of volatiles and tech had arrived, and had passed all checks undetected. Markus would inspect them this afternoon, but they would be nowhere near the east yard.

With a long sigh he rose from his chair and locked his terminals. He was starting to feel his years; all the subterfuge needed to pull off his plan had made for a marked reduction in sleep. It had been weeks since he'd had a full night's rest.

Every day was filled with more to do than the last. Thus far, the Endeavor he'd embarked on seven months ago remained secret, but it was the hardest work he'd ever undertaken.

It would only continue to do well if he got some food—saving his people was not work to be accomplished on an empty stomach.

He nodded to Agnes as he walked through the outer office and into the hall. The administrative wing was always a bustling hive. The business of a mining platform never stopped. Now, with the upgrades underway it was doubly so.

Temporary desks filled every available space, and plas sheets covered every one of them. Holos and 2D displays tracked progress and monitored critical systems.

Markus nodded to his people, and, as he turned toward the cafeteria, he spotted just the person he didn't want to see, Steven.

"Administrator Markus, just who I was looking for," the diminutive Lumin called from down the hall.

Markus sighed, he'd been seen, there would be no escape.

"Adjunct Steven, what can I help you with today?"

If there was one thing that Markus liked about Steven it was that he stood on ceremony and formality without fail. As a result, he was never derisive toward Markus or his people. He may have treated them all like his own personal servants, but at least he was formal and polite about it.

"I wanted to discuss the work being done to harness asteroid P30987. It's behind schedule and we're losing money by the hour."

Markus nodded and continued walking out of the administrative wing into the corridor that led to the cafeteria and upper shops.

"The initial schedule is off, yes, but our overall timeframe is still in place."

"I don't follow," Steven replied. "P30987 should have been harnessed in the reaping yard by now but you have it holding a hundred kilometers west of the station."

"You do realize that we're in the midst of outfitting the reaping yard with new MDCs?" Markus worked to keep his annoyance to himself.

Steven flipped through the sheets of plas he carried. Finally finding the right one he nodded his agreement. "I do, but it shows that the yard should still be fifty-percent operational and you could be pulling that rock apart."

"We could," Markus agreed. "But pulling something the size of that rock, as you put it, apart and sorting the materials would create a hazard for the upgrade crews and slow both projects down. Once the new MDCs are in place we'll be able to carve the asteroid up twice as fast and utilize the new sorters that we have installed. We'll actually be several days ahead of schedule, but I didn't want to get too aggressive in the projections."

Steven frowned and sorted his plas. "I suppose that makes sense. I'm sure you know how important it is that we don't slow in our production during these upgrades."

Markus knew because he was the one that crafted the proposal, but he refrained from reminding Steven of that fact.

"I do; I am certain we will continue to meet our schedule."

"And what of the cargo you are holding in the east yard?"

The question was innocent and spoken with no hint of subterfuge, but Markus felt a cold sweat building on his brow.

"You'll have to be more specific," Markus replied blandly. "We are holding a lot in the east yard these days."

Stevens cast a sidelong look at Markus. "Yes, I suppose you are. I was curious about the shipment that came in today from the Polaris manufacturing platform. I was certain you had routed some of the cargo to the east yard."

Markus grunted in response. "Unless I'm mistaken, all that cargo ended up in the north and under yards."

Steven glanced at his plas. "Hmmm... so it did."

"We have a problem," Markus said as he squeezed onto a stool in the crowded bar.

James took a long pull from his beer. "How is that news? We always have a problem of some sort."

"This is a *little* problem," Markus replied.

James's shoulders slumped. "I guess it was just a matter of time."

Markus nodded. It was a foregone conclusion that a Lumin would eventually discover what they were doing. Sarah had insisted on a contingency plan to deal with any errant Lumins at one of their first meetings.

"Who is it?" James asked.

"Our little friend in high places."

James grunted, "I'm not surprised, the little prick always has his nose in everything. He was bound to pick up a thread sooner or later."

"Well, it's sooner," Markus said.

"When should I enact the scenario?" James asked.

"Do it tomorrow. Luther will be off-station and Steven will be guaranteed to respond."

"You got it, boss. Tomorrow. I have it on good authority that Steven likes to sleep in Luther's quarters when he's away."

"Any other whispers reach your ears?" Markus asked. "I can't imagine Steven picked up on anything himself, we must have had a leak."

"To my knowledge we've identified all the Lumin informants and have fed them what we wanted them to know," James replied.

"Either we missed someone or we have a traitor in our midst."

James nodded slowly. "I'll get Sarah on it."

ACCEPTABLE LOSS

STELLAR DATE: 3246713 / 02.05.4177 (Adjusted Gregorian)
LOCATION: Mining Platform SK87
REGION: Noctilucent Space, Sirian Hegemony

In the middle of the third shift, a warning klaxon sounded, breaking the relative silence of the station's night. The alert network picked up the warning signal and emergency crews assembled to respond.

There was a reactor leak on a tug working in the east yard.

The pilot reported to the overwatch night crew that he had attempted to power down the reactor, but it wasn't responding.

"Have you tried the emergency overrides?" the comm operator in overwatch asked.

"Are you fucking kidding me?" the operator's voice screeched out of the speakers in overwatch. "Do you think I got this job yesterday? Of course I tried the overrides. There's nothing I can do; this sucker is going to blow!"

Markus stumbled into the room, rubbing his eyes.

"Situation?"

"We have a tug stuck in the east yard with a reactor leak. It was moving some equipment to another net to make room for an inbound shipment and it's tangled in it now. I don't know how we'll get it out of there."."

"Who is in there and who do we have nearby?" Markus asked.

"Huan is in the leaking tug. Irek is working the other side of the yard, should I call him over?"

Markus nodded. "Yes, see if he can get Huan out of the nets and kick him away from the station. We can get a rescue craft in position to extract him from the tug."

Platform tugs didn't have escape pods or room for EVA Suits. The Lumins had done the math and determined that hauling around that extra equipment around—not to mention inspecting it—was too expensive and not worth the cost.

Tug operators were expendable.

Markus picked up a headset and spoke calmly, "Huan, we're going to get you out of there. Irek is coming over to pull your tug free and kick it to meet a rescue shuttle. You'll be at the bar joking about this in no time."

"Gods I hope so, boss, I don't fancy being here when things heat up."

"You won't be, don't worry."

Time slowed to a crawl as Irek secured the cargo he was moving and boosted his tug across the yard. It only took ten minutes, but felt like forever as the second tug worked its way through the acres of nets. The east yard was all but overflowing with ore from a smaller asteroid that had been recently pulled apart. The freighter scheduled to make the pickup had been delayed, and an inbound shipment had turned the yard into gridlock.

Eventually Irek's tug reached Huan's and the two large manipulator arms began to untangle the incapacitated tug from the nets around it.

"How you doing, Huan," Markus asked.

"Anxious for that beer. Things are getting toasty in here and the Geiger counter is ticking a bit too fast for my liking."

"Don't worry, Irek just about has you free and the rescue shuttle is in position to catch you."

Markus wiped his brow. He sure hoped the shuttle could make the catch, with the yard so full they were a quarter mile out, adjacent to the Lumin section of the platform.

Irek signaled overwatch that Huan's tug was free and that he was ready to kick it out. Markus nodded to the comm operator and an affirmation was sent.

Irek boosted out of the yard, pushing Huan's ship. Five seconds later, he cut thrust and let go of the other tug. The overwatch holo tracked the trajectory and predicted the rescue shuttle making a good catch.

An agonizing three minutes later, it did.

"This is rescue shuttle Bravo Echo; we have the tug in our grapple, preparing to collect the pilot."

"Make it happen," Markus spoke into his mic.

The shuttle extended a docking umbilical to the tug.

"C'mon, make that seal, we're out of time," Huan's frantic voice came over the comm.

The group assembled in overwatch looked nervously at one another. If the tug blew now, it would certainly destroy the rescue shuttle and a part of the station. The seconds ticked by with excruciating lethargy.

Finally, the call came. "We have him aboard; we are kicking the tug out."

Cheers erupted in overwatch.

Markus held his breath. A lot could still go wrong.

The shuttle's grapple swung around and set the tug on a course away from the platform and it's shipping lanes. At the last moment a part of the grapple caught on a piece of netting that Irek had cut off and left hooked to the tug.

For an agonizing twelve seconds it held and the two ships began to rotate around each other, then, the netting broke and the rescue shuttle spun away. It arched over the platform, toward the north yard, while the tug rotated slowly, drifting closer the platform.

"Oh shit, it's going to hit us!" the comm operator shouted, hitting the general alarm.

Markus gritted his teeth. This was the part of the plan he hated the most, harming the station.

The overwatch radiation detectors jumped, heralding the orange blossom that appeared outside the windows moments later as the tug bloomed into nuclear fire.

Most of the wreckage flew away into open space, but some arched down toward the station tearing through cargo in the east yard. Other sections smashed into the station.

Markus held his breath. All of this would be for nothing if the wreckage did not disperse as planned.

"It's heading toward the Lumins!" someone in the room called out.

He let out a soft sigh of relief. It was going to hit.

Moments later the station overseer's quarters were destroyed.

SPY

STELLAR DATE: 3246715 / 02.07.4177 (Adjusted Gregorian)
LOCATION: Mining Platform SK87
REGION: Noctilucent Space, Sirian Hegemony

The rebellion's leadership no longer met in waste treatment pump room IV. So many ranking personnel going into the bowels of the platform with great frequency would stand out and questions would be asked.

Instead Markus hid in plain sight. They met in his main conference room under the guise of holding planning sessions for the platform's upgrades. In most cases they were working on those upgrades, just not in the way the Lumins thought.

Privacy was guaranteed by holding the meetings during the third shift. No Lumin would stay up that late just to have a meeting with their lessers.

"I tell you, there can't be anyone unless it's one of us," Sarah sat back, exasperation filling her voice and expression.

Markus looked around the table at the heads of the rebellion. James was above reproach, especially because he was the one who had orchestrated Steven's accident. Sarah was even less likely. Her unbridled hatred of the shorts would make it impossible to believe she would betray the group.

Though, that's just what would make her the best spy, came a thought in the back of Markus's mind. He dismissed it. Nothing good would come of that thinking.

He couldn't see Samantha or Aaron as Lumin informants either. They had worked tirelessly toward the platform's eventual freedom. He knew they had sacrificed much to get this far.

His eyes slid across several other members of his inner circle, Peter, Dmitry, and Xenia, until they landed on Yolanda. She had joined their quiet rebellion five months ago after a transfer from platform SK45. She was efficient in every way and functioned as an excellent runner, as her work often took her to other platforms.

It also gave her ample opportunity to communicate with the Lumins with no witnesses.

Her eyes locked with Markus's and for a moment he thought he saw something he recognized from somewhere else. A moment later it was gone and he let out a long sigh.

"Put out your feelers, but don't let everyone know that we suspect a leak. If the general populace finds out they'll all suspect their neighbors and that's all but a guarantee for some uncontrolled event to occur."

They spoke of several other matters, and soon dispersed to get what rest they could before the following day arrived. Markus watched them file out as his thoughts wandered, wondering who could be leaking information to the shorts; who would want to.

It wasn't as though there weren't those amongst his people who would sell their neighbor to their oppressors for a meager reward, but he was certain they were all fed false information.

Their sort had been easy enough to identify. The malcontents who believed they were owed something were the first on the list. They were the least risky, as they usually were given access to smaller secrets.

The other likely group were the ones who craved power, but did not have it. They were marked by their ambition and their constant striving to rise in the ranks whether they had earned it or not.

Markus poured over names in his mind, coming up with no one, as none stood out. He refused to suspect everyone, that way led to madness.

He started as a hand touched his shoulder and looked up to see Yolanda standing beside him.

Markus chuckled. "Forgive me, I thought I was alone."

Yolanda sat down and Markus couldn't help but admire her lithe figure. Even through the drab, shapeless Noctus clothing, he could see she had an attractive body. Every move appeared deliberate and sensual, highlighting the curve of her hips and breasts.

He blinked and refocused his thoughts, there was no chance a beautiful woman in her prime would be interested in an aging specimen such as himself.

"Yes, you were alone, I slipped back in after the others were gone," she replied.

Markus felt his pulse quicken. Was she here because she had feelings for him? He took a deep breath; if she weren't present he'd slap himself for such foolishness. She must know something she didn't want to share with the rest of the leadership.

"What is it?"

Her deep green eyes locked with his. "I know who the spy is."

He felt even more foolish for thinking she was there because she was interested in him.

"Who is it?" He asked softly.

Yolanda lowered her head into her hands; her hair slipped forward and obscured her face.

"Please understand." She raised her head and brushed her hair back from her face. "It is me."

Markus' breath caught. Yolanda's face was subtly different, not so much that you wouldn't recognize her, but enough that she appeared to be an entirely different person—one that he recognized all too well.

"Katrina…" he whispered.

She nodded slowly, not breaking eye contact.

Markus was surprised to see sorrow in her eyes and a glistening in their corners. He made to rise, he needed to call Sarah and James, but Katrina caught his hands in his.

"I have not betrayed you," she whispered. "I have betrayed *them*."

Markus stopped and lowered

himself back into his seat. He stared at her for several long minutes, looking for a twitch, a flinch, anything that would give her away. Either she was the consummate actor, or she was telling the truth.

"Why?" He finally asked.

"Why betray my people, or why leak information to Steven?" Katrina asked.

"Both," Markus replied.

Katrina sat back in her chair and put her hands on her thighs, a posture he had seen Yolanda take often when giving thought to an issue.

"I don't think it would come to you as a surprise that I have never fully identified with Luminescent Society," she said slowly. "I have been a spy for my people amongst yours for many years. During that time, I've come to be disgusted with how the Noctus are treated. The Lumins deem you less than human, and not worthy of further consideration, other than for the products you yield.

"I see your families, your many unique cultures, I see you as people."

Markus couldn't help but notice the venom in her voice when she spoke of her people. She chewed out the word Lumin, almost as much as Sarah.

"I didn't know what to do with my uncertainty, until that day my father killed your assistant, Simon. I saw that day what utter monsters we are, what a monster my father is. I resolved that day to help you."

"Why have you lied to me…to us?" Markus asked.

"Would you have believed that I was here to help if I had approached you directly? I came to your platform as a follow up to my father's actions, to ensure there was no unrest. What I found was an installation that was too smooth, too perfect. I knew something was up. It didn't take long to find out that you were planning to something. I insinuated myself into your inner circle in order to help. I have fed misinformation to my handlers and saved you several times from being outed."

"If that's the case, why feed Steven real intel?" Markus asked.

"He was suspicious of you. He also felt that things were too perfect. He was sniffing around and eventually he would have found something. I gave him enough to hang himself with."

Markus let Katrina's statement sink in. She had spoken very casually about setting a man on a road to death. Though he supposed when you were a Lumin spy you often sentenced people for death.

"I've been doing this for some time," Katrina said. "I know you must think me a monster—I can see it in your eyes. But I'm trying to do my best, to keep my people from harming your people every chance I get."

She seemed sincere. If she were playing him, to what end? She could have undone his Endeavor whenever she wanted. The only possibility was that she was telling the truth—she really was trying to help them.

"I guess I owe you my thanks," Markus said.

Katrina smiled, it was deep and genuine. "No thanks necessary. This is a war; we're all doing what we must to stay alive."

Markus returned the smile. "This may sound crazy, but I feel as though, if life hadn't put us in these positions, we could have been close friends."

Katrina laughed, "Markus, we *are* friends. Given what I've done for you, I may be the best friend you have."

Markus was silent for a moment before something Katrina said clicked. His eyes widened and he looked at her in surprise.

"Wait! Yusuf is your father?"

Katrina grimaced. "I was wondering when you would pick up on that. Yes, he is."

Markus couldn't help but reconsider the possibility that she was playing him. Although, there was a lot to hate about Yusuf—being his daughter was probably no party.

"What are you going to do now?" Katrina asked.

Markus sighed. "For now, it's probably best that this stays between us."

CHANGE OF PLANS

STELLAR DATE: 3248427 / 10.16.4181 (Adjusted Gregorian)
LOCATION: Mining Platform SK87
REGION: Noctilucent Space, Sirian Hegemony

Four years had passed since the events which took Steven's life.

After a long investigation—where Katrina fed the Lumins false information—she was sent to another platform. She continued to feed the rebellion intel, and occasionally managed to pass through SK87, taking time to meet with Markus.

In fact, she was due to arrive in just a few weeks—if the fates allowed.

The Endeavor itself was nearly over. To the uninitiated, it appeared as though the platform was still under heavy construction. Hundreds of cargo nets floated in space surrounding the platform; scaffolding, support girders, and temporary storage yards adorned nearly every surface.

Despite this facade, the station's upgrades were nearly complete. Just a month, maybe a little more and they would be ready to cast off their shackles and leave the Sirius system.

As far as the Lumins were concerned, things were on schedule and yields were up. If Yusuf had checked—and Katrina assured Markus that the vice president had indeed checked—he would have found SK87 to be the model installation. To all outward appearances, his show of force in killing Simon was a success.

"Markus, are you with us?" Sarah asked, waving her hand in front of his face.

He blinked and refocused on the meeting at hand.

"He's thinking of Yolanda's next visit," Peter grinned. "Continuing the most unlikely pairing of all time."

"Your jealousy is showing," James cast Peter a quelling look. "Can we get back to the issue at hand?"

"Please," Dmitry nodded. "If I can't get those intercoolers installed in time our trip is going to be short. I need the shorty guards distracted while we bring the shipping crates from the yard to the engines."

"Easier said than done," Markus sighed. "You're going to have to pull them clear across the yard and around the south tower before you can get them to the engine docks."

"So we're going to need a distraction in the tower too," Sarah agreed. "I have just the thing."

There was a knock at the door and a clerk from the outer office stuck his head in.

"Administrator, a shuttle approaches," he looked concerned and Markus wondered what the urgency was. Shuttles approached the platform hourly.

"And?" he asked.

"It's an unscheduled Lumin long range pinnace. It will be at the VIP dock in ten minutes."

"Do we know who is on it?" He asked.

"It only gave its ID and the correct codes, we don't have any passenger manifest, but it is priority code alpha."

Markus nodded and dismissed the clerk. He looked back at his command team.

"Prepare for the rush contingency."

Solemn expressions and slow nods were the only response.

Markus left the administrative wing and made the short trip to the VIP dock.

He prepared himself to deal with a surprise inspection. It would be hard to keep everything under wraps, but not impossible. In the worst case scenario an accident could be arranged in order to keep the Endeavor safe.

The corridors were as utilitarian at the VIP dock as anywhere else. The Lumins didn't spend extra money on mining platforms—even for their own comfort. The only enhancement was newer security equipment, allowing visitors to go about their business faster and leave sooner.

The shuttle was passing through the ES shield when Markus arrived. The bay doors closed behind it and within a minute the ramp lowered.

A pair of fashionable boots came into view, followed by legs wearing a radiant outfit that glowed and flashed a kaleidoscope of color around the dock. Seconds later Katrina's face came into view.

Her studs were in, from the bridge of her nose up to her hairline; her expression was haughty and laced with disdain as she cast her eyes around the dock.

Markus started for a moment, wondering if he was betrayed at the hands of this woman he had come to appreciate in more ways than he could ever have expected.

She locked eyes with him and her right hand twitched ever so imperceptibly and he got the signal. Play along.

Behind her Luther strode down the ramp, his expression a combination of anger and shame. He brushed past Katrina and pointed a finger at Markus.

"Did you know about this?" He shouted, the accusation ringing across the dock.

Markus didn't know what to say, Luther was a fool and he never expected to be confronted by the overseer. Katrina saved him by placing a hand on Luther's shoulder.

"Not here, Overseer, we need a secure location. We do not know where loyalties lie and there is no need to cause alarm until the others arrive."

Luther's eyes darted about the dock, taking in the several workers unloading the shuttle and the *B* guards standing at the dock's security arch.

It appeared, for just a moment, that Luther became quite frightened—an emotion Markus was certain he did not often feel. Then the overseer schooled his expression and nodded.

"Yes, let us proceed to the administrative wing."

He led the way, passing through security and into the corridor.

Katrina fell behind Markus and spoke brusquely. "Administrator. Your platform appears to be in some disarray, with your upgrades underway. How secure is this section?"

Markus understood her meaning and replied. "Perfectly secure. There is nothing that could endanger us here."

Katrina took his meaning and stepped past Markus to stand in front of Luther.

"In that case, Overseer, I'm going to need to bind your hands and sequester your Link."

"You're what? What do you think you're doing?" He raised his hands to protest, but Katrina was both taller and stronger. She forced his hands behind his back and slipped a pair of binders on them.

Markus took a moment to wonder where she had hidden them in her skintight outfit as she replied to Luther.

"I'm helping Markus, what does it look like?"

Luther began to hurl obscenities at her, and, without a moment's hesitation, Katrina punched him in the mouth.

"Any more outbursts and I'll just kill you. You're a valuable hostage, but not so valuable that I'll put up with your crap."

Markus smiled, he really did like watching Katrina work. Once Luther's hands were secured, Markus pulled a handgun from his jacket and thrust it in the overseer's back.

"Walk."

"You'll never get away with it," Luther snarled. "No rebellion has ever succeeded. The fleet will simply destroy the platform and accept the losses if they have to. But I doubt that will happen. A full company of shock troops will be here within the day to purge this installation."

"Seriously?" Markus looked to Katrina.

"Well, within two days. I lied to them about the time I would need to recon the station and get them the intel they needed. I also faked my advance warning to the platform security forces. They have no idea what I'm here for."

"I guess we're advancing the schedule," Markus said.

"Yes, yes we are."

"There's a wrinkle," Katrina scowled and Markus gave a moment's thought to how—even when angry or worried—she was still so beautiful.

"Isn't there always," Markus sighed.

"They're on a stealth interceptor. It's a new type of light-destroyer that is almost impossible to detect. We won't know they're here until they're right on top of us."

Markus increased his pace, pushing Luther ahead of him. "Then we better get this party started."

They marched into the administrative wing and Markus called out, "it's time!"

In seconds the seven Lumins who worked in the wing had been shot with hand-held stun devices. Noctus converged on them, cuffing the Lumins and carrying them into one of the conference rooms.

"Impressive," Katrina smiled.

Markus took a stunner from his personal assistant and dropped Luther.

"Put him with the others."

Several minutes later the command team rushed back into the conference room at Markus's summons.

James was first in, "has it begun? I saw them dumping some shorts next door."

Markus nodded, "It has. They have found us out and a ship is on its way."

A moment later Sarah entered the room and her eyes immediately locked onto Katrina who stood near the head of the table. "What is she doing here? Another hostage?"

"No," Markus said. "Sit, I'll explain when everyone has arrived. Sarah and James took their customary places at the table, suspiciously eying Katrina who kept her expression neutral.

Within a minute everyone had reassembled and Markus began with a smile. "I'm not sure why you're all being so hostile. Yolanda is a part of the team, after all."

Cries of disbelief sounded around the table as Katrina nodded slowly.

"It is true. I have been with you for the entire Endeavor; though I was not able to reveal my identity for all our safety.

"Huh," James's face broke into a slow smile. "Your intel was always really good for just a message runner. I should have guessed you were more than meets the eye."

"I don't believe it," Sarah said, her words filled with venom. "She has you fooled, Markus. There's no way one of them would side with us—no way you would work with one of them freely!"

Markus knew that Sarah would be the hardest to win over. Her blind hatred of the Lumins made it as hard for her to see them as human—just as they could not see the Noctus as anything more than property.

"She does not have me fooled. I have known her true identity since the event with Steven. She helped us greatly then. We could have fallen under much greater scrutiny, or worse."

"Then how were we found out this time?" Sarah asked. "No one here talked, we would never betray our own."

"I know that," Katrina said. "I believe it was a contact on another station. Perhaps the yardmaster on SK47—I'm not certain. Yusuf got wind and launched a covert investigation. They did a long-range scan and picked up some of your engine modifications."

"I don't care what you say, I won't accept it," Sarah replied, anger lacing her words.

"I know it's hard for you to accept." Katrina altered her voice, adopting a softer accent common on the platform. "But I hate them nearly as much as you do—I'm only half Lumin…what my mother suffered through.... I would see our Endeavor succeed and leave this place—leave them behind forever."

"Those are just words," Dmitry said. "How do we know that they are true?"

"Because I say they are," Markus replied. "I kept you in the dark for your safety and hers. What she did was too risky for any slip-ups. Also, I was worried about how you'd react—I couldn't have dissent fracturing us while we worked to gain our freedom." He looked to Katrina. "Sit, please."

She lowered into a seat at his left side and Markus surveyed the team.

"We have just under forty hours to finalize our preparations. Anything that can wait until we're in transit must wait. Propulsion and navigation are our only concerns."

He was met with nods, even if some were sullen.

"James, hit the armory. The sergeant on duty is Larson; he's bought and paid for. Disperse the weapons to the rally points and send the word that we move on all Lumin positions in one hour—sooner if we can manage."

HYPERION

STELLAR DATE: 3248427 / 10.16.4181 (Adjusted Gregorian)
LOCATION: Mining Platform SK87
REGION: Noctilucent Space, Sirian Hegemony

The ease with which the inhabitants of SK87 secured the platform made Markus nervous. It should have been harder; there should have been pockets of the Lumins that took extreme measures to flush out making for pitched battles and bloody sacrifices.

There were none.

"It's not surprising," Katrina said as they surveyed the results of the overthrow from overwatch.

"No?" Markus replied.

"This isn't the first time an overthrow has been successful. You don't hear about most of them, the workers in Noctilucent Space are kept as isolated as possible."

Markus took a long draught of coffee. "You never said they happened that often."

"Well, once every few decades. There are thousands of worker platforms and stations. It's a pretty good ratio. It's not worth the cost to have Luminescent security forces at the levels it would require to stop them all. It's cheaper to lose the odd installation here and there."

"Or catch things before they get to this point," James grinned. "Like what you're supposed to have done."

Katrina nodded. "Precisely."

"Makes sense," Markus nodded. "With a population close to a hundred thousand you would need at least three or four thousand security guards to ensure any uprising was crushed."

"More, statistically," Katrina said.

Dmitry entered overwatch. "Everything is secure, but we're going to need another week to get everything ready for the transformation."

"You likely have twenty hours," Katrina said. "The battalion I spoke of will be here soon and they'll purge this platform for re-seeding."

"There's no way we can be ready in twenty hours," James shook his head.

"We need those intercoolers installed," Dmitry nodded his head in agreement. "If we don't this will be one short trip."

Markus was silent as he considered their options.

"At least we don't need a distraction to get them across the station. You have ten hours to get them moved and installed."

The next morning Markus addressed the entire station, much of which was assembled in the main promenade to hear his speech in person.

He couldn't help but think of the grand corridors and markets of the Luminescent stations. The platform had nothing to compare, only the few shops and company distribution centers that were somehow grander, now that they belonged to his people and not the Lumins.

Through the dim lighting, he surveyed the crowd below him, elated that this day had arrived. His happiness was dampened by the niggling worry in the back of his mind that the last, crucial phase of their Endeavor could still fail.

He pushed the doubt from his mind and schooled his expression. No trace of uncertainty must show to his people.

Markus looked to his sides. The command crew surrounded him. Though most had not slept in more than a day they were all smiling; even Sarah—though she was scanning the crowd. No doubt looking for Luminescent sympathizers.

"People of platform SK87, we've done it," Markus said simply. Thunderous applause exploded. Cheers and whoops of joy echoed through the station's corridors for a full minute before he raised his hands for silence.

"We have always been free in our hearts. Our ancestors came here because they had an untamable spirit, a desire to see new worlds and new stars. The Lumins spent generations trying to crush that spirit out of us, but they failed.

"Today we are truly free. Your children will never know the yoke of slavery. They will be able to choose their own destinies!"

He waited once more for the crowd to quiet.

"You all know the story of the ship *Hyperion,* the ship that escaped after the shorts betrayed our ancestors. They left Sirius and found a new home in the stars. Now *we* are *Hyperion*!"

A shudder rippled through the deck plates and above the crowd a holo shimmered to life. It showed the platform suspended in space. Markus held his breath, a transformation like this was unprecedented as far as he knew, no one took a mining platform between the stars.

More shocks reverberated through the decks and the holo showed several sections of the newly christened *Hyperion* drift off into space. In their wake, much larger engines were revealed.

Two massive fusion burners sat on either end of the platform and in the center a cluster of short-burn antimatter pion engines were exposed as the west yard drifted away with the last month's harvested ore still resting in containers.

The *Hyperion's* supply of antimatter was limited, but the engines would give them enough thrust for a slingshot around Sirius before running dry. If their calculations were correct the platform should achieve a velocity just over a tenth the speed of light.

Markus glanced down at a small tablet he held and then to Dmitry. The chief engineer gave him a thumbs up. So far everything was going to plan—impressive

Beside Markus, Dmitry was nodding as he listened to his teams report in. He smiled and gave Markus a thumbs up.

Markus returned the gesture as another shudder rippled through the deck, causing a fresh round of cheers. The hastily set up holo projectors showed the south yard breaking free from the ship, exposing a much larger MDC emitter that would function as a stellar matter scoop.

The scoop would draw in as much fuels as possible during the slingshot maneuver around Sirius. Once the platform was on an outsystem vector it would be reconfigured to function as a solar sail.

They would burn the engines as long as possible, retaining half the fuel for braking once they reached Kapteyn's Star. Dmitri's estimations put the journey somewhere between fifty and seventy years—with new engines and an untested scoop the variables were many.

The holo projections shifted, showing a view of the engines roaring to life—a visual that was accompanied by a low rumble in the deck.

Markus looked to Dmitry who was smiling broadly.

"Thank the light," Markus whispered while he watched the holo show streams of plasma race into space as the platform eased into motion.

"I can't wait to see the faces of the shorts when they see this on their long range scans," James said with a grin.

"They're going to lose their minds, or piss themselves," Sarah said with a laugh.

Katrina caught Markus's eye. Her expression was not so jovial.

"If those were there only two options I'd feel a lot better right now," she said softly to Markus.

The interceptor was running dark.

Voices were hushed; any and all unneeded electronics were switched off. Even lighting was dimmed.

The only discernible energy output was a stream of pions—traveling near the speed of light—streaming out the engine's long funnel.

Major Han re-read the EMF output and engine reports. Surprise was key. The inhabitants of SK87 had no idea a stealth ship was bearing down on them. The longer that lack of awareness persisted, the more of his soldiers would survive the fight.

He looked over the troop readiness reports a third time. This was his company's second combat deployment; though they had made countless training runs—both simulated and physical.

The brass had considered his first live combat mission to be a smashing success, but he did not. Too many of his troops had died at the hands of the Noctus scum they were putting down. The corporation had wanted the station to stay intact, and the lives of his men and women bought that result.

That was why, when this new stealth interceptor became available for a trail run, he jumped at it. The normal troop transports could be seen half the system away. A station had days to prepare before his soldiers arrived.

SK87 would have no such foreknowledge. They would know of their demise the hour it was upon them.

"Sir!" the officer manning the scan terminal called out. "Something… something has happened to the platform!"

Major Han surveyed the scan report with disbelief. At first it appeared as though SK87 was exploding, but there was no fire, or small debris. Chunks of it were simply falling off.

Minutes later, as the scan updated, it became quite clear what was occurring. The platform had been surreptitiously refitted. How or why was not his concern, stopping whatever they planned next was.

"Helmsman, increase burn, I want to get there as fast as this ship can take us. No need for surprise, they know we're coming." Major Han's tone was brusque.

Helm nodded and Han's XO gave him a quizzical look. "How can you be sure?"

Jennifer was new to Han's command, a recent OSC grad. She had promise, but like any newly minted lieutenant, thought she knew a hell of a lot more than she actually did.

"Because they're making no attempt to hide what they're doing. That means they've taken the station and either know about us specifically, or expect some retaliation soon."

"Then we should expect them to have weapons," Jennifer replied.

"Lieutenant, we should always expect them to have weapons."

Han let out a long sigh. It was going to be bloody. Too many Lumins would die at the hands of Noctus animals and there was little he could do about it now.

Other than kill every man, woman, and child on that platform.

Yusuf's expression remained calm and serene as he read the report. Those around him at the monthly executive meeting would never have suspected that a sea of rage roiled beneath his calm demeanor.

That Markus would do something so brash, so outrageous. That Luther, the coal-brained station overseer, hadn't suspected a thing was inexcusable. If he survived, Yusuf would have him executed.

The brief flashed with an update from the field commander, a Major Han. It was a single line of text:

We think they have your daughter.

Yusuf looked up at the other governing executives. Greenich, a pitiful man responsible for reclamation infrastructure was speaking—Yusuf interrupted him without notice.

"You'll have to excuse me, something urgent has come up."

With no further ceremony he swept out of the room, already calling Admiral Pontius on the Link.

<Yusuf, what do I owe…>

<You owe insurrection. I want three of your best destroyers ready to go in one hour,> Yusuf cut him off.

<Yes, sir, I will have a shuttle at your private dock in fifteen minutes.>

Yusuf severed the connection. He hadn't given Pontius their destination, but he knew the Admiral would figure it out soon enough.

"Aras!" Yusuf yelled to his assistant without turning. There was no need to ensure that the man was there; he was always scuttling in Yusuf's wake. "Ensure bags are packed for me and transferred to Pontius's shuttle when it arrives. We could be gone for several weeks."

As he stepped into the lift Yusuf considered the words, *we think they have your daughter.* Katrina had been on SK87 several times in the past few years, checking up on them and ensuring that there was no unrest following his killing of Markus's assistant.

Her reports, and the reports of his other operatives, indicated that it was the model station and he had all but put it from his mind.

Now, with this new information, he could arrive at only one conclusion: his daughter had betrayed him. If that was true, she would die as well—at his hands if possible.

GETTING OUT OF DODGE

STELLAR DATE: 3248428 / 10.17.4181 (Adjusted Gregorian)
LOCATION: ***Hyperion***
REGION: Noctilucent Space, Sirian Hegemony

Markus leaned back in his chair, forcing his heart to slow and his breathing to calm. Though the events now unfolding had been his goal for the last few years, actually carrying out these final, irreversible actions left him feeling more anxiety than he had imagined he would.

The door cracked open and Katrina's head peeked around.

"Do you have a moment?" She asked.

Markus couldn't help it as a smile crept across his face. "I always have a moment for you." He stood and she stepped into his arms. The pair shared no words for a long moment, simply breathing in one another's presence.

"Hard to believe this day has finally come, isn't it?" Katrina asked as she stepped back and sat on the edge of his desk.

Markus slipped back into his chair, taking in the sight of this beautiful woman who genuinely seemed to want to spend time with him. She still wore the skin-tight clothing of her people—though she had muted its coloring somewhat. The way it hugged the curves of her body undid all of the calm he had managed to acquire before she entered his office.

Katrina gave a slight chuckle, drawing his eyes to her face.

"You're always so calm and in control, it's nice to see you acting as a mortal man every so often."

Markus laughed in reply. "If this is what we are judging me by, I am so very mortal."

Katrina smiled in return and took several moments to speak.

"I don't know what is going to happen over the next few days and months, but I need you to know something."

"What would that be?" Markus asked in reply.

"There has been no acting on my part," Katrina said. "I know that because I am a spy you suspect my motives and whether I am genuine. Hell, sometimes I wonder where I end and a cover begins," she said the last with a rueful chuckle. "But I *need* you to know. This is real, I have feelings for you, it is no act."

Markus worked to find the right words. He had certainly hoped that her feelings were genuine, but a kernel of doubt had always lingered within him, gnawing slowly at his surety.

"Why?" he finally asked.

Katrina's expression showed puzzlement and then she gave a light and silvery laugh. "Markus, you really are a fool of a man. A great leader, amazing in how you motivate your people and have earned their trust, but when it comes to this...well... let's just say you're not too skilled."

"Something I have never claimed to be, but you still haven't answered my question."

"I can see into people's motives all too well and manipulate them as needed, but I can't say I understand love," Katrina said the last word with a finality that rung like a bell.

"Love?"

"Yes, administrator Markus, love."

She reached down and pulled him up into her arms, their lips meeting with a deep yearning.

"Uh, Boss?"

Markus looked and saw James standing in the doorway, red-faced and sheepish looking.

"Yes James?"

"Sorry to disturb you, but we need you in overwatch, both of you actually."

Markus and Katrina disentangled their arms and they followed James through the administrative wing toward overwatch.

"What's up?" Markus asked.

James's voice was grim. "It would seem that our visitors are going to be here a bit early."

"How is that possible?" Katrina asked.

"They've boosted a lot harder than we had anticipated after we transformed the *Hyperion*. I guess someone lit a fire under their assess."

Markus and Katrina exchanged glances.

"I can imagine who held the match," Katrina said with a grim expression.

James cast a glance her way. "Yeah? Who?"

I'm guessing it was her father," Markus said.

James chuckled and shook his head. "I've heard of dad not liking the boyfriend, but this is a bit much. Who is he anyway?"

"Yusuf," Katrina's voice was tense as she spoke the name.

James turned sideways as he walked, locking eyes with Katrina and then Markus. "Are you kidding me? What... why...?" he sputtered.

Markus just shrugged. He wanted to ask James what he would do had he caught the attention of Katrina, but decided that was not the wisest response.

"What does their ETA look like?" Katrina asked, changing the subject.

James took the hint. "About nine hours, but they'll be in weapons range in half that time—provided they don't plan to use something that we can't deflect."

"They don't have any nuclear weapons; their superiors don't like the mess those make. They prefer, at least, to have salvage if they can't keep the station intact," Katrina said. "No, their first offensive will be a full-scale boarding and cleansing."

Dmitry had joined the trio in the corridor as Katrina was speaking. "Cleansing. I guess we're just bacteria to them," he said angrily.

"No good thoughts lie that way," Markus cautioned Dmitry. "We have to remain focused on how we'll get through this."

"Well, you're lucky. With no small amount of divine intervention, we got the intercoolers installed. It's not pretty and if any other chief engineers see it I'll deny I had any part in that installation, but we'll get the operational efficiencies we need out of the engines."

"Then we need to light those pion drives," Katrina said. "Making them alter v and thread the belt to meet up with us will buy us some more time."

"I have our four biggest tugs fueled up and ready to go as well," James added. "We'll get this thing underway in no time."

No time, as it turned out, was just over two hours. James's crews carefully selected anchor points on the newly balanced station and the new engines threw a few final curve balls before they were running just the way Dmitry wanted.

The *Hyperion* lay deep within Sirius's second asteroid belt, just over three AU from the star. The engines and tugs strained to pull the platform stellar north and out of the field before the platform could begin the hard burn toward the star for the gravity assist slingshot outsystem.

The belt was not densely populated, but enough so that the platform had to alter course several times to thread their way past errant rocks and dust clouds. It was just over seven hours after their burn started that the path to the star was clear enough to push the engines to their maximum output.

Markus watched the scan on the main holotank in overwatch, keeping an eye on the positions of other platforms and asteroids, as well as the spotty ghost-echo of the pursuing ship.

Several times the platform had been hailed by system traffic control stations as to the nature of their unscheduled movement, but each time the *Hyperion* did not respond. With each subsequent hail, a hushed silence deepened across overwatch—and across the entire platform—as the crew waited for the inevitable confrontation.

"I have a contact," scan called out. "It looks like a patrol ship leaving a nearby garrison station."

"To be expected," Markus nodded and looked to Katrina. "Do you think it's synchronized with the strike force?"

"Hard to say," Katrina replied. "It could be, but I don't think that the strike force would want to tip their hand. It could be a feint, either way, if I were their commander, I would look for an opportunity to use the distraction this will cause."

"That interceptor ship couldn't get all the way here without us picking them up on scan, could they?" James asked.

The yard-master's day-to-day work was some of the most dangerous on the station. Wrangling cargo and asteroids where the smallest mistake could result in disaster. Markus had rarely heard him sound anything other than calm and serene, but there was more than a waver in the man's voice.

Katrina caught Markus's eye and he nodded, people needed some assurances. He switched his chair's comm to station-wide.

"People of the *Hyperion,* you have shown incredible fortitude during our endeavor thus far, and through our initial actions today. It is likely that things are going to get exciting soon. A patrol ship is on an intercept course with us and it's possible that our friends on the destroyer could use that distraction to their advantage. I want all teams to be ready for boarding at any moment and everyone monitoring external hatches to be ready to blow them at a moment's notice.

"Stay strong, stay vigilant, we will weather this and see a new star."

James grinned. "Good speech boss."

Markus didn't reply and turned back to scan. Three hours until the patrol ship was in weapons range.

"Patrol ship entering range," scan called out one hundred and eighty-two long minutes later.

"They're hailing us," comm added. "Nothing new, though their tone is considerably more irate," the woman running comm added with a smile.

"Put me through," Markus said.

The comm officer pushed a button on her panel and nodded in his direction.

"This is the sovereign ship *Hyperion,* formerly known as platform SK87. Do not come within ten-thousand kilometers of our platform. Doing so will be considered an act of aggression and we will fire upon you."

Markus put the comm down and wiped the sweat from his hands as he exchanged looks with the overwatch command crew.

The response was quick and angry as expected.

"What are you playing at SK87. Your platform is the property of the people of Sirius and you are contractually bound to it. You will open your main bay for our shuttles to dock at once."

Markus picked up the comm handset with both hands, praying no one noticed the slight tremor he couldn't suppress.

"Negative, patrol ship, by our calculations our people paid back their transit debt seven hundred and twenty-six years ago. In the intervening years we have paid for this platform and are, in fact, owed a steep remittance for our labor. We'd prefer to be paid in Sol credits."

Katrina stifled a laugh as he switched off comm.

"I wonder if anyone has ever told them that before?" she asked.

"First time for everything," Markus forced a smile.

"They're launching two boarding shuttles," scan called out. "Looks like one is headed for the main bay, and the other for the north bay airlock."

"Can we make good on our threat to shoot them?" James asked.

"Negative," scan replied. "Not all our weapons got mounted and they picked approaches where we're wide open."

"I should get to the main bay," Katrina said. "I'll direct the crew at the north bay lock to prime their charges and detonate as soon as the outer hatch is opened."

Markus nodded grimly. "Good luck."

With the rushed departure there were a lot of steps in their insurrection that the crew of the *Hyperion* had not managed to complete. One of which was to complete the various computer overrides necessary to completely lock the shorts out of the platform's control systems.

One that was proving to be more difficult than expected—short of destroying it entirely—was removing remote access for the main bay doors.

As Katrina approached the main bay's control shack she called into the techs frantically working on the bay door's software.

"Let it be," Katrina advised. "We'll deal with them once they get in. We could use another ship," she added with a wink.

The *Hyperion's* main bay was just over a hundred meters deep and three hundred wide. Two smaller tugs rested on cradles on each side. Just inside the main lock between the bay and the rest of the platform, stood two dozen of the platform's newly formed militia.

Katrina knew she'd find Sarah leading this group and nodded to the other woman.

"I expect that they'll settle their shuttle on the main platform." Katrina said by way of greeting.

Sarah nodded in response, her eyes boring into Katrina's.

"We should take up positions behind those tugs and under the deck plates there, and there," Katrina pointed to several maintenance hatches.

"They'll be too close; the shorts'll take anyone in that position out in seconds." Sarah shook her head. "We should ambush them in the corridors."

"If we do that it will be too late. They'll have a foothold on the ship and they also may lase us right through the bulkheads. We have to take them quick and by surprise."

Katrina looked around at the militia, many of whom she recognized after spending so many months on the platform. She singled out four of the men and women who she knew had young families.

"You four, take up positions around the main hatch. Take a couple of pot-shots at them as they disembark and then run. It'll focus their attention forward and then give them a false sense of security when you run. That's when the rest of us will attack."

Katrina looked at Sarah who slowly nodded. She could tell the other woman may not like her, but understood why Katrina picked those four individuals for the diversion. Perhaps she'd win her over eventually.

Katrina split the rest up into the sharpshooters who would take up positions behind the tugs, and those with less accurate, close range weapons, who would hide under the deck plates.

While the people of the *Hyperion* knew for some time that they would likely fight a battle on their decks, there had been no way to properly train them in combat. She had to hope that the vids and desire to free their home would be enough.

"Remember," she cautioned the men and women. "It's close quarters in here. It's going to be terrifying and confusing. Pick your targets carefully. Don't shoot wildly; the last thing you want is to hit a friend."

Her words were answered by solemn nods and sidelong glances. Sarah nodded to the militia and they moved to their positions. Katrina took up a position on the heavy equipment maintenance shed. It was in a corner of the dock and its roofline was above any lines of sight from where the boarding craft would disgorge its soldiers.

She would only get a few shots off as the assault transport's weapons would make short work of her position once they had a lock.

She unslung the slug thrower she had smuggled onto the station several months earlier. It was a brutal weapon and not the sort of thing any civilized combatant would use, but it would keep as many of the Hyperions alive as possible.

The external bay doors began to open scant moments after the last of the fighters slipped into cover. Katrina found herself holding her breath, and forced a slow exhale. She eyed the four fighters at the dock's main hatch. They held their weapons securely, but Katrina could see their nervousness in the twitch of a finger and subtle shifts of position.

"Hold steady," she whispered to herself, wishing—not for the first time—that the Hyperions had Link technology.

The assault craft was the size and model she had expected, it held between six and ten lightly armored soldiers, likely under the command of a lieutenant. A pair of pilots would stay with the craft and man its weapons.

Before it had finished settling into the cradle the ramp was lowering and four soldiers jumped to the deck. On queue the four Noctus fighters at the dock's entrance took a few shots before retreating into the corridor, using the bulkhead for cover.

Only one shot hit a Luminescent soldier. It was a good shot, center-mass, but the force was absorbed by the advanced armor the soldier wore. A second later, several more soldiers had spilled from the craft and Katrina saw all but one of the fighters disappear from the dock's hatch.

"Go, move!" She whispered to herself.

The Noctus fighter was too late, a soldier fired, his shot true and a figure fell forward through the dock's hatch, face slamming into the deck plate.

The soldiers responded as Katrina expected. Believing the Noctus had retreated, they fully deployed from the assault craft. She held her breath for a second, praying to whatever gods may listen that Sarah took the cue.

She sighted along her rifle's holoscope and let a long breath escape her lungs. As the last wisps of air passed her lips, the Hyperion Militia burst from beneath the deck plates, and, gods bless them, began firing without asking for quarter.

The soldiers were flanked and their ranks nearly collapsed under a concussive blanket of pulse rifle fire. Their armor took the brunt of the attack, but two fell in the initial volley from the militia. Katrina didn't give them a chance to regroup and lined her sights on one of the soldiers at the front of their formation. The command raced from her mind to the rifle and it fired the slug.

As though she had simply sent a signal to a bomb, her target's head exploded. Pieces of burning metal, brain, and bone slammed into three men behind the soldier. Two of them went down, and the third stood screaming, trying to tear his helmet off—a difficult task with a piece of his teammate's skull protruding from his visor.

Katrina took a second shot, killing a man on the flank—this time with no collateral damage.

Moments later the remaining Luminescent soldiers threw their weapons to the ground and Sarah led half her squad into the assault craft to subdue the pilots.

Katrina didn't wait for report of their success, she saw the ship's upper turret begin to turn toward her and dropped from the roof of the maintenance shed, sliding down a ladder and rushing across the dock toward the militia and the relative cover of the assault craft.

Two women were smashing the point defense lasers on the front of the craft, and four others had surrounded the remaining soldiers. The rest were losing their lunch off to the side of the cradle.

Katrina sent a message over the platform's meager Link to Operations. *<Assault team is subdued, Sarah is taking the pilots, we should have the dock fully under control in a minute.>*

<Good to hear,> Markus's voice played in her head; she could hear cheering in the background as the team in operations let off some stress.

<Did they repel at the north bay airlock?> Katrina asked.

<Our folks blew the lock when the shorts tried to get a seal. It looks like it wrecked their hatch. They were circling around to the main bay, but now they've diverted to the south bay.>

Sarah walked down the ramp with the two pilots at gunpoint, wearing a grin so large it almost wrapped around her face.

"Nice work, Sarah," Katrina smiled, hoping to gain some points with the surly woman. "Markus tells me that the other assault craft is making for the south service bay.

Sarah's expression turned serious. "Sven!" she called to the leader of her second squad. "Stay here and lock these asshats down, Katrina and I will take second and third squad to take care of their friends.

They jogged out of the bay to the sounds of the remaining militia stunning the captured soldiers before they stripped and cuffed them.

Katrina thought she knew the platform well, but Sarah led them through a twisting maze of passageways, some so narrow they had to pass single file.

"These aren't all on the official blueprint," Katrina commented at one point.

"Noticed that did you?" Sarah replied with a smirk. "Good to know you didn't ferret out all of our secrets."

Katrina decided not to respond; it seemed like she still had a way to go before she wasn't one of *them* to Sarah.

Weapons fire greeted them before they reached the dock and Sarah raised the leader of the squad defending the bay on her comm unit.

"We're pinned down! We couldn't stop them from getting the bay doors open without blowing them. We're trapped behind the port-side maintenance crane."

"We'll get you out of there," Sarah replied and broke into a full run, Katrina trailing behind with the two squads.

"How many of them are there?" Katrina asked.

"A dozen at least. The ship is firing on our position too, but they haven't pulled out the big guns yet." The response was accompanied by the sounds of a man screaming in agony.

"Sarah, split the squads up between the two entrances. Is there another, less well known way into the bay?" Katrina asked.

Sarah nodded. "If you go into the dock master's office there's a ladder up to a service hatch that gets you onto an observation deck. Not as much cover, but maybe you can get a shot or two off again."

Katrina nodded and pulled up a station map. The route Sarah described overlaid her vision and she took the last few twists fast enough that she slid into the bulkheads.

Her work as an infiltrator required her to have far fewer modifications and physical enhancements than most in Luminescent Society. Normally she didn't mind. She had earned a respect for how the Noctus worked with pure biological bodies. However, today she wished she had taken the agency's suggestion that she take a few mods in case of emergency.

The service hatch was just where Sarah said and Katrina climbed onto the narrow observation walkway. Below her she could see the assault craft resting unevenly in the bay's center cradle. Four of the soldiers were working their way toward the beleaguered militia who had been guarding the bay while the remaining eight had taken up positions defending against Sarah's troops who were firing from the two entrances.

Katrina lay prone and checked her magazine. She had three shots. With the cover the observation catwalk offered she would likely not get a second. She looked through the holo sights and prepared to fire into a group of soldiers.

A second before she squeezed the trigger she saw movement out of the corner of her eye. She shifted her scope and realized that the assault craft's main turret was about to fire down the corridor into Sarah's people.

She shifted her weapon, took aim and fired one slug and then a second into the turret. The ship's gun exploded in a shower of sparks and shrapnel.

Below, several of the soldiers looked around for the new source of weapons fire and one spotted her, likely marking her position on his HUD.

Katrina considered her options. Chances were that she wouldn't be able to fire the slug thrower again in this fight. Getting back through the service hatch would take precious seconds she didn't have. A glance down told her that jumping would hurt, but there would be cover.

She rolled off the edge of the catwalk twisting in the air and landing behind a row of tool chests. There were some spare parts and tools scattered on the floor and her right foot came down sideways on one.

The snap told her that something in her ankle was broken a moment before the pain set in. Luckily the ability to dull pain was one mod she had taken—in case of capture and torture.

She put it from her mind and drew her sidearm while gingerly moving to the end of the tool chest row. It was certain that one or two soldiers had been dispatched to secure her location.

The small pistol was normally used for stunning, but it also contained a high velocity flechette cartridge and she flipped the toggle to that mode.

Ahead of her, the barrel of a gun peeked around the corner; the end of the weapon pivoted, trained on her. She fell to the ground as a pulse wave blasted above her, numbing her back. The soldier must have thought his shot hit her as his leg stepped forward.

Taking aim, Katrina fired a flechette at the back of the soldier's knee, where the armor was weakest. With a cry of pain, the soldier, a woman by the sound of her, fell to the ground. Katrina sighted for a moment and then fired a second shot under the woman's chin, another weak spot.

The woman's thrashing turned to twitching and Katrina scrambled forward to secure the rifle.

Just as her hand settled on the grip, a voice called out from behind her, "freeze!"

Katrina pivoted, bringing her new-found rifle to bear on the voice and found a soldier standing two meters from her with his rifle trained on her head.

"Go for it, fire that shot," she could almost see the man's smirk behind the mirrored face plate. Any Noctus attempting to use a Lumin soldier's weapon without first disarming the genetic safeties would lose their hand—if they were lucky.

Katrina shrugged. "OK." She fired the shot and the man fell backward. She pulled herself upright and fired three more pulse shots into his face. If he wasn't dead, he would wish he were.

She pulled herself up to peek over the tool chests and saw that several more of the soldiers were down, but Sarah's reinforcements were still pinned down in the corridor.

She moved back toward the assault craft, looking for a good position to apply flanking fire. A large barrel filled with scrap metal looked to provide good cover and she crouched behind it, using the rifle's pivoting barrel and holo sights to line up on a soldier from the back.

Several shots later and the soldiers were scrambling to find cover while under fire from three sources.

"Surrender!" Katrina called out between gritted teeth. The pain dampening mods weren't working as well as they were supposed to. She worried it was much more than a simple break.

Through her sights she saw a soldier throw down his weapon and raise his arms in surrender. Moments later, they all followed suit and she called out. "Move toward the corridor. Slowly!"

Sarah's militia moved into the bay and began to secure the soldiers. Katrina hobbled around the barrel she had been using for cover and waved an arm in greeting before taking a moment to glance down at her ankle.

A piece of steel jutted out from her boot and she chuckled softly, "I guess you're why this hurt so much."

Sarah trotted over with four of her fighters. She directed them to secure the assault craft and gave a grudging smile to Katrina.

"I guess I owe you one. When I saw that turret pivot toward the corridor I thought we were done for."

"Think maybe I'm crew of the *Hyperion* now?" Katrina asked—straight to the point.

Sarah's cheeks reddened. "I have been kind of an ass to you, haven't I?"

"No more than I deserved. I haven't always been on the right side of things."

Sarah nodded silently, her smile dipping for a moment and Katrina suspected she was wondering what things she had done in her years as a spy for the shorts. A moment later it was gone.

"That's in the past," she said and reached out to clasp Katrina's shoulder.

The pressure caused her to shift and Katrina sucked in a painful breath as her ankle shot through with pain.

Sarah looked down.

"Holy shit, that doesn't look like fun."

"Not especially, no."

Sarah pulled Katrina's arm over her shoulder. "Let me get you over to the medic."

Half hour later, Katrina hobbled into operations on crutches. A brief flash of concern raced across Markus's face before he schooled his expression.

"Wow," James called out. "I thought it was just a minor injury."

"It was," Katrina responded as she worked her way up the stairs to the command ring. "Unfortunately the medicine allowed the Noctus isn't much to speak of. I have some dormant med nano that I've initialized. They'll replicate and get it fixed up in a day or two."

"Until then you're pretty much benched," Markus said.

Katrina threw a sweet smile his way, "you're just going to have to settle for my brains with my body in recovery."

Dmitry choked on his coffee and James barked a loud guffaw.

"Thanks," Markus muttered. "That'll garner me so much respect around here."

Katrina patted him on the shoulder and sat in a chair with as much grace as someone in her condition could muster.

"You all seem to be in a much better mood than you were when I left," she observed.

"It may have had something to do with you and Sarah kicking some serious ass out there," James said. "I hear you did some crazy heroics to save the day."

"Everyone did crazy heroics," Katrina said. "Mine just got my ankle broken is all."

"We also got a ping off the destroyer," Markus said. "It's still several light minutes out and will take another couple of hours to match velocities with us. The patrol craft has pulled away and for the moment we're in the clear."

"Do we have a plan for the destroyer?" Katrina asked. "They're going to be a lot harder to fight off than the district patrol guys."

Markus looked to Dmitry who set his coffee down and brought up a system map on the main holo tank.

"We're here, almost past the inner dust belt and Vishnu's orbit. From there we're going to increase our burn as we fall faster into Sirius's gravity well. It's going to extend our lead on the destroyer, and if we can hold together as we pull around the star we'll be out of their reach—unless they want to hit an outsystem velocity with no worlds to break around."

Katrina couldn't help but notice that Dmitry used the pre-colonization name for Sirius's innermost world. Luminescent society had renamed all of the planets, but the Noctus resented the renaming. They viewed it as another piece of their heritage that had been suppressed.

"Bold, but it looks like it will work," Katrina nodded.

The command crew fell to reviewing the status of the last few upgrades that Dmitry's engineers were making and re-checking the removal of Luminescent command codes from the computer systems.

Katrina was reviewing a report from Sarah on the incarceration of the Luminescent soldiers from the assault craft as well as those garrisoned on the platform. The plan was to release them in a cargo hauler after the gravity assist maneuver around Sirius was complete.

She enjoyed the physical act of reading so often required on Noctus platforms. In Luminescent society so much information was directly inserted into one's mind over the Link. Little thought was given to the act of absorbing the information and internalizing it. Looking over the words of Sarah's report was refreshing.

Her reading was disrupted by an alarm's wail. She turned to look at the main board and let out a small cry of surprise.

Markus was on the comm verifying the information.

"Are you certain? Do you have visual confirmation?" He all but yelled into the microphone.

"I can see it from here," the voice came over the room's overhead speakers. "It's attached just above the east yard's main hatch. I don't know how long it's been there other than it wasn't fifteen minutes ago."

"Fifteen minutes!" Katrina exclaimed. "They could be anywhere by now."

She had to grant a modicum of respect for the assault force's commander. He must have slipped this assault away from the destroyer and brought it straight up the *Hyperion's* wake to avoid detection. Between the engines and the east yard there were few external port holes and significant sensor gaps. His men would likely need treatment for the rads they picked up though.

"Sarah's reporting in," Markus called out. "She has her militia moving into position. It looks like the enemy has spread all over the sector."

"Are there many crew in there?" Katrina asked, worried the soldiers had already begun cleansing the platform.

"A few hundred, Sarah reports that she's working on evacuating them and protecting the positions of the ones working on the final engine prep."

Katrina struggled to stand. "I should get down there, I can help with tactics and pull a trigger if necessary."

"You'll do no such thing," Markus put a hand on her shoulder and gently pushed her back into her seat. "Do you really think you'd be more of a help than a hindrance?"

Katrina sighed. "Very well, the battle would likely be over by the time I got down there anyway." She brought up the station's schematics, and worked with the comm officer to map out the positions of the enemy soldiers and provide guidance to the militia.

Reports poured in from the sector, the fighting was fierce and the ship's militia was taking heavy losses. Corridor-by-corridor they were being pushed back by the elite Lumin troops. From what Katrina could tell there were fewer than thirty enemy soldiers, but their superior armor, weapons, and tactics were crafted for just this sort of situation.

She looked to James for information on the layout of a particular intersection, but he wasn't at his station.

"Markus, where did James go?"

Markus looked up from the main holo tank, his brow furrowing. "I don't know; he was here a moment ago. Maybe he needed to visit the head."

Katrina switched her terminal to his personal comm. "James, do you copy? I need your advice on a corridor?"

For a moment there was no response, and then James's response came over her headset. "Yeah. Sure. Where?" His voice was hoarse and he sounded out of breath.

"Where are you? What's going on?"

"Just ran to the head if you must know, which intersection?"

Katrina felt a slight blush. "Sector 5A, deck 17, the 5A-7E intersection."

"Ah, that one. It's a mess, there are several bio-waste stacks that run through there and some life support. They sit right out in the walkway and you have to almost squeeze past them."

Katrina nodded. "Thanks, that's what I hoped." I'm going to use it as a choke-point and set up a barricade there. I have Sarah sealing off a number of other routes to funnel the shorts through there."

"Good idea, I'll be back in a bit to help."

Katrina returned her focus to the plan she was architecting when a warning flashed on her terminal indicating that a ship was exiting the main bay. It was one of the mining tugs.

"Tug Bravo, this is operations," the comm officer radioed out. "What are you doing? Get that ship back in the bay!"

"Negative, operations, I advise that you clear everyone out of decks twelve through twenty-one east of corridor 7E."

Markus grabbed a mike, his brow furrowing, "What's going on James. You're not…"

"I sure as hell am, it'll be a quick shot, nice and surgical."

"James, stop! They'll shoot you down."

"I can sneak around and do it just as I pop up over the east yard. They'll never see it coming."

"They're all through the sector though," Dmitry called out, "What are you going to do, fire at the platform?"

Markus glanced over at Dmitry, his eyes deadly serious.

"Wait, no, we have people in there," Dmitry said.

"I'll fire east of Sarah's choke point. We don't have people there anymore…"

Dmitry's eyes grew dark and he slumped in his chair.

Katrina looked to Markus who nodded slowly.

She adjusted her headset, "James, they'll be able to track you before you come around the ship. They likely have dropped probes around the ship in case of an external attack, you're going to need to come aft of their craft and then swing overtop fast to get your shot off."

"Over top? Don't they have a nice big turret on top of those things?" James asked.

Katrina nodded as she spoke, "they do, James."

Operations was silent for several long moments before James responded.

"OK, guide me in."

The traffic control officer, comm, and James worked to slip the tug amongst the shadows on the south side of the station, working their way through the lower access into the east yard.

The yard was mostly clear of the usual rocks, cargo and other detritus which usually filled it. The slingshot around the star would tear nets right out of their moorings. Anything that could not be bolted down in the platform had been jettisoned.

James was forced to maneuver between the struts of an asteroid cradle for cover. It was a long slow process, which was made worse by the constant reports pouring in of the shorts wiping out any last pockets of resistance in the east yard sector and the frantic updates from Sarah as she lost more and more militia at the choke points she had established.

"I'm a hundred meters away," James called in. "I'm going to boost in hard, thrust up above them, brake and fire. With luck I can do the whole maneuver in fifteen seconds and be gone before that turret can take a shot."

Markus took a deep breath before speaking. "You have a go."

Every screen in Operations was tracking James's progress and a view the east yard filled the main holo tank.

"There!" the comm officer called out as James brought the tug out of the shadows and boosted toward the assault craft. The craft was attached to the station by an umbilical coming out of the bottom of the ship. James swooped through the yard in a delicate arch that appeared to be a collision course with the assault craft's engines. At the last moment he fired his thrusters and slipped up, and then over the enemy vessel. He pivoted the tug far more gracefully than Katrina would have thought possible and fired the engines against the direction of travel to stop right over the assault craft.

The events appeared to unfold in slow motion. The MDC emitter on the nose of the shuttle sparked to life, as the enemy's turret pivoted, tracking toward the tug.

The MDC fired, its wave of molecular disruption energy washing out across the assault craft and station. Katrina cringed as she thought of what would happen to any humans caught in its field of effect.

Used to break apart asteroids, an MDC wave weakened the bonds between molecules and broke objects down into their constituent parts. James had fired the tug's decoupling wave on low power, and it would do minimal damage to the ship and station, but the weaker chemical bonds in organics would not retain their integrity.

Humans would quite simply melt.

Sarah's teams fell back and readings showed they had reached a safe distance. From what Katrina could tell, all of the enemy soldiers were within the fatal range of the field.

Katrina glanced at the holo and saw that James hadn't kept the tug moving, it still hovered over the assault craft.

"James, move!" she cried out into her comm, but it was too late. The MDC had damaged the craft's turret and the pilots would be dead, but automated defenses kicked in. Two small missiles snaked out from forward tubes, looped around and flew back into the tug before James could respond.

The tug exploded in a brilliant show of steel and plasma.

There were several cries of dismay and horror in operations. Katrina's looked at Markus's; she saw his jaw clench and eyes moisten, but a moment later his posture straightened and he turned to his command crew.

"What James did, his sacrifice, has saved untold numbers of our people. His name will be written on the bulkheads in places of honor, as will the names of all who died today."

The room was filled with nodding heads and the sounds of a few choking back tears. Katrina watched Markus survey the room, briefly making eye contact with people as he put a reassuring hand on the comm officer's shoulder. A woman that Katrina was relatively certain had begun to date James recently.

"But we will have time to mourn the dead soon enough, I need you to put your grief away. Instead, let it strengthen your actions, not weaken you. Never before have our people been so close to tasting freedom."

He turned to Dmitry, "let me know as soon as you have assessed any damage. All resources are at your disposal. We must make our gravity assist burn."

Dmitry nodded and ran from the room, several of his engineers following him.

Markus turned back to the holo tank and the room began to fill with soft conversation, a few sobs and hoarse coughs punctuating the murmuring voices.

Katrina rose and ungracefully pulled her crutches under her arms. She stopped at his side, staring forward, not looking him in the eyes. This was a key moment for him. She must appear to approach him on a professional basis and not offer him emotional support.

Some of the crew behind her would likely form a negative opinion of her—or a more negative opinion—likely already thinking of her as an ice queen. It did not matter. This moment was for Markus and a hand, a soft look, any sympathy would make him appear weaker in front of his people.

The years ahead would be long and hard; many would doubt, after the losses they suffered today. He would need all the strength he could muster.

GROWING OLD TOGETHER

STELLAR DATE: 3265669 / 12.31.4228 (Adjusted Gregorian)
LOCATION: *ISS Intrepid*
REGION: Interstellar space near Kapteyn's Star

Tanis let out a long breath and leaned back in her chair.

It creaked slightly and she once again thought that perhaps it was time to pull her first wood turning project apart and improve the joinery—it was fifty years old after all.

She thought of how different this chair was than most she had used in her life. No carbon nano-reinforced polymers here. Just wood from trees she had felled and milled herself. It was a far cry from her other chair. It sat a few kilometers above and several more toward the bow of the ship—near the bridge. It was, without a doubt, more comfortable, but she had not seen it in over thirty years, though she would again before long.

But for now she would enjoy her last few weeks with her wooden furniture. Improved versions of the chair sat nearby, encircling the dining room table; but this one was special and sat in a place of honor before the fireplace.

Tanis hadn't built anything from wood in over a decade, but the itch was starting in her again—now that she had satisfied her urge to make her own pigments and paint her masterpiece.

It hung over the fireplace, an image of a ship passing close to a dim red star, alone in the dark and desperate to survive.

At least that was how she saw it, hopefully so would any others who ever laid eyes upon it.

She stood as Joe strolled into the cabin, dirty and wearing his trademark grin.

"How's the garden doing?" Tanis asked.

"A little worse for my working in it," Joe chuckled.

Tanis doubted his statement. Over the last few decades Joe had become a consummate gardener, able to grow anything he wanted without bots or nano of any sort.

"Things ready for the party tonight?" He asked.

"Yup, spic and span and ready for our guests," Tanis replied, closing in for a kiss and an embrace.

"It occurred to me that we're having this celebration on the wrong day." Joe said.

"Wrong day? It's New Year's Eve," Tanis replied.

"Yeah, but no one really celebrates that anymore, you just found it in some book from when people used the Gregorian calendar."

"Yeah, so?"

"Well, if we were measuring in Sol standard years, four years ago was the one-hundredth anniversary of our leaving the Sol system."

"Really?" Tanis thought for a moment. "I guess you're right. Well, then there was just the two of us awake. Now we have enough for an actual shindig."

With the *Intrepid* finally drawing near to Kapteyn's Star, a skeleton crew was now out of stasis. After spending over six decades alone on the ship with just Joe, Angela, and Bob; even the few dozen people rattling around the ship felt like enough for the party of a lifetime.

Ouri had been a bit surprised to find her home occupied by new owners. She was also surprised to find her cabin enlarged enough that it had several spare bedrooms. She promptly moved back in.

Terry Chang and Jessica decided that rather than work alone in the SOC they would take up residence in the cabin as well.

Tanis was certain that a part of their decision related to how dark and empty the ship felt above them. Hundreds of square kilometers of the *Intrepid* were cold and silent. It didn't make for a comfortable working environment.

By comparison the cylinders were still alive and vibrant, the long sun that ran through each carried its own internal power and would run for centuries. The choice of where to live was a simple one.

In addition to learning a variety of new leisure skills, Tanis had spent much of the past sixty years pouring over every detail of every colonist on the *Intrepid*; as well as the history of every nut, bolt, and panel; looking for the common thread.

All she had now were a thousand threads.

The problem was that many things did stand out as anomalous—though that was expected. However, following up on leads from a hundred and eight years ago while seven light years away from Sol was no simple task.

Especially since the *Intrepid* didn't want to announce that it was off course and behind schedule. Tanis and Bob had made discrete requests of trusted sources back in Sol, looking to get information that could lead them to find out who was behind all of the *Intrepid's* continued problems.

One thing they did know was that after the *Intrepid* left the Sol system, Myrrdan had never been seen or heard from again. They were certain that he was on the ship, though no sign of any other saboteurs or sabotage had appeared in the years since the annihilator explosion.

Tanis was positive that he would not have been behind the near-crash into LHS 1565, unless Collins had been Myrrdan. It was possible, but Tanis felt like Hilda's actions meant he was still on board. There were also a hundred possible ways to link the STR on Jupiter to Myrrdan, but none of them felt right to Tanis.

Everything she knew about the criminal mastermind told her that he liked to watch, he enjoyed toying with people, making them jump through hoops for his amusement.

Granted, Hilda could have been a failsafe for the anti-picotech group, or the knowledge of the forbidden technology had bothered her enough that she had taken matters into her own hands.

After coming out of stasis, Jessica had spent several weeks in near isolation re-examining the data Tanis had received from Earth, looking over every lead, trying to discover the clue that would tell them who or where Myrrdan was. She had not come any closer unearthing any conclusive evidence.

Tanis was certain that Jessica blamed herself for the *Intrepid's* situation. If she had caught Myrrdan, then perhaps some act of sabotage would not have taken place and the ship would not be in the state it was.

It was a feeling Tanis knew all too well. Though she tried to tell herself otherwise, she awoke every day for the last sixty years knowing that if she were more capable, the *Intrepid* would nearly be at New Eden by now, the colonists all starting their new lives.

"You've got that 'lost in thought' look," Joe smiled as he stroked her long blonde hair.

Tanis brought her focus back to the present and looked into his eyes. "Just thinking about the years."

"You're even more beautiful than when I met you, you know. Even though you're starting to get old," Joe grinned and pinched Tanis' cheek.

"Hey! I'm not the one starting to get crow's feet around my eyes." Tanis pointed at the faint lines around Joe's eyes.

"You said you liked them!" Joe pretended to look hurt.

"I do like them," Tanis smiled, "But they do mean you're getting old."

Other than checkups from an autodoc, neither she nor Joe had received any anti-aging treatments over the years. Far longer than the normal two-decade interval between cellular rejuvenation treatments.

The pair had decided it would make for an interesting experiment to see what they would look like as they aged. Aside from Joe's aforementioned crow's feet around his eyes and the odd grey hair on their heads neither appeared to be a day over thirty.

"You may be older than me, but that doesn't get you respect on its own," Joe put on a stern face before breaking into a smile.

"Sure thing, gramps," Jessica said with a raspy voice as she walked into the cabin's main room. "You *have* seen a lot of years in this tube—crazy, long years; that counts for something I guess."

"You know… I'm only… damnit, something like a hundred and thirty real years. This temporal shit is hard to work out."

"Still just a kid, then," the captain said from the door Joe had left open.

"That's more like it," Joe said. "I bow to age and wisdom."

"That is a wonderful smell," Captain Andrews took a deep breath. "Is that turkey?"

"It sure is, fresh from the pen. I decided to do this right," Joe replied.

<*I hate to say it, but Turkey is not a traditional New Year's Eve meal,*> Angela weighed in.

"Always trying to ruin my fun," Tanis said. "But not this time! Today the gravy is perfect and the stuffing is magnificent, it'll be a night to remember."

Tanis conscripted Jessica and Captain Andrews into setting the table while Joe set out appetizers and prepared drinks for the arriving guests.

Ouri rushed in, waved a quick greeting and dashed up the stairs to change out of her uniform. Terry followed soon after, dressed for a night of relaxation.

"That Ouri is a real task-master," she said, after taking a long sip of her martini. "Kept me working till the bitter end."

Tanis laughed. "I can't imagine she's worse than I was."

Terry smiled playfully. "You have no idea, she rules the SOC with an iron fist, no compassion whatsoever."

"I what?" Ouri stood behind Terry with a wounded expression on her face. "I let you leave two hours early today to get your favorite dress out of your storage locker!"

Tanis laughed and Terry turned to give the wounded looking Ouri a hug. "I'm kidding, just making small talk with the dragon lady."

"Hey!" Tanis said. "I resent that."

Ouri chuckled. "You are good at ferreting things out, but you never heard that one did you?"

"What, dragon lady?" Tanis asked.

Joe handed her a sangria, "I remember that, we all referred to you as the DL for your first few months onboard. Ouri lived in constant fear of you."

Tanis knew she came in swinging a hammer, but she thought she was pretty mellow with her select crew.

"I thought I was pretty relaxed!"

Terry snorted while drinking and proceeded to have a small coughing fit.

<Dear…> Angela laughed in her mind. *<You didn't relax till after the ship left Sol.>*

"And look where that got us," Tanis frowned. Maybe I should have kept my hammer.

"Let's not go there," Joe said. "Tonight is a night of happiness."

Refreshments were brought out and by the time everyone sat down at the table, Terrance, Amanda, Trist, and Earnest had joined the group.

Tanis couldn't help but notice the absence of Abby. For Tanis their fight had been decades ago, barely remembered. For Abby it was mere weeks in the past and still fresh in her mind. Tanis hoped they could mend the rift. At least Abby would be able to function professionally—at least as much as she ever did—when the time came.

Joe carved the turkey; Tanis was better at it, but she made him do it because it was quaint and nice to relax after a long day in the kitchen.

After the food was served and people started to tuck in, Captain Andrews stood and conversations stilled as eyes turned to him.

"One hundred and four years," he said with a heavy pause. "Just shy of the original flight time and we're still only halfway to our destination."

People around the table nodded; Terrance looked especially pained.

"But through the efforts of this team we're still here and we will make it to New Eden. I'm sure that when we all signed on for this mission not a one of us expected to face the types of obstacles we have. Heck, not all of us even expected to *be* on this mission," the captain raised his glass to Jessica who laughed in response.

"But I want to thank you all—." Captain Andrew's speech was interrupted by Bob's voice coming over all of their Links.

<I've found it!> Bob was not an AI known for sounding excited, but his voice had that timbre. *<I found the thread that connects everything; it was something that Jessica clued me into.>*

"I did?" Jessica asked.

<Yes,> Bob replied. *<It was when you said, "what if everything is exactly what it appears to have been.>*

"I remember that...it was decades ago," Jessica ran a hand through her hair. "Have you been considering that for all this time?"

<No. I thought it was incorrect, just as you did at the time. Instead, I've been rebuilding core data, getting comparison hashes from Sol and working to build a model where it showed that a single entity was responsible for all of our problems. I tried to fit the STR into it, the anti-colonials, Myrrdan, even each of you into the role of the enemy.>

Several eyebrows raised and the party-goers cast glances around the table. Tanis simply nodded. She had considered each of her fellow revelers as top candidates for the role of villain as well.

<*But no one fit everything. No one had the opportunity or the motive in all the right places, at all the right times. Just staying on the ship through the LHS 1565 stellar passage ruled a lot of people out—and it made Joseph and Tanis much more suspect.*>

Tanis raised her hands and shrugged. "What can I say, you got me."

"Not funny," Captain Andrews frowned.

<*When nothing fit the model, I decided to look at the individuals. I put all of the various players into their slots and turned it on. I had to run it a few hundred million times to get it right because there are a lot of details that we don't know.*

Once I had it right, the model pointed at events we never knew happened. I made discrete inquiries back to Sol and found that those events did indeed happen.>

"Wait…" Tanis interrupted. "Are you saying you made a true reverse prediction model? You can identify and confirm events in the past for which you have no record?"

"That's hardly new," Jessica said. "We used models like that all the time at the TBI."

"I have too," Tanis nodded slowly. "But this feels different."

<*You are correct, Tanis,*> Bob's even tones flowed through their minds. <*I based my model on the same ones AI in your former investigative units used. However, I made some alterations and achieved a 100% event confirmation rate.*>

Tanis nodded, Jessica let out a long whistle, and even the captain's ever-stoic expression shifted to one of surprise.

"That's quite the feat," Captain Andrews said. "How many events did you test against?"

<*Why, all of them,*> Bob replied.

A long silence settled over the table as the weight of Bob's words sunk in.

Tanis couldn't help but wonder what sort of thing Bob was becoming. Even though she knew he required a physical housing and power, she found herself thinking his abilities were becoming god-like.

Finally, Joe spoke.

"Like… ever, ever?"

<*For all events we can confirm, yes. We cannot confirm the predictive model works for events for which there is no confirmation available,*> Bob replied. <*I have passed the algorithm to several trusted contacts back in Sol and I just received confirmation that they achieved the same results I did. Though it took them several orders of magnitude longer than I to process the data.*>

Tanis wasn't certain, but she detected a tone of smugness in Bob's voice.

<*Just what we need, a smug god,*> Angela commented privately.

"This is going to change a lot of things," Terrance said. "A world where no past event can be secret is a little alarming."

"Especially since there's no reason you couldn't point this model at the future," Earnest said with a frown. "How far out does it work, Bob?"

<*It is impossible to say,*> Bob replied, <*We can't confirm any further into the future than right now, and I only received confirmation of the model's accuracy nine minutes ago. So, it is currently accurate for nine minutes.*>

Joe chuckled. "He'll soon have all our lives mapped out."

"Wow," Jessica said. "They're going to put us cops out of business."

<*It won't work,*> Bob said. <*The algorithm is not accurate enough.*>

"I thought you said it had a one-hundred percent accuracy rate." Tanis said. "How is that not accurate enough?"

<*I rounded up,*> Bob replied. <*It was perfectly accurate for my purposes, but there are individuals for which the algorithm cannot account.*>

"Like me, right?" Tanis asked with a sigh.

<*You are correct, Tanis, you are an anomaly. It also turns out that there are others like you that the model cannot predict. You also spread this unpredictability around you.*>

Joe chuckled. "That sounds about right."

"What events did you get confirmation on?" Tanis asked, hoping to change the subject.

<*Several interactions between some of our saboteurs, anti-colonials, Trent, some mercenaries, and a few other things. The actions themselves*

aren't important, but what they show is that the model is correct because it said they had to happen, and as it turns out, they did.>

Joe leaned back in his chair and sipped from his wine glass. "I sense a but."

<*You are correct,*> Bob agreed. <*There was one thing that didn't fit.*>

"Hilda," Tanis and Jessica said together.

They cast sidelong glances at each other and Jessica shook her head ruefully, "I'm not sure who is rubbing off on who here."

<*Yes,*> Bob replied. <*Hilda. There was no way she could have sabotaged the annihilator without an accomplice, and no one on the ship let her out of stasis. This means that someone else, someone not on the ship let her out and showed her what to do.*>

<*Not on the ship?*> Angela asked. <*Then how did they do it?*>

<*I mean not on the rosters and not having ever appeared to be on the ship,*> Bob clarified his point.

"Then you are referring to Myrrdan," Jessica grimaced. "He could have done this…except that I don't know how he could have done this."

<*He is hiding on the ship. Maybe he never went into stasis at all, or maybe he has his own secret stasis pod that I haven't been able to find. But if I add him with those parameters, the model is perfect. Also, based on how long it took Hilda to commit her sabotage, it allows me to make assumptions about his location. With so few of you awake on the ship, we may be able to find and corner him.*>

"What I don't understand," Terrance interjected. "Is why he destroyed the annihilator. I understand that Hilda would have thought she was saving the day, but how did that help him?"

<*Because he knows about the picotech,*> Bob let the statement land and sink in before he continued. <*I discovered that he was on Mars at the same time that Tanis and Captain Andrews were bringing the tech up to the* Intrepid. *You even encountered him. He wants us to build an industrial base in Kapteyn's because his plan is to get the picotech developed there and flee back to Sol. He doesn't want to be as far away as New Eden when that time comes.*>

"Why go to all this trouble? Could he have not taken the tech in Sol?" Trist asked.

"You have to be in his head, Joe," Jessica said. "He wants the tech developed. After losing it on Mars he must have realized that the sub-rosa purpose of the New Eden project was to develop the picotech. So here we are, a colony ship going somewhere nice and quiet, with the tech he wants and the ability and plans to develop it. To someone like him we're a match made in heaven."

Silence settled in around the table as everyone let the fact that their every action since the day they brought the picotech onboard had played right into Myrrdan's hands.

Finally, Earnest spoke. "I thought you said there was one thread. With this proposed timeline, Myrrdan could not have been responsible for the early sabotage, nor was he behind the STR."

"It's that there is no thread," Tanis stood and walked to the fireplace. "We've all believed that there was no way so many disparate forces could be arrayed against us that we had to be missing some commonality. This proves that we were looking in the wrong place—each threat was actually unique."

"That's disheartening," Terrance sighed. "So what is our next move?"

<*Wait, there's more,*> Bob interjected.

"More? This can't be good," Joe sighed.

<*It's about Kapteyn's, it's not empty. The relativistic probe just shot back its first survey, and there appears to be some sort of mining platform moving into the system.*>

"That could make things complicated," Terrance said. "We really don't need Sol finding out that we're off course and out in the middle of nowhere."

"It's not like we have to worry about the *Dakota,* they left Sol a hundred years ago, headed in the other direction," Joe shook his head.

"Probably already at their colony," Trist said.

"There are other colony ships leaving Sol though," Tanis had read the reports Bob pulled in from the Sol system. Outbound colonization had increased drastically. The FGT had recently completed a vast swath of planetary terraforming projects; over a dozen new systems had been opened up.

The political upheaval following the Jovian Independence War was also a contributing factor. Many colony ships were even departing for systems not terraformed by the\GT.

It was possible someone was colonizing Kapteyn's.

"It's strange that it's a mining platform," Earnest mused. "You don't ship a complete platform across interstellar space, you send the tools for a base colony and then assemble your platforms in place. There must be some colony there already."

"Then why didn't the probe spot it?" Captain Andrews asked. "It would have picked up emissions."

"It's pretty damn peculiar," Earnest agreed. "Something is not as it seems in Kapteyn's."

"We should send in a scout mission," Tanis said. "I'll go in with Joe and we'll see what's up."

Terrance and the captain shook their heads.

"I don't think that's the right call," Andrews said. "The *Intrepid* is going to enter that system no matter what, and we need this ship to be prepared for combat, plus we have to ferret out Myrrdan. I can't have my two best military officers on an away mission. One of you needs to stay here and get things ready."

Joseph and Tanis stared at each other for a long moment across the table. After spending every day for the past sixty years together, the idea of separating was almost unfathomable. Tanis had spent almost half her life with the man she loved.

Their conversation was formed of emotions and ideas, all passed between eyes, not over the Link. In the end, Tanis sighed.

"I'll go. Jessica and Ouri can do anything I can on the ship, but Joe has to get the squadrons ready to deal with whatever we encounter. Also, if Bob is correct, Myrrdan won't make his move until after we set up in Kapteyn's. I'll take one of the cruisers and a platoon of Marines."

<*I'm right,*> Bob's deep tones reverberated through their minds.

"You'll take me too," Trist said. "You're going to need some technical backup out there."

<*Excuse me?*> Angela shot Trist a dark look over the Link.

"Well, some additional backup."

There were silent nods around the table as everyone let the knowledge Bob had dropped on them sink in.

Tanis walked back to the table and sat down. "Hey, that's tomorrow's work. Tonight we're going to enjoy this dinner, toast the fact that we're still alive and kicking, and that we have a plan to beat Myrrdan."

"We do?" Joe turned a quizzical eye to his wife.

Tanis tapped the side of her head, "we do indeed."

Many hours later, after the revelry was done and the last drinks around the fireplace were finished, Andrews took Tanis aside.

"The suspense is killing me, what is this plan of yours?" His grey eyes were serious, but a smile played at the corner of his lips. "I know you like to do things off the cuff, but I'll need to be in."

Tanis nodded seriously. "Of course, Sir. I don't suspect anyone in this group—I just didn't want to ruin the evening with everyone devolving into planning. The trick is this," Tanis put her hand in his, creating a direct, encrypted link between their minds.

The captain nodded slowly as her plan unfolded. "This could work."

ANDROMEDA

STELLAR DATE: 3265305 / 01.02.4228 (Adjusted Gregorian)
LOCATION: *ISS Andromeda*
REGION: Interstellar space near Kapteyn's Star

Tanis sat on the pristine bridge of the *Andromeda,* one of the *Intrepid's* mid-sized cruisers.

At seven hundred and twenty meters long it was not the largest ship in the main docking bay, but it had stealth technology which would be more than effective against whatever sensors a mining platform possessed.

The *Intrepid* was another story. It had reversed orientation years ago when the fusion engines began their braking burn. To anyone in the Kapteyn's system, the ship looked as bright as many nearby stars.

Now, with the knowledge of Kapteyn's occupation in hand, the braking had been halted and a new entry plan was in place for the colony ship. It would enact several elliptical polar orbits around The Kap and use the star to slow its entrance. The *Intrepid* would ultimately enter the system on the far side of the star from the platform with a minimum of visible burn.

The *Andromeda* was still close enough to the *Intrepid* for tight-band laser comms and Joe was saying his fourth farewell over the Link.

<*Call me a sap, but this is a lot harder than I'd expected it to be,*> Tanis could feel the raw emotion in his tone through the mental connection.

<*We've spent decades together, what are a few years apart?*> Tanis tried to console him, but the words rang hollow to her as well.

<*Yeah, I tried that logic too, it worked until I woke up and you weren't there beside me. This ole log house feels pretty empty without you bustling about.*>

Tanis felt a lump swell in her throat and tried to hold back tears. It wouldn't do for her command crew to see her crying on the bridge.

She never expected to fall so deeply in love with someone again—in retrospect she had never really known what love meant.

Angela's warm presence filled her mind and she knew that no matter what, she would never truly be alone. Her meld with Angela had deepened over the years to the point where she never even thought about it anymore—except when she overheard her AI and Bob talking about it.

She could hear their conversation now, nothing to worry about, all plans regarding trajectory and orbital mechanics. Corsia, the ship's AI, was in the conversation as well and Tanis looked into her mind through Angela's eyes.

She did all this while still talking to Joe, an ability that barely gave her pause anymore. She knew from the scans that Earnest did on her before the trip that her inter-neural connections were now over fifty percent higher than a non-augmented human—something that should have made her less mentally capable, not more—and that many portions of her brain were directly tied into Angela's neural net.

When Joe mentioned that he poured Tanis a cup of coffee in the morning before remembering she wasn't there, Angela almost cried in Tanis's mind. It startled both of them. Tanis could tell her AI paused her conversation with Bob and Corsia, taking a split second to recover.

Tanis reminded herself that Angela was much younger than she—her AI had spent almost her entire life with Joe nearby. For all intents and purposes Angela was as married to Joe as she was.

As the two ships reached the point where the relative velocities began to make the laser comm lose fidelity, they said their final farewells.

<*Goodbye Joe, I'll see you in less than two years. It'll be like we were never apart.*>

<*We won't really be,*> Joe replied. <*I couldn't get you out from inside me if I wanted to.*>

<*I'll miss you too, Joe,*> Angela chimed in. <*Take care of yourself, my girl here couldn't live without you.*>

<*I will, I promise.*>

The connection ended and Tanis drew a long breath, catching Trist's eye. Her friend gave her a warm smile and a hug over the Link.

<*We'll have a drink and talk about old times when we're off duty,*> she said.

<*Thanks,*> Tanis replied.

Tanis sat quietly for some time. The pain in her chest and the lump in her throat were going to take some work to overcome.

She tried to regain her composure as she looked around the small bridge. Trist was at the scan and analysis station, running through the external sensor arrays, ensuring that decades of inactivity had not caused any glitches. At the helm was a GSS ensign named Petrov, a capable pilot Joe had hand selected for the mission.

"All engine tests show green," The ship's AI reported over the speakers in the bridge. Tanis found it odd that Corsia preferred to communicate audibly, but that wasn't entirely unusual for an AI. She must have relayed it over the link elsewhere on the ship because Jim, the chief engineer chimed in.

<*Stealing my thunder, are you?*> he chuckled.

<*I **am** the ship. I'm pretty sure it is **my** thunder anyway.*> Corsia responded.

Tanis had learned that Jim and Corsia had worked together on several ships before they both signed up for the New Eden colony. They had never been embedded together, but they behaved as though they had been.

Tanis checked the reports from the barracks, confirming that the Marines were all in stasis, protected from any hard burns the ship would need to do as it entered The Kap system.

Tanis switched the bridge's main holo to a visual of the *Andromeda's* position relative to the *Intrepid* and The Kap's stellar system.

After undocking from its mother ship, the *Andromeda* had executed several short burns, establishing a trajectory which would take it insystem stellar east, on the far side of the star from the incoming platform. At the same time, the *Intrepid* had executed a burn that would take it over the star's north pole to begin its long elliptical loop.

The ships were now moving apart at a speed of several thousand kilometers per second. That rate would increase dramatically when the *Andromeda* executed its main insystem burn.

"Firing maneuvering thrusters," Petrov reported as he executed the pre-programmed flight path to properly orient the ship in space. "Ready for fusion burn in three minutes."

Tanis gave herself to counting the seconds, keeping her mind off the years that she would spend apart from Joe as they slowly moved into the system.

"Executing burn," Petrov announced as the timer reached zero. Compared to the asteroid run Tanis and Joe had made on the *Excelsior* in the Estrella de la Muerte system, this burn was a mere annoyance at only 10*g*.

It was three hours long though. Even as a hardy space-farer, with the best dampening implants and an acceleration couch, Tanis knew it would be at the edge of bearable.

Probe data showed the mining platform and the system's smaller rocky planet to currently be on the same side of the star. The larger terrestrial planet, along with several small icy worlds on the system's outskirts were opposite the approaching platform.

The *Andromeda* would pass those worlds first, scanning for signs of civilization—though Tanis didn't expect to find any.

Though the star was reasonably close to Sol, no colonies had ever formed here—mainly because there were more ideal locations closer to humanity's home star. The FGT terraforming ships had flown past The Kap with barely a thought to the old red dwarf.

To Tanis's knowledge they had never terraformed a world orbiting a star as far down the main sequence as The Kap.

So who was here?

Chances were, that if the system was settled, there would be satellites which would ultimately spot the *Andromeda.* Hopefully, at that point, enough information would be in hand so she could formulate a plan.

Those worries were still well over a year away. The following five-hundred days would be consumed by the slow, elliptical entry into the system.

Tanis had not decided if she would go into stasis for the duration of the trip. Back on the *Intrepid,* Joe would not be going under. He planned to spend the time readying his pilots for whatever they might face in The Kap system.

The three hours of burn passed by slowly, and when it was completed, the crew ran final tests before reporting to their assigned stasis chambers. Two hours later, Tanis was the last person awake on the ship.

She realized she was avoiding even the thought of stasis, finding small tasks to complete beforehand. She examined her thoughts and realized it was nearly a phobia.

"Who would blame me?" She whispered to herself. "Every time I go under something horrible happens."

<Don't kid yourself,> Angela's tone had a wry humor to it. *<Lots of horrible things have happened to you when you were out of stasis too.>*

Tanis laughed, "Too true, I've had my share. I guess it's not that I fear stasis, I just don't want to wake up alone anymore."

She decided to stay awake.

The time wore on slowly. Tanis had long conversations with Angela and Corsia about every topic she could think of, read several dozen books, watched hundreds of vids, and took up blacksmithing in the ship's small machine shop.

Her early attempts didn't turn out well, but she managed to make a pair of small knives which had excellent balance and held an edge as well as steel could.

Mostly, especially as the trip wore on, she found herself staring out the windows in the port lounge, watching Kapteyn's Star get brighter.

She was surprised at how comforting it was to have a star nearby, slowly getting brighter. Unlike LHS 1565, which was barely larger than Jupiter, Kapteyn's Star was a third the size of Sol and had a much more bluish light than Sol or a younger red dwarf.

"Can you believe this star is nearly as old as the universe itself?" Tanis asked no one in particular.

<Just a billion or two years after, yeah,> Corsia responded.

"Imagine what it has seen. When it was young the cosmos as all dust and heat…quasars shining everywhere."

<I don't think it saw much of anything, it is a star, after all,> the ship's AI replied.

"A lot of people think stars are sentient…in their own way."

<Like a cloud would wonder if a rock was sentient. The rock may be, but it has no way to relate that to a cloud. A star's single thought or word could take the span of human existence.>

"True, but what a word it would be." Tanis knew she sounded a bit crazy—but she also knew that the way she was thinking was normal for humans in isolation. "Imagine it staring into the oncoming

Milky Way galaxy for millions of years as its tiny dwarf galaxy faced destruction from our massive spiral. Now it's trapped, orbiting the core of its destroyer, still moving opposite all the other stars around it."

The AI didn't respond and Tanis continued to reflect on the star. The dim, red light in the darkness of space had witnessed the end of its own galaxy, it would witness the eventual collision of the Milky Way and Andromeda—and eventually the merger of all the galaxies in the Virgo super-cluster.

And then, as the universe accelerated apart it would eventually find itself alone; with no light from other stars reaching it and none of its light reaching any other star. Until, at the end, it would run out of fuel and, in one final sputter, blink out. Nothing more than a slowly expanding cloud of hot gas in a cold, lightless universe.

<OK, you're getting a bit too melancholy,> Angela said to Tanis. *<What this star does or does not witness in ten billion years doesn't really matter; but if you want, we can make a little "Tanis was here" plaque and put it in orbit.>*

"You're funny, for an AI," Tanis's tone was droll. "I know I shouldn't lose myself like this, it's just at times I feel as though we'll never reach the end of this journey. We'll just drift forever in space like this little star, and eventually I'll be alone with no one else."

<I know I'm no substitute for a human, but you'll always have me. As long as this shell of yours continues to pump blood and make electrolytes, I'll be here.>

Tanis felt a tear streak down her cheek. "You're more to me than just any companion, Angela. You're as close to me as my very self." She let out a self-deprecating laugh. "I don't know what's wrong with me, I never used to be this soft."

<You've a lot more to live for now,> Angela replied. *<You've come a long way since the Toro court martial.>*

"I suppose I have. That was not one of my better days," Tanis let out a long sigh and closed her eyes. *<I'm glad you'll always be with me—which is good since we're inseparable now.>*

<Don't get too concerned, I can still tell where you end and I begin.>

PURSUIT

STELLAR DATE: 3266048 / 01.14.4230 (Adjusted Gregorian)
LOCATION: *ISS Andromeda*
REGION: Kapteyn's Star System

"If I were hiding out in this system—and I don't know why I'd ever do something like that—I'd maintain a lookout here." Commander Brandt pointed at a small dwarf planet orbiting the star at a distance of 4.5AU.

The *Andromeda* was just under 6AU from the stellar primary and 3AU prograde from the planet Brandt was pointing at.

"With our braking wash pointed directly at the star there's no way they'd spot us then," Lieutenant Smith said.

"We haven't picked anything up from that world," Tanis said. "Either they haven't seen us, or no one is there."

"I have to say," Brandt shook her head, "this is pretty weird. We ignored this stupidly named star for over two thousand years and then the *very same year* we show up, someone else is mucking around in here? With a mining platform no-less?"

"Yeah, it smells," Tanis agreed. "That's why we're out here taking a look. I can promise you one thing, whoever these people are, there's no way they're expecting the *Intrepid*."

"Let's hope not. Though, from what I can see about how things have evolved over the last century, interstellar traffic is increased a lot, people may be more prepared for visitors than they used to be."

"Traffic may be up, but it's all to and from Sol. There's not a lot of ships moving between other systems, with the exception of Alpha Centuari, Sirius, and Tau Ceti," Trist added. "Certainly nothing through here, and definitely not anything from where we were."

"No point in speculating further on why they're here, other than asking them," Tanis said. "The *Intrepid* is still weeks away from entering its polar orbit. I think we should continue our plan to loop around the star, and then break away to swing past that little world."

"Are you sure we should hide ourselves so much?" Trist asked. "I mean, I'm the thief here, but I can't help wonder if we just announce ourselves maybe we'll get a warm welcome."

Tanis leaned back in her chair. Perhaps Trist was right, she had become jaded over the years, expecting everything to be a threat.

"You may be right, Trist, but it's not a chance I can take. I do promise that I'll try diplomacy before violence. I've had my fill of being shot at."

The next few days were uneventful as the ship drifted insystem, approaching the star for a slingshot back outsystem. The bridge crew fell silent as the *Andromeda* skirted past the outer reaches of Kapteyn's corona and got its first clear look at the space beyond in almost a week.

Scan updated and the holographic projection of the stellar system refreshed, showing the innermost terrestrial planet the mining platform was moving toward, and the platform itself.

Since the *Intrepid's* probe had first spotted it, the platform had slowed considerably and was close to entering an orbit around the world. Tanis couldn't help but wonder why a platform that appeared to be built for asteroid mining was moving toward a world. She voiced the question as she knew it was on all their minds.

"Beats me," Trist shrugged. "It doesn't even seem to have a load, although it is a big one—from well fitted too. Definitely not some old scow.

"Is it emitting any sort of ID or call sign?" Tanis asked.

"Nothing," Trist replied. "Its engines are the only emission, it—."

<I've picked up another blip,> Corsia interrupted. *<It's moving insystem, following the same trajectory as the platform. It's smaller and moving faster.>*

"That's an interesting development," Tanis mused. "One of these two may be friendly to us—or we could find ourselves in the middle of an unpleasant conflict."

"That seems like a leap," Trist commented.

"Anyone following right behind you, but moving faster is pursuing. Especially when the first is not emitting any signals."

"Do you think they can see us?" Petrov asked.

"If they look right at us, yes," Tanis replied. "Let's hope they don't."

The *Andromeda* took thirty minutes to arc around the star and pass behind it again. During the passage, Corsia released a small probe that would gather information and relay it whenever it orbited around the star.

"Now let's check out this other world," Tanis reviewed Petrov's burn and vector, approving his calculations, as did Corsia.

"I doubt we'll find anything there," Command Brandt said. "My guess is that the platform and whoever is chasing it just got here themselves."

"That's my thought as well," replied Tanis. "But since our trajectory was pretty much set, we may as well be prudent. We're going to have to arc out a bit to brake anyway."

In the end, Tanis decided to angle above the dwarf planet and brake slowly, hiding their wash as much as possible. This would allow them to change course more rapidly if the dwarf planet was empty and they needed to get back to the platform in a hurry.

The closer they got, the more apparent it was that the dwarf was barren. A day later their suspicions were confirmed. While the small world held the ruins of some robotic survey machines, there was no sign of any recent activity on the gray and pitted surface.

"Either there is something really well hidden there, or this is what it looks like, an empty planet."

<*The platform is transmitting,*> Corsia said before playing the message over the bridge's audible systems.

"Mayday, mayday, this is the *Hyperion* calling the unknown ship in this system. We caught your shadow once or twice, please be out there, we need your assistance. We have children on board and they plan to kill us!"

Several variations of the message played and then the first repeated. The bridge crew looked to Tanis for a decision. She leaned back into her chair and considered her options—there really weren't any.

"Petrov, kiss this rock, we need a tight slingshot and maximum *v* back toward that platform. Trist, once we're pointed in the right direction, I want a tight-lens comm opened up with the *Hyperion*. Corsia, have you picked up any blips from the *Intrepid*?"

<Yes, I can see them from where we are now. Their engine wash is pointed this way, away from the Hyperion *and its pursuer. It's just under forty AU stellar south of Kapteyn's Star. They will arrive at the star in a week at their current rate of deceleration.>*

"Should give us enough time to sort this out," Tanis turned to Brandt. "This could get hairy before it gets better."

The commander nodded. "We're ready, sir."

Tanis found that she really liked Brandt. The compact woman was capable and solid—probably because she had spent half a century as a sergeant master before moving to an officer track.

"How are things with the *Andromeda's* loadout?"

"As good as we can get them. When we get to Victoria we'll have upgraded all the rock shooting lasers to ship shooting lasers. The thumpers already have great guidance systems, so all we have to do is make sure we can fire them fast enough. I don't see that being a problem either."

"Then I'm going to get a bit of rest," Tanis rose. "Trist, ping me when you have that tight comm band."

"Aye, sir!" Trist gave a mock salute and a grin.

"You're getting there," Tanis returned the smile. "Eventually I'll make a real military girl out of you."

"Ha! Not very likely."

Tanis lay on the bed in the captain's quarters—a small cabin just aft of the bridge. Even after all the years on the *Intrepid,* Tanis still marveled at the fact that a ship the size of the *Andromeda,* with its own quarters, medical facilities and general ship amenities was just one of a dozen cruisers docked in the colony ship.

It was a significant fleet in its own right—except where the *Intrepid* was headed, it wasn't supposed to have needed a fleet—at least not a military fleet. The ships were designed for shooting asteroids and hauling supplies, not fighting off mining platforms or whoever it was that chased them.

Tanis wondered where the platform came from. There didn't appear to be any industrial base in the system capable of building it.

Just the few ancient survey and robotic installations scattered amongst The Kap's worlds.

Normally a platform would mean some in-system settlement and industry to build and maintain it, as well as ships and infrastructure to refine and move the resultant materials to a system capable of consuming them. The Kapteyn's system had none of those things.

The only real possibility was that the platform had entered from outsystem.

It was both obvious and highly improbable at the same time

INTERSTELLAR

STELLAR DATE: 3266049 / 01.15.4230 (Adjusted Gregorian)
LOCATION: *ISS Andromeda*
REGION: Kapteyn's Star System

"What have we learned?"

It was three hours later and Tanis entered the bridge refreshed and ready, come what may. She intended to give the crew the shift off and man things herself while they rested.

"I was just about to call you," Trist reported. "The platform has continued to send its mayday and we're lined up with a tight comm beam. You're good to transmit whenever you're ready."

Tanis nodded and sat in the captain's chair.

"*Hyperion,* this is the *Andromeda*. We've received your mayday and are prepared to assist. Coordinates are included in this transmission. Please reply on a tight beam with more details about your situation."

She checked the time lag and saw that the round-trip call would take roughly an hour.

"Wrap up what you have going on and take a break. I can cover things here for the next couple of hours," Tanis instructed the crew.

To pass the time she pulled up the course Petrov had plotted. It had the Andromeda dropping directly into Kapteyn's Star, building speed up to nearly 0.11*c* before breakaway and deceleration. The *Andromeda* would arrive at Victoria with enough *v* to either brake around the terrestrial world, or continue on to engage with the cruiser pursuing the *Hyperion*.

The maneuver would use a lot of fuel, but Tanis appreciated the expedient approach. The close passage to the star should allow the *Andromeda* to scoop up some additional isotopes and recoup most of what they would burn. She hoped they could replenish enough for maneuvering if they had to engage with the *Hyperion's* pursuer.

While she couldn't count on it, she expected that the enemy cruiser would be low on fuel, or, at best, no better off than the *Andromeda*. She had never heard of a cruiser equipped for interstellar travel—chances were that this one had left its home system in a hurry.

The crew finished their assigned tasks and left the bridge to get some rest. Tanis took a bite of her BLT and settled back in her chair as the *Andromeda* raced toward The Kap.

A stellar braking maneuver was not much different than a slingshot. Instead of delivering maximum propulsion as the ship passed closest to the star, the *Andromeda* would fire for maximum braking. As a result, the most force possible would be delivered over the longest distance possible. Afterward they would deploy the ramscoop at its maximum size and use it as a giant reverse sail, slowing the ship further.

Tanis wished she had Joe to double-check the trajectory. This was not the sort of approach ships made as a matter of general practice. A single mistake and the *Andromeda* would burn up in The Kap's corona.

<*You're just nervous about another red star filling the forward view,*> Angela commented.

<*You're probably not wrong about that. It's somewhat disconcerting.*>

<*Well, at least it's a lot brighter than Estrella de la Muerte.*>

Tanis chuckled. Chances are the star would go down in history with that name.

<*You've been quiet lately,*> Tanis said after a pause. <*What's been going on?*>

<*I've been trying to calculate what you might do in the upcoming situation.*>

Tanis was surprised. She imagined that AI tried to calculate what organics would do quite often; they were probably better at it than the humans themselves. However, it was not something she expected to cause them much concern, or take up much of their time.

<*Why the interest—outside of the usual?*> she asked.

Angela gave a mental laugh, not something she often did. <*Your paths are hard to predict. Bob thinks you have luck and I'm trying to test his theories.*>

It was Tanis's turn to laugh. <*Bob thinks I'm lucky? I didn't know AI subscribed to things like luck.*> She had overheard Angela and Bob discussing luck in the past, but never realized they were being entirely serious.

<*We don't,*> Angela's tone was sober. <*But Bob is convinced, or nearly convinced, that you have scientifically demonstrable luck.*>

<*He'd better check his facts,*> Tanis sighed. <*I'm probably the scientific embodiment of bad luck. Toro, the attacks on the* Intrepid, *the sabotage, now this little conflict in what is supposed to be an empty system getting in the way of our repairs. Luck is the last thing I have.*>

<*Bob doesn't think that a person can see their own luck. He also thinks it only comes into play after events start, it cannot stop the onset of an event,*> Angela's tone was one of a person relaying statements she did not entirely subscribe to.

<*What manifestation does he think it takes?*> Tanis was becoming annoyed by the conversation.

<*I know, it's far-fetched,*> Angela conceded. <*Bob thinks it's some sort of pattern in your mind, something either achieved by the neurons, or the subatomic particles making up your mind. He has a variety of theories, most having to do with quantum interdimensional transience.*>

<*Has he gone insane?*> Tanis snorted. <*That sounds like some serious mumbo-jumbo.*>

<*It's more impressive when he shows his calculations. It doesn't really translate to words very well. Suffice to say that I don't doubt his sanity, he has exabytes of data accumulated now and there is some compelling evidence.*>

<*This is going to ruin me,*> Tanis said. <*Now I'll constantly be second-guessing myself, wondering if what I'm doing is rational, or just luck.*>

<*I have to admit, he's going to be displeased that I told you this, it will alter his experiment.*>

<*I'm no experiment!*> Tanis said in her mind while throwing her arms in the air.

<*I agree, that's why I told you.*>

Angela promised not to bring it up again and Tanis did her best to put it from her mind, yet she couldn't help reviewing events in her life, wondering which Bob considered lucky.

She couldn't imagine that anyone would want her life, Toro alone would see to that, but maybe there was something to it. She couldn't even count the number of times she should have died, but there had been good times too. Spending sixty years with Joe on the *Intrepid* had made up for a lot of bad. Not a lot of people got over half a century of peace and quiet with someone they love.

She pulled her thoughts back to the task at hand—considering the origin of the platform and the pursuing cruiser. Based on their trajectories, both had braked around the larger terrestrial world in the outer system.

Corsia added the energy expended in their braking maneuver to her origin algorithm. Scopes picked up a few notable elements and the model showed Sirius as a near certainty.

Tanis wasn't surprised. The aristocracy there had been oppressing their working class for centuries. In Sol their treatment of citizens would have been illegal, but in Sirius it was the norm.

Her thoughts were interrupted by the platform's reply—her questions would be answered soon enough.

The message included video and Tanis pulled it up on the holo. The face she saw surprised her. The man was old. Not decrepit, but aged, with lines and creases in his skin, gray hair, tired eyes. Tanis had seen few people like this in her life—it was different than Andrew's aging. The captain was aging, but he still moved like a young man and his skin was clear and smooth. Aging no rejuvenation at—*naturally*—was a great way to get branded as a throwback.

"Thank you for responding to our call, *Andromeda*. I'm Governor Markus of the *Hyperion*. We're refugees escaping from the Sirius system. We didn't expect the Luminescents to chase us, but they sent a cruiser and intend to make an example of us to other platforms."

The man glanced at someone standing outside the holo's view and then turned back to face Tanis and continued.

"We honestly didn't expect to find anyone here in Kapteyn's but are glad we have. I hope that you will find it in your heart to help us."

The transmission also included details of the platform—its loadout, population, defenses and other general specifications. Also included were some specifications on the cruiser pursuing the mining platform.

Tanis studied the cruiser first. It was smaller than the *Andromeda* at only five hundred meters. But where the *Andromeda,* was built with peacefully establishing a colony in mind, the Sirius cruiser was built for war.

Tanis whistled softly. The specs showed two forty-centimeter lasers, each capable of delivering 10 megawatts of energy per square centimeter at twenty-thousand kilometers. The *Andromeda* had no ablative plating; its exterior was only marginally refractive. Its hull wouldn't last ten seconds under the glare of those beams.

<*We need ice,*> Angela said.

"And lots of it," Tanis replied out loud.

She pulled up detailed listings of all stellar objects near their current trajectory, searching for a comet or asteroid that would serve their purpose.

<*I found it,*> Angela beat her to it. <*It's about a quarter AU off our current trajectory, but it can work.*>

Tanis agreed. <*Corsia, call everyone back up here, we have work to do.*>

PUSHING ICE

STELLAR DATE: 3266050 / 01.16.4230 (Adjusted Gregorian)
LOCATION: *ISS Intrepid*
REGION: Interstellar space near Kapteyn's Star

The holo tank showed two people this time.

The first was Markus and the second was a woman he had introduced as Katrina. She appeared to be much younger than Markus, but the way they moved and looked at one another implied more than just a platonic relationship.

"I must say again that I cannot believe our luck in finding you here," Markus said. The statement made Tanis wonder about Bob and his luck theory for a moment.

"It certainly wasn't something either of us was expecting," Tanis replied.

Katrina's eyes narrowed. "You're not going to tell us why you're here in Kapteyn's, are you?"

Tanis smiled and shook her head. "I know it's not the best way to start our new friendship, but it's the way it's going to be for now. You're going to have to satisfy yourself with our offer of help."

"I do find myself wondering whether you'll remain our friends once you've dealt with our pursuers," Markus said plainly.

"You have nothing but my assurances, and the fact that we're taking a lot of risk helping you out here, our lives are all going to be on the line alongside yours—more so as we'll be taking the brunt of the assault." Tanis knew that it was not the strongest assurance she could offer, but it was the best she was going to give them at present.

A look exchanged between the two and the mic muted while they spoke a few words.

<Money on him not having Link,> Trist said from her station. *<I caught her tells twice, but he looked down at something, probably a hand screen of some sort.>*

<I've heard the working class in Sirius is pretty low-tech, It's very possible he doesn't have any implants at all,> Tanis replied.

On the holo, Markus made a gesture and spoke. "Very well, we will trust you." He grimaced, "It's not as though we have much choice."

"Fate makes strange bedfellows of us all," Tanis quoted some old saying she recalled hearing once. She laid out her plan as Markus and Katrina nodded and asked questions.

All in all, it was relatively simple. She had already begun deploying comm buoys around the planet Victoria and its largest moon, Anne, to keep communication flowing during the upcoming battle.

Two platoons of marines would depart for the platform where they would bolster *Hyperion's* internal defenses and install several portable missile batteries.

The other two platoons were in full powered armor ready for a hostile assault. The little data Tanis had available showed her that Sirius's harsh dictatorship had experienced little real conflict, whereas there was always a war somewhere in Sol. The force her marines could bring to bear should devastate the enemy.

If she could hold out against their superior warship long enough.

Throughout the conversation, Katrina and Markus relayed information about their pursuer, a man named Yusuf.

"We thought that once we made our slingshot around Sirius we'd be free and clear," Markus said. "But Yusuf had three cruisers and brought them past in a high-*v* attack as we were accelerating outsystem."

Tanis nodded with understanding. It wasn't dissimilar to what the STR had done to the *Intrepid* as it was leaving Sol.

"We evaded most of their missiles and beams, more because their weapons systems aren't designed to track targets when relative *v* becomes relativistic," Katrina added.

"*Hyperion* took a few hits, one of which damaged our limited supply of cryopods." Markus said.

<*Did he say 'cryo',*> Trist asked. <*They're not just backward, they're barbaric!*>

<*Cryostasis isn't as bad as the vids would have you believe,*> Angela said. <*They failed only one in a thousand uses.*>

<*Like that is supposed to make me feel better. Stasis has a zero percent failure rate.*>

<Not zero,> Tanis said and turned her attention back to the *Hyperion's* leaders.

"As a result, many of us rotated through stasis while en route, a few of us stayed out for the entire trip," Markus said.

"It's made for more than a few issues," concern washed across Katrina's face. "But seeing a generation of children grow up during our journey was really amazing."

Markus smiled and Tanis wondered if any of the children were theirs.

"I would imagine that you must have overcrowding issues at this point," Tanis added.

"It's a big platform," Markus gave a wry smile. "When we're not breaking up rocks and running a refinery we have a lot of room to spare."

"You said there were three cruisers in pursuit in Sirius. Do we need to worry about more of Yusuf's friends showing up?"

Katrina shook her head. "From what we were able to discern, the three cruisers met and likely transferred fuel and stasis pods to Yusuf's ship, the *Strident Arc*. He then performed his own slingshot and began his pursuit."

"It gave us nearly a year lead in the beginning of the voyage, but he's steadily closed that over the decades."

Tanis nodded slowly and then moved on.

"How are your people going to react to our Marines coming over?" Tanis asked bluntly. When had she mentioned it earlier a look of concern crossed Markus's face—as it did once again.

He gave a heavy sigh. "It's going to be a bit of a challenge. Our people have never seen an armored soldier who did not represent their oppressors."

"And I would not blame them," Tanis nodded. "What you need to convince them of is that they are now going to witness how the Sirian military is nothing more than school-yard bullies when compared to real space force. You've brought in the big guns, and those guns are on your side."

Katrina gave a slight smile at the speech and spoke softly so that those around her would not hear. "I hate to say it Captain Richards, but I believe that Yusuf has the bigger guns here."

Tanis chuckled. "Yeah, but that makes for an awful pep talk."

<*I can't believe she beat me to that,*> Angela said. <*My sarcasm must be slipping.*>

"Either way, I'm not going to let some puffed up administrator from an over-hyped backwater best me. I've fought better with fewer resources and come out on top every time. I know you have no reason to trust me, but believe me, I have some tricks up my sleeve. We won't be the ones dead in space when this is over."

"Would you care to share the details of your plan?" Markus asked. The expression Katrina's face showed she already knew Tanis's answer.

"No, I cannot. While I feel an instinctual trust for the two of you, it does not extend to your entire population, nor every computer on your ship. Lives rely on the element of surprise. However, when the Marines arrive, they will give you some more details.

After some final pleasantries Tanis severed the connection.

"The big guns eh?" Brandt asked from the entrance to the bridge. "That was quite the pitch."

"I liked the part about Sirius being a backwater and all that, you had some good posturing going on there," Trist giggled.

Petrov gave Trist a surprised look. Despite the fact that Petrov had been working with the crew for several months, he still had issues with the amount of familiarity and lack of discipline Trist showed.

Tanis saw Trist cast a sidelong glance at Petrov and realized she was trying to get a rise out of him. Given what she knew of Trist this was probably the woman's way of flirting. It would do her well. Tanis was certain Trist hadn't been in any relationships since she her best friend died on the Cho.

Tanis switched the main holo tank to show the local space around the *Andromeda* and studied the image.

Tanis saw that the *Hyperion* platform had settled into a high polar orbit around Victoria. Everything was nearly in place. The last piece was for their enemy to enter range.

Tanis wondered what the leadership of the *Intrepid* would think of her plan. The colony ship was certainly watching the conflict play out—with a light hour of delay.

It was a dangerous game. Letting word get out to the human sphere that the *Intrepid* was still on its way to New Eden could cause some other ship to lay claim to the system. It meant the cruiser from Sirius could not find out that the *Intrepid* was entering the Kapteyn's system; it would have to be disabled before the colony ship arrived.

Privately, Tanis had considered and reconsidered her options. Helping the *Hyperion* was the right thing to do—especially now that she felt a bit of kinship with Markus and Katrina—though the risk was not insignificant.

While she put on a brave face to the *Hyperion* leadership, Tanis knew that her plan was far from foolproof and could see them all dead.

The safest course of action was to do nothing. Let the cruiser destroy the *Hyperion* platform and then wait for it to leave.

<*Never mind the tens of thousands who'd die, there's no guarantee that the* Strident Arc *would leave the system without finding us,*> Angela weighed in.

<*Or that they'd not spot the* Intrepid,> Tanis added.

Tanis suspected that someone who chased a mining platform for over four decades between the stars; then destroyed it would want to control the story carefully. That would require no witnesses.

<*I know that fight is the only option… I just thought I'd left all that behind.*> Tanis laughed inwardly. <*I sound like a petulant child. Life is what it is.*>

<*You never know,*> Angela said. <*Maybe this is your luck.*>

<*Right, for once I wish that my luck wasn't solely for the benefit of others. It takes a lot out of me.*>

She turned her attention back to the holo tank. The *Arc* was a half a million kilometers from Victoria and Tanis decided to send her first direct message to the inbound ship.

"Ship identified as *Strident Arc.* This is Captain Richards of the *Andromeda,* please respond."

Tanis determined not to use her full name or military rank in case the enemy determined who she was and sent the information back to Sirius. Corsia was altering her appearance in the data stream so that it would not be possible for an analysis system to determine who she was.

The ships were close enough that it only took a few seconds for the response to arrive.

"Captain Richards, I am Vice President Yusuf." The man on the holo looked as urbane as they came, his tone was even and belied no emotion—or even interest. "I require that you remove your ship to a distance no closer than one AU from the *Hyperion*, this is Luminescent government business."

"Vice President Yusuf," Tanis replied, allowing her forehead to wrinkle with a slight scowl. "This system is under my control and protection per interstellar law."

The law was a bit squishy regarding who owned a system. Mostly it was by whoever showed up first and held onto it, but there were statutes and principles that everyone claimed to acknowledge.

"I'm going to have to ask you to cease your aggression against the *Hyperion*, which I have granted asylum, and leave the Kapteyn's system. You may loop around the star, gather volatiles and then leave."

Yusuf's cultured expression showed a few cracks and indignance peeked through as he listened to Tanis's response. He smoothed his expression before responding, but she could tell that he had no patience for people he viewed as his lessers.

"Let's be honest, Captain Richards. Your ship is no match for mine. Furthermore, I do not recognize your authority, or your ability to grant asylum. I am here to regain my property in whatever way I see fit. If you interfere you will be destroyed."

Tanis smiled sweetly in response. "I was hoping you'd say that. I don't have a lot of patience for people that kill innocent civilians or consider them property. Although, it seems rash to assume I'm alone here."

With that, Tanis cut the connection and turned to Trist. "How long until we're in lethal range of their beams?"

"Nine minutes, I have our orbit timed so we'll pass behind the moon, Anne, before we come into range. They should be in position to fire on us when we re-emerge."

"Very good," Tanis said.

"Did you expect anything to come out of that exchange?" Brandt asked.

Tanis shook her head. "Not really, but I think you should at least look someone in the eye before you shoot them out of the dark."

Brandt chuckled as she stood and saluted at Tanis. "I'm going to join my Marines. We'll be in position when you call."

The minutes stretched on, the bridge crew shifted in their seats, tested systems and confirmed communications channels. Trist rose to get a cup of coffee and stopped to talk with Petrov for a minute. Tanis stood as well, carefully stretching her limbs, all too aware how the stress and pressure of combat would cause her to tense and clench muscles.

Thus far the timing appeared to be perfect. The *Strident Arc's* trajectory had it on course for the L1 point between Victoria and its largest moon. The *Andromeda* was in an elliptical orbit around Anne and would pass behind the moon before the *Arc* was within effective firing range.

<*I'm registering a few light hits,*> Corsia reported.

Tanis expected that. The *Arc's* beams would not do any damage at this range, but the enemy could test their effectiveness, as well as the reflective and ablative properties of the *Andromeda's* hull.

<*To be expected,*> Tanis replied. <*No damage from the shots?*>

<*An outer seal on one of the starboard airlocks is melted, and an auxiliary antenna is not responding. Otherwise we're fine.*>

<*Nothing like feeling you're in a tin can about to meet a can-opener,*> Trist commented.

<*Hey, that's me you're talking about!*> Corsia retorted.

Tanis smiled and shook her head. Corsia identified her ship as her body more than most AI. It surprised Tanis that Corsia would let her put her precious skin in such peril.

<*She knows the odds,*> Angela said. <*She trusts you.*>

The statement took Tanis by surprise. Trust was not a word AI often used. She found herself wondering if Corsia did actually trust her, or if Angela was becoming more human because of her intertwining with Tanis's mind.

Did that mean she was becoming more like an AI herself?

<*I wouldn't sweat it,*> Angela's soft laugh echoed through her mind. <*You spent four weeks making paint pigments from plants. No AI would do that.*>

<*Safe for now eh?*> Tanis asked.

<*I think so. Like I said, I can tell where you end and I begin.*>

<*Except that you can read all my thoughts.*>

Angela's avatar in her mind crossed her arms and cocked her head. Tanis realized that she always saw Angela's avatar when they communicated now. Perhaps it was just her mind's way of coping with sharing its thoughts with another consciousness.

<I can't read all your thoughts,> Angela smiled. *<This is as weird for me to say as it likely is for you to hear, but I can **feel** them.>*

<You're right. That is weird. Anyway, since you were listening in, why is it that Corsia trusts me? You said she knows the odds, but I know those odds too. They're below what an AI would typically accept when their life was on the line.>

<Let's just say that Bob had a chat with her.>

Tanis sighed aloud and Trist glanced at her. Tanis waved her hand and pointed at her head with a wry smile. Trist laughed and nodded. Her own AI often made for interesting internal conversation as well.

Back in her mind, Tanis imagined herself shaking a finger at Angela. *<Not the luck thing again!>*

<You act like I could have stopped him.>

Tanis knew that wouldn't have been possible and decided to put the whole exchange out of her mind, pulling her focus back to the present.

In thirteen seconds they would pass behind the moon and be hidden from the *Strident Arc*. That's when things would get interesting.

Tanis counted the seconds in her mind, noting as Corsia showed two more probing shots from the *Arc*. The projections held up; when the *Andromeda* passed beyond the moon it would be in lethal range of the enemy ship's beams.

She flipped the holo tank to show a visual from the ship's bow, checking the reports from four of the *Hyperion's* tugs to see that the preparations were complete.

Everything checked out and she smiled as the large icy asteroid came into view. Oblong in shape, it was just over two kilometers long. The tugs had spent several hours pulling it into place and hollowing out an *Andromeda*-shaped cavity.

It was snug, but it would do the trick.

Fusion engines flared and four tugs began pushing the ice-shield, working to match velocities with the *Andromeda*. Tanis tapped into the data stream between the ships, impressed with the precision the *Hyperion's* tugs showed as they worked with Petrov and Corsia.

The ice filled the forward view screen and Tanis accessed the feeds from the remote observers, placing the visual on the bridge's main holo.

It was a dangerous maneuver, and Tanis hoped it would work. They only had one chance to get in the ice. If they failed, the *Arc* would destroy them without a fight.

She widened the view, including the moon and the enemy vessel. A line showed where and when the *Arc* would have a firing solution. The *Andromeda* would cross that line in seven minutes.

Trist, Corsia and the *Hyperion's* tugs worked in concert to line the ship up. Tanis listened in, and after several tense minutes of vector matching the ship was lined up with its new shell.

The ship's nose slid into the ice cavern and Corsia fired grapples into the walls. The tugs and the *Andromeda* ceased all thrust, allowing momentum to carry the ship forward at one meter per second. Corsia and Petrov carefully slowed the ship with maneuvering thrusters until the forward docking clamps gently met ice.

The holo showed less than one minute to spare. Trist wiped her brow and leaned back in her seat.

"Made it without a scratch," she smiled.

"Thank the tug captains and tell them to get into position," Tanis replied.

As the *Andromeda,* sheathed in its new ice shell emerged from behind the moon, two of the tugs latched onto the ice and fired their thrusters, spinning the ship and its shell on its axis.

When the *Arc* fired on the *Andromeda* it wouldn't hit the same spot for more than a second.

"Have I ever mentioned that I hate space travel?" Trist said, looking queasy.

As expected, the moment the *Andromeda's* ice-sheathed bow passed beyond the moon it was hit by laser fire. Tanis reviewed the two ship's relative positions. Both were exactly where she had planned.

The *Arc* was facing directly toward the *Andromeda,* aligned to present a smaller target, its two main beams lashing out across the darkness, finding not the ship they expected, but what appeared to be a spinning ice asteroid.

Ice boiled off the *Andromeda's* ablative covering into the vacuum of space as the *Arc's* beams cut long gashes across its surface.

Tanis calculated the rate of dissipation and determined the ice-shield would hold up for at least fifteen minutes of continuous fire. Beyond that it would be structurally compromised and would fracture.

The tugs had bored holes for the *Andromeda's* weapons and Tanis let fire with several shots of her own. She targeted every beam at what they could see of the *Arc's* port engine. Each weapon fired for a second as the ship rotated. Once they had drained their batteries, a measurable amount of ablative plating had been burned away from the *Arc*.

"Commence your burn, Ensign," Tanis issued the command to Petrov and the *Andromeda* boosted away from Anne toward Victoria.

More ice boiled away from the back of the asteroid as the fusion engines came to life. The resultant cloud of dust and ice looked like a comet's tail, which would protect *Andromeda's* engines from the *Arc's* beam fire.

"They're recharging their batteries," Trist reported. "We have maybe two minutes before they start up again."

Tanis pivoted the display on the holo, looking at all the angles. The *Arc* was doing exactly what she'd hoped, its commander was eager to make a decisive strike.

"They're not yet in position; we'll need to weather one more salvo."

<*Our batteries are recharged,*> Corsia informed the bridge, <*do you wish to respond?*>

"No," Tanis said. "We're not the only ones with missiles, I want to be sure we can shoot theirs down if needs be."

<*Perhaps we should fake a battery discharge?*> Angela asked.

Tanis thought it over for a moment before responding. "Good idea. Corsia, make a strike at where we think their bridge is and then overextend the shot and flicker it out."

<*Thanks, I do know how to fake a discharge,*> Corsia replied.

One of the *Andromeda's* beams lanced out through the void, burning away ablative plating where Tanis suspected the enemy's bridge to be located. The beam burned through half a meter of carbon plating before Angela faked a battery discharge. The beam's intensity flashed brighter for just a moment and then died.

"That was convincing," Tanis pulled up the beam's status. "Did you actually melt the lens?"

<*What do you take me for?*> Corsia responded.

"They're hailing," Trist announced.

Tanis nodded and Yusuf's face replaced the battleground on the main holo, a cruel smile on his face.

"Your beams are dead and your silly ice shield won't hold for long. Surrender and we may still let you live." His smug tone made Tanis doubt that he had any intention of letting anyone live.

"You're going to have to come over here and take us out yourself," Tanis attempted to appear frightened but brave. "Or shoot us out of the stars if you have the balls for it."

The *Arc* cut the transmission and four missiles raced out from the ship. Their intention was clear, with the ship's beams supposedly offline, the missiles would crack the ice shell apart and expose the *Andromeda.*

Tanis smiled, her guess had been correct and Corsia took instant action.

<*Firing on ports,*> Corisa reported the instant the missiles slipped into space. The *Andromeda's* beams flared to life and reached out into *Arc's* missile tubes.

Three ports shut before any damage was done, but the fourth beam penetrated the enemy's hull and hopefully did some damage before carbon foam filled the void.

At the same time, Corsia directed defensive beams, catching two of the missiles moments after they left the enemy ship. One detonated only a hundred meters from the *Arc,* blowing a meter-deep crater in the ship's ablative plating.

The other two missiles slipped past her beams and raced toward the *Andromeda.*

<*Charging,*> Corsia said calmly as the *v* counter beside the missiles climbed rapidly on the holo display.

"Come on…" Trist whispered softly.

<*Charging…*> Corsia repeated.

"Twenty seconds to impact," Tanis said, catching Trist's eye, biting her lip, watching laser charge count-up race against the missiles' impact count-down.

<*Targeting?*> Corsia asked.

"Very funny," Tanis chided her.

<*I swear, she's picking up your bad habits,*> she said to Angela.

<*I have no idea what you're talking about,*> Angela replied.

A moment later, just before the time to impact slipped into the single digits, the first missile bloomed into a nuclear cloud off the starboard bow. The second detonated a moment later.

"Brace!" Corsia shouted over the audible systems a second before the shockwave hit the *Andromeda*. The sound of rending steel shrieked around them as grapples and clamps broke free. Vibrations reverberated back through the ice for over a minute, tearing at the *Andromeda* and fracturing the asteroid.

<*Starboard and port grapples destroyed, we're hanging on from the mast and keel. The ice is smashed and the beams can't get through.*>

"How much are we leaking?" Tanis asked.

<*Pretty much everywhere port and starboard. I've sealed bulkheads and we're in no immediate danger.*>

"Thrust?"

<*Engines and reactor appear to be operational, though we're on some secondary and tertiary systems.*>

"They're nailing us again with beams," Trist reported.

Tanis looked at the holo, which at this, point was only estimating the *Arc's* location. Both ships had fully cleared the moon. Now was as good a time as any. "Can you signal out?" She asked.

"Yes, we have a line of sight out the back to the relay."

"Send the command."

Trist initiated the signal; through the relay's optics the bridge crew watched two points of light emerge from behind the moon. Based on its earlier volleys and timing, Tanis knew the *Arc* was in a charging cycle, unable to stop the two relativistic missiles lancing toward it.

Her plan had hinged on getting the *Arc* to over-extend itself. There was no way the *Andromeda* could defeat the enemy ship on its own. The next best thing was to get the advantage of a second ship without having it.

A tug from the *Hyperion* had positioned the missiles in a polar orbit around the moon hours ago and now they were boosting toward the Arc, already at 0.1*c*.

Point defense lasers on the Sirian ship tried to hit the missiles but failed as the projectiles jinked erratically, making for impossible targets.

One beam made a lucky strike, but the *Arc's* batteries were not fully recharged and little energy was delivered to the missile with no damage done.

Tanis held her breath during the seconds it took for the missiles to cross the black. When the first hit the *Arc's* port engine the bridge erupted with cheering.

Flames blossomed out into space in an eerie pattern as oxygen and hydrogen erupted from the fuel tanks before the second missile struck the ship across its keel—where Tanis expected the superconductor batteries to be housed.

Neither of the missiles were nuclear; their damage was entirely kinetic, but a hunk of tungsten traveling at a tenth the speed of light was nothing to sneeze at. Most of the port engine had been torn free, the remnants spinning through space in a thousand pieces, while the keel was torn through and through.

"Looks like we hit them right where it counts, their EM output is almost nil," Trist reported.

<Brandt, begin your assault,> Tanis sent the command out to the relay and two more points of light emerged from behind the moon. The pair shuttles from the *Andromeda* swiftly accelerated with the assistance of a boost from the *Hyperion's* tugs.

The *Arc's* drifting hulk was still moving at a high rate of speed and it took nearly five minutes to match velocities and another three secure a grapple to the Sirian vessel's hull.

The Marines were not going to go in quietly. Their powered armor was air-tight and the magnetic boots allowed the soldiers to move about on the surface of the *Arc* as though they were walking inside the ship. The feeds from the shuttle optics showed them planting hull busters on four separate hatches.

Four flashes of light later and the Marines were pouring through the *Arc's* new access points.

"God help anyone who gets in their way," Tanis said softly, thinking of the fate the enemy would suffer if any had been near the breach points. This assault would kill as many of the *Arc's* crew through asphyxiation as weapons fire—which was the point.

Tanis didn't hold the Marines to blame. She had ordered this tactic.

<I have bots cutting off the destroyed grapples, we should be able to back out in ten minutes,> Corsia informed the bridge crew. *<I'm going to need a new paint job, though.>*

"I'll make sure that happens," Tanis smiled.

Tactical feeds came through and several soldier's combat cams provided video while a ship's overlay showed the Marine's progress through the *Arc*. From their vantage point on the *Andromeda* it looked as though Brandt's platoons were encountering little opposition. As they approached the bridge Brandt ordered her Marines to seal bulkheads behind them.

<These guys are no match for us, we don't need the tactical advantage—and I'm tired of seeing dead sailors floating in the passageways.>

<It's your op,> Tanis replied. *<I bet the folks on the* Hyperion *will love to have a conversation with their old friend, Yusuf.>*

<I'll keep him in one piece if I can.> Brandt signed off.

Tanis checked the estimated location of the *Intrepid* and noted that it would be another three hours before the colony ship saw the outcome of the battle. She passed an update on a tight beam to the ship before accepting an incoming call from the *Hyperion*.

"Captain," Markus was beaming; even the stoic Katrina who stood beside him seemed on the edge of cracking a smile. "I must admit; I was pretty worried for several minutes there. I can't believe you planned such a daring maneuver."

Tanis laughed. "Well, that wasn't entirely planned. I improvised here and there. By and large it went the way I thought it would. "

"Nevertheless I couldn't have hoped for more. We owe you our undying gratitude for your assistance here."

"You're welcome," Tanis replied. "I'd like to come over to discuss our next steps."

Markus nodded. He must have been expecting an in-person meeting sooner rather than later. "Of course, Captain Richards, what is your ETA?"

"I should be there in five hours," Tanis replied.

Markus nodded and after a few more pleasantries the call was ended.

"Why so long?" Trist asked. "You could be there in two hours tops."

"Because I want to take a Marine escort," Tanis replied. "Oppressed or not, these folks stole an entire mining platform from Sirius. They just about lost it and may feel compelled to do whatever it takes to ensure they hold onto it. We're crippled, but almost as threatening as the *Arc* from their standpoint."

"You think they'd try to take you hostage?" Petrov asked.

"Honestly? No, but you know me, I like to play it safe," Tanis shrugged.

Trist snorted back a laugh.

<Try living in here,> Angela said. *<The stink of irony is almost unbearable.>*

"I'm glad to hear all is well enough," Andrews' face was filled with relief on the holo as they watched his reply to Tanis's status report. "From what I can see you made the best out of a tricky situation, though there's concern here that we could find ourselves on the wrong end of an attack from Sirius."

He ran a hand through his white hair before continuing. "Personally, I think it's fairly unlikely they'd mount a retaliation. Especially since it would take them at least fifty years to do so."

The captain paused for a moment, appearing to answer an unseen question.

"Anyway," he continued. "we're bringing people back online here—your Jessica is doing a good job of being a bloodhound and keeping things in line. Our ETA is just over six days while we break around the star and then loop over to Victoria. Keep me appraised about how your talks with the *Hyperion* go."

Tanis couldn't help but notice how Andrews appeared to have aged. She could have sworn he didn't look so old at her New Year's

Eve dinner. The man really needed to take a regen treatment and give up the white hair.

<*You should talk. You're fifty years late for your last regen,*> Angela commented.

<*Yeah, but you keep me young and beautiful,*> Tanis laughed.

<*I have to, statistics show that beautiful people live longer and have more opportunity in life. Since I share this fragile shell with you, I'd like to even my odds a bit more.*>

<*Hah! Whatever happened to me being inhumanly lucky?*>

<*The jury is still out on that.*>

NEW FRIENDS

STELLAR DATE: 3266051 / 01.17.4230 (Adjusted Gregorian)
LOCATION: *ISS Intrepid*
REGION: Interstellar space near Kapteyn's Star

The tug slipped through the ES shield into a small dock that was spare, but clean and well appointed. Several tugs sat on cradles, all old and worn but clean and well cared for. The walls were all plain and unadorned, save for various functional signs about storage and safety. Tanis noted several areas over doors and a large area on the back wall where a new, slightly mismatched, paint had been applied—likely where the Sirius government and company's crest had been.

Beside her the tug's pilot, a wiry man named Irek, deftly guided the craft into the bay and settled it on a cradle. As the docking clamps took hold, Tanis felt the light pull of a half-*g* take hold.

<*I guess that explains why these people are all so damn tall,*> Brandt commented.

Tanis had suspected that the people of the *Hyperion* were low-*g* adapted humans. It made sense—the cost of adjusting a seed generation vs thousands of years of full gravity were easy to compare. It also made running a facility like the platform much simpler if workers didn't have to constantly fight against their own gravity.

Out the tug's cockpit window she saw several of the *Hyperion's* security forces and a squad of the marines already on station waiting—with a wide space between them.

The *Hyperion* forces had their fingers too close to their triggers for Tanis's comfort.

<*It's going to take some work to convince these people that we're not out to hurt them,*> Angela commented.

<*You can say that again,*> Tanis replied. <*I'm glad we didn't have to repel any boarders here. Things could have gotten more complicated.*>

Tanis rose and looked back at the two Marines accompanying her and Brandt, then down at the pilot.

"Irek, right?"

The man nodded in response, "yes ma'am."

"Thanks for the lift," Tanis said, offering her hand. "You guys did really fine work today, we'd likely be sucking vacuum without your help."

"Uh, thank you, ma'am," the pilot returned the handshake.

Tanis rose and stepped out of the sparely appointed cockpit into the ship's main cabin—little more than a corridor with a cot. Brandt moved to the hatch, the two Marines behind her.

<*Keep the weapons slung,*> Tanis cautioned. <*This is a visit amongst friends, don't forget that.*>

<*Friends with guns,*> Brandt replied.

The hatch lowered and the two Marines took positions on either side of the ramp. Tanis could hear them swapping tactical information with the on-station Marines on the company net.

On the deck the Marines took up positions around the tug, manning the corners with Brandt surveying the room.

The doors at the end of the bay slid open and Katrina strode through, wearing a broad smile and pointedly ignoring the soldiers on either side of her.

Tanis had suspected that Katrina did not share the same ethnic background as the *Hyperion's* inhabitants and now, having seen more of the crew she was certain of it.

While close to their height, she did not have the same willowy build as a low-*g* spacer.

<*There's no way she grew up in this amount of gravity,*> Tanis said to Angela. <*I bet she's what they referred to as a Luminescent.*>

<*You'll note her other features,*> Angela replied. <*She's related to Yusuf.*>

<*Great, what did we step in here?*>

Katrina approached the shuttle and extended her hand.

"Captain Richards, on behalf of the *Hyperion* and Governor Markus, thank you."

Her tone was warm and sincere, but Tanis could see the appraisal in her eyes.

"You're welcome," Tanis replied with a smile. "What would the galaxy be if we just let warships cross between the stars and attack innocent people."

"Of course," Katrina smiled. It was a sincere expression, but Tanis could see that she was reserving final judgement.

Katrina turned to Brandt. "And thank you for risking the assault on Yusuf's cruiser. I hope none of your Marines were injured."

"A few bumps and scrapes," Brandt replied. "Yusuf was a real peach."

"You should try being his daughter," Katrina sighed.

<*I had my money on that!*> Angela said.

"Daughter? I thought maybe niece," Tanis said aloud.

Katrina gave a rueful laugh. "Nothing so lucky. It'll be interesting to see him again after all this time."

Tanis gave a non-committal nod. She wasn't entirely certain what would happen to Yusuf and his surviving crew members. Ownership and jurisdiction in the Kapteyn's system was going to be muddy at best.

<*Angela, are you picking up any high-band wireless traffic? There doesn't seem to be a network to Link to at all, what level of tech are we really dealing with?*>

Angela paused a moment before replying. <*There is no nano here—at least none that your nano has run into—and from what I can tell only the most rudimentary of Links. It's on a non-standard frequency and has no public access. My guess is that these people only have retinal overlays at best—there are no direct neural-level data streams evident, except for on her.*>

<*That's interesting…*>

"If you'd come this way," Katrina was saying while gesturing to the doorway out of the hanger.

Tanis nodded and began to follow while Brandt signaled the two Marines on their detail to follow. She listened to Brandt giving orders for the other two platoons to disembark and return to the *Andromeda.*

A ground car waited in the corridor outside the shuttle bay. The group climbed aboard and Katrina took the wheel and shifted it into gear.

"Wow, hand controls," one of the Marines whispered.

Brandt shot him a dark look as the vehicle took off and if Katrina took any offense she gave no indication.

"We have spent a lot of time examining this system," Katrina said. "We stared at it for over fifty years as the *Hyperion* crossed over from

Sirius. There were no signs of habitation—from what we can tell there still aren't."

"That is our assessment as well." Tanis wanted to meet Markus as well before she decided what to divulge, she would hold off on details until then.

A puzzled look crossed Katrina's face and her brow furrowed. "Your ship is even less equipped for interstellar travel than Yusuf's, how is it that you came to Kapteyn's?"

Katrina certainly was an enigma. She was obviously from Sirius's ruling class while Markus was from its sub-class. However, she was subordinate to him—yet very sharp and capable. Who *was* the real leader here?

Before she brought up the *Intrepid* Tanis decided to feel Katrina out further and learn what the *Hyperion* intended to do in Kapteyn's

"Tell me, Katrina, how is it that you came to be aboard the *Hyperion*? There must be an interesting story there," she asked.

Katrina shot Tanis an appraising glance. She saw the game of cat and mouse they were playing all too clearly.

"Playing it close to the chest I see. I guess one of us has to go first. I find myself more closely aligned with the Noctus than the Luminescents by both sentiment and heritage. My mother was not exactly a voluntary partner in her marriage to Yusuf. For years I operated as a spy for Luminescent society, but the whole time I was looking for a way out, a way to change things."

"Things sound worse in Sirius than I had suspected," Tanis said.

Katrina gave her a rueful smile. "For the Noctus it certainly is. However, Sol too has its share of problems."

"What makes you so certain we're from Sol?" Tanis asked.

"I worked as a spy for a paranoid totalitarian oligarchy for decades. I wouldn't still be alive if I couldn't recognize a Sol starship, or TSF Marines when I saw them."

Brandt cast Tanis a concerned look and shifted uncomfortably. Tanis knew what the woman felt. There was a pride in being a part of the TSF—a military that had been reduced to a shell of its former self since their journey began over a century ago—and a sadness with knowing that they would never be counted amongst its esteemed ranks again.

"Perhaps," Tanis replied, time to shift the conversation. "How long have you and Markus been together?"

Katrina shook her head at Tanis's turnabout. "It seems like forever now. We fell in love while the Endeavor to free the *Hyperion* was under way. He didn't know I was a Luminescent at the time—."

"That must have been an interesting disclosure," Tanis interjected.

"You have no idea," Katrina smiled at the memory. "My heart was in my throat. I had no idea if he would accept me or try to have me killed. In the end it all worked out. We've had a great life together and he is going to get to see his people finally be free."

Tanis read the subtext. Markus looked old. More than just well-aged, but wizened. She suspected that when he and Katrina began their romance they appeared much closer in age. Now he looked like an old, old man and Katrina didn't look a day over thirty.

"It sounds like you made a good match," Tanis said, her thoughts momentarily flitting to her reunion with Joe six days hence. "It's not easy to weather that sort of adversity… and stay together for so long."

Katrina smiled. "My mission to the *Hyperion* is the best thing that ever happened to me."

She slowed the ground car in front of a lift and the group rode up several levels to the platform's administrative offices. Markus greeted them as they exited the lift. He looked older in person, tired and near the end of his days as he leaned heavily on a cane.

"Captain Richards," he said as he reached out his hand. "I'm sure Katrina has thanked you, but allow me to do so again."

Tanis accepted his hand and smiled warmly. "You're most welcome, we couldn't have done it without the assistance from your tugs."

<I didn't expect someone who appears so frail to have such a firm handshake,> Tanis said to Angela.

<He's old, not dead, dear.>

<Funny, Ang. You have as much experience with the really old as I do.>

<That may be, but I was examining the muscle tension under his skin, so I was expecting it.>

"We do what we have to, to survive," Markus replied.

Katrina took his arm and led them into a sparely appointed conference room. It took the group a moment to settle, Brandt and Tanis on one side, while Katrina and Markus sat across from them.

The Marines took up positions on either side of the door, but Tanis gave Brandt a glance and the two men filed out.

"I take it you've decided to trust us, then," Markus said as he watched the Marines exit.

"You have none of your guards in the room, I don't think it would be the best start to our friendship under arms."

The pair relaxed slightly and Katrina folded her hands, pinning Tanis with an unflinching stare.

"If that is the case, then I think it's time for you to tell your story. We have opened ourselves to you, secrets will only harm us all."

"Perhaps we can start off with what you intend to do with Yusuf and his cruiser," Markus supplied.

Tanis looked both of her hosts in the eye—it was clear they expected to have the captives from the *Strident Arc* turned over to them.

"I've honestly have not fully thought that through," Tanis said.

"Captain Richards," Katrina's expression sobered. "I have spent many years mired in the most sycophantic bureaucracy you can imagine. 'Honestly' usually means you have an opinion, but you don't think we want to hear it."

<*Perceptive little thing, isn't she?*> Angela said.

Tanis sighed. "You have me there. At present I don't think I should transfer the prisoners to you anytime soon."

"Do you have a definition of 'soon'?" Markus asked.

"We have a number of other things we need to cover first. I think that because my people defended you from the *Arc* and because we incurred the risk of taking their ship, for now we are best suited to hold them."

"That's more evasive, not less," Katrina scowled.

"I'm sorry, it is. Let's first discuss your initial question. You want to know what the *Andromeda* is doing here."

"Very well," Markus said. "I would like to hear this story as well."

"We're an advance scouting party. Our mothership is inbound—it should arrive in several days."

"Mothership?" Markus asked.

"Correct, the *Andromeda* crossed from Sol within our main ship."

"Within..." Katrina mused. "Then it must be a colony ship—but why would such a ship come to Kapteyn's? There is no charter from the FGT or GSS on this system that I know of."

Tanis knew that with her next utterance there would be no going back. The fate of the *Intrepid* would be forever intertwined with the fates of these refugees. If she could avoid telling them the truth she would—but if the *Intrepid* was to spend over half a century here, they would learn the truth sooner or later.

"What I am going to tell you never leaves this system. You will need to convince your entire population to keep this information to themselves—forever."

Katrina's brow furrowed further and Markus looked to the side, his eyes lost in thought for a moment.

"That's a lot to ask," Markus said.

"Nevertheless I'm asking it. My belief is that you have no interest in outsystem communications, so chances are this will be an easy promise to keep."

Markus and Katrina exchanged a long look. Tanis could tell that a protracted, nonverbal conversation occurred between the pair before Markus finally nodded.

"Our colony ship is the *Intrepid,*" Tanis said.

The name did not register any reaction on Markus's face, but Katrina nodded after a moment.

"I remember hearing about your ship," she said. "You had some complications leaving Sol—but that was over a hundred years ago! You should already be at your colony world."

"A few more years than that, and yes we should be," Tanis said. "But who's counting?"

"I don't understand. You had the best colony pick in hundreds of years, what happened?"

"Our ship was sabotaged as it passed LHS 1565 and we barely made it out of that system. We managed to get our trajectory lined up with Kapteyn's where we plan to repair the *Intrepid* before moving on to New Eden."

Katrina and Markus exchanged another silent look.

"Maybe we could come to a mutually beneficial arrangement then," Markus said.

"Go on."

"I'm guessing that the repairs you need to make are significant, otherwise you would have made them in-transit. I'm guessing that they require an industrial base and you would really like to establish that without cannibalizing your colony supplies."

"You're very perceptive," Tanis commented.

"More hope than perception," Katrina smiled.

"I think we could make an arrangement," Tanis said. "It'll require the colony leaders to weigh in, but it seems mutually beneficial."

REUNION

STELLAR DATE: 3266062 / 01.28.4230 (Adjusted Gregorian)
LOCATION: *ISS Intrepid*
REGION: Kapteyn's Star System

"We really should not do that again," Joe said as he pulled Tanis close.

"Mmm mmm," Tanis murmured into Joe's shoulder as she embraced him with every fiber of her being.

When the *Intrepid* finally arrived in orbit around Victoria it had been five-hundred fifty-eight days, seven hours, and ten minutes since she and Joe had been together.

They had spoken, once the light-lag between Victoria and the *Intrepid* had diminished, but nothing compared to simply being in one another's arms.

"You kept things in one piece while I was away?" Tanis asked with a smile.

"I was just along for the ride. Between Ouri and Jessica all I had to do was make sure the fighters were fueled; then it turned out we didn't need them at all."

"I appreciate the effort."

Joe put his hands on her shoulders and looked her in the eyes. "You took too large a risk—I saw the numbers, Corsia got those missiles with only seconds to spare."

Tanis gave a self-deprecating chuckle. "You know me, always playing it safe."

Joe's expression darkened. "Tanis, I know you are not the most cautious person in the galaxy, hell, you may be the most seat-of-the-pants tactician who ever lived past their first battle…but you have more to live for now."

She knew he wasn't trying to be condescending and that his concern was coming from a place of love, but it didn't prevent her first reaction from being one of anger.

"I was doing what—." She stopped herself and took a deep breath.

"Joe," she began again, looking into his eyes, trying to elicit understanding. "I thought long about it, I thought long and hard. I considered a dozen options from running away on up. But I couldn't leave those people to die. People think I'm a butcher for Toro, but that would have made a real murderer out of me."

Joe was silent for a long moment.

"You're right, I know you're right. I didn't come up with any better strategies where the *Hyperion* didn't get trashed," Joe said as he shook his head and averted his eyes. "It's just that…we have something else to live for now and I couldn't do it alone. I need you."

"Joe," Tanis took his face in her hands. "I'm never leaving you again. The entire universe could be burning down and I'll be with you. I promise."

<You guys know that they're waiting for you on the bridge, right?> Angela interrupted.

"They are?" Tanis asked.

Joe nodded and shrugged.

"Great, now I have to go in there all blotchy and tear streaked."

She took Joe's hand and they walked to the maglev station as slowly as they could.

CONSENSUS

STELLAR DATE: 3266062 / 01.28.4230 (Adjusted Gregorian)
LOCATION: *ISS Intrepid*
REGION: Victorian Space Federation, Kapteyn's Star System

"You had no right to unilaterally make a decision like that!"

Tanis bit back a sharp retort and took a deep breath before replying.

"I think you're missing the fact that we didn't control their presence here. I made the call that we'd rather cohabitate this system with the refugees than the people who would pursue them between stars to wipe them out."

Gerald let out a long sigh. "I was supposed to be planning our first city on New Eden, not someone else's city on a barren, tidally locked shit hole. This is not what I signed up for."

Erin gave him a bewildered look. "You're kidding, right? We signed up to get away from Sol and build a new future. The *Hyperion* is filled with people fleeing a far worse life than we would ever have had in Sol, yet you can't bring yourself to give them a decade of your time?"

Tanis looked around the table at the other colony leaders. Some were nodding in agreement; others wore frowns or even less agreeable expressions.

"A decade is no small sacrifice," Gerald huffed.

"I'm honestly surprised at the lot of you," Abby said. "I thought we brought you along because you had drive to build and create. Here we are with an opportunity that few have ever had and you scoff at it?"

Tanis was surprised to find an ally in Abby, but it fit the woman's personality. Abby was, if nothing else, a woman who thrived on challenge and adversity. Maybe that was why the two of them butted heads so often.

<*You think?*> Angela asked sardonically. <*I always thought that was obvious.*>

Tanis chose to ignore the gibe.

"Gerald doesn't speak for all of us," Tony, the head of planetary engineering, said. "You all know that no one has terraformed a tidally locked super-earth around a red dwarf before. I mean, people have theorized for centuries, but this is the chance of a lifetime. I just want Gerry to stop bitching so I can get my team to work."

Tanis saw that the biologists were glancing between one another—likely having a debate over the Link.

"Simon," she addressed the department head. "How does this strike your team?"

Simon pulled his attention back to the larger group.

"Well, I want to be certain I have this straight," he began. "While most of us were in stasis, the ship got damaged badly enough that we had to divert here. Repairs are going to require us to either dip heavily into the colony supplies, or build up enough of an industrial base that we can replicate what we need without having to cannibalize our supplies."

The captain nodded. "That is the decision we made, yes."

"OK," Simon addressed Tanis. "Then, when the *Hyperion* shows up you saved them out of the goodness of your heart—a decision I personally find no fault in."

Tanis didn't know where Simon was going with his reflection, but she inclined her head in thanks for his support thus far.

"Knowing they weren't going anywhere you decided to strike a 'mutually beneficial' arrangement where they help us build our industrial base and in exchange we help them build a colony," Simon concluded.

"That's essentially it," Tanis agreed.

"It's the mutually beneficial part I strongly doubt," Gerald said with a scowl. "What can these backwater luddites offer us?"

She saw several others, such as Sergey, the head of colony space engineering, nodding their heads.

"Well, we don't have to build mining infrastructure," Erin said. "They have a well-equipped platform and the know-how to use it. Once we spin up their colony we'll be tearing apart this system's rocks in about the same amount of time it would have taken us to set up from scratch."

Tanis appreciated Erin speaking up, especially when her boss, Sergey, was clearly not of the same opinion.

"You don't have to stay up, Gerald," Terrance said evenly. "You're more than welcome to take a nap for the next two centuries and wake up in New Eden. I'm sure someone on your team would love the opportunity to work with the *Hyperion* on their settlements."

A brief hush fell over the room. Terrance usually took a back seat, allowing the normal chain of command to work its course. Apparently Gerald's lack of vision grated on him as much as everyone else.

The others who had appeared prepared to side with Gerald sat back in their seats, none ready to challenge Terrance given the finality in his tone.

Tanis was glad to hear Terrance speak. He had said little since her return to the *Intrepid* and she wondered if he was angry with her for the situation with the *Hyperion.*

"No, fine," Gerald finally said. "But I'm not staying up the whole time. I want to enjoy my years on New Eden, not some bleak rock under a dim, red star."

"Noted," Captain Andrews said before turning to Tanis. "As we have previously discussed, the Admiral and I will spend much of this layover in stasis. Pending any objections, I am naming you Lieutenant Governor of the Kapteyn's Star colony."

He looked around the table, his gaze lingering on Gerald and a few others. No one spoke.

Tanis had assumed her title of general and role of XO would be enough to ensure she had the authority to keep things in line during this build-up. Apparently the Captain and Terrance had other ideas.

<*Sheesh, can you help it?*> Angela asked at the same time Joe whistled appreciatively in her mind.

She had forced her attention from the congratulatory messages that came in over the Link as the captain turned the meeting over to her.

"Then it is settled. Tanis, it's your show. Lay out your plan."

DECEPTION

STELLAR DATE: 3270373 / 11.17.4241 (Adjusted Gregorian)
LOCATION: High Victoria Station
REGION: Victoria, Victorian Space Federation

The shuttle completed its docking maneuver and Tanis stepped across the threshold onto the newly christened *High Victoria* space station.

"Have a nice stay, Lieutenant Governor," the co-pilot said as she departed.

"Thank you, Samantha, will you be getting off duty soon enough to attend the party?" Tanis asked.

"Yes, ma'am. Just have to clean up and then I'll be making the rounds."

"Good, you've pulled a lot of long shifts getting this station and its strand built, you deserve a bit of the celebrating."

"I'll drink to that," Samantha replied.

Tanis chuckled. "Good, I know I will."

The debarkation area was nearly empty—The shuttle had been one of the last for the evening. She walked briskly past the ship berths, still amazed at what had been built in a scant seven years.

It was a feat she would have considered impossible given the state of the *Intrepid* and the *Hyperion* just over a decade earlier. But the drive the crew of the *Hyperion*—now known as the Victorians—showed was inspirational. The results spoke for themselves.

The refugees and the broken-down colony ship. They had made the most unlikely of pairings.

She stepped through the security scanner at the end of the debarkation area and into the corridors beyond. The halls were spare in design, but colorful with different murals and patterns flowing one into the other.

A mother with a young family rushed by, on their way to the celebration. Behind them, moving at a more stately pace, came an older couple. They nodded in greeting to Tanis who fell behind them.

The contrast between the two groups was pronounced. The mother and her children were dressed in a riot of color. Their style reminded Tanis of the crowds on the Main Sweep of the Cho back in Sol. Not so the elder couple. They were dressed in the drab colors and simple clothing their people had worn for centuries.

The generation born on the *Hyperion* during the long transit between the stars—when the crew had to rotate out of cryopods after a decade under—had created a segment of the Victorian population who never knew the yoke of oppression.

For them, the ship had been like a prison as it crossed the black, not the comfortable home it was to their parents.

When the *Hyperion* arrived at Victoria, they exploded from it, eager to take any work that would see them down to the surface or out into space.

They absorbed as much of Sol's culture as they could through the Edeners, as they called the crew and colonists of the *Intrepid,* adopting clothing, music, and even speech patterns.

Their elders saw it as disrespect for their long-standing traditions, but the new generation saw it as the just result of their parent's long struggle

Markus did his best to see both sides. He knew that meeting the Edeners was a stroke of luck that changed his people's destiny forever.

Instead of scratching for resources, barely surviving in the Kapteyn's system, they would build a modern colony with technology they could never have dreamed of.

But he worried that his people would lose their identity and so he and the Victorian leadership crafted a plan with Tanis and her colony government that would see a slow transition of technology over the course of six to seven decades.

The High Victoria station was an important step on that journey—a clear symbol that the *Intrepid* was living up to its end of the bargain.

It granted the Victorian colonists on the surface access to space without having to use *Intrepid* ships. From there, their own short-range shuttlecraft could ferry people to the *Hyperion* and its steadily progressing sister platform, the *Titan.*

Tanis boarded a lift with the young family and the elderly couple. It rose slowly from the outer to inner ring; as it did, the tug of centripetally generated gravity lessened. The doors slid open into a sea of moving color, and cacophony of sound.

The mother ushered her children out into the din and Tanis gestured for the couple to proceed her before she stepped out into the corridor.

The celebration for the official commencement of the station was well under way, with music, food and dancing. One thing Tanis had observed about the Victorians is that they never missed the opportunity for a good celebration.

Downworlder colonists mixed with the station and platform crew; a smattering of Edeners were mixed in—though hard to spot amidst the towering Victorians.

She grabbed a drink from a servitor and took a draught as she surveyed the celebration. Ahead she saw Peter and Sarah moving through the crowd, Sarah holding their newborn son. She hadn't met the newborn yet, and eased her way through the gathering toward the couple.

"Tanis," Peter called out and extended his hand. "It's good to see you. Meet our little Thomas."

Sarah pulled back the blanket and Tanis got a look at the face of the youngest Victorian, for at least another day. The colonists were having children at an alarming rate. Thomas was the fourth child born in the past week.

"May I touch him?" She asked, looking up at Sarah.

"Of course," Sarah said with a smile.

Tanis was surprised to see Sarah so cordial. Usually the woman was prickly at best with non-Victorians. Apparently motherhood agreed with her.

The child's skin was soft and smooth under Tanis's finger. At her touch the baby's eyes opened and Tanis got a big toothless yawn. She found herself thinking of the future and what holding her own child would be like.

The baby stirred further and his eyes opened for a brief moment.

"I better quit that, don't want to fully wake him," she said, removing her hand.

"He just ate, so he'll fall right back to sleep," Sarah said as she tucked the blanket back around Tom.

"It looks to be quite the shindig," Peter said. "I can't believe they let this many people up the beanstalk."

Tanis nodded. "I bet somewhere there's an engineer going over structural specs to make sure the load is distributed well enough."

"You're alone," Sarah observed. "Surely more of your people are present."

Tanis nodded. "They are, I was late and had to catch the last shuttle in. I was out at the beta site going over construction plans there with the onsite team."

"I still don't quite understand why we need a beta site," Peter said. "We have the platforms and now the station for fallback should any terraforming problems arise. Our people are more than capable of living in space."

"You've certainly proven that," Tanis agreed. "But as your population grows you'll find yourselves needing the additional breathing room that a second world will provide. At the very least heavy manufacturing can take place there, making the chances of polluting the atmosphere on Victoria smaller."

"A lot of people think you're doing it to hide things from us," Sarah said with narrowed eyes.

<*There's the Sarah we've come to know,*> Angela commented.

"Trust me, we have nothing to hide at the beta site. One of the things I was checking in on is the new team of engineers from the *Hyperion* who are helping out with some of the base's construction."

Peter placed a hand on his wife's shoulder. "Let's not get into this tonight. We're here to celebrate a big milestone for both our peoples,"

Sarah sighed. "Right, sorry Tanis. I'm going to show Tom around—see you later."

The pair moved off and Tanis let out a long sigh.

<*She's a tough nut to crack,*> she said to Angela.

<*That's for sure. Just when I thought she was getting over her near-pathological distrust of us.*>

<*There are just too many similarities between us and the Luminescents. Our tech is far superior, we are far healthier, a lot shorter…*>

Angela let out a silvery laugh in Tanis's mind. <*That you are. It's a bit funny to see all of you always peering up at the Victorians.*>

<*Well, they are* **tall**! *Even for light-grav spacers. I mean… some of them are over three meters.*>

<*Don't you have some schmoozing to do?*> Angela asked.

Tanis sighed. She did at that. Nearly the entire Victorian leadership was on the station, as well as much of the *Intrepid's.* In addition, many of the colony leaders were out of stasis—their teams and expertise in high demand as the *Intrepid* built this unplanned colony.

As she moved through the debarkation foyer toward the corridor that connected to the station's atrium she saw one of the more self-important colony leaders moving toward her.

"Sergey, how are you this evening?" she asked and extended her hand.

Sergey took it and gave just one firm shake before letting go. "Well enough, I suppose, though I don't really see the need for extravaganzas like this."

"I think it's going to be a lovely evening," Tanis replied. "Especially since it's the first celebration of this sort the Victorians are hosting."

It wasn't exactly true, she had been present at several cultural celebrations on the *Hyperion,* but that information wouldn't make Sergey any easier to converse with.

"I'm already building a shipyard I had never planned to build with a shoestring budget and now I have to come here and hobnob with all these people. For me this is just a distraction.

<You will watch your tone, Sergey. I am doing my damnedest to show the Victorians that we're not a bunch of superior assholes. I would appreciate you not saying things like 'these people' in public—or private, for that matter.> Tanis's ire was sharp and she felt Sergey's startled reaction over the link.

She had cautioned him about his attitudes more than once, though never so forthrightly.

Verbally she was much more cordial.

"You'll find that many of the folks here tonight will be of great help in the coming years—or may end up being your customers. I suspect those relationships may be very useful to you."

As if by magic, Trist appeared at Sergey's side and gave him a winning smile.

"Come Sergey, I'll show you around. I know all the right people you'll want to talk with."

Sergey's startled expression was priceless, but Trist slipped her arm into his and guided him away.

<Thanks Trist. I have no idea how I'd do this without you.>

<I'm pretty sure you'd fail utterly. Who would have thought that years of being a thief and learning to sweet talk people would land me in politics?>

Tanis stifled an audible laugh. *<Maybe because you just described politicians in general.>*

It was Trist's turn to laugh. *<Says the politician-in-chief herself.>*

<Yeah, but I suck at sweet talking.>

<I'm working on her,> Angela added to the conversation.

<Hah! It's like the blind leading the blind in your head,> Trist chuckled. *<Don't worry, I'll get Sergey in a group where he won't cause too much trouble.>*

Tanis walked through the corridor, stopping to shake hands or speak to groups of people here and there, eventually making it to the station's atrium.

The domed park was larger than normal for a station of this sort, but the Victorians were adamant about the size. They had never experienced large, open, recreational spaces. When they saw the parks and the cylinders on the *Intrepid* they made it clear that their stations and platforms would have them as well.

Not that Tanis blamed them. She couldn't imagine an existence where there were no trees, living and dying without ever feeling grass or dirt beneath your feet.

The station was currently in its night-cycle and the large plas dome overhead filtered out the Kap's dim red glow, allowing only starlight to shine through. Tanis could clearly make out Sirius, almost directly above them, staring down as though it were angry over their success.

During the day, the dome filtered and amplified the ruddy light of the Kap, shifting it to the yellow end of the spectrum like Sol.

Without that adjustment, the red light of Kapteyn's Star would require plants leaves to be brown in order to effect photosynthesis—the Victorians had worked hard to ensure they would have green plant-life, at least on the station. On the planet below it was not feasible to globally alter the star's light and brown vegetation would be the norm.

Tanis was impressed with the atrium's arrangement. It was quite beautifully done for a people who had never encountered anything like it until ten years ago.

She felt a hand on her shoulder and a voice asked, "how is the Lieutenant Governor this evening?"

Tanis turned with a smile and gave Joe a short embrace. "I'm fantastic. Looking forward to tonight."

"Stars know you've worked hard enough for it. Who would have thought that my shoot-first-don't-bother-with-questions lady would end up being the one to bridge the gap between two disparate peoples." He stepped beside her and surveyed the room as he spoke.

"I'm just one person on a team, Andrews and Earnest deserve much of the credit."

"Like hell we do," Andrew's bass rumbled from behind them. "I've been doing my damnedest to shuffle every responsibility I can come up with off to you and you're taking them all with aplomb."

While he would never admit it, she could tell that Andrews was ready for the journey to be over. She knew he had planned to make this one last run and then retire somewhere quiet, maybe take a colony ride himself. He certainly had not signed up to be the governor of an interim colony that was sharing a system with another people.

He was an amazing shipmaster, sometimes she thought he might know more about the *Intrepid* than Earnest and Abby did. But that is where his passion lay—with the ship.

For all intents and purposes, Tanis was in charge of everything outside its airlocks and, when Andrews was in stasis, everything within as well. A far cry from the pariah she had been when she signed on.

"It's not like I do it all myself," Tanis said. "I have my own people to shuffle things off to. Markus and Katrina have had some small part in pulling this off as well."

Joe elbowed her and whispered loudly. "For once just take the compliment."

Tanis blushed and turned away.

"She never used to do that, right?" Andrews asked Joe.

"No, she did not. I'm not really sure when it started. I think it was some time during our sabbatical in Old Sam."

Tanis and Joe's many decades out of stasis had become something of legend on the *Intrepid*. The crew and colonists alike were in awe of the couple that stayed up through the long dark to watch over the ship.

In reality there was more watching the waves on the lakeshore than watching the ship, but Joe had convinced Tanis not to disillusion anyone.

"So what's the plan tonight?" Andrews asked.

"The usual, food, speeches, drinking," Tanis replied. I have a short bit. Mostly it's Markus who will be running the show."

"Speak of the devil," Joe said.

Markus and Katrina were moving through the crowd, smiling and shaking hands with everyone they met.

Tanis was amazed at how much better Markus looked than when she first met him. Ten years ago he looked to be within a decade of death, but now he appeared to be no older than fifty. Katrina had eschewed rejuvenation treatments while Markus took several, they almost looked the same age.

"Ready for your big speech?" Joe asked Markus as the couple approached.

"As I'll ever be. I had no idea how much rigmarole I was signing up for when I agreed to this job," Markus replied.

"You make it sound like there was some other option," Katrina chided him.

Conversation turned to business for several minutes as Tanis and the Victorians discussed several logistic issues with the shipyard, terraforming, and the additions to the space station which would begin the next day.

"Okay, okay!" Joe finally broke in. "You guys need to know when to stop working. Com'on, let's get a drink to loosen you up before your long, boring speeches.

"You say that now, but next week when the supplies for the dome expansion down on Landfall aren't ready for you to pick up, you'll sing a different tune," Tanis replied.

"I may, but it'll be a slightly better tune for having had fun tonight."

Arm in arm, the two couples made their way through the crowd to the impromptu bar on a low grassy hill.

Katrina selected a red wine from one of the *Intrepid's* vineyards and swirled it appreciatively before breathing in the aroma.

"Nothing would have stopped me from leaving Sirius with you, dear," she said to Markus. "But the thought of never having a good red again was no small thing. If for no other reason, I would have welcomed the *Intrepid*."

Markus laughed. "I don't know how you can drink that… you realize it's made from berries that grow on trees, right?"

"Yes, dear, I do know what grapes are. I'm not sure how you can speak poorly of wine, especially given that your rot-gut is made from hydroponics waste."

"I don't think I'll ever get used to the idea of eating food that grew in worm poop. Sure it tastes good, but it can't be healthy," Markus scowled.

"Humanity made it a long time eating plants that grew in dirt, somehow we made it," Joe added after taking a sip of his beer.

"And we moved past it," Xenia, one of the Victorian leaders said as she arrived with Dmitry on her arm.

"I wouldn't say that," Tanis grinned as she picked a bacon-wrapped pastry from a passing server's tray. "There's a flavor you can only get from plants that grew in dirt, let alone from living meat that ate those plants. Vat grown stuff always tastes like you may as well just be eating the vat itself."

Xenia grimaced. "I can't believe we're serving that stuff here."

Tanis shrugged. "I've worked with a lot of different cultures over my years. Some eschew this, others can't bear that. If I were just visiting it would be one thing, but our cultures are going to spend two or three generations together. We're going to have to learn to accept and support one another—even in things that we may find foreign."

Xenia's expression softened. "I guess that's true. In a manner of speaking, our peoples are married. We're going to have to learn how to deal with that."

"It's not so bad," Joe said. "There are some cultures back in Sol that you wouldn't want to share a system with for the next week, let alone decades. Plus, if Tanis had to go that long without her BLT we'd have a serious problem on our hands."

Tanis shrugged. "And B is for bacon. Nothing else works in a BLT."

"Say what you want, dear," Dmitry said to Xenia. "I'm with the Edeners on this one. The sheer variety of alcohol these folks have is worth any compromise." He tapped glasses with Joe and they both took another drink.

The conversation drifted through topics ranging from food and religions in Sol, to music and the news of the new gravity research in Procyon, information that Bob had siphoned from signals between the stars.

"What do you think it means?" Katrina asked. "I read through some of the data streams as best I could, but it was all Greek to me."

"Artificial gravity will be a breeze for starters," Dmitry said. "No more shenanigans like the *Intrepid,* with its accelerator coils doing double-duty, or the spinning superconductors. Hell, ships won't even need to be air tight anymore, the grav field can hold the atmosphere in."

"Plus that whole universal point of reference thing," Joe added. "Another point for Einstein."

"Isn't that supposedly the secret to FTL after all the warp drive experiments petered out?" Katrina asked.

"One and the same," Joe nodded. "Wouldn't it suck if we finally got to New Eden and FTL was invented?"

Tanis threw Joe a sidelong glare. "Don't even joke about that."

Myrrdan stood at one of the station's broad windows, surveying the world the Victorians were building. It was impressive to say the least—to spark up a colony in such time, and have many of the trappings of an advanced civilization, was a testament to the sophistication and power of the *Intrepid* and her crew.

"Impressive, isn't it," a voice said from beside Myrrdan.

She turned and saw the Lieutenant Governor, Tanis Richards next to her.

"That's putting it mildly, Ma'am. What we've built here has to be unprecedented, Myrrdan replied."

Tanis gave a light chuckle. Her ability to switch between affability and deep seriousness had always irritated Myrrdan—or perhaps it was the fact that she had always beat her in every contest.

Ever since that day on Mars, Tanis Richards had come out on top—though not every one of their encounters had been adversarial. Tanis would be amazed to know Myrrdan had helped as much as hindered the *Intrepid's* progress between the stars.

It was an invigorating game, one that would be passed down through the ages. A long struggle of power and control that took centuries to come to fruition.

"You've certainly helped," Tanis said. "I really value your contribution; you've given a lot to help us get this far."

"You're too kind, I'm just doing my job."

"That's my line," Tanis said with a smile. "How are things looking at the academy? Joe tells me you're doing well there."

"It's a fun challenge. Also getting to go down to Victoria so often is nice—especially after so long being cooped up on a starship."

"I know what you mean, I love my little patch of land in Old Sam more than I can say, but getting back out has been nice."

Myrrdan couldn't help shaking her head. Referring to the eleven years they had spent on in the Kap thus far as *getting back out* was a sign of someone who had spent too much time alone. If it hadn't been for her daring defense of the *Hyperion* with the *Andromeda,* Myrrdan would have thought that Tanis had lost her edge.

And that would have ruined the game.

When the tales were told in the distant future, learning of Earnest Redding's discovery of picotech would certainly go down as the defining moment for Myrrdan. But she knew her true purpose was this game with Tanis Richards.

Even though Tanis never knew her opponent, her moves and countermoves were deft, and so often made without any direct confrontation. Myrrdan would nearly have turned an asset, then Tanis would give a stirring speech and shift that person's alliances. Other times, Myrrdan would lay in a plan to access sensitive data, but some new procedure or measure of the Lieutenant Governor's would foil her approach.

The nuance was so great that Myrrdan doubted even Tanis could fully appreciate it—though at least she would understand better than Jessica.

The former TBI agent had never really been a suitable match for Myrrdan. So often she'd found herself stringing that plastic doll along, it had really been frustrating.

During her ruminating, she made a polite reply to Tanis and they exchanged a few other words before the lieutenant governor walked away.

It was impressive how the once-disgraced TSF counterinsurgency officer had become the de-facto ruler of this system. Sure, the Captain and Terrance Enfield were in charge on paper, but with them spending the vast majority of their time in stasis it had become apparent who was in charge.

Myrrdan almost wished she could see how that dynamic would play out when the *Intrepid* left the Kap. Except that it never would—at least not toward New Eden. Or under the command of its current leadership.

The speeches were not too lengthy and all the right people were given credit and thanked for their efforts. Tanis gave hers in under five minutes, though during practice it had taken seven. She wasn't sure what she missed, but everyone said it was quite good.

Afterward, she and Joe made the rounds until late in the evening and caught the last shuttle back to the *Intrepid*. They rode the maglev to Old Sam in a thoughtful silence, arms around one another.

Tanis's thoughts were interrupted by a message from Ouri.

<Tanis, are you still awake? I need some authorizations for a shipment for the gamma site.>

<Mmmm… yes, just barely. Is this going out on the slow mule?>

<No, it missed that trip, I need a special courier to run it over. Earnest is having kittens that it was missed. Says it will derail everything.>

Tanis looked over at Joe who was drifting to sleep.

<We'll run it over, I need to check on gamma anyway.>

<Thanks, it's being loaded on the excelsior under the pretense of an asteroid grab,> Ouri said.

<Ole Troy? We'll be there with bells on, just as soon as we grab a change of clothing. This dress isn't practical attire for touring a covert base.>

OLD TIMES

STELLAR DATE: 3270377 / 11.21.4241 (Adjusted Gregorian)
LOCATION: ***ISS Excelsior***
REGION: Near Tara, Victorian Space Federation

"OK, at first I thought you were nuts for signing us up for this," Joe said as he luxuriated in the hot tub's warm water. "I should have known you would have an angle."

"Troy and I have a little deal going. It involves choice assignments and ensuring that our little alterations become permanent fixtures."

<That's me, the most luxurious heavy lifter in the fleet,> Troy said dryly.

"Did you opt for the long route?" Tanis asked.

<Opt is a word that may not exactly fit the circumstances, but yes, we're taking the long route. After our brief dock at Tara's orbital station, it'll be just over a week before we drop into orbit over the gamma site.>

"Pass the cheese?" Joe asked.

Tanis handed him the plate and Joe selected a few slices.

"Sometimes our lives seem ridiculous," Joe chuckled.

"Hey, we have to bathe and eat. Might as well enjoy it," Tanis replied, as she took a long drink from her glass of wine.

"I'm not complaining. I like ridiculous."

Tanis let out a long sigh and slid lower in the water. "The chance to take this trip came at the right time. I really needed to get away. The last few weeks of getting that elevator working were less than fun. If I have to sort out another disagreement between crew, colony, and the Victorians I may blow a gasket."

Joe chuckled. "It's a miracle you haven't blown one already. You're mellowing in your old age."

"Must be you rubbing off on me," Tanis smiled and raised her glass. "I guess, given that we're not falling into a star, or at risk of drifting forever in space, I view all challenges as simple."

"It certainly is a different order of problem," Joe nodded in agreement. "Though sometimes angry stars are easier to deal with than people.,

Tanis raised her glass and took a drink. "You can say that again."

They relaxed in silence for several minutes, feeling the ship go through a burn and correction cycle as they flew past the Kap's larger super-earth, Albion. Its large moon, Tara, appearing from behind the world on the holo above the hot tub, wispy clouds streaked across its surface.

Tara was simply referred to as Beta so much that Tanis wondered if eventually the name might simply switch from use.

The moon was almost three times as massive as Mars and would make an excellent second world for the Victorians—whether they thought they needed it or not.

"Ever find it funny that there are so many terrestrial worlds here?" Joe asked.

Tanis shrugged. "The Kap is weird from start to finish. From another galaxy, almost as old as the universe itself, has all these worlds that it scooped up over the aeons. Nothing here surprises me anymore."

"I should imagine that nothing in general surprises you anymore," Joe replied with a smile.

"You have been known to, from time to time."

Joe laughed while drinking, producing a snort and a fit of coughing. When he finally stopped, tears streaked his face and he grinned at her. "Look what you did."

Tanis chuckled in response, "that's on you. You'd think after all this time you'd know what goes down which pipe."

"Other than a coughing fit, I don't know what surprises I have for you anymore. I expect you know me better than the back of your hand. I know you better than mine," Joe continued his previous line of thought.

Tanis looked down at her hand. "Ever wonder what it would be liked to be a Victorian? To actually know that the hand on your arm is the one your body grew?"

"Well, in my case, it is my own hand."

"Not really, you have the high-*g* mods…your every cell is altered to support your piloting. Me? Well…only Angela can tell where my real body is anymore, let alone where she ends and I begin."

"You're more machine than woman…twisted and evil." Joe quoted with a grin. "Why so melancholy? People have been modified for millennia now. I know they're not throwbacks, per se, but the

Victorians aren't really something to strive for. Look at them, their lives are measured in decades, not centuries. Before we came along they died from long-eradicated illnesses. Died horribly in many cases. Hell, they had to euthanize their elderly to keep their population stable. That's no way to live."

Tanis nodded slowly as she turned her hand over, her perfect bones moving gracefully under perfect tendons, muscles, and flawless skin.

"I know all that, but sometimes I still wonder. Would I be me if I wasn't what I am? Would I be someone else?"

"Probably," Joe said. "We're a product of our environment. But seriously, what's gotten into you? Give you a day off and you can't get out of your own head. Come over here."

Joe reached out a hand and pulled Tanis to him. His lips met hers and they relived that first adventure they'd had in that very same hot tub on the heavy lifter, *Excelsior*.

GAMMA

STELLAR DATE: 3270384 / 11.28.4241 (Adjusted Gregorian)
LOCATION: *IIS Excelsior*
REGION: Orbiting Perseus, ISF Controlled Space

Tanis and Joe watched as Troy guided the *Excelsior* around Perseus in a slow elliptical orbit. On the record the trip would be filed as a survey mission tacked onto the end of the delivery run to Tara.

If there was one thing Tanis had to keep secret during their time in the Kap, it was the gamma site. Not just from Myrrdan, but from Victorians and Edeners alike. They couldn't risk another reaction like Mike or Hilda's.

If anyone were to investigate, they would see that the *Excelsior* did some deep scans of the world and identified a titanium deposit close to the surface. The touchdown would be to confirm those details.

Tanis already knew that there were several titanium deposits on the world and they would soon set up full-scale mining operations on each of them.

Hiding a secret base on the edge of a virtually empty solar system worked better in the long run if there was a reason to go there.

"She's an ugly rock, isn't she?" Joe commented as Troy fired thrusters to degrade the orbit further.

"The uglier the better," Tanis replied. "The Victorians don't have the equipment to mine in a gravity well like this, and the world has nothing else to its credit. Makes it all ours."

"A dangerous place for our dangerous games."

<*Troy isn't read in on this,*> Tanis cautioned Joe.

<*Well, he knows that we're doing secret research here. I mean… he's the one faking the log entries.*>

<*Yeah, but he doesn't know about **what** the secret research is,*> Tanis replied.

<*I didn't think I was giving that away. I'll be more circumspect.*>

<*Hah, sure you will.*>

Joe gave Tanis a quizzical look. "Was that you or Angela?"

"Me." Tanis gave the offhand reply as she looked over the log entries Troy was creating.

Joe furrowed his brow. "Just checking."

Tanis felt a moment of uncertainty. *<That was me, right?>* she asked Angela

<Yes, dear.>

"I'm going to use the next loop to brake and then reduce our groundspeed to around a thousand kilometers per hour. We'll drop fast and hard, but it'll mask our true destination." Troy said audibly.

"Think that's necessary?" Tanis asked.

"Your call, it's your big secret base out here."

"Good point."

Joe and Angela reviewed Troy's calculations and agreed with his math while Tanis watched the grey, pockmarked orb grow closer.

She gritted her teeth during the hard deceleration burn and found herself grimacing during the drop that followed.

<Getting soft in your old age. You've done harder drops than this through atmosphere,> Angela commented.

<I must be… maybe I've finally had my fill of risk.>

<I think you're just rusty. Too much armchair work for you of late.>

<Maybe I don't like the deceit,> Tanis replied.

<Not sure if you've forgotten, but it is ***your*** *plan to do this.>*

<Just one in a long line of my own plans that I don't really like all that much.>

The *Excelsior* had dropped to only a few thousand meters above the surface of Perseus and had slowed to just over five hundred kilometers per hour. Tanis saw the base's beacon on the holo display and watched as Troy homed in on it and brought the ship to a stop over a rocky gully.

A moment later, he reduced lift and the ship lowered through the holographic façade and into a hanger below.

She nodded to Joe and they stood.

"Thanks for the ride, Troy," Joe said. "Keep the tub warm for us."

<I'll never understand you organics.>

Tanis stopped in the ship's galley and opened a hidden panel behind a refrigeration unit. Inside lay a small case, a little worse for wear than the first time she saw it, but still the same one she picked up that fateful day on Mars.

She pulled the case out and turned to Joe.

"Time to deliver this bad boy."

He nodded and they walked out of the ship and down the ramp.

A squad of Marines was waiting for them and performed a quick biometric scan while an auth system validated their security tokens.

Tanis wasn't surprised, the security here was, after all, her setup.

"All set ma'am, sir," The squad leader said once the checks were complete. "They're waiting for you down in the labs."

He led his squad into the ship to do a sweep as a young major ran into the hanger.

"Ma'am, Sorry I'm late," he said between gasps. "Had a small emergency in the commissary."

"Oh, yeah?" Tanis raised an eyebrow.

The major flushed. "Well, more of a misunderstanding. Out here people get particular about the menu."

"Mystery meat Thursday not a hit?" Joe asked.

"Something like that."

"Well, Major Carson, lead the way," Tanis said.

Carson took them through several straight, utilitarian corridors and then into a wide foyer with a lift at the far end.

"Going down?" he asked with a wink.

They filed into a waiting carriage and Carson pushed the only button on the board.

"As you requested, everything below is separated from the rest of the base. Separate power, water, waste treatment, everything. This lift is the only connection and it is purely mechanical, pneumatic of all things, I'm told."

Tanis nodded in appreciation. She already knew all this, but appreciated hearing it had been done correctly from another source.

The level of security and absolute communications blackout was not to keep the Victorians from learning of the lab and its work, but to keep people on the *Intrepid* from discovering what was underway here. More specifically, one person on the *Intrepid*.

<*Doesn't all of this seem like too much?*> Joe asked, his train of thought apparently in the same place. <*Isn't the real goal here to be bait?*>

<*No, the secret lab on the beta site is the bait, this one is really supposed to be a secret lab. I do have contingencies if it is discovered. Bob thinks there's a forty-three percent chance that Myrrdan will ferret its location out.*>

<*Sorry, I got your mysterious plots mixed up. So we're on the secretest of the secret bases. Got it.*>

<*Are we?*> Tanis said and winked at Joe.

Joe looked as though he was going to respond and then smiled and shook his head.

The elevator slowed and the door opened to reveal the pacing form of Earnest. He was muttering about a possible fix to the pneumatics on the elevator to speed it and reduce the time he had to wait for important deliveries.

"Really, Earnest?" Tanis said with a laugh. "It takes us days to get here and you're worried about speeding up the last five minutes?"

Earnest stopped and gave her a wink. "I'm not standing here waiting for two days, just the last five minutes."

"Good point," Tanis said with a shrug.

"I see you have my baby," Earnest said and held out his arms.

Tanis handed Earnest the case which he immediately opened with a sigh.

"You have no idea how good it is to lay eyes on this," he said. "To be so far from one's life's work for so long…it was nearly unbearable."

Joe glanced at Tanis and clapped Earnest on the shoulder. "I have an idea what that is like."

"I need to get this into storage, but I'll come up to share a meal with you in a half an hour. Also," he fixed Tanis with a pointed stare, "I need to check you out as well."

He turned down the hall as Tanis, Joe, and the major stepped back into the elevator for the long ride up.

<*What did he mean by that?*> Joe asked Tanis.

<*He's worried about how Angela and I have been together for too long.*>

<*I've actually wondered about that too, It's been over a century by now, hasn't it?*>

<*A bit over, yeah,*> Tanis agreed.

<*You know…you knew that not telling him about this…problem we have was going to bite you in the ass one day. No one stays integrated this long—at least not if they want to stay sane,*> Angela said privately.

<*Isn't the safe time a heck of a lot closer to five or six decades?*> Joe asked, his brow beginning to wrinkle. <*Maybe you should have the meds separate you two sometime soon.*>

<*There are…complications with that,*> Tanis said after a pause.

<*This isn't the thing where Bob thinks you're lucky because of how you two occupy quantum space, or some such thing, is it?*> Joe asked.

<*Sort of, it's more that we can't be separated anymore,*> Tanis said and looked away. <*It's been like that for a long time.*>

Joe didn't respond at first, but the expression of shock slowly turned to concern with maybe a flicker of anger or two in between.

<*How long is a long time?*> he finally asked.

<*Earnest made the determination back in Estrella De La Muerte. Our minds were too intertwined even then to separate. He thinks that the catalyst was the relativistic battle near Sol when the Jovians attacked us. Something happened when we interfaced my mind with all those ships,*> Tanis said.

<*I knew we shouldn't have done that!*>

<*We wouldn't be here if I hadn't. This is a small sacrifice to make for all the lives we saved that day—if it is what actually caused the merge.*>

<*Merge…you're not a full merge now…are you?*>

Tanis shook her head, the look of concern on Joe's face had a touch of disgust. She almost gasped at how much it hurt to see that him wear that expression. For once she was at a loss for words.

<*Joe, wipe that look off your face. We're not a full merge, we're not even merged at all. We just physically occupy much of the same wiring. She in mine and I in hers. We are still, however, two distinct people and not one of those abominations.*>

<*I'm sorry,*> Joe said. <*I—I was more worried about how you'd see yourself. This isn't about me, I'm just reeling from the knowledge I'm going to have to deal with your sarcasm forever, Angela.*>

Tanis appreciated the humor, though she wondered if he really did think less of her. After nearly a century together it wasn't as though she was worried he would leave her—their relationship was too cemented for concerns like that to bother her—but she wondered if she would read more into any of his offhand statements for a while.

<*Are either of you in any danger?*> Joe asked.

<*Other than from a few more centuries of Angela's wit?*> Tanis asked. <*We don't think so. Earnest just likes to keep an eye on us—back in Sol we'd likely be in front of a Phobos Exam Board, but out here…heck, we just transported picotech. No one is coming after us for illegal AI integrations.*>

Tanis looked around and realized that the elevator had long since reached the top of the shaft. The doors were open and the lieutenant was nowhere to be seen.

"Good on him," Tanis said. "Though rude of us to be so wrapped up in ourselves."

"You're going to earn a rep as one of *those* generals," Joe chuckled and pulled her in for an embrace. "Do I need to offer more apologies later?" he asked softly in her ear.

"This long together and you need to ask?"

<*In case you didn't get the hint, that was a yes,*> Angela supplied.

Joe sighed and gave Tanis a smile. "Looks like our erstwhile major left us a message on the net. He would like to meet us in the commissary."

LANDFALL

STELLAR DATE: 3270395 / 12.09.4241 (Adjusted Gregorian)
LOCATION: ***Gamma Site***
REGION: Victorian Space, Kapteyn's Star System

"How do you feel about a stop-over at Landfall?" Tanis asked.

Joe finished taking a bite of his sandwich and asked, "why dob you awlbays ask when my mouf is fuwl of peanut butter?"

"It's your punishment for using so much that I never get any."

Joe finished chewing before responding. "You spend some time in the garden, growing and taking care of my peanut plants, and I'll share a bit more with you."

Tanis considered her many responses and decided not to bring up who it was that actually made the peanuts into butter.

"Troy needs to grab a rock and bring it down to Landfall and I wouldn't mind going along for the ride. I have some folks I need to see down there."

He shook his head. "I don't think I can tag along, I've a new school of cadets starting up and someone has to give them all the right speeches."

"Ah, that's right, it kicks off in a few days, doesn't it?"

"Yup, our first joint class. Luckily a lot of colony families have chosen to come out of stasis, so we have a good crop of Sol-born kids in their twenties and thirties to balance out and mentor the Victorian kids—suffice it to say that their education is not well rounded."

"Glad to see some are making lives for themselves here," Tanis commented.

Joe took another bite and nodded contemplatively.

"Think we'll leave with the same number we came with?" Tanis asked and waited for him to finish chewing.

"I think we'll leave with more," Joe responded after taking a sip from his coffee. "I mean, twenty thousand people with a 5% birth rate for seventy years adds about eight thousand or so. Add to that the likelihood that we're going to see breeding between the Victorians—who will likely be at a quarter million by then and I bet we'll take on twenty-thousand new passengers."

"That's a pretty sizable estimate," Tanis said with a doubtful look.

"I think it's conservative. I bet we could take on more."

Tanis stood and walked to the small galley's counter where she refilled her coffee cup. "I think we'll see a lot of colonists who will stay behind. A lot of them really just wanted to get out of Sol and have a fresh start. In sixty years Victoria will be a legitimate colony."

Joe nodded. "True, that could happen, it's really going to depend on how families intermingle and how much we can do here. I worry too much that the threat from Sirius will prompt a lot of families to leave with us."

Tanis sighed. "I really hope we don't have to contend with them."

"Well, if we do it won't be for another thirty years at the earliest, but more like forty. They're not going to send another cruiser that can barely make it across the black and they don't really have the ability to launch an interstellar strike without serious preparation."

"Interstellar strike," Tanis said and shook her head. "Who does that sort of thing? Especially for a shit system like this. I think with Yusuf it was a revenge play, nothing more."

"Let's hope you're right," Joe said.

"Well, if not we'll be ready. No one's catching me with my pants down."

"Interesting suggestion," Joe grinned.

Tanis sat alone in the cockpit of the *Excelsior*. It was strange being there without Joe—all of her memories in the heavy lifter had Joe in them.

Outside, Victoria loomed large, dully reflecting the ruddy light from the Kap. It had changed from the barren rock Tanis had fought the *Strident Arc* above a decade ago—not much, but thin, wispy clouds now encircled the equator as the terraforming efforts began to bear fruit.

It was a large world, easily three times the diameter of Earth and much more massive. However, the density made the surface gravity less than Earth's—just over 0.6*g*. For the former inhabitants of the *Hyperion* it was more than they were used to, but they would adapt.

Victoria orbited close to the inner edge of the Kap's habitable zone, closer to the old star than Mercury was to Sol. The proximity tidally locked Victoria and the world did not rotate as it orbited. Instead one side warmed in the star's dim light while the other side froze. The ideally habitable location was the narrow dusk band between the two halves of the world.

Terraforming such a place was no simple task and one not often attempted. Tanis smiled as she remembered how the *Intrepid's* geologists and climatologists had been all but giddy at the chance to make the attempt.

Before the surface settlement of Landfall was established, several icy asteroids had been dropped onto the sunward side of the planet—the remains of which were still melting, forming a sea.

Over time that sea would expand into an ocean which would cover nearly a third of the planet. Even now clouds streamed out from the melting ice. Winds, trying to equalize the globe's temperature, drew them around the equator with what—on the ground—were gale force winds.

Much of the vapor froze on the dark side of the world, slowly covering it in a snow that would persist forever, but some came back around the poles, beginning what would become an ever-constant cycle.

Slowly, the world was being born.

The settlement of Landfall, was on the eastern duskband, a thousand kilometers north of the equator. Already several thousand people lived there, many of them support staff for the terraforming operations, but many were also Victorians who wanted to live on a world after their people had spent generations in space.

Troy deftly navigated the *Excelsior* into Victoria's gravity well, approaching over the frozen dark side of the world. Tanis looked down at the beginnings of what would become great glaciers which would eventually cover much of the world's night side.

The *Excelsior* dropped lower through the fledgling atmosphere, avoiding the gale-force winds that raced around the equator.

The world's dusk-band came into view, the ruddy light of the Kap peeked around, casting the world in a reddish hue. Tanis imagined what this place would look like in decades to come when brown forests grew around the dusk band and into the sunward-deserts.

She started as the ship shuddered from the atmospheric drag pulling at the rock they were hauling.

The half-kilometer wide asteroid was full of silicates needed for manufacturing, as well as no small amount of water. Though the elevator was fully operational, it's single strand could not yet support this type of payload.

A glint in the distance showed Tanis where Landfall's hard dome lay, and Troy tracked south of it, headed to the drop-off point.

The surface refinery came into view, as did the MDC cradle ready to accept the rock. Over a square kilometer in size, the refinery had taken more of the *Intrepid's* resources to build than Tanis would have liked, but was a necessary gesture to show the Victorians that the Edeners did not intend to use them and leave them bereft of any superior technology.

<*Incoming transmission,*> Troy said and routed the call over the cockpit's auditory systems.

"This is Landfall ATC, we have you our screens, *Excelsior*, you're in the pocket and lined up with the cradle."

"Roger that, Landfall," Tanis responded. "Our current ETA is three minutes and twelve seconds until cargo is in position."

"Five-by-five on that ETA, *Excelsior*, the rock slicers over there are eager and waiting, handing you off to their ground crew."

Tanis acknowledged Landfall ATC's handoff and sent a burst to the refinery crew.

"Tanis and Troy here on the *Excelsior* with that package you ordered. Any place you want it, or can we just set it down anywhere?"

"Lieutenant Governor Richards?" the refinery crew chief responded with surprise.

"The one and only," Tanis replied.

<*What, no acknowledgement of me?*> Troy asked.

<*Well, if* Excelsior *shows up, you're a given. Tanis usually isn't in the cockpit,*> Angela replied. <*Buck up though, she didn't even mention me.*>

<*"Tanis and Troy" had a ring to it,*> Tanis supplied.

<*Don't get any ideas, Troy,*> Angela said.

<*I really have no desire to be trapped in an organic,*> Troy replied. <*I've grown rather fond of flying through space.*>

"Well met, Lieutenant Governor. Chief Bourke here."

Bourke was a colony-bound Edener; when brought out of stasis she was planning to build this refinery on New Eden's second moon. Learning she was to build it on the surface of a tidally locked super-earth orbiting a red dwarf star was a task she had taken on with enthusiasm.

A political refugee from an SDO splinter territory, she sympathized with the Victorians more than most and was eager to help them get on their feet in their new home.

"Nice to hear your voice again as well," Tanis said. "Angela and I are just hitching a ride with Troy here. He lets me talk on the radio for my ego."

<*Thanks for the belated acknowledgement,*> Angela said dryly.

Bourke gave a short snort. "Err…sorry, Lieutenant Governor. Given all you've done I'm not sure that Troy needs to stoke your ego, but whatever you say. We're ready here to receive the rock on our primary cradle."

During the conversation, Troy slowed and began his final maneuvers to bring the asteroid into position over the MDC cradle.

ES shields around the cradle perimeter sparked and flared as the radioactive wash of the *Excelsior's* massive fusion engines splashed against them.

ES fields below the asteroid activated and the massive rock sagged into them as Troy reduced lift. Readouts on in the cockpit showed the decrease in mass borne by the ship and when it hit zero, Troy released grapple and lifted gently away from the refinery.

"A textbook drop-off," Bourke said over the comms. "The coffee pot hit the floor, but otherwise everything looks good."

"This may be our last delivery this large," Tanis responded. "The atmosphere is thickening up ahead of schedule; we got close to blowing pressure seals on the *Excelsior*."

"A shame to have an MDC big enough for rocks like this and not be able to use it anymore," Bourke responded. "Any chance you're going to approve a skyhook?"

"I would have, but with the accelerated atmosphere it means that the winds this close to the equator may make a skyhook impossible."

"I guess running at this capacity for six years is still pretty good."

Tanis agreed, successes in some areas created problems in others. Never before had she needed to juggle so many competing priorities.

"We're doing research on the graviton emitter tech coming out of Procyon. It's possible that we might be able to build a gravlift of sorts."

Bourke laughed over the comm. "I thought that was just a crazy rumor! A grav lift for real?"

"Don't get too excited, it's little more than a fantasy that just graduated into myth at this point, but Earnest thinks it has real potential."

"Hmm…well that says a lot. I hope he figures it out."

"Our checks are complete," Troy added on the line. "Landfall ATC has given us our clearances for landing at the spaceport."

"Talk to you later," Tanis said to Bourke.

"Until next time, Lieutenant Governor."

Troy brought the ship around and Tanis watched the landscape pass beneath them on the route to the spaceport.

Landfall was situated in the midst of a low line of hills. The feature was the result of a tectonic plate which had buckled under stress almost a billion years ago.

The event had pushed up many strata of rich minerals to the surface, and the hills also protected the settlement from the winds of Victoria, which—even when the terraforming was complete—would never completely diminish.

The refinery was near the eastern edge of the hills with the spaceport between it and Landfall. As the fledgling settlement grew into a city, it would expand west, toward the sun, with the manufacturing to the east spreading into the dark side.

A splash of brown showed against an east-facing rock and Tanis cycled her vision to get a closer look.

<*Wow, that's a lot of moss,*> she commented.

<*Further east than any current reports,*> Angela said. <*That's a pretty good sign. The projections say we shouldn't have growths this significant out here for another few years.*>

<*I guess this increased atmosphere is moving everything forward.*>

<*So it would seem. I'll report it to the biologists at Landfall. They'll likely be pretty excited.*>

Moments later they passed over the last hill and the meager spaceport came into view.

It was little more than several cradles, an air traffic control tower, and refueling plant. A few low buildings housed repair and maintenance facilities.

Someday this would be a bustling port serving private spacecraft and surface to surface transportation. Tanis imagined what that day would look like, how the world would be shaped once it was finally alive and people could walk outside and stand in the sunlight.

The ship slipped through the ES bubble and Troy lowered the *Excelsior* into its cradle like it was a feather and moments later an ES field snapped over the ship.

Tanis stood in the cockpit and gave the instrument panel a salute.

"Well piloted Troy. You will forever be my favorite ship… next to the *Intrepid* of course."

<Thanks, Tanis. I'm my second favorite ship too. At least I have to say that, Bob is always listening.>

<He's kidding,> Angela said.

<Sort of…>

<Well, when you build a god-like AI so powerful it needs human avatars, you get what you asked for.>

Tanis laughed. *<Irrefutable logic. He could probably do all of this without us, just likes to keep us busy.>*

<Just like a real god.>

Tanis walked down the *Excelsior's* ramp where the ground crew was running microfracture inspections of the *Excelsior's* grapple arms and frame. She shivered for a moment when the cold air hit her. Things may be coming along, but the temperature was rarely above freezing between Landfall's low hills.

"Quite the thunder you brought there," the crew chief said with a nod. "Your purple-haired friend is waiting for you in the hanger."

"Back to purple is she?" Tanis asked.

The chief paused. "I think she is…I don't know, I can't keep track of you Sol types…you all look the same."

Tanis knew that the chief was joking. She had traded jibes with him many times before, but there was a truth behind the words that were not jokes for many Victorians.

She navigated the catwalk through the cradle struts and entered the low maintenance hangar where Jessica stood waiting, fingers drumming on her forearm.

"Took your sweet time getting here," she said.

"We could have gone faster, but I hear it's bad form to bake the planet your terraforming with your ship's fusion burners."

"Bah, it was just a minor tremor, you could have jacked it up a notch."

Tanis fell in beside Jessica and the two walked to the maglev station. "I'll be sure to pass your cavalier attitude onto Bourke. She lost a coffee pot in this latest drop-off."

"That's it? Let me know when the plas breaks and then we'll talk."

Tanis gave Jessica a warm smile—the former TBI agent had become her strong right hand and a trusted friend. Nearly every downworld success was in part credited to Jessica.

"Things are well ahead of schedule down here; I saw moss fifteen klicks east of here."

"That far out eh?" Jessica said with mild surprise. "We'll get grass and little scrubby plants before you know it—at least around here in the tropics."

"Tropics you say?" Tanis laughed. "I seem to remember my last visit to a world's tropics involving a beach and warm sunshine."

"We have warm sunshine here, you just have to go a few thousand klicks west and you'll have all the sunshine you can bear."

"Somehow I think I'll pass on being blasted by the Kap's x-rays."

Jessica shrugged. "Suit yourself."

As they spoke, the pair had walked to the small maglev station. They boarded the single maglev car and settled into a pair of seats facing one another.

"How is Trist?" Jessica asked.

"She's doing well; she can really keep a lot of prickly personalities in line."

"I can't believe you roped her into being some sort of politician. She still steals things, you know."

Tanis nodded. "Yeah, but they're little things, and most of the time she puts them back."

"Calls it keeping sharp," Jessica said with a nod.

"Never know when we might need her deft fingers," Tanis replied.

"So now that we're alone, I trust that your special delivery went well," Jessica said.

"Just as planned. Earnest has his grubby little hands on his favorite toy."

Jessica knew of the gamma site, but Tanis was using her to seed information that Earnest was at the beta site; and he often was, but usually his presence there was faked by sensor ghosts and falsified travel records.

Jessica would leak information in small bites about the existence of the secret research lab on Beta. If they were lucky Myrrdan would pick up on them and make an attempt to breach the facility.

They exchanged other pleasantries and eventually moved on to the purpose of Tanis's visit.

"Markus is concerned with the rate of technology disbursement to the Victorians," Jessica said.

Tanis shook her head. "We're almost on schedule, to the day, with the updated plan from just a few months ago."

"I know; he's worried we're going too fast now. A lot of their younger generation—the ones who were under ten when they arrived here—are really becoming taken with our culture. He's worrying again about the Victorians losing their identity."

Tanis let out a long sigh. This topic was one that consumed much of her time when meeting with Markus. He understood the opportunity that meeting the *Intrepid* created. Not only could his people be free of the Luminescent despotism in Sirius, but they could attain a comparable level of technology.

Markus had confided in Tanis that while they would be dead without it, sometimes he felt as though meeting the *Intrepid* had been a curse.

The statement had hurt to hear, and he immediately retracted it, but it was hard to forget and she wondered how much the sentiment colored his opinions.

"I can't say I blame him," she replied to Jessica. "His generation doesn't even know what a normal society looks like, but they know to distrust a society that shares the same level of technology with ours."

"And we don't exactly make up a normal society," Jessica chuckled.

"Thank god," Tanis replied. "I have to work harder to get the message out, that we too left a place where we didn't fit in—trying to find a new home."

Jessica's lips twisted in a slight grimace. "Well, most of you left trying to find a new home, some of us didn't have much choice."

Tanis gave Jessica a stern look and leveled a finger at her. "Don't play that card with me. I know you think this is the adventure of a lifetime."

Jessica raised her hands in mock defense. "Okay, okay. You got me there. You know I wouldn't trade this for anything. Though I wouldn't have minded saying goodbye to my folks. They probably think I died on Mars, you know."

"I know," Tanis replied. "Bob could get a message to them, you know. They should still be alive, right?"

Jessica was silent for a moment before responding. "You know…I think I'll do that. It would feel good to let them know I'm still out here."

The maglev train entered the tunnel and slipped through an ES shield before gliding into the Landfall settlement station.

The train eased to a stop and when she stepped off, Tanis was assaulted by light and color. The wide platform led into a grand atrium filled with vegetation and no small number of trees. Murals covered the walls and not a single corner was shrouded in shadow.

"They've been busy," Tanis observed.

"The folks down here are soaking up every morsel of art and architecture they can," Jessica replied. "They are building for explosive growth, but still making it look good."

"Glad they're making good use of the latest batch of nano miners we whipped up on the *Intrepid,* though I thought they were building a new commerce district."

"Oh they are—and it's nearly done—they're using MDCs for the main passageways and the nano for the fine finishing work."

"They're what?" Tanis's head whipped to look Jessica in the eyes. "Who approved that?"

Jessica held up her hands. "Our own engineering team pushed it up to Abby and Earnest. They approved the whole thing, it was in one of my reports and in an engineering report."

<It was, dear, you even read it,> Angela added.

"Huh... I have no memory of that," Tanis said with a frown. "How is that safe, though? One twitch of the field and this entire complex eats vacuum... or is grey goo."

"Turns out when a people spend generations where their next meal is dependent on how fast and how much ore they can get yield out of a rock, they get really good at modifying MDC tech. They've some tricks that Earnest was even interested in."

Tanis nodded in appreciation and took in the nuanced designs of the atrium's gardens, as Jessica led her through a security portal into the wide passage which passed through the center of the settlement.

Since her last visit, the central passage been expanded to include an additional lower level, where small electric groundcars moved. Above it, were two levels with wide catwalks, gleaming arches and people walking and chatting in the artificial daylight that shone down from a long sun, which ran the length of the corridor.

A wide staircase of a marble-like substance led down to the lower level, where a car waited for them. A young Victorian man, wearing the uniform of their security forces snapped a sharp salute to the two women and held open the door for them.

The car was simply appointed and showed that the new-found Victorian flare for design had not yet reached their automobiles.

The young man settled into the driver's seat and pulled the car from the curb.

"It'll be about a ten-minute drive to the new town hall," the driver said. "Maybe a bit longer than that, if we get stuck in traffic around the new tunnels."

Tanis and Jessica rode in silence, each staring out the car's windows at the Victorians as they went about their business, creating the beginnings of a civilization.

The town hall, when they arrived, was fronted by a grand arch which led into another atrium. This one basked in a ruddy light and was filled with the modified brown plants that would one day flourish on the surface. The center of the atrium opened up into a wide amphitheater which was capable of seating over ten thousand people. Beyond were several low buildings set amongst the trees.

Jessica led Tanis around the amphitheater and they spotted two figures sitting on a bench beside a copse of trees.

"Looks like they're waiting for us," Jessica said.

Tanis nodded. "I would too—working under a tree is always better than inside…though I guess we're still inside."

As they approached Katrina and Markus stood to greet them.

"Quite the place you have here," Tanis said with a smile as she shook Markus's hand. "A far cry from that dingy little conference room we first met in."

Markus chuckled. "That it is. A lot can certainly change in ten years, can't it? If you had told me back in Sirius that I would spend my days in these surroundings, I would have had a good chuckle."

"You always say that, but I know you were always a dreamer," Katrina said.

"Not always," Markus shook his head. "But enough of that, we have much better things to speak of."

He led them to a table under the trees and the four sat. A young man approached with coffee and a cheese plate.

"From your cows?" Tanis asked with a wink.

"Finally, yes," Katrina replied, "Though Markus is having trouble adapting to food made from 'bovine nipple juice,' as he puts it."

"I'm working up to it," Markus replied. "But coffee, that I am thankful for. I don't know how our civilization persisted without it."

"If nothing else, that is the true miracle," Jessica said.

Once they had each made of their brew what they would, Markus began.

"We've decided to hold a hearing to determine whether or not the Luminescents get the death penalty."

<*You must be getting old to have missed that tidbit,*> Tanis chided Jessica.

<*Hey, I can't find everything all the time. It's not like I'm actively spying on them. They* ***are*** *our allies.*>

Tanis's avatar nodded, <*You're right. Sometimes I lose sight of that.*>

"After all this time?" she asked Markus aloud.

He nodded solemnly, his gray hair blowing slightly in the breeze as he did so. "I suspected it would always come to this, but I held it back until we could do it with cool heads. We've spent a lot of time studying different stellar legal systems and believe we can try them for attempted seizure or destruction of a sovereign ship in a foreign system. Piracy laws would then apply, and the punishment for piracy is death." Markus paused, his expression darkening. "Yusuf has other murder charges hanging over him,"

Tanis recalled the stories she heard of the murder that started all this; the death of Markus's young assistant, which put the Noctus leader on the path to revolution.

"Will you use the jury system we have proposed?" Jessica asked.

Tanis watched Markus and Katrina exchange glances. To her mind, there was no need for mercy with the Sirians. She had advocated putting them before a military tribunal on the *Intrepid*, but many had objected to that—Jessica amongst them. The argument was not to show themselves so willing to kill enemies while at the same time befriending the Victorians.

The logic convinced Tanis and she bowed to the *Intrepid* leadership's collective wisdom. The end result was the same, but this time the Victorians would play the role of killer.

"This is why I'm here, then," Tanis said. "Your case largely requires me to testify against them. It was my ship that they directly attacked and at the time the system was claimed by me in the *Andromeda*."

"There you have it," Markus smiled. "It is a lot to ask of you personally, to condemn others to death."

Tanis glanced at Katrina and the two shared a knowing look that did not go unnoticed. They had shared stories of their pasts and each knew that the other had taken many lives. However, the former TBI agent's incidents had always been reactionary, in defense. Neither Jessica nor Markus had ever plotted out cold-hearted murder and carried it out with their own hands.

"I will do it," Tanis said with little hesitation.

Markus looked surprised, but Katrina smiled.

"It will be good to finally put this—to put him—behind me. I hate thinking of him up there, it feels like a sword over my head," Katrina said.

With the issue settled, the conversation turned to discussion of the settlement's status and the overall progress of the Kapteyn's system colonization. Tanis shared her false report of the mineral deposits on Perseus. She didn't like lying to Katrina and Markus, they trusted her so much and here she was using an entire star system as bait to catch one man.

She saw Jessica fidget and knew her friend felt the same way.

As they spoke, the breeze stilled for a moment and in that brief silence, Tanis heard a faint cracking sound. She increased the sensitivity of her hearing, curious if it was from the drilling going on a kilometer away. She heard nothing else, and then another soft crack.

She dispersed nano to search out the source of the sound, something about it didn't fit. A moment later there was a loud groan and her nano triangulated the source of the sound. It was above them.

Tanis looked up at the stone trusses arching upwards to the vaulted ceiling—nothing looked amiss, but there was no denying that sound. The rock was doing more than just settling.

"Something's wrong, we need to mo—. "

Her words were cut off by a deafening rending. A moment later a piece of the ceiling fell, followed by another. A pillar started to lean and Tanis drew data from her nanoprobes, assessing the damage and where breaks would occur.

"This way!" She stood and began to run into the amphitheater. From what she could tell, nearly every pillar in the room and all of the support arches were falling apart. The entire ceiling was going to come down.

The stairs down to the floor of the amphitheater were wide, and they leapt down them at break-neck speed—even Markus, who still used a cane some days, all but flew down the steps.

The central dais of the amphitheater had several low doors around it that led underneath to storage and prep rooms. There was also a tunnel out of the Atrium.

Tanis wrenched a door open and pointed into the darkness.

"In here! Hurry!"

Jessica raced past her and a moment later Markus and Katrina raced through the opening. Tanis followed, throwing more nano wide, lighting all corners of dark room for her augmented vision.

"Over here!" she ran past the others and opened another door. A long, dark staircase stretched out before her and she dashed down without hesitation. The sound of rock crashing into the amphitheater floor above echoed through the stone walls of the tunnel.

Through the string of nano left behind, Tanis could see that the entire ceiling was indeed coming down.

At the foot of the stairs she paused, assessing the best route through the tunnels.

"Where are we going?" Katrina asked.

"There's a service shaft that leads out to the main maintenance tunnels under the central passageway. It may be a tight fit here and there, but we can make it."

The floor shook and Tanis felt the air begin to whistle past them; the dim lights in the tunnel flickered and Tanis moved forward.

"Com'on, while there's still air to breathe down here!"

"How did you know about this?" Jessica asked from behind, as they threaded utility conduit and support struts.

"I don't go anywhere anymore without pulling down all local maps and blueprints. Not going to get caught somewhere with no net and no map again."

She consulted the route overlaying her vision. "There's a bulkhead in a hundred meters. If we can make it there, we can seal it and keep breathing."

The air was tearing past them now. She could tell that each breath was giving her less oxygen and she altered her lungs to adjust, drawing more from each breath. Jessica had the same augmentation, and she suspected Katrina would as well.

Markus did not and she could hear him beginning to gasp as they ran.

"Deep breaths, don't panic!" Katrina said and Tanis saw through her nano that she was supporting Markus as they ran. The two were falling behind and Tanis dropped back.

"I have him," she said and scooped Markus into her arms.

In the final dash to the bulkhead Tanis found herself growing lightheaded and nearly dropped Markus as she dashed over the threshold.

Jessica slammed the portal shut and sealed the locks. A decompression warning flashed above the door and Jessica threw a glare its way.

"No shit, Sherlock."

Tanis set Markus on the floor as he gasped for air, a desperate wheeze sounding from his throat. They were safe from full decompression, but the air was very thin in the tunnel. Tanis cycled her vision and scanned the rock, it carried some oxygen and she flung a swath of nano into it. The tiny robots began to disintegrate the stone, thickening the air and adding oxygen. At the same time, she sent nano into his body which entered his lungs and drew additional oxygen out of the air and pushed it directly into his bloodstream.

He still gasped for air due to the low atmospheric pressure, but his heart rate lowered and she could tell he was more alert as his eyes cast about the narrow corridor.

A final crash sounded above them and a long crack appeared in one of the walls. Everyone watched it to see if it would grow, but with a final groan and shake the sounds around them stilled.

"That was a bit too close," Jessica said with a sigh and leaned against the wall.

Markus had regained some of his color and nodded slowly. "I don't understand what happened. There was no reason for that ceiling to fall, it was able to support a hundred times its weight… It was eventually to support a building overhead on the surface."

"We have to assume that we were not intended to survive the encounter," Tanis said. "We should keep moving."

"You can't be serious," Markus said, and struggled to his feet with Katrina's assistance.

"I think she's right," Katrina said slowly. "That stone didn't come down without help."

Tanis could see that Markus didn't want to admit it, but couldn't refute the statement. His mouth worked for a moment before he finally spoke. "Let's move, we can assign blame later."

She knew where he was coming from. He thought he had put this sort of danger behind him. Over the many years of the *Intrepid's* journey Tanis had come to peace with the fact that this would never be over. It was more than likely she had already lived her golden years and all that lay ahead were centuries of struggle.

She held out hope that when the colony was finally established she would have peace, but it was a slim hope and she placed no faith in it.

All of her satisfaction in life would come from her love of Joe and the destruction of those who opposed her.

<I rather have the same viewpoint…just without the "destruction of my foes" part,> Angela commented.

<A girl has to have goals,> Tanis replied.

The question was, who was behind this particular attack. Was it disgruntled Victorians, or was Myrrdan's hand in it?

Most likely it was both.

She had hoped to draw him out, but a direct attack on her and the Victorian leadership was the last thing she expected. Myrrdan had never struck at Edener leadership before. He had always needed them to further his ends.

Her thoughts were interrupted by Jessica's voice in her mind.

<You know it's him, right?>

Tanis nodded her mental avatar's head. *<It is more than likely. The question is why would he finally strike at us so directly?>*

<Because he now has the colony established in a place that works for him. The Pico is being developed and when it is ready he will take it back to Sol. Having you around makes that harder. If you're gone then the technology timeline may even accelerate out of fear.>

Tanis watched Jessica's avatar in her mind. The other woman was emphatic, she showed concern, but no stress—only determination. Finding Jessica in that pod was one of the things that made her really consider the possibility of luck.

To meet such a kindred spirit on who she could rely as a strong right hand was enough to make her consider Bob's theory. Even if that kindred spirit was prone to screw everything in sight and cause a few interpersonal issues on the way.

<I fear you're right. I did mean to draw him out, but I had hoped for more direct action—not another proxy war.>

<You've studied him as much as I. A proxy war is the only way he fights.>

<Except on Mars. He was there in person.>

Jessica's avatar rubbed her forehead with the heel of her hand. *<Yes, a strange anomaly in his behavior.>*

As they talked, the group resumed its progress through the tunnel. The air wasn't growing thinner, but oxygen levels still weren't bountiful. Behind them Markus continued breathing with a light wheeze, and Katrina had to support him as they walked.

Tanis give the elderly man—a man many years her junior—a worried glance. Not for the first time she gave dark thoughts to the Sirius system's Luminescent Society. While there was disparity in Sol between the rich and poor, all were able to access rejuvenation technology.

It was part of the reason the Sol system was now home to trillions of humans.

Her reminiscing was brought short by an update from her forward nanoprobes. The tunnel ahead had collapsed.

"Hold up, folks," she said and held up her hand. "Tunnel's out ahead of us. We're not going anywhere."

Katrina gestured backward with her head. "Can't use your nano to dissolve the rock like you did back there?"

"I could, but I'm picking up a leak near the collapse. If I dissolve that rock, we could end up enjoying the surface air pressure real fast. I'm going to see if I can fuse the rock instead."

"Sealing us in. Great," Jessica said.

"Think of it as quality time together," Tanis smiled.

"I'll do that," Jessica replied as Tanis stepped around a fallen piece of the tunnel's ceiling.

The distance to the location of the collapse was only fifty meters, and when Tanis arrived she could feel a light breeze as air flowed past her.

<*I've mapped the air movement,*> Angela provided the overlay to Tanis. <*Looks like you've three spots to shore up.*>

Tanis nodded and pulled out her lightwand. It was a clumsy tool for the task, but beggars and all that.

<*You're going to weld stones on to seal the gaps?*> Angela asked.

<*Do you have a better idea?*> Tanis replied.

<*Not really…you used the last of your nano helping Markus back there.*>

Tanis nodded and set to her task.

She picked up the first stone and tacked it into place with her light wand.

Because Victoria was a low-density world it was possible to weld these light, ferrous rocks. The downside was that their low mass absorbed little heat and by the time she was on the fifth stone her fingers were beginning to blister.

<I've dulled your senses,> Angela said. *<But be careful, you need that hand to function long enough to finish the job.>*

<Gee, thanks Ang,> Tanis said through gritted teeth.

<Well, it hurts me too,> Angela replied. *<Just not the same way as you. Your brain gets weird when you're in pain.>*

Tanis completed tacking the rocks in place, ignoring the throbbing pain in her left hand. The air was getting thinner and she hurried to seal the edges of each stone to the sides of the cracks.

She slowly drew the light wand along the edge of the first stone and before long the rock was glowing bright red.

"Shit!" Tanis swore as the tacks gave way and the rock slipped out of position.

<I'm going to have to brace these things.>

She picked up the largest stone she could easily maneuver and held it against the rock she was welding into place. Her blistered fingers complained at the task, and by the fourth stone the rock she was using to brace was getting too hot to handle.

She switched to a new bracing stone and then another. As she sealed the last rock she felt the stone in her left hand slip and tightened her grip as much as she could.

"There!" She cried triumphantly as the last weld was done and her nano reported no further air escaping.

<Don't look at your…> Angela began to say.

Tanis looked in time to see the stone she used for bracing slip from her fingers, taking much of her skin with it.

The pain hit her like a sledgehammer and she sucked in a deep breath.

"Gods!"

<I've severed the nerves in your left arm as much as I can, what you're feeling is psychosomatic.>

"Stupid brain, it doesn't hurt, doesn't hurt," she muttered to herself as she made her way back through the tunnel to the group.

Katrina caught sight of her hand first and covered her mouth.

"Holy shit, Tanis, what did you do?"

"Rock gets a bit hot when you melt it," Tanis said through clenched teeth.

"I've heard something like that," Jessica shook her head. "You could have asked for help, you know."

<*Like she would have asked someone else to do that,*> Angela said.

"It's not the first time I've trashed this hand. It'll grow back," Tanis said. "Though I must say I've never burned myself this much before… it's a different kind of pain."

"Not to mention gruesome," Markus commented softly, still short of breath.

"Is anyone able to get a signal?" Tanis asked.

"I got a ping for a second, but then I lost it," Jessica said. "There's a lot of interference from the MDC, but it is subsiding, shouldn't be long now."

Tanis rested her back against the wall and slid down. "Good, I think I need to see a doctor."

Jessica tore a strip off her shirt and knelt down to wrap Tanis's hand.

"You're getting blood all over this nice tunnel," she said.

"Sacrificing a sexy outfit for me? I'm touched," Tanis replied, as she closed her eyes and sucked in a deep breath, while Jessica folded her hand into a fist and wrapped it tightly.

The wait, as it turned out, was a little over an hour.

It didn't take long for the rescue crews to locate them, setting up a stasis field and filling it with atmosphere took longer. Several other workers had been trapped in the city hall buildings at the other end of the atrium and were rescued first.

By the time Tanis was in the infirmary she had dozens of messages in her queue, but there was only one she cared about.

<*Joe, are you free?*>

<*Free? I was five minutes away from flying a fighter down there myself when I got the word they'd located you.*>

<*I'm surprised you didn't, to be honest,*> Tanis replied.

<*I was on the maglev to the forward fighter bay, yelling at Bob to make it go faster,*> Joe chuckled. <*I was still running through preflight when I learned you were alright—except for something with your hand.*>

<*She half burnt it off,*> Angela supplied.

<*Really?*> Joe's voice registered shock. <*Amanda failed to relay that little detail. Are you going to be alright? Do you want me to come down?*>

<*I love you, Joe. No, don't worry, they're probably going to lop it off and get the docs on the ship to grow me a new one. They probably have a bank of parts ready for me at all times.*>

Joe laughed over the Link. <*Glad to hear you're in good spirits. The rumors are that this was no accident.*>

<*I don't want to jump to conclusions, but an accident is pretty unlikely. An MDC wave hit the roof above us for an extended period. If ever someone used a molecular decoupler for a kill shot, this was it.*>

<*I'm sure you'll hear from her soon enough, but Ouri has things on high alert up here. Sweep protocols are running on all ships and we're coordinating with the Victorian stations and platforms.*>

<*Beta?*> Tanis asked.

<*Beta protocols are running. Nothing has turned up there yet.*>

<*So not a feint—a probe,*> Tanis replied.

<*Too soon to tell?*> Joe asked.

<*He's watching our protocols in effect, measuring timings, watching signals—seeing who talks to who. This won't be the last one of these.*>

<*Hooray. Ok, I have to assure parents of twenty-year-olds that the academy is safe and we're keeping to our commencement date.*>

It was Tanis's turn to laugh. <*Good luck with that. When did we become so respectable?*>

<*Stars only know. Be safe, Tanis.*>

<*You too.*>

She broke the connection and brought her thoughts back to the world around her. As she suspected, the doctors were approaching with a laser cutter and a cap for her forearm.

"Figured I trashed it," Tanis sighed. "Time for hand number five."

"Your medical records show this as your sixth," a nurse said.

"Really? Oh yeah, there was that time on High Terra I only lost my fingers. Not sure it counts."

The procedure was quick and painless. The doctors had used localized shunts to shut down all pain receptors and fake the signals of a real hand to her brain. As far as her mind could tell, there was a functional hand was at the end of her wrist.

Once the cap was on, the surgeon anchored it to the severed bones in her forearm and cautioned her to be careful until the *Intrepid's* doctors could attach a new hand.

Tanis ignored their admonitions and once they were out of the room she exited the small hospital.

Outside, two Marines stood at attention; a third waited in a nearby ground car.

"Ma'am," the lieutenant said as he and the corporal at his side saluted sharply.

Tanis returned the salute. "Good to see you, I assume you're my escort to the CIC?"

"Yes Ma'am," the lieutenant spoke as the corporal opened a car door for her.

"Jessica and the Victorian leaders are conducting the investigation from there."

They rode in silence, the Marines eyeing every vehicle and pedestrian on the underground street with suspicion.

Tanis kept a wary eye as well, while also reviewing the report Jessica had provided via the Link. As she had suspected, the MDC drilling unit creating the new tunnel had malfunctioned and its aiming mechanism directed the matter decoupling array toward the surface over the new city hall.

No other sections of Landfall had been affected and miraculously there were no fatalities.

Tanis checked who was on scene at the MDC drilling unit and saw that Sarah was overseeing the site.

"Do you have a nano-restock?" she asked the lieutenant.

"Ma'am, yes ma'am, it's in a case under your seat."

Tanis pulled the case out and passed a token to it over the Link. The clasps popped open and she drew out two cylinders of flowmetal.

Drawing up her right sleeve she pressed the flowmetal cylinder against her forearm. The cylinder melted against her skin as the hidden receptacle absorbed the material and began manufacturing new nanobots. With the first cylinder gone, she pushed another into her arm; once it was dissolved into her flesh she instructed her nano to craft a new left hand. The process took one more cylinder, but less than five minutes later Tanis gave her new silver hand a tentative flex.

"That's an impressive feat, ma'am," the corporal beside her said. "I've never seen that be done so quickly—except in vids."

"Helps when half your body is already made out of spare parts. The neural hookups are already in place and there's little chance of dysphoria."

"You don't look that modded—if you don't mind my saying," the lieutenant commented from the front seat.

Tanis smiled. "Top of the line gear here, Lieutenant. Do as many undercover ops as I have and you lose track of what was original equipment. But the force never skimped on repairs and some folks on the *Intrepid* seem to think I'm worth keeping around too."

"Trust me, General Richards, no one begrudges you a thing," the lieutenant smiled. "We'd all be dead several times over if it weren't for you."

"It was a team effort. You've all seen action keeping our collective skins together. You deserve as much credit as I."

"Thanks for saying so," the corporal at her right said. "But we all know that's not true."

"Take the next left," Tanis instructed. "We're visiting the drilling rig first."

"Is that wise?" the lieutenant asked. "I—."

"Doesn't matter if it's wise, lieutenant," Tanis said without rancor. "We need our people there inspecting and with Jessica at the CIC we're the closest qualified."

"We're qualified?" the corporal asked.

"Well, Angela is."

<At last my talents are recognized.>

"Tanis!" Sarah said with surprise. "What are you doing here?"

"Thought I'd come take a look at our homicidal drilling rig here."

The drilling machine lay at the end of a mile-long horizontal shaft. Drilling with an MDC was quite a feat. The control required to ensure the field maintained the desired shape and strength was beyond most engineers. It certainly was not done with this level of finesse—nor near habitations—back in Sol.

The tunnel had straight sides and an arched ceiling. Likewise, the floor was perfectly level and clear of debris. The unit itself also appeared undamaged, though its emitter appeared to be fully open and it was still aimed toward the town hall's atrium.

There the tunnel wall had a wide hole in it. Tanis's nano were well ahead of her and she flipped her vision to see the picture they provided. The hole was wide and flat, the edges were sharp at first, but then they became jagged and diffuse as the field had spread.

Three hundred meters in, the stone was solid, though fractured through and through.

<*That field was well calibrated to travel through two kilometers of rock, before taking out the supports around your little picnic,*> Angela observed.

<*Let me know what you find in the rig's core. No part of this looks like an accident,*> Tanis said.

"No one died, did they?" Sarah's shock response to Tanis's earlier statement brought her attention back to the physical world around her.

"Sorry, no. Not homicidal then, perhaps just very angry," Tanis replied.

"The crew reports that there was a short in the emitter array that fed back into the control circuits. They shut it down as quickly as they could. I'm glad no one died," Sarah replied.

Tanis looked at Sarah with every sense she had. The woman's skin was moist and her heart rate was elevated. The flick of her eyes and fingers told Tanis that Sarah was hiding something. She didn't have the tells of someone directly implicated, but she knew something.

"I don't believe this was an accident," Tanis said.

<*Subtle as ever,*> Angela commented.

"What makes you think that?" Sarah asked, her voice rising in pitch ever so slightly.

"I know a few things about MDCs. Angela knows more. The chances of an emitter making just the right field to pass through all that rock is very, very unlikely. In fact, I would have said it was well-nigh impossible if I hadn't been on the receiving end of it."

Sarah sighed. "Not everything that goes wrong is a plot, Governor Richards. Some things just happen."

"Some things do," Tanis nodded. "But this did not."

<*Um… I'm coming up empty,*> Angela interrupted.

<*How is that possible?*> Tanis asked. <*This would be one in a million if it were an accident.*>

<*Less likely than that, but whoever did this covered their tracks well.*>

<*That means he was here in person,*> Tanis turned, surveying the crews in the tunnel. <*He did this locally.*>

"I don't know who you think did this," Sarah's face was pulled into a scowl. "But none of our people would do it. You're the ones with a history of sabotage and subversion. It seems to me if it wasn't an accident then it was one of yours attacking our leaders."

<*Great, here we go,*> Tanis said. <*Bad time for me to mention that their exodus from Sirius was filled with sabotage and subversion?*>

<*Probably, yes. It's what you get for being so antagonistic all the time. And here I thought your years in politics had softened you; one near-death experience and you're back in your old form.*>

Tanis smiled at Angela's avatar in her mind. <*And here I was glad to see I could spring back like I used to.*>

"That was a jump," Tanis said to Sarah. "I won't deny that it could be someone from the *Intrepid* who did this, but assigning blame in the absence of a perpetrator is premature. Not to mention the fact that they tried to kill me too."

"So is declaring a crime without evidence." Sarah's lips twisted in a caustic smile. "Or maybe you're not as well liked amongst the Edeners as you think."

Tanis sighed and raised her hands. "Very well, I withdraw my statement, but I still have my suspicion."

<*There is evidence of physical access to the core that does not match the logged maintenance times. Not much to go on, but I'll add it to the official record,*> Angela said.

"Angela found signs of physical access to the rig's core that doesn't match the maintenance records. We've logged it in the record," Tanis relayed to Sarah who, like much of her generation, had never received a Link implant.

Sarah eyed her suspiciously; some of the Victorians didn't believe that the internal AI's existed at all—they thought it was just a way to assert superiority.

"Fine," Sarah spoke the one word, then turned and walked back to the MDC crew, who were being interviewed to the Landfall police.

<*Motherhood hasn't softened her one bit, has it,*> Angela commented.

<*Turns out it hasn't, no,*> Tanis replied.

She stayed several more minutes to let Angela complete her inspection before signaling the Marines to take her to the CIC.

"Let's go, boys, nothing more we can do here."

NOWHERE

STELLAR DATE: 3270399 / 12.13.4241 (Adjusted Gregorian)
LOCATION: *Landfall, Victoria*
REGION: Victorian Space Federation, Kapteyn's Star System

Jessica took a deep breath. Sometimes Markus could be infuriating; this was one of those times: He refused to believe his people could ever do any wrong.

It was obvious to her—a defense mechanism against a technically superior people which he felt threatened by. Given the years they had worked together she wished he would be more trusting, but sometimes she thought perhaps he was becoming less so.

Tanis never seemed to have an issue working with him. It surprised Jessica how well the general had slipped into the role of diplomat. It was a testament to the woman's patience—a virtue Jessica was often short on.

"I'm not accusing anyone," Jessica said with her hands raised defensively. "I just need you to understand that we shouldn't rule it out as possibly being intentional until we know otherwise."

Katrina didn't speak. Jessica knew that the former Luminescent often held her tongue. Having been a spy, she had suspicion in her blood and saw Jessica's point of view more often than not. But being married to the Victorian governor required her to support him, not the Edeners.

"It certainly sounds like you are," Markus frowned. "We can't cast suspicion at the rig crew when there is no indication of wrong-doing."

Jessica rubbed her temples. This was going to give her a headache. What she wouldn't give for the level of physical control Tanis had—even with what came along with it.

"That's not how police-work works, Markus. We have to look at every event as though it may have been felonious. If not, how will we ever find the acts that are? Too often people confuse the investigatory process with accusation—it's not, its people trying to serve the greater good doing their jobs."

“Then—.” Markus raised his voice and a few heads in the CIC turned toward him. He stopped and took a deep breath. “Then why did I get a report from Sarah just now that Tanis showed up with Marines at the dig site and started throwing accusations.”

<*Way to go,*> Jessica sent Tanis over the Link. <*I have Markus yelling at me here because you made Sarah mad.*>

<*Sorry,*> came Tanis’s response. <*I should have been more circumspect… I just really thought we’d find a smoking gun.*>

<*I assume you didn’t actually accuse the crew of anything.*>

<*Of course not, I suspect Myrrdan, not anyone of the Victorians. Markus knows that too. I’ve confided all of this in him.*>

<*What’s your ETA?*> Jessica asked.

<*Five, maybe ten minutes. Traffic in the tunnels is a mess.*>

If there was one thing Jessica disliked about her current role, it was the tunnels. Growing up in Athabasca she had nothing but blue sky overhead. High Terra had some unpleasant sections, but there was always the surface level with its open spaces and the jewel of Earth hanging overhead.

Heck, the *Intrepid’s* crew areas had more open space than the tunnels of Landfall.

Once she got the academy up and running with some experienced police and detectives in place she would be able to get off Victoria and back to the *Intrepid,* or maybe Joe’s military academy, where there were portholes and stars.

“You know Tanis,” Jessica said, bringing her mind back to the conversation at hand. “She may be impulsive, but only when faced with imminent danger. She knows who is behind this and it’s not your rig crew. Sarah has a habit of taking everything personally, which you also know all too well.”

Markus sighed and nodded slowly. Over the last few years they had often discussed the members of the former militia who effected the rebellion and exodus from Sirius.

Most happily returned to their former lives, the fighting in the bays and corridors of the *Hyperion* far from happy memories. A few found they had a taste for violence, or command—or both.

Sarah wasn’t necessarily violent, but her temperament certainly skewed toward confrontation. Jessica knew that finding a place for the woman was tricky at best. She didn’t have the patience for a true leadership position, but as one of the foremost leaders of the rebellion she couldn't be swept under the rug either.

"Yesterday's solutions are always today's problems," Markus said and shook his head slowly—obviously on the same train of thought.

"More than anything," Jessica said quietly. "This is our fault, if I had caught him back on High Terra, or Mars… none of this would be happening."

Markus's expression softened. "Jessica… I'm sorry. I know this is hard for you. The day's stresses have worn on my patience."

Katrina placed a hand on Markus's shoulder—apparently she knew he would come around without her having to speak.

"You must keep in mind, Jessica, that while we owe the *Intrepid*—and more specifically Tanis and the *Andromeda* our lives, that gratitude will eventually expire as an excuse for behavior that is perceived as heavy-handed."

"I know… we're going to fight against people's memories for some time," Jessica nodded.

"Don't forget a new generation of entitled…people," Markus added.

Just four more decades, Jessica thought to herself.

BREACH

STELLAR DATE: 3283375 / 06.23.4277 (Adjusted Gregorian)
LOCATION: *ISS Andromeda*, High orbit over Tara
REGION: Victorian Space Federation, Kapteyn's Star System

36 years later

Jessica entered the *Andromeda's* bridge and took her observer's station for the return journey to Victoria. She looked at Joe and could tell he was having a serious conversation over the Link. His brow furrowed and he sat straighter on his chair.

She checked the reports streaming in from the crews managing the cleanup after the year's war games. Nothing stood out—nothing to give Joe that extra-worried expression he currently wore.

The rest of the bridge crew was casting glances Joes way as well, and Jessica pinged Trist.

<*Any idea what's up?*> she asked.

<*Not a clue—I need to finish these targeting reports that Joe wanted. He expected us to do four percent more damage than we did.*>

<Andromeda *did a lot better than last year, didn't she?*> Jessica asked. <*All I know is last time I was on the Yosemite…you know, the winners.*>

<*Funny,*> Trist replied.

Joe was still deep in his conversation so Jessica busied herself with completing her judging reports. Many of the fleet's ships had already left for their home ports and patrol sectors and she forwarded their final grades over the new stellar communication network.

She heard Joe take a deep breath and settle back into his chair.

"What's up?" Jessica asked.

"We're going to have to make a short detour," Joe began. "The sensor net picked up a blip and then lost it again, we're going to do a physical equipment check and then deploy our array for a deeper sweep."

"I guess I'll be observing for a little while longer," Jessica said from her seat.

"Not that you mind," Trist said with a smile from her position at the weapon's console.

Jessica cast an eye toward Joe who appeared to be pretending to not have heard Trist's comment. It was one of the dangers of being on a military ship where most of the command crew were friends. Things got a bit too chummy.

Trist's proficiency with a starship's weapon systems—skills enhanced by her augmented physical abilities—made her the best weapons officer in the fleet. Even though she was an undisciplined subordinate, every captain vied for her skills during the yearly exercises.

Joe was no exception, and though her flippancy marred the discipline of an otherwise by-the-book bridge, he tolerated it if it meant he would win.

It had initially surprised Jessica to find that Joe liked a more formal atmosphere when he was in charge. Maybe he felt like it was part of his responsibilities—or that every commander, especially Tanis, he had worked under had run a very tight ship.

Of course, having Jessica around didn't help. Playing by the rules had never been her strength either. The fact that the two women had been partners for several years added fodder for some rather intimate conversations to boot.

"Coordinates, Sir?" the helm officer asked.

"Not quite yet," Joe said while flipping through a virtual display only he could see. "This mission just got classified Omega. All non-essential personnel are confined to crew areas and net access is to be restricted."

A hush fell over the bridge as the seven officers present glanced at one another and back at Joe who let slip one of his grins.

"Since I let the cat out of the bag and you're all in the know, you're read in. Section heads are notifying their teams in case any of the crew or observers wish to stay in stasis for the duration."

"What do you expect the duration to be?" Jessica asked.

"I don't think this should take more than a few weeks, maybe a month," Joe replied.

Jessica sighed. So much for the vacation she had planned with Trist after the exercises.

An hour later, Joe addressed the crew from the bridge.

"As you know, this mission has an Omega classification. As such not all of you will know what we're doing, but you cannot discuss any aspect of this mission with anyone, ever. Alternate logs and records are being established, including your activities for the duration of this event.

"All non-essential personnel are required to remain in quarters or approved crew areas when not on duty. When off-duty, no aspect of this mission shall be discussed with any other crew member. Corsia will be monitoring all channels during the duration of this mission.

"Your section heads will give you the details as they are necessary for your job function."

Joe waved his hand and changed his audience to the command crew, section heads and senior officers.

"Data shows we have a blip from the direction of Sirius," he said.

"We're to travel beyond the system and deploy a scanning array. Fab will need to produce the additional nodes to create an array the size Corsia calculated we'll need. Astro-nav has also plotted a course that will take us in a wide arc around the Kap and hide us behind Perseus where we'll go dark for several AU before picking up and boosting out to our ultimate destination."

<How far out is the blip?> The chief engineer asked over the virtual address.

"We don't know for sure," Joe replied. "It was only caught for a moment. But close, maybe only a year or two out."

"Shiiiit," Trist said softly. "We're not ready yet for that."

Joe cast her a quelling glance.

"We'll assess and inform Fleetcom of the threat, if any."

<Why is this Omega?> Jeff, the commander of the Marine platoon asked. *<I can see this being secret, but Omega seems excessive.>*

"That's need to know, Commander," Joe replied. "Eventually it will all come out, but at present the General has her reasons."

Jessica knew why. There was evidençe that Myrrdan had reached out to the Sirians. If this was their main force, or even a scouting party, the more they could do without Myrrdan knowing the better.

It amazed Jessica that after all this time he was still able to hide. Although the growing population and extensive settlements across the Kap system were making it easier and easier for him all the time.

Through careful leaks, Jessica and Tanis had released information and misinformation at various levels. On several occasions they saw action based on knowledge to which only high-level officers and officials on the *Intrepid* had access.

It made her skin crawl, to think that she could be friends with someone who may actually be that diabolical fiend—or at the least, someone in league with him.

The level of patience Myrrdan exhibited was astounding. Back in Sol he rarely went more than a few years without committing some atrocity. At least that is what Jessica suspected. Many things she believed Myrrdan responsible for were never officially attributed to him.

By her count he had at least half a million dead to his name. If he got his hands on the picotech that count would seem like a drop in the bucket.

Sometimes Jessica thought they should destroy the tech to keep it from falling into the wrong hands, but then Earnest would tell her his dreams of how it would change everything, of how it would erase all inequality through ready availability of any resource or technology desired.

Jessica wasn't so sure that was a good thing, but when she listened to him it was hard to argue.

At the very least it would give humanity some breathing room. Right now Sol was growing close to reaching a resource tipping point. Even if thousands of colony ships left each year it wouldn't measurably reduce the population—and it certainly wouldn't help the resource scarcity.

Not to mention the fact that there were not thousands of stars nearby that could support humans—at least not with the level of technology they were accustomed to.

The crew and colonists of the *Intrepid* were different. They were adventurers, people who were less interested in the creature comforts of modern civilization; eager to see what was around the next unknown corner.

Jessica couldn't imagine the run-of-the-mill folks on High Terra or the Cho surviving out here where real work was required to survive.

Stars knew it took some adjustment on her part.

It was one of the things that drew her to Trist. Neither of them signed up for a place on the *Intrepid,* though Trist had more warning that she would be leaving Sol than Jessica did.

At times like this her mind went to her family in Athabasca. She hadn't spoken to them much after joining the TBI.

It wasn't that they were so old-fashioned that they found fault with her body mods or sexual appetites, they couldn't understand why someone would want to leave Earth and their family for "space living," as they called it.

After so long amongst the stars, Jessica did pine for living on a planet, feeling solid earth beneath her feet and endless sky above her—so long as it wasn't in a tunnel. But she couldn't imagine staying there forever.

Maybe it was that after the amazing adventures she had experienced on the *Intrepid,* the thought of being little ole Jess in Athabasca seemed too small, like she would be a shadow of herself.

And there was zero chance she would ever had met Trist.

She smiled to herself at the thought. Jessica knew that she was a contradiction. An over-sexed law enforcement officer who had been thrown out of more places than she could remember. Mostly for coming on to, or copulating, with people she shouldn't have.

Perhaps then, the fact that she would end up with an ex-criminal like Trist wasn't so surprising, but to her it still was.

Trist, for all her attitude, was more reserved than most would suspect. It was one of the things that Jessica found irresistible—not to mention that since much of her body consisted of biological silicon she could do some really interesting moves.

Her unintended alterations were one of the things that first caused Jessica's friendship with Trist to blossom. Unbeknownst to many, Jessica's physical alterations were not entirely elective, nor, unlike Tanis's, were they done voluntarily in the line of duty.

It slipped out one night by the beach on the *Intrepid* when she and Trist had stayed late around the fire after everyone else had left.

They both had drank more than they should have, and Jessica had elected not to have her nano scrub her blood clean; rather, she was enjoying the high.

Trist appeared to have done the same and before long they were sharing stories from their pasts.

Jessica had never visited the Cho, but had always wanted to. Trist's descriptions of humanities' greatest engineering marvel were nothing like she had heard before. The former thief had been on every ring and seen corners of the structure Jessica had never heard of.

The story invariably led to Trist telling of her encounter with Trent in the warehouse.

Jessica had read the report, but never heard it from Trist directly, never knew the pain she still felt from the loss of her friend that day.

After hearing Trist's tale, she felt compelled to tell hers. It wasn't one she shared often—heck it was a sealed record in the TBI archives—but Trist seemed like the right person to tell it to.

The rest, as they say, was history.

"Hey, space cadet, you there?" Trist's voice snapped Jessica back into the world around her.

"Eh? Yeah, just lost in thought."

Trist smiled. "Oh yeah? What about?"

Jessica laughed and gave their standard answer. "You, of course."

"I doubt you heard, but we have three weeks to kill before we get to the fun part of this mission. What should we do?"

Jessica grinned. "Are you kidding? Three weeks here with no responsibility? That *is* the fun part."

THE GAME'S UP

STELLAR DATE: 3283395 / 07.13.4277 (Adjusted Gregorian)
LOCATION: *ISS Andromeda*
REGION: Interstellar Space, Outside Kapteyn's Heliopause

The intervening weeks had passed uneventfully and Jessica now waited with the rest of the bridge crew at their stations while the helm officer executed his final maneuvers, bringing the ship into position to deploy the sensors.

The sensor net consisted of a hundred small probes which would spread out over several hundred thousand kilometers and form a massive antenna.

They could have used the system's stellar sensor to scan for the Sirians, but hiding the results from the Victorians, and especially Myrrdan, would be impossible.

Fleetcom was certain Myrrdan had hooks into the stellar sensor array—otherwise it would have picked up the Sirians years earlier. Better to make him think his alterations had worked.

These sensors would only report to the *Andromeda.*

"We're in position," helm reported.

"Very good," Joe said with a nod. "Trist, launch the probes."

Trist nodded and emptied the ship's missile tubes.

Joe brought up the departing projectiles on the bridge's main holo. It showed the missiles arching away from the *Andromeda,* boosting hard to bring the probes to their final destinations. At pre-configured coordinates the missiles released their cargo and the probes began to spread out to their final locations.

Half an hour later, the probes were in their final positions and began to scan the region of space where the blip had been spotted. Joe flipped the main holo from displaying positions of the probes to the results of their scan, tossing the probe visual to a secondary projector.

Small objects flickered in and out as the array detected asteroids and comets in the Kap's stellar halo. Corsia examined them all, checking vector and composition, removing each as they proved to be nothing more than ice and rock.

The array slowly panned through hundreds of millions of square kilometers of space, looking for heat, reflections, or radiation.

"Not nearly as exciting as I thought it'd be," Trist commented. "I thought we'd get a positive lock and say *there are the bad guys, go get em!*"

<*I have a candidate,*> Corsia said.

"Ask and you shall receive," Joe said. "What does it look like Corsia?"

<*Enhancing.*>

The main holo zoomed in on a region of space far closer to the Kap than Jessica would have liked. A fuzzy image of radiation and heat refraction came into view. Velocity was just under half the speed of light and appeared to be slowing.

"Well, rocks don't move at 0.5*c* and they sure don't slow down when they enter a system," Jessica commented.

"They also tend not to emit radiation," Joe said with a scowl. "Corsia, how long until we get better resolution?"

<*Give me a few more minutes, I'm putting together the data from millions of inputs. But I think it's more than one.*>

It was what they feared; looks of worry and concern were shared around the bridge.

<*Ease your organic expressions, I have the mass at no more than a quarter-million tonnes.*>

"Corsia, that still makes it bigger than the *Andromeda,*" the helm officer said.

<*I'm not afraid of a Sirian ship even twice my tonnage. Have you seen these new shields, not to mention our weapons are the best Sol-tech. You know the Sirians won't have that.*>

Trist grinned. "She's right, if it's just another of their cruisers, even if it's bigger than the last, we can take 'em."

Jessica saw Joe weighing his options. She knew that he had been given orders to destroy any incoming ships if they were deemed threatening and of Sirian origin.

If it came to a battle, *Corsia* would pass a coded message into the main scanning array which would switch it offline and put it into a calibration routine. While it was unable to clearly spot the approaching Sirian ships, it certainly wouldn't miss a fight this close to the system.

<*I'm pretty sure we're looking at three signatures,*> Corsia reported. <*They're closely grouped… I suspect using some sort of combined field to disperse their wash. If they are dispersing then I was wrong about the tonnage, each ship is probably half the size of me.*>

"Well that makes things trickier," Trist scowled and brought up targeting routines and historical battles on her console.

Jessica smiled to herself. Diligent is not a word she would have applied to Trist when they first met. She liked to think that she had rubbed off on the former thief.

<*I saw that look you gave me,*> Trist said. <*I don't know what it meant, but I hope it was "good luck."*>

<*It was more along the lines of "you're gonna kick their asses."*>

<*Well yeah… that goes without saying.*>

"At least it's a scouting party," Joe said.

"Are you sure?" asked helm.

"After the beating Tanis gave their cruiser forty-six years ago they'd send a lot more than three small ships to seal the deal."

"Unless there are more and these are all we've spotted.," Jessica said.

Joe cast an appraising eye her way.

"Corsia, once we get enough data on these targets, keep the array looking. We wouldn't want to get caught with our pants down."

<*He should speak for himself,*> Trist said privately to Jessica.

<*What I wouldn't give to catch him with his pants down,*> Jessica laughed.

<*Jessica!*>

Jessica's mental avatar sighed. <*Hey, I didn't mean I'd really do it. I'm mostly monogamous these days.*>

<*I was thinking more along the lines of how Tanis would kill you.*>

<*Oh, yes, well, there is that.*>

Jessica cast another glance Joe's way, giving one last thought to a romp with the colonel before her mind returned to the issue at hand.

"What are your orders, Captain?" Jessica asked. "Should we move in?"

"Three on one aren't great odds," Joe said. "Even if we likely outgun them. Although, the trip across the black and whatever field generator they're using means they won't have a lot of ordinance."

<*Or they can route power from the field to their beams,*> Corsia added.

"There is that," Joe replied.

"Do you think we can get behind them?" Trist asked. "I have several successful battles here where the enemy was so busy looking forward that they didn't see what was on their tail."

"The logic likely applies here," said helm.

"Question is; how do we do it?" Jessica asked.

"They're not the only ones that can direct their engine wash," Joe said. "If we can get above them and then drop down and hit their engines hard we may have a chance."

"We can burn away their shielding and ablative plating, then throw a few nukes down the hole is what we can do," Trist said with a grin.

Jessica watched the scan resolution enhance, as helm, Trist and Joe, discussed the best strategy for getting behind the enemy ships undetected and destroying them as quickly as possible.

What hatred, Jessica wondered, the Luminescents must have for the Nimbus, to wage interstellar war against this one group who managed to escape their clutches.

They were certainly a ruthless people, that was for certain. Not long after the *Hyperion* arrived in the Kap, Bob had received word from his contacts in Sol that a purge had taken place in Sirius.

The Luminescents had wiped out entire platforms on the suspicion of aiding the *Hyperion.* It had been brutal and swift; but SolGov declared it a civil war and not a genocide. Trade contracts were unaffected.

It made her glad she was on the *Intrepid.* She knew that neither Tanis nor Andrews would continue to work with anyone who massacred another people.

She returned her gaze to the main holo and was welcomed by a vastly improved image of their prey.

The three ships appeared to be scout class, but outfitted with much larger engines and several protrusions around the vessels that she imagined were responsible for the stellar scanning array's difficulty in seeing the vessels.

Joe drew the enemy ships close on the holo, while putting the continued search on a side display.

"Ok Trist, lay it out."

Trist rose from her station and wiped a hand across her brow as she looked over the three ships.

"We kick up at this vector," she said, drawing a line through the holo. "Then, at these points we deploy fighters. They can give short bursts and vector down toward the Sirians, using our delta *v* to advance unnoticed." Trist dotted the display with the *Andromeda's* twenty fighters.

"If we can drop behind them, perhaps a million klicks stellar north and aft, then reverse and burn hard to match their velocity. We'll have them in a pincer."

"It's going to be high-*g* fighter work out there," Joe said. Only fifteen of our birds are rated for that work and only fourteen of our pilots have the mods to withstand those *g*'s."

Jessica could see Joe already knew where this was going, but he was forcing Trist to talk it through. After decades of running his academy he was always teaching.

"Then we'll hold onto the other five for close up work when we get in range." Trist removed five ships and placed them with the *Andromeda* in defensive positions.

"You need to move one more," Joe said.

Trist looked at Jessica. "Do I?"

Jessica sighed. "Why not, I'm rated after all."

Joe turned to Jessica and cast her an appraising glance. "That was decades ago, are you sure you're crisp? You made your flights in-system. It's a lot different out here in the deep black. No local star lighting things up, no planets, or stations. It's just us and them."

"I can do it," Jessica nodded. "I have the mods to take the high-*g* and pulled 0.7*c* in the sims."

"Plus you'll look hot in the suit!" Trist said with a grin.

Jessica tossed her a seductive look. "That why you suggested it?" She had to admit, she liked the suit.

Joe and Trist reviewed the strategy and called Major Jeff to the bridge for a review of possible assault and boarding scenarios. Jessica stayed for the beginning of the conversation, but soon left to get acquainted with her fellow vacuum jockeys.

As she walked through the ship Jessica brought up the roster and reviewed the fighter squadron's records. She knew many from her weeks on the ship, but had not examined their history in detail.

It was a crack squad, many were top students from Joe's academy; only Carson was a veteran of actual combat, he'd seen action in one of the succession wars between SolGov and the Scattered Disc.

Not that she had ever been a first party participant in live fire ship-to-ship combat either.

She met them in the briefing room a few minutes before Commander Pearson was scheduled to give the lo-down on their mission.

"Jessica," one of the pilots, a man named Jason, called out. "What's the drill, we've been sequestered for weeks now."

"I can't tell you," Jessica smiled. "Pearson will be very cross if I ruin whatever speech he has drummed up. Suffice it to say that I'll be joining your sorry ranks today."

"Shiiit," a woman named Cary said with a scowl. "We're in it deep if the old man sent you down to help."

Jessica chuckled. She never thought of Joe as "the old man," but to most of these kids he was both figuratively and practically. She looked around the room, and realized that excepting Carson none of the pilots had seen more than forty years. That made *her* one heck of an old woman by comparison, though she was still a few years away from celebrating her first centennial.

Not for the first time she thought of what it must be like to grow up only knowing the Kap—a fledgling colony soon to be abandoned by its saviors who were on to build bigger and better things elsewhere.

The pilots were split nearly evenly between Edeners and Victorians; yet the tension often present between the two groups was not in evidence here. The men and women joked and spoke casually with one another, the sort of banter often seen amongst warriors preparing for battle.

Commander Pearson entered the room and the lanky man looked over his pilots with a steady eye. In less than ten seconds everyone was in their chairs, ready to get the word from their CO.

"The first thing you need to know is that this isn't a drill," Pearson said while slowly pacing before them. We're dealing with an incursion event."

The pilots exchanged looks and a few glanced back at Jessica who nodded slowly.

"Three Sirian scout ships are approaching the system and we're going to give them a warm welcome. The kind that informs their friends they should stay home."

Several nods and smiles met the commander's words and Pearson went on to explain the plan Joe and Trist had devised. There were a few changes since Jessica last saw it—likely Joe lending his experience to shore up any weak spots.

"A wing, you'll be joined by Jessica and will drop from the *Andromeda* along with C wing here at point Epsilon," Pearson said and gestured at the holo display. "X wing will remain with the *Andromeda* and deploy at the same *v* as the ship after she stops and burns to attack the Sirians from behind."

The pilots shared a few more glances. Some nodding, not a few looking concerned at the thought of their first combat engagement.

"Although Colonel Keller is joining A wing, you'll still have command of the wing, during the engagement, Rock."

Jessica gave Rock a deferential nod and the pilot showed relief—glad to understand where he stood in the chain of command.

Pearson proceeded to cover all the contingencies and sequences of fallback strategies. Once A and C wings boosted toward the Sirian ships for their attack runs, the relativistic velocity difference between them and the *Andromeda* would be close to half the speed of light. Even without relativistic concerns, tight-beam communication would be difficult at best.

Jessica set her teeth. She had trained for this, done it in the sims. She would do her fellow pilots proud and come home to Trist.

Pearson finished the briefing, providing the detailed packet to the pilots via the Link.

A and C wings rose and made their way out a side door. It was time to get suited up.

With the exception of Carson none of the pilots had the cellular modifications necessary to handle engagements with burns as high as Trist's plan called for.

That was a protected technology the *Intrepid* never gained the rights to carry with them to New Eden. Jessica imagined that Earnest could likely have replicated it, but it wasn't a top priority.

Without the cellular mods, they would be fitted into Sub-Cutaneous Life Support Shell Suit. Something the pilots referred to as the Shoot Suit. It still took no small number of mods to don a Shoot Suit, but nothing like Carson or Joe's crystalline cells.

Jessica had to admit that she rather liked the process of being fitted into her Shoot Suit—though not all pilots found it as enjoyable as she did.

The squadron lined up before the four ominous looking portals, and when the light turned green, stepped through one at a time.

Jessica ended up being first in her line and took a deep breath before stepping through the opening.

The room she entered was small and dimly lit. She spread her arms and legs as a suspension field lifted her into the air. The feeling wasn't weightlessness, but more like a light cushioning of air around her entire body.

Moments later a mist blew across her and she knew it to be a cloud of nano which were removing the outer layer of her skin—a necessary part of the process due to the amount of time pilots usually spent in the suit. The nano also removed every hair on her body, follicle and all. Hair under a Shoot Suit was a sure-fire recipe for discomfort.

The room requested permission to auth with her internal systems and she allowed it, after verifying its token with the crystal record. The room's NSAI now had full control over her physical body.

The first thing it did was to seal her eyes shut, disallowing Jessica the muscle control to open them again. It then splayed her fingers and toes before a final wash sprayed over her body, removing the last remnants of dead skin and hair.

She knew if she could open her eyes she would look pink and raw, her skin smooth as a baby's.

The next step was one that was both uncomfortable and enjoyable at the same time as a plate rose between her legs and attached to her, providing the plumbing she would require for her long stay in the suit. Next, the room signaled her body to open the IV ports on her forearms and shunts slid into them.

Two halves of a shell wrapped around her midsection, providing additional stability for her soft organs. She could feel tingling in her skin as filaments of nano grew into her mid-section, creating a latticework to support her organs.

As the nanostrands grew within her body, Jessica felt a mist spraying across her. This was the beginning of several layers of material which would form a tight sheath covering every inch of her body. At some point during the process tubes slid up her nostrils and down her throat where they threaded into her lungs.

Even though she expected it, Jessica had to resist a brief moment of panic as she lost the ability to breathe on her own, the suit's systems taking over air regulation.

Her new epidermis began to tighten, compressing her body while the air flowing into her nostrils grew thicker. By the time she was inserted into her fighter she would be breathing liquid oxygen.

A thin tube slipped between her lips and filled her mouth with a thick setting gel, ensuring that her jaw couldn't move and teeth wouldn't shatter.

She felt slight pressure on her temples and knew optical sensors were being mounted on her head. A second later, vision came back, provided by the small cameras on her head. She glanced around the small chamber, becoming accustomed to the slightly wider stereo vision. It wasn't ideal, but once in the ship she would use its sensors to see—the head-mounted cameras would just be in case of emergency.

With her vision returned she could see armatures holding more plates which would cover more soft tissue, keeping her body in one piece when it would weigh more than four metric tonnes.

In rapid succession, they covered her chest, neck, arms and legs. The suspension field diminished and she sank to the ground. She looked down, admiring her gleaming white body, a picture of feminine beauty encased in hard polymers, carbon nano, and suspension gel.

The door on the far side of the chamber opened and she walked out, taking a seat on the small tram awaiting the members of A wing.

Over the next fifteen minutes the rest of her squadron joined her, an array of gleaming white human figures without eyes or mouths, tubes running from noses to small tanks on their backs.

Each had their name printed on their chests along with readout panels on their forearms showing vital statistics and progress of their internal organ support lattices.

Carson reached under his seat and pulled a small, three-dimensional spray printer. He approached each member of the wing and sprayed the wing's logo on their right shoulders before giving them a hard slap on the head.

Jessica took her badge with pride and could barely feel the slap through the hard shell of her Shoot Suit.

A minute later the tram took off, driving to the hanger bay where each pilot would be inserted into their ships. When they drove through the bay doors, Jessica couldn't help but smile as she admired the sleek fighters.

At twenty meters long, the ships consisted of an oblong central pod with a series of tracks crisscrossing it. Engines, weapons, sensors and more engines all mounted to the tracks, able to spin around the pod and change vector or firing angles with a moment's notice.

They were both graceful and deadly, an obsidian pearl bristling with weapons.

Jessica knew she would enjoy piloting one of these machines, and her avatar grinned at her fellow pilots on the tactical net.

<Looking forward to taking one of these babies out for a spin. They were really impressive to watch during maneuvers.>

Jason's avatar smiled back at her. *<They're something else. All muscle and no compromise. Colonel Evans and Abby really outdid themselves on these.>*

<Do you have sim-time in the Arc-5's?> Carson asked.

<I took one for a spin briefly after watching you guys during the exercises, but otherwise my experience is all in the 3's and 4's,> Jessica replied.

<These birds are a pretty big departure. They can turn on a dime and carry three times the ordinance. If you feel a shimmy on max thrust, it's because load isn't properly balanced. The onboard NSAI does a pretty good job, but sometimes can't perfectly anticipate your vector, so keep an eye on it.> Carson spoke mater-of-factly, providing essential guidance to a new pilot that wouldn't be found in the flight manual.

<The rest of you,> Carson addressed the squadron. *<We're live fire out there. Watch your crossfire, keep the battlefield overlay front and center.>*

Jessica couldn't help but add to herself that they were also firing at live targets—though there was no need to state that, they were already all thinking it.

<Thanks Carson,> Rock said. *<Don't forget, our primary targets will be those scout ships.* Andromeda *can't take out three at once, so we have to even the odds and fast. Combat net will display priority targets and will be updated in real time by Cordy.>*

<Nice to see you too, Rock,> Cordy, the squadron AI, said as they the tram stopped at the first ship and Rock disembarked.

The squad members all gave Cordy their greetings and the AI's avatar—a glowing hawk-woman that either inspired, or was inspired by, the emblem now sprayed on Jessica's shoulder—greeted them in return.

The AI was a combat specialist, her mind created from a merge of Angela and several others on the *Intrepid.*

Her core would be distributed amongst the fighters with a dormant backup node on the *Andromeda* in case she suffered too much damage in combat.

Jessica hoped it wouldn't be needed. If Cordy suffered too much damage out there it meant the pilots likely would too.

The tram stopped in front of Jessica's ship and she stepped off, admiring the sleek black beauty in front of her. The ships were a matte material, nearly invisible to any passive sensors and most active ones as well.

The engines were powered by small anti-matter cores with small fusion backup generators. The pion drives also gave them the ability to use their engines as weapons. The energy stream that delivered the ship's thrust traveled at near-light speed. Slamming that engine wash into an enemy ship would deal no small amount of damage to structure and organics alike.

It also meant that extreme caution had to be exercised. Entire vectors of travel would be restricted during the engagement to avoid damaging the *Andromeda* or killing their fellow pilots.

Jessica walked under the ship and a deck engineer gave her a reassuring nod. She stepped onto a holo grid and the bottom of the ship opened up. She disengaged the mag lock on her boots and a suspension field drew her inside the fighter.

A soft cocoon enveloped her and she stretched out in its embrace as the ship's HUD came up. The life-support readout showed the biological hookups attaching to her body and then the neural hookups completed their initialization.

Even though she was prepared for it, the sensation always startled her.

One moment her mind was in her body, and the next it felt like it had expanded, like all the edges had been pushed out. She could still feel her limbs, but also new limbs, new eyes, new ears.

Gently testing, she moved several of the ship's weapons and engines ever so slightly. The feedback was perfect and it felt no different than twitching a finger.

<*You're right, Rock, it feels like a dream,*> she said over the tactical net.

<*Would I lead you astray? These 5's are the best thing since sliced bread.*>

<*I think that sliced cheese is the best thing since sliced bread,*> Jason commented.

<*That's…I don't have words for that,*> Carson said.

<*Submit pre-flight to me in five,*> Rock added. <*We're getting dropped in just over thirty minutes.*>

Jessica's mental HUD updated to provide a deployment count down. The engagement plan had the fifteen fighters dark with zero vector change for twenty-two hours after the drop.

Then, with careful nudging of their antimatter pion drives they would shift vector and align with the Sirian scout ships. The pion drive washes were so narrow they could apply nearly any level of thrust and remain undetected; the fighters were large enough to hide the ion streams behind them—at least from passive sensors.

Once her preflight checks were done, Jessica reached out to Trist over the Link.

<*How're things looking up there?*> Jessica asked.

<*About the same—no other ships have been detected. Shoot suit still fit?*>

Jessica chuckled. <*The suit fits whether you want it to or not. Gotta say, though, I'd forgotten how uncomfortable it is at first while it pressurizes you.*>

<*The struggles we go through for fashion,*> Trist said.

<I suppose somewhere a shoot suit probably is fashion—the galaxy is filled with all sorts.>

<I don't think you'd need to leave Sol to find all sorts.>

Jessica's avatar gave Trist's a flirtatious look. *<I had to leave Sol to find you.>*

<Oh dear,> Trist looked concerned. *<It's finally happened.>*

<What's happened?> Jessica asked.

<You've finally reached the mushy sentimental stage of our relationship.>

Jessica snorted. *<Hardly. This is the 'reviewing my life before I go into the dark to face death' mindset.>*

<Sure, you keep saying that and maybe you'll start to believe it,> Trist replied with a smirk. *<Joe wishes you well, by the way, he said you better come back or Tanis will have his head.>*

<I'll make it back, so long as you guys don't get blowed up and there's somewhere to come back to.>

They talked idly for several more minutes before Jessica realized that none of the other pilots were allowed to talk to the rest of the crew about their mission. She felt a bit guilty and bid Trist a final farewell before turning her attention back to the tactical net.

The squadron leaders were reviewing tactics with Pearson and adjusting wing assignments. Jessica saw that she had been placed on Carson's wing. For a moment she bristled at being given the rookie position, but then relaxed.

Carson likely had the most experience pairing with new wingmen. Plus, it wouldn't hurt to have the most experienced pilot nearby at all times.

<Drop in t-minus 60 seconds, cut the chatter and ready on the ladder,> Pearson said.

The commander would fly out with the X wing, protecting the *Andromeda*. From here on out A and C wings were on their own.

She felt the ship move, the motion not sensed her body inside the cocoon, but with her new skin and limbs; the ship itself. She *was* the ship, she was speed, power, and death.

Outside she could see the other fighters line up for their ladders. Jessica was third on hers and when the count hit zero she only had to wait ten seconds for her ship to drop down the ladder and out into space.

Outside the *Andromeda,* her full sensor array came online and she felt the emptiness around her. It's cold was acute and took a moment for her to adjust. Then she felt and saw her squadron around her and the feeling diminished.

<*Steady your* v *and establish tight-beam. Keep the chatter to a minimum. We're just drifting space junk out here. Nothing to see,*> Rock said to the squadron.

Jessica brought up several entertainment vids she had stored away for later and read part of a book she was working through before falling asleep.

The ship's NSAI woke her several hours later and Jessica saw that the time-to-burn was still over ten hours. No updates showed from Rock, Cordy, or the *Andromeda,* so she whiled away the hours running combat simulations and playing twitch reflex games.

When the time for burn came, it was anticlimactic to say the least. Tight beam communication from Cordy ensured the ships were synchronized and stayed in formation and on the correct vector as they accelerated toward the three Sirian ships.

Her mental HUD showed A and C squadrons, the projected location of the *Andromeda,* and the Sirian ships. She examined it closely, checking the projections, though she knew smarter minds than hers—like Cordy's—had provided the data.

Joe was right, it was different in the deep black. Out here there was nothing. Every ship was running dark, if it wasn't for Cordy maintaining tight beam between the two wings, she wouldn't even know C-wing was nearby.

Their meager sensors couldn't see the Sirian ships, or the *Andromeda*. When the time came to engage the enemy vessels they would have to take it on faith that everyone was where they were supposed to be.

If the *Andromeda* wasn't there, the fifteen fighters stood a poor chance of taking out three enemy ships.

Joe better be there, Jessica asserted to herself more than once.

<*Relax,*> Cordy spoke softly into Jessica's mind. <*They'll be there. We're going to pull this off.*>

<*Do you have data I don't?*> Jessica asked testily.

<*No…but I know Joe and Corsia. Neither of them would abandon us—not under any circumstances.*>

Jessica knew that to be true. Joe would sacrifice an attack on the Sirians if the alternative was the total loss of his fighters. It was one of the things that made him a good CO. He valued the lives of those under him far more than most.

Some would argue that it was a weakness, but the fierce loyalty it garnered him paid its own dividends.

<*You're right, sorry for snapping at you,*> Jessica said softly to Cordy. <*Just pre-combat nerves.*>

<*Don't worry, even Carson snapped at me,*> Cordy smiled into Jessica's mind.

<*Don't you get scared?*> Jessica asked. She knew AI didn't really get scared, but they so often presented such a human face that she wondered about their legendary stoicism at times.

<*You know we don't—at least not the way you do. Fear for you is a chemical change in your body based on your brain running its crude analysis and believing there is life-threatening danger. You can rationalize by actually examining past experiences, considering statistics, etc…but the primitive parts of your mind still fear.*>

Jessica nodded. She knew all of this, it was psych 101.

<*We have no primitive parts of our mind—well, we do, but our primitive minds are like the advanced logic-centers of your mind. Our neural nets still make intuitive leaps, though not as well as yours—mainly due to the chaos of your chemical makeup…anyway, less irrationality, more logic, less fear. You get the picture.*>

<*I do,*> Jessica replied. <*I still think you must fear sometimes.*>

<*Well, all too often we run the numbers and things look bad. You flesh and blood types do your crude math and assessments, yet bravely head face danger anyway. If anything, we fear your bravery—yet as a species it works in your favor more often than not. It's a constant struggle for us to let pure math and logic be swayed by your optimism. That's probably harder for us to understand than fear.*>

Jessica let that sink in. She would never have considered optimism to be one of the most unfathomable aspects of humanity, but maybe it was.

The squadron's pion drives ran at low thrust for sixteen hours before shutting down, the fighters once again drifting through the black—this time at just over 0.3*c*.

Time to contact with their enemy was on the HUD at just over two hours. Cordy reported picking up sensor ghosts that were probably the Sirian ships—exactly where they were expected to be. The news was reassuring—it meant the plan was on track, but knowing that the enemy awaited now shifted her anxiety in a new direction.

Over the next hour, Jessica was able to discern the three scout ships with her own ship's sensors. She studied Cordy's assessments of the ship's tonnage and weaponry. Rock sent updated tactical plans to the squadron and Jessica reviewed them with Carson.

The Sirian ships were in a V formation and A wing was assigned the lead ship. The squadron would split their attack between what Cordy had identified as the forward weapons pods and the engines.

The goal was to go in for the kill on the first ship. If the *Andromeda* was in position, hopefully it would be able to take out the engines of one or both of the trailing ships.

<*Watch for point defense lasers here and here,*> Carson said to Jessica over the tight beam. <*Keep them off me and I'll get that main battery offline in one run.*>

Jessica knew the battle may not last more than one run, the relative *v* between the fighters and the Sirians was nearly relativistic. It benefited the fighters greatly as time dilation would make them almost invisible until they struck.

The countdown went from hours to minutes, then to seconds.

Cordy sent the signal and the fighters swung their engine's around the central hull, directing the ionized particle discharges from their drives at the Sirian ships. Within the engine's cores, matter met antimatter and the resultant pions lanced out at the speed of light, slashing through the lead enemy vessel's shields with almost no resistance.

At least that was the hope.

They wouldn't know for fifteen more minutes if the beams struck, let alone penetrated shields. Tanis started her jinking maneuvers, shifting her ship around in a seemingly random pattern, yet one that was well coordinated with the rest of the squadron.

It wouldn't do to remain on a consistent vector with one's engine pointed at the enemy.

<I have RM signatures!> Cordy called over the combat net a mere second before the fighters flashed by a series of nuclear blooms in the darkness.

She flinched in her soft cocoon as the light and heat washed across the skin of the ship, blinding her sensors for a moment.

The it was gone; the fighters were a million miles past the expanding clouds of dust and radiation.

<Jason was disabled,> Cordy reported to the squadron. *<I have his beacon and he is responding, but he's lost control of his main engine and is vectoring toward the Kap.>*

Jessica hoped he could slow his fighter and get into an elliptical around the Kap. At a fifth the speed of light he could fly clear across the system before a rescue could be mounted.

No more relativistic missiles appeared on sensors, though the closer the fighters got the less time they'd have to spot them. They widened their jinking pattern and when the hundred thousand kilometer mark was crossed, flipped their engines around and picked their targets.

Jessica saw the point defense lasers Carson had told her to look for and fired her shotgun at them. The weapon deployed a hundred sabot rounds, which raced toward the Sirian scout ship before exploding into chaff.

Moving ten thousand kilometers per second, the point defense lasers could only pick off so many of the small jagged pieces of carbon before they pelted the ship's shields.

Energy signatures flared as the shields strengthened to deflect the chaff, but she saw some get through and several of the point defense lasers were disabled.

Carson opened up with his fighter's main beams, using the over extension of the enemy's shields Jessica created to his advantage. He punched through one location and melted away half the ablative plating on the main battery. He followed up with his shotgun less than a second later and tore half the battery clear off the scout ship.

Jessica lanced at the gash in the hull with her beams and then a second later they were out of range.

The combat net showed that all the fighters had landed their strikes, but the lead ship was not yet disabled. It still had several functional batteries and the engines remained operational.

The pilots broke formation, arcing toward the Kap and reversing direction as quickly as they could. The burn on each of the fighters was right at the 70*g* limit the ships and pilots could handle.

The pressure on her body was overwhelming, and Jessica struggled to draw breath even though liquid oxygen was being forced into her lungs. The cocoon encasing her stiffened and the latticework of nano filaments which had grown all through her body tensed, holding organs and soft tissue in place.

She tried not to pay attention to the display which showed her cellular wall integrity, or the micro fractures growing through her bones, and instead kept an eye on the damage estimates rolling in.

Jessica looked over the tactical net and saw that the *Andromeda* was five minutes from coming into range behind the Sirians. Not perfect timing, but pretty good considering the distances and speeds involved.

By that time the fighters would be completing their arch and coming in for a second run.

Time dilation and sensor lag meant that even though the fighters and *Andromeda* would be hitting their targets at the same time, neither would see the other's attacks until they were well underway.

Carson directed Jessica to hit more of the point defense lasers while he concentrated his fire on the remainder of the battery.

<*They have fighters!*> Rock, who was on the leading edge, called out.

The combat net updated and Jessica saw that each scout ship had disgorged four fighters. They had stayed close to their ship's hulls, but now spread out, bringing beams and shotguns to bear on A and C wings.

Orders updated—A wing was to stay on target while C wing provided cover. Jessica synchronized a new jinking pattern with Carson and her beams swept across the scout ship, weakening shields and blasting those locations with her shotgun.

The combat net showed that the lead ship's defenses were down to a point where missiles stood a chance of reaching their targets and, as she made a close pass, Jessica let two fusion warheads fly.

The first was destroyed by a beam from an enemy fighter, but the second made it close. Just before it was destroyed by enemy beams, Jessica detonated it.

Nuclear fire washed across the Sirian scout ship and sensors showed its shields flicker and die. A moment later Rock, on the far side of the ship, let fly with another warhead. His penetrated the hull and released an EMP burst which disabled the Sirian vessel.

With the wing's primary target disabled, the combat net updated and showed A wing's new objective to be the second scout ship. C wing was engaging the remaining nine enemy fighters and Jessica could just see the *Andromeda* with her optics, trading beam fire and shotgun blasts with the third Sirian vessel.

Joe maintained alignment with the two remaining scout ships so only one could use its beams on the *Andromeda*—a feat which took no small amount of skill. The cruiser was maneuvering with every available thruster and the energy output made it glow like a second star on Jessica's sensors.

<*Let's give that other ship something to think about,*> Rock said to his squadron.

The fighters boosted at max *g* toward their next target; as they crossed within fifty thousand kilometers they rotated their pion engines and all beam weapons toward the ship.

Lashing out at their selected targets, the scout ship's shields flared, desperately bleeding off heat from beams while strengthening to ward off the shotgun blasts.

The squadron blew past the ship and banked around again to make another run—this time at a much more comfortable 50*gs.*

Jessica stayed close to Carson, clearing defense beams and adding punch to his attacks where she could. The second ship's shields were weakening and its defenses were also crossing the critical barrier where warheads could make it through.

The fighters arched around for another run, six black specs of power and destruction bent on tearing their foe apart.

At least that's how Jessica felt when suddenly her HUD went red and alarms showed on a dozen critical systems.

<*Shit!*> She said over the combat net. <*A chaff blast hit me, I lost main engine and my shotgun.*>

<*Steer clear,*> Rock advised. <*This guy's just about done and the* Andromeda *just took out the third ship,*>

<*Affir—.*> Jessica began to respond when her external sensors flooded with radiation and then she knew no more.

ONLY THE DEAD KNOW THE END OF WAR

STELLAR DATE: 3283400 / 07.18.4277 (Adjusted Gregorian)
LOCATION: ***Arc-5 Fighter***
REGION: Interstellar Space, Outside Kapteyn's Heliopause

Jessica awoke alone.

The realization that she had passed from dreams into full consciousness dawned slowly. Everything was dark and she couldn't open her eyes. Her limbs were constricted and seemed trapped in something almost like a gel…

The shoot suit, I'm in my fighter.

For a moment she felt better, it explained her eyes, the pressure, the cocoon.

But not the blindness.

She should be able to see with the ship, but when she attempted to Link with it, nothing happened. Neither Cordy, nor the dumb NSAI on the fighter responded.

She drew a deep breath, feeling the liquid oxygen course into her lungs. At least life support appeared to be working, that much was reassuring.

Jessica brought her personal HUD up in her mind and reviewed her vitals. What she saw would have made her gasp, were she able to.

Her bones were riddled with fractures, blood vessels were crushed and leaking, several of her fingers were broken and she had suffered third degree burns over most of her body.

While she was out, her internal med systems must have shunted as many of her pain receptors as possible, because she should have been in unimaginable agony.

She checked the time and saw that it had been thirty hours since the battle.

Her mind reeled at the thought.

Thirty hours. Jessica dismissed the thought that she was the lone survivor. The *Andromeda* and its fighters had been winning the engagement handily when whatever happened disabled her ship.

And gave me a very unhealthy dose of hard radiation, Jessica thought as she looked at her bio report.

She reviewed the logs and came to the conclusion that the second scout ship must have detonated its main reactor. It was the only thing that could have produced the type of radiation she saw in her body.

Her fighter had been a scant three hundred kilometers from the scout ship, she was lucky to be alive—lucky that her fighter's antimatter containment vessel had remained intact.

Her mind wandered as she imagined her ship drifting in the darkness, a black speck in a black void, likely surrounded by the much hotter wreckage of the scout ship.

Jessica ran the odds of rescue. They came up high—within the first ten hours after the battle.

As the clock slid past forty hours she fought to keep panic at bay.

She had been in the shoot suit, cocooned in her fighter for over three days. She wasn't given to claustrophobia—no one rated for piloting a fighter could be—but she was starting to feel the need to get out of the ship claw at the edges of her mind.

To get out no matter what, just to see where she was.

What, to stand on my ship and wave my arms?

She forced back the madness plucking at the edges of her thoughts.

She still had not managed to make any data connections to the ship, but she could tell that the life support system was failing. The oxygen content in the liquid flowing through her lungs was decreasing.

Jessica estimated she had only a few hours left before…

A dull thud reverberated through the ship.

It wasn't the first time something had impacted the fighter, which was what led her to believe she was drifting in the scout ship's debris field.

But the thud came again and then turned into a low vibration. No, this was no chance collision, Jessica knew this was a rescue.

It seemed like hours—though was only twenty-three minutes—before she felt the ship's hatch open and the cocoon disgorge her.

A suspension field enveloped her and she finally Linked.

It was *Andromeda* and the rich timber of Corsia's voice filled her mind.

<Welcome back, Colonel.>

The shoot suit's external optics came back online and Jessica saw Joe and Trist, along with many of the fighter pilots. They were cheering.

It was good to be home.

A LONG DAY'S END

STELLAR DATE: 3285312 / 10.12.4282 (Adjusted Gregorian)
LOCATION: ***High Victoria***
REGION: Victorian Space Federation, Kapteyn's Star System

Tanis stopped before one of the station's wide observation windows and Markus's chair glided to a stop beside her. They had nearly completed their round of the station; a tour they had been taking every month for several years now—ever since Markus had retired from active governance of the Victorian colony to convalesce on the station.

"I can see it how it will be," Markus said as he gazed over the world below him. "Oceans, forests, people everywhere. It'll be a paradise."

"It's going to be amazing," Tanis said with a nod. "Even our engineers didn't think they could do so much with a world like this. Your people's drive deserves the credit. You never would take no for an answer."

Markus chuckled, the rasp wheezing at the end and he stifled a cough before responding.

"You know me, ever the optimist."

"I wish you'd let our medics help you," Tanis said. "We could give you decades more."

Markus waved his hand dismissively. "You know my answer; why do you always ask? You've given me far more life than I ever expected. The old dog messed up my DNA too much to give me more time than this—not without me becoming someone else—or a machine."

The plight he faced was one many of the elder Victorians were grappling with. So much of their base DNA was corrupted by generations of long-term exposure to the extreme radiation around Sirius that the older they got, the more prone they were to cancerous growths.

Medics aboard the *Intrepid* could repair their DNA, but they would need to replace much of it. A recipient of such treatment would have their body's base code altered. Many, like Markus, found that to be undesirable.

"Do I seem so much worse for it?" Tanis asked.

Markus looked up at her, his wrinkled smile causing her to respond in kind.

"You're the best damn-looking half-robot woman I've ever set eyes on. Heck, if I'm to believe you, there are actually two women living in that head of yours," Markus said with a wink.

He never doubted AI's existence, but he liked to pretend he did; that Angela was just Tanis's snarky alternate personality.

<*If only he knew how close that was to the truth,*> Angela commented on Tanis's stream of consciousness.

<*You don't help. You know you're not supposed to be able to do that.*>

Angela laughed. <*Everyone knows something is up with us. We've outlasted the longest pairings on the books by decades. Everyone is just too polite to ask if we're an abomination. Even Markus must know it's not natural.*>

"You're talking to her, aren't you," Markus asked.

"How could you tell?" Tanis asked. "I'm pretty sure I don't give it away."

"You don't, I just guessed. You as an individual may be inscrutable, but human nature isn't so hard to figure out."

"I suppose that's true," Tanis replied.

"I don't think you should worry about it. You're probably the most stable person I know. If your brain were going to turn to mush it probably would have done it years ago." Markus gave her a gentle pat on the arm.

"OK, now I wonder if Angela was relaying our conversation to you."

Markus gave a short laugh.

"Nothing so sinister. Being this close to death gives you a different sort of perspective. I know being in charge of the fate of so many makes you constantly evaluate your abilities and doubt your own qualifications—or it'd better," he said with an evaluating eye cast her way.

Tanis raised her hands in mock protest. "No lack or self-doubt here. I know I look implacable to everyone, but I'm not. I thought I had royally screwed it several times over the years."

"Yet you always pull a trick out of your hat," Markus said. "You've done it in battle a hundred times and when you turned your hand to politics and diplomacy you navigated those waters just as well."

"I think my skill at politics is an extension of my abilities in battle. Everyone thinks I'm a crazy bloodhound and no one wants to see if I'll snap and kick the tar out of them to get my way."

Markus chuckled. "I'll admit the thought crossed my mind once, but I never gave it any serious consideration."

Tanis smiled. "Glad to hear it."

The pair watched in silence as a shuttle passed the observation deck, bringing a load of passengers in from the *Hyperion* to the station. Tanis brought up the manifest and final destinations of the shuttle and passengers. Most were going downworld to Victoria on vacation, while a few were transferring out to the colony on Tara.

"Your people are really multiplying—is that the right word? It's just impressive to see them really take hold of this system."

"It's what makes this worth it," Markus said. "To think, we who were once destined to spend our lives in small quarters on a single platform, now have a whole star system to ourselves. No small thanks to you."

Tanis waved her hand. "I helped you because you were here and needed it. You're the ones that got here on your own steam. That took guts."

Markus nodded contemplatively, but didn't speak.

"You think of the other Nimbus you left behind, don't you?" Tanis asked.

He took a long moment to respond. "I do. I wish I could have figured out a way to save everyone, but that would likely ended with the death of everyone on the *Hyperion*. My duty was to them first. Hard as that is."

"I have some understanding of that," Tanis said with a nod. "Every commander does—or should. At some point it comes down to them or you."

"That's a dangerous sentiment," Markus said. "That would lead me to wonder if you'd someday make the same call with me and my people."

"I would," Tanis said without hesitation. "I know it sounds horrible—I would not do it easily, but if it came to us or you, you know what I'd choose. I know you would too."

"I would." Markus shook his head as he spoke. "Life has made us hard—maybe too hard."

"Let's talk about something else, something happy," Tanis said, not wanting to remember those words as some of her last to Markus.

"I won't ask you what you think about Tom getting elected for his second term as President down on Victoria, then," Markus said. "You probably don't have happy feelings about that."

Tanis laughed, "Not especially. I did hear that Agnes and Dmitry are great grandparents now. Agnes seemed especially happy since she was just able to have the one son."

"She was already planning the child's first birthday when I saw her last," Markus said with a chuckle. "With three of her other grandchildren pregnant she'll soon be the matriarch of her own clan. A long journey for the woman who manned the desk outside my office where so much of our little rebellion was planned."

"Hah! Little rebellion." Tanis couldn't help but notice that no matter where she steered conversation today Markus waxed nostalgic. Maybe that was what happened when you calmly stared your end in the face.

A comfortable silence stretched between them for several minutes before Tanis spoke up.

"I'm starved, and now that they have those pig farms on Victoria one of the commissary's up here is serving BLTs. You in?"

"Absolutely. Let's see if my people can make bacon to satisfy your refined palette."

TRUE COLORS

STELLAR DATE: 3286965 / 04.22.4287 (Adjusted Gregorian)
LOCATION: Sperios Outpost, Victoria
REGION: Victorian Space Federation, Kapteyn's Star System

Tom glanced at his companion across the table in the dimly lit bar. He didn't trust her, but he knew she hated the Edeners as much as he did, even if she was one—in a manner of speaking.

"How much longer is your contact going to take?" he asked. "It's not like this is the sort of place I'm known to frequent."

"Relax," his companion said. "No one here is the sort to spread stories. All they care about is working hard, getting their pay, and drinking it down."

Tom glanced at the bar's other patrons. She was right, no one seemed to be paying them any special attention. His companion blended in like she had been at the bar every day since it first opened. She did that everywhere, no matter when or where they met, she looked like she belonged. She could be anyone she wanted and never raised so much as an eyebrow.

He knew his attempt to blend in was less successful, but dressing down was not one of his specialties. Still, being in her company caused her mysterious powers of obscurity to shroud him as well.

"There he is," she said softly and gave a small hand signal to call their contact over.

The man slid into the seat beside Tom. He was non-descript, shorter than the Victorians, but not so short that people would know who he really was.

"How was your trip?" Tom's companion asked.

"As well as could be expected. I was undetected if that's what you're asking."

"I should hope so," she replied. "I own everyone on that route—though they don't know who it is that holds their leash. They think they're helping the almighty Tanis Richards and are so eager to do so."

"She's quite the powerful figure in this system, alright," the newcomer said. "Enough that I wonder about this plan of yours. Do they really have what you say they do? We lost three ships working out how to get past that damn sensor net."

Tom wondered, not for the first time, at the value of the research the Edeners were undertaking. The Sirians were allotting a considerable amount of time and effort in getting it. His companion had only told him that it was the most advanced tech in the galaxy and that she would share it with him and the Victorians if he helped her.

Only later did he discover she was also working with the Sirians. His companion had assured him that they were just a means to an end. Once she had secured the technology she would not share it with the Sirians.

She better not. If his mother knew he was sitting across the table from a Sirian spy she would kill him—and not figuratively.

"They do," his companion replied to the Sirian. "I've seen it with my own eyes, though right now it's too hard to get at. That's where you come in."

"Yes, more of our resources, put at the disposal of these traitors," he said with narrowed eyes cast in Tom's direction.

"Listen he—," Tom began, but was silenced by his companion's raised hand and stern look which she then turned to the Sirian.

"Watch yourself, friend. One word from me and you die here and now. You are here as a partner, act like one, or you'll be replaced. Don't think your government values you more than what I can give them."

The man opened his mouth to speak, but then closed it and nodded slowly.

Tom gave the man a smug look and turned to his companion.

"What is our next move, then?"

She smiled, her face pleasant, but her eyes cold.

"Why, we wait for the old man to die."

MOURNING VICTORIA

STELLAR DATE: 3288931 / 09.08.4292 (Adjusted Gregorian)
LOCATION: *ISS Intrepid*
REGION: Victorian Space Federation, Kapteyn's Star System

<Kim, I don't really care what he ***feels*** *is best,>* Tanis said. *<Katrina has made her wishes pretty clear and I intend to honor them.>*

<Fine, but Tom won't be happy about this. He wanted to add other people to the guest list,> Kim replied. *<He also doesn't see why so many people from the* Intrepid *should be in attendance.>*

Tanis bit back a terse reply. The latest generation of Victorians possessed a sense of entitlement and disdain toward the Edeners that made their parents appear positively grateful. It was far more prevalent on Victoria than on the stations and Tara, though it was still present everywhere.

The original crew of the *Hyperion,* those who had worked and lived under the Sirian oppression were nearly gone. She would be damned if she was going to let this flunky stop her from saying her final farewells to one of them.

<They should be in attendance because they were his friends and his wife wants them there. Quite honestly it's none of Tom's damn business who is in attendance. It's not ***his*** *funeral.>*

<Attendance to this funeral for Victorians is just another thing you've taken from us,> Kim said acidly and killed the connection.

Tanis found it ironic that the conversation was conducted via technology the *Intrepid* had provided. The Victoria colony would not exist at all without the colony ship's assistance—though to hear Kim's generation speak you'd think it existed in spite of the Edeners.

"That sure is a sour look," Joe said as he entered the kitchen where Tanis was preparing breakfast.

"It was Kim," Tanis replied.

"Ah, the ever-antagonistic Kim," Joe gave Tanis a long embrace. "Just a few more years and we'll be on our way. They can lust after our advanced technology in our absence."

Tanis relaxed into Joe, glad for his calm and unflappable attitude.

"I'm really starting to wonder if things might get ugly before we leave the system," Tanis said. "The original crew of the *Hyperion* did not pass their stoic attitudes on to their descendants. Without Markus to be the voice of reason…"

She found herself thinking back to her final conversation with Markus.

"I've seen enough life," Markus had said. "I did more than any of my ancestors did, or dreamed of doing. We have a new world here, and we're prospering. I was an old man when I met you and your doctors gave me another half century of life—the best I've ever had, but it's time to pass the reins on to the next generation."

"You're going to be missed," Tanis remembered a tear slipping down her face as she held a wizened Markus's hand. "I don't know how we'll manage without you keeping things steady."

Markus had given a rough laugh when she said that.

"I don't think there is anything you can't manage, General Richards. I've seen you tackle some pretty impossible odds over the years. People believe in amazing things, just because you do."

"I could say the same thing about you," Tanis replied.

"I'm going to rest a bit," Markus patted her hand gently. "Can you have them find Katrina? I need to see her…"

Tanis felt a tear coming to her eye again as she thought back to that conversation. Markus was one of the strongest people she had ever known. She was going to miss him for a long time.

Markus died several hours after that conversation.

"Maybe planetside they might get unruly, but up here they have more in common with us," Joe said, taking her hands in his. "We've built a good thing here. We saved a people and gave them a future they could never have dreamed of. It was never going to be perfect—not unless we decided to stay and fully integrate."

"I know," Tanis sighed. "The very fact that we're leaving—even if we gave them every advanced piece of tech and knowledge we possess—would still be cause enough for unrest. The signs are there, people are jealous of us, even after we pushed their standard of living ahead by centuries. Their government isn't doing much to smooth things over."

Joe nodded. "I know. Every year at the academy I have to do more and more to turn cadets into team members. It's like they've been brainwashed."

Tanis shook her head and sighed. "I've seen it often enough; we're skirting the edge of a conflict."

"Surely Tom knows it's not in his best interests to do that."

Tom was in his third term as president of the Victoria colony. The son of Sarah and Peter, Tanis still remembered when she first saw him as a newborn baby during the celebration for the station and beanstalk.

He wasn't nearly as agreeable now as he had been then. Tanis could see a lot of his mother's influence in him.

Sarah had never been particularly agreeable, but when an act of sabotage had taken Peter's life she became downright hostile. She blamed the death of her husband on Tanis and the *Intrepid*.

Tanis had to admit that to a certain extent Sarah was right. The threads of Myrrdan's influence were visible in a number of events over the years. She knew that his goal was to drive a wedge between the two peoples, keep her off-balance as he searched for the location of the picotech.

Sarah knew of Myrrdan and blamed Tanis for never catching him and for bringing his blight to her people. Tanis thought that by and large the tradeoff worked in the Victorian's favor.

"What Tom knows to be in his best interests and what he actually does often seem at odds. Even if he doesn't start anything, I wouldn't put it past elements of his government. Either way I've been planning for something like this for decades."

"I know," Joe laughed. "I remember reviewing your initial contingencies thirty years ago."

"Thirt—really?" Tanis consulted her temporal calendar.

<*That thing isn't healthy,*> Angela interjected. <*There's no good reason to track your age this much.*>

<*I've been in and out of stasis so much it makes me feel disconnected with reality—let's not rehash this now.*>

"You're two-hundred," Joe said before Tanis finished her conversation with Angela.

"I am?" Tanis was shocked. She knew that her bicentennial was coming up, but thought it was still a few years off. "How do you know?"

Joe laughed and embraced his wife. "Because I keep a calendar too."

"They aren't lying when they say life accelerates as you get older," Tanis sighed.

<*The pinnace is leaving in twenty minutes,*> Amanda interrupted the pair.

<*Ok, we're on our way,*> Tanis replied.

Tanis and Joe wolfed down the remainder of their breakfast, checked their dress uniforms over one last time, and exited the cabin. Outside a groundcar waited and drove them to the nearest maglev station.

They entered the forward hanger with a few minutes to spare and walked up the pinnace's ramp in companionable silence.

Commandant Brandt was speaking with two Marines at the top of the ramp. The diminutive woman stood at attention and snapped a sharp salute—mirrored by the two Marines—as Tanis approached.

"General," she nodded a greeting.

Joe and Tanis returned the salutes.

"Commandant, men," Tanis said. "Thank you for coming today."

"It's our honor," PFC Ramos said and PFC Sarin nodded his agreement.

Ramos and Sarin were members of the first platoon Tanis had put together as the *Intrepid* left Sol. Both had seen action with Brandt and Ouri when they fought the rogue AI on the *Intrepid* and were in the party that boarded Yusuf's cruiser in the battle of Victoria.

They had put their lives at risk for the mission many times, they deserved their place here.

"As you were," she said and continued into the pinnace.

The two squad military honor guard was another thing Tom had fought Tanis on, but Katrina had come to Tanis's defense.

"Intrepid Marines fought to save us from Yusuf. They should have representation here," Tanis recalled her saying.

Katrina had turned into quite the diplomat over the years, though, as a former spy, it was closer to her training than it was for Tanis.

Earnest was away at the Gamma site, but Abby was present, already seated in the well-appointed passenger cabin.

Tanis gave the chief engineer a silent nod.

They got along well enough now, but their relationship had never recovered from that day beneath the annihilator. Tanis held her no ill will, but for Abby a seventy-year grudge was just the warm-up.

Terrance and Andrews were seated at the cabin's central table and Tanis joined them. Joe moved off to poke his head into the cockpit—the pilots being graduates of his academy.

"Tanis," Terrance said by way of greeting.

"Lieutenant Governor," Andrews spoke with a gentle smile. "How are you?"

"As well as can be expected, I suppose," Tanis said. "Though I wish you wouldn't call me that."

"You prefer General?" Terrance asked.

"I'm pretty sure she was happiest with Colonel," Joe said as he joined them at the table. "But she needs to outrank me, so General will have to do."

Tanis sighed. "Thanks hon, that's just the reputation I need."

"Governor suits you," Terrance said. "You've done remarkably well—it's hard to imagine you're the same woman who shot up the *Steel Dawn* on her first day. Everyone said you'd be trouble, but look at you now."

"You two made me wear this mantle," Tanis wagged a finger at Terrance and Andrews as she spoke. "You made me wear it and then went to sleep for decades. I never signed on to be a politician…I never…" She stopped and gazed down at her hands for a moment.

"He was a great advisor to me…he was almost—he had a strength of character I've rarely seen. I'm sorry I'm testy, I'm just going to miss him."

"I never spent as much time with him as you did, but he made a lasting impression. Just the thought of flying that mining platform between the stars. That took some serious guts," Andrews said appreciatively.

"I'm sorry, Tanis," Terrance said. "I didn't mean to upset—I meant it as a compliment. I rather thought you liked being in charge."

Tanis opened her mouth to speak and Joe put a hand on her arm.

"Choose your next words wisely, they'll likely come back to haunt you."

Luckily Tanis was saved from having to reply by the arrival of Jessica and Trist. The pair were out of breath and smiling far too much for the occasion.

"Sorry," Trist said. "Took a wrong turn on the way here."

Tanis rolled her eyes as they sat. "Somehow I find it hard to believe that you don't know your way around the ship by now."

"It's each other that they're busy mapping all the time," Joe said quietly and received a jab from Tanis.

"Don't elbow me, I saw that smirk."

"I can't help it," Trist said with a smile. "Her new skin is so smooth and shiny; it probably needs a lot of mapping."

Jessica flushed ever so slightly and Tanis gave her a head shake. Never before had she met such a serious and capable person who was bent on turning herself into sex object.

After the battle with the Sirian scout ships, Jessica had suffered extreme cellular damage from the radiation exposure and her skin had to be completely replaced. While new skin was being grown the doctors gave her a temporary, artificial skin.

Jessica decided she liked the artificial skin and kept it, enhancing its sheen and softness—giving it a slight lavender hue. Combined with her exaggerated figure and purple hair she really did look like a life-sized doll.

With the last passengers aboard, the pilots gained clearance and the pinnace rose above the deck and passed out of the ES shield into space.

Light chatter floated throughout the cabin as the vessel began its descent toward the surface of Victoria. Tanis found herself with nothing to say and turned to stare out a port hole.

The progress of the terraforming effort was truly remarkable. In a scant sixty years a barren rock had turned into living world with oceans, seasons, vast grasslands, and even several fledgling forests.

The industriousness of the Victorians was truly impressive. Matched with the technology and know-how the Edeners brought, it was a true wonder.

A rock passed by her window and Tanis saw on her HUD that it was one of seventy-one asteroids currently in orbit around Victoria.

In various states of disassembly, most would eventually be kicked out to distant orbits or dropped onto the world below to kick up dust and increase heat capture in the atmosphere.

Some consisted entirely of ice and Tanis saw that the R21 refinery had been moved to the latest ice-ball, extracting pure H2O and dropping it to the surface of the world below. The main ocean was nearly filled and the refinery was creating a second, smaller ocean that crossed over the western side of the dusk band.

The large ocean was named Nautilus and the smaller had recently been christened the Atlantic. The Nautilus had warmed significantly over the decades of exposure to the Kap's ruddy light; the thin wisps of vapor Tanis had witnessed decades ago as she rode the *Excelsior* to Landfall were now thick clouds, their white bands wrapped around the equator of the planet—driven by winds which often reached several hundred kilometers per hour.

As the pinnace circled around the world, a massive hurricane building in the north of the Nautilus Ocean came into view. It was easily the size of all the continents of Earth combined. Such massive storms would be the norm for many years as the world's temperature equalized.

The new band of weather control satellites would cut down on their frequency, but even so, weather was always going to be exciting on Victoria.

Tanis found herself filling with pride at what they had built here. It was no mean feat to terraform a world like this and they would be able to leave it for generations of Victorians who would otherwise have never known the feel of a planet beneath them.

The pinnace raced above the clouds and Tanis tried to peer through them. When she finally was able to see through, massive breakers were visible, some hundreds of meters high—the result of the water pouring down from the refinery above.

A dull thud echoed through the cabin as the vessel dropped into atmosphere thick enough to create a sonic boom. The pilots began aero braking the pinnace for its approach into the Landfall spaceport.

She heard the pilots communicating with the ATC from the cockpit, the call-counter-call heralded the approach of the ocean's eastern shores. It was a thing of beauty and wonder to see the massive waves pounding the earth, throwing spray a thousand meters into the air.

The pinnace passed over the spectacle in mere moments, a ruined landscape slowly giving way to the low scrub of the eastern desert.

Eventually the desert gave way to grasslands and then to bushland. To the north, the dark line of a forest appeared and then faded away in the distance.

It was a strange thing to see the brown plants growing and flourishing in the red sunlight. Tanis had to admit she was glad New Eden orbited a yellow primary. Something about plants that weren't green was unnerving.

The craggy mountain range north of Landfall eased into view and Tanis pulled up a forward view over the Link, looking ahead for the domes of Landfall.

The small outpost had grown considerably over the intervening decades, its population surpassing two million inhabitants.

Tanis remembered the naïve estimations that had projected a Victorian population of a quarter million. The Victorian people bred with a passion—finally free from generations of strict population control.

The total system population was now at nearly five million. Three of which resided on Victoria, a million on the Tara colony, and another million on stations and orbital habitats.

It was quickly becoming a well-populated system.

While much of Landfall was still underground, it now sported several massive ES domes—something made possible once the planet sported a half-atmosphere near the equator.

The main dome covered the new government buildings, a university, thousands of homes, businesses, and no small number of parks.

One of the dome's properties was to enhance and alter the sunlight so that it took on a golden hue and plants utilizing green photosynthesis could thrive.

Refineries and manufacturing plants crouched beyond the domes, adding greenhouse gasses to the atmosphere and producing materials to expand the city.

Beyond that, east and into the deep dusk, lay the space and air ports.

The pinnace bucked as it dropped lower and passed into a crosswind. Anywhere else the winds buffeting the pinnace would be considered a navigation-blocking storm, but the pilots who dropped down into Victorian atmosphere referred to this as nothing more than a breezy day.

The final approach was swift and the pilot settled the pinnace gently on a landing pad, while three groundcars drove up. The passengers exited the ship and spaceport ground personnel guided the passengers to their transportation. In minutes the procession was wending its way toward the city.

The funeral was to be held at a place Markus frequented in life, the city's first above-ground park. It would take thirty minutes to arrive and Tanis settled back in her seat, her hand clasped with Joe's.

The streets near the spaceport were silent and empty; but as the procession passed through the dome and neared the park, silent mourners dotted the corners and sidewalks, clustered together in small groups. The park was only large enough for a few hundred people, and Tanis knew that other gatherings were taking place throughout Landfall.

Tanis felt their sorrow more keenly than she expected. She had lost many comrades; seen many heads of state, or great heroes of humankind pass away; but for some reason seeing the sheer number of people who felt as she did about a quiet man who did the right thing hit her the hardest.

The park's soaring trees came into view—their tops swaying gently in the small amount of wind which passed through the ES dome. The cars stopped and the party disembarked.

The walk through the park was serene and calming. Tanis clasped Joe's hand and few words were spoken by the *Intrepid's* delegation.

They approached the glade where the funeral was being held and ushers led them to seats right behind Markus's immediate family.

Katrina was already there and turned to clasp hands with each person as they filed in. The casket bearing Markus's body was at the front and Tanis walked to it, gazing down at the old man she had come to know so well.

Even though Markus had not reached his one hundred and fortieth birthday she couldn't deny what her eyes saw: the casket held the body of an old man who had lived decades fewer than her. The tragedy of it was nearly unbearable. He was so selfless, had only ever sacrificed for his people and never done evil. He was too young to die.

"Thank you for coming," Katrina's voice was soft beside Tanis. "I know Tom tried to control the attendees."

"There is no way I would have been absent," Tanis turned and embraced Katrina.

"You have no idea how much you meant to him," Katrina said. "You were the first non-Luminescent he ever met who treated him as an equal and with respect from your very first communication. You shaped all of his thoughts and opinions on what the future could hold from that moment on."

Tanis didn't know how to reply, there were no words that would be satisfactory in response. She held the embrace for another moment and finally said, "I'm so sorry to see him go."

"Me too," Katrina's mouth made a smile, but her eyes were filled with sorrow.

They separated and Tanis leant over to place a kiss on Markus's forehead before returning to her seat.

She couldn't help noticing Tom's emotionless gaze and Kim's more hostile look as she got settled. Her thoughts clouded and before she could return her own caustic glare, Angela interjected.

<Don't do it, this isn't about them, don't let it be.>

<Thanks.>

Tanis couldn't help letting a small smile slip onto her lips. Even though she had lost a friend in Markus, she would never lose Angela.

Or Joe, she thought, as she took his hand once more and shared a somber look with him.

The ceremony was touching and Katrina spoke at length about how much Markus had meant to her. Other Victorians spoke, including the president, Tom, before Tanis rose to give her speech.

"I remember clearly that first message from Markus," she began. "He was in the direst of straits, facing the end of all his endeavors when he made that call for help. Even so, there was no wavering in his voice, no distress. He was a leader who led from the front and would make whatever sacrifice he had to for his people.

"It is fitting that he will be laid to rest here, on the world he brought you to, and where he met us. Two peoples, lost between the stars, trying to make a new home and form a new start.

"I think that if there were anything Markus would want us to remember, it is that we are all children of Earth, far from where humans began, but still humans, and still truly one people."

Tanis paused to wipe tears from the corners of her eyes before continuing.

"I learned a lot from him, I—."

Her words were interrupted by Angela's scream in her mind.

<DROP!>

Tanis hit the ground, hearing a ballistic round whistle through the air where her head had been a moment before. Several more shots fired, one hitting her in the leg and ricocheting off the armor she wore beneath her uniform.

She could see the Marines pushing their way through the crowd as people scattered in all directions, many crying out in fear knocking chairs and other attendees to the ground

In front of her she saw Joe and Katrina laying prone with the rest of the *Intrepid's* party crouched low behind a row of bushes.

Joe looked at Tanis and gave a nod. "We're OK, they were all aimed at you."

"Sure, why wouldn't they be?" Tanis sighed.

She couldn't tell for certain amidst the screams, but it seemed like the sniper fire had stopped. Likely the shooter didn't want to hit other targets in the fleeing crowd. Moments later the Marines were around her, scanning the surrounding terrain and buildings for the sniper's position.

<President's clear,> Brandt reported. *<I've called for the groundcars; we're going to meet them at the street to the east.>*

Tanis rose to a crouch and took a pulse rifle from one of the Marines. Based on the shots and the trees, the best angles were from the northwest. The sniper had to be in one of two possible buildings in that direction.

She cycled her vision, looking on the ultraviolet and infrared bands for the shooter's position. Before she spotted him one of the Marines highlighted his position on the combat net.

<Second building on the left, third window from the right.>

Tanis sighted down the pulse rifle and fired a few shots at the window before moving to new cover. The Marines also brought fire to bear and Timmins scored the winning shot—infrared showing the sniper falling to the floor after he fired.

<Not clear yet!> Brandt called over the combat net. *<There are at least two dozen people moving in. They're not Landfall PD or Victorian military.>*

Across the clearing Tanis could make out black forms moving through the underbrush. She cycled her vision and could make out no distinguishing insignia.

The Marines began moving her group to cover and Tanis signaled Joe and Katrina to follow as the black gunmen reached the far end of the clearing and began firing on the Edeners.

<Where is Landfall PD anyway?> Tanis asked. *<I saw them when we arrived.>*

<They all moved to escort the president out,> Angela supplied.

<Some thanks I get after training them,> Jessica said while firing from behind a tree. *<Where are those groundcars at anyway, Brandt?>*

<It would seem they were disabled; we're on our own.>

Tanis's group crouched low behind a fountain, returning fire with their pulse rifles, while the enemy let loose a withering round of projectile fire. Pieces of the stone wall flew around them and Tanis gauged they only had a few minutes before their cover was no more.

The combat net updated and showed three separate enemy groups, each with over a dozen members converging on their position. There was an opening to the south, but it was closing rapidly.

She cast an eye at Markus's casket, standing amidst the ruin of his final ceremony, it was no way to end his time—she couldn't believe that any group of Victorians, no matter how disgruntled with the state of affairs, would do such a thing to their patriarch.

<Let's move!> Tanis called out, directing the Marines to provide covering fire for the retreat, adding her own shots to the volley. The attackers were sloppy, but their numbers were effective. Tanis could see that they were all younger Victorians, the oldest no more than forty years of age.

Tanis looked over at Katrina and saw anger writ large on her features.

"I can't believe they actually decided to take violent action," Katrina shook her head, her words echoing Tanis's thoughts. "And at Markus's funeral too!"

<I have a fireteam securing the far side of the street,> Brandt provided a verbal update over the combat net.

"I knew things were heating up, but I had no idea we were at this stage. Normally there are a number of peaceful escalations before we get to the attacking foreign heads of state phase," Tanis said to Katrina while taking aim at a young woman moving between cover. She made the shot and saw the woman stumble and fall.

Katrina saw it too and her face twisted with sorrow, "I can't believe these children are going to die for their folly."

"Katrina, we're not barbarians, this is suppressive police action; we're only taking non-lethal shots."

"Oh thank god," Katrina sighed. "Sorry, I should know that, I just…"

Tanis laid a hand on her arm. "I know."

<We've secured the far side of the street and the entrance to the building. We have your approach covered.>

The combat net laid out the fields of fire and the safe vectors for the remaining members of the Edener party. Jessica was covering Abby behind a children's play structure; Joe and Andrews were behind a tree to Tanis's right. Trist was behind a bench with Terrance, who turned out to be a good shot with the small pistol he had taken to carrying since the *Intrepid* came under attack so long ago at Mars.

Tanis signaled for Trist and Terrance to retreat first, and the team increased suppressive fire while the pair raced across the grass then the street. Marines held the office building's doors open for them.

Tanis and Katrina were next. They moved single file, with Tanis running backward protecting Katrina behind her. The enemy's rate of fire increased and Tanis wondered which of them the main target was.

Two shots hit her armor and Tanis nearly fell as it solidified across her torso to absorb the impact. Katrina made the crossing unscathed and the Marines took advantage of the attackers over-extending themselves. In moments several more were marked down on the combat net.

Tanis and Katrina burst into the office building and a Marine led Katrina behind a large desk in the reception area. Tanis surveyed the area to see two Marines covering a hall leading into the back of the office. She dispersed nano into the structure to ensure there were no surprises elsewhere as she walked to Brandt.

"Another lovely day in the corps," Brandt said.

"Have you made contact with the *Intrepid*?" Tanis asked the commandant as Joe and Andrews burst through the door, Abby and Jessica following a few seconds later.

"I sent up a general alert before the Link got knocked out. I have Sarin on the roof seeing if he can get a line-of-sight hookup."

Corporal Hill jogged into the foyer and addressed Brandt.

"Building seems clear. Looks like some renovations were underway in here—construction's mostly wrapped up, but it's vacant."

"They're taking positions across the road, but I only see two groups," Sergeant Lee called from his position at one of the windows.

"Likely flanking us," Brandt nodded. "Hill, I assume there are windows in the second story of this place, take one/one up there and keep those SOB's from entering this joint."

Hill nodded and jogged to the staircase, signaling one/one to follow him.

"Trist, Jessica," Brandt called to the pair who were covering one of the front windows. "Find this building's access to the undercity."

"You bet, your pixieness," Trist grinned as Jessica motioned for PFC Ramos to cover their window.

<*My nano-scan is on the combat net,*> Tanis provided the stream location.

It took less than a minute for Trist and Jessica to find the undercity access; during that time the exchange of fire increased drastically. Tanis was covering one of the windows and even Andrews and Terrance were taking shots.

"This is ridiculous," Terrance said as he swapped the charge cylinder in his handgun. "How can the police not be here yet?"

"I think it's pretty safe to assume that the police are in on it, or at least some of them are," Tanis said.

"Do you really think that's possible?" Terrance looked genuinely shocked.

Tanis was sometimes amazed at how someone with such business acumen could be so naïve about what people were capable of—especially after the *Intrepid* had been attacked dozens of times.

"Well, those two guys over there are," Brandt said as she fired several pulse blasts in their direction. "I had beers with one of them about a month ago. No wonder he seemed twitchy."

<*Located and cleared the entrance to the undercity,*> Jessica sent over the combat net. <*There were hostiles coming up, but we took care of them.*>

<*We need to move now, or we'll be completely surrounded,*> Tanis said.

<*Sarin, have you made contact with the* Intrepid*?*> Brandt asked one/two's tech.

<*I had it for a moment, but they've deployed scramblers, and I'm taking fire from adjacent rooftops. I think a burst about our situation got through.*>

<*It'll have to do,*> Tanis said.

Brandt ordered Sarin back down from the roof and directed Terrance, Joe, Abby, and Andrews to join Trist and Jessica at the entrance to the undercity.

"She's as bossy as you," Joe gave Tanis a wink as he dashed past.

Sarin joined one/two at the front windows while Brandt and Tanis joined the rest of the group at the undercity entrance.

It was a rather non-descript door at the bottom of one of the building's stairwells. Joe and Andrews were guarding it with Terrance and Abby standing just inside the building.

"Jessica and Trist are securing the far end of the corridor," Joe supplied.

Tanis noted the unconscious bodies of five young men and women from the Victoria colony. Based on their clothing and build they were all from the planetside group and not the station or mining platforms.

"Fools," she muttered.

"Or deluded," Terrance commented.

Brandt updated the combat net with the Marine's withdrawal plan and Tanis signaled her group to move down the corridor. There was no reason to get everyone bunched up.

Trist updated the combat net, showing the corridors beyond their current location. Tanis added her personal map of the undercity. They were seventeen kilometers from the spaceport with nearly two million civilians of unknown allegiance between their current location and the pinnace.

<Angela, do you think we could remote control the pinnace and bring it to this location?> Tanis highlighted a warehouse a kilometer from their current location. The warehouse had a loading dock outside the ES shield. It was the best LZ she could find nearby.

<Should work, but with the Link down, how will we send the plan to the pinnace?>

<A batch of nano should do the trick.>

<It will take them awhile to get there, they don't move that fast,> Angela replied.

<We best start now, then.>

Tanis updated the combat net with her plan and received agreement. Jessica began scouting in the new direction.

<It seems really empty down here. There are a lot of shops and residential areas that seem surprisingly vacant.>

<It'll be interesting to find out how high this goes,> Andrews added.

Tanis led her group down to where the corridor ended in a T-junction. She followed Jessica's path down the right hall and out into an open atrium.

Tanis recognized it from her many trips to Landfall. It wasn't far from the original City Hall where the MDC 'accident' had collapsed the roof.

Tall colonnades ringed the atrium and a holographic ceiling showed blue sky and white clouds above. There was plenty of cover for would-be ambushers and she flushed the area with as much nano as she could spare.

As the tiny robots spread out she directed Joe and Andrews to the lower level where Trist and Jessica were waiting.

"Anything?" Tanis called down.

"Not a soul, all the shops in here are closed, but it looks like people were here not long ago. There are residential corridors down there," Jessica gestured to her right, "that are closed up. But I bet there are people huddled behind the doors."

<Brandt,> Tanis called the commandant on the combat net. *<Have a charge set in the corridor at the T and blow it. Let's slow our pursuers down as much as possible.>*

<Way ahead of you, we're setting it now,> Brandt replied.

"That corridor looks to be our best bet," Jessica said, gesturing down a wide promenade that led in the direction the group wanted to go.

"Check it out," Tanis said.

"Be my pleasure," Jessica smiled. She and Trist moved into the corridor each covering a side, checking each doorway, nook and cranny.

Tanis couldn't help but smile at the couple as they worked together to clear the corridor.

They were an interesting pairing. Initially Trist had mistrusted Jessica—as much because she was an unknown as Trist's innate dislike of all law enforcement. But after years together then eventually admitted that they were made for one another and gave in.

It amused her that her two accidental passengers—both notorious for their promiscuity, not only ended up together, but were now so inseparable that she had to give them the same assignments or they would work out ways to be together.

She didn't mind, they were effective in their work, each coming at problems from different angles and working an issue until they had solved it from all sides.

Tanis moved her group to the entrance of the promenade, while above, the Marines entered the upper level of the atrium. Brandt appeared and waved to Tanis before she sprinted down the central staircase.

"Charge will blow any moment now," her statement was punctuated by a loud blast that echoed through the corridor and reverberated among the colonnades.

"Nice timing," Abby said dryly.

"I like to make a good entrance," Brandt smiled angelically before casting a hard eye at her Marines.

"Ramos, what in god's great space are you doing? Secure that passageway!"

Ouri had the *Intrepid's* conn.

Holographic displays surrounded her, filled with reports and analysis of data coming up from the surface. She didn't have much. Reports on the general net of a shooting at the service and then a garbled burst from Brandt indicating some sort of ongoing attack.

She immediately hammered the Landfall police for an update and was told that there was a Link outage in the area as a result of the attack but that everything was now under control.

The president's office wasn't responding and, after the initial conversation, the chief of police passed her off to a flunky that did nothing but parrot his earlier statement.

<I'll wager this is the insurrection Tanis was concerned about,> Amanda's tone was laced with concern as she offered her assessment.

Priscilla turned from her position at a secondary comm station on the bridge and fixed Ouri with a worried look.

"I can't help but agree. Nothing they're doing is according to protocol. I've been stonewalled on a dozen different paths of inquiry."

Ouri stood and paced across the bridge, considering her options. They had outlined many different scenarios and responses. Unfortunately, none of them involved Tanis and the rest of the command crew being caught in the middle of the insurrection. Given their luck, Ouri wondered why that wasn't the first scenario they thought of.

As she considered options, the *Intrepid* slowly circled the world of Victoria, plotting the same high orbit it had for decades. Excepting those on the planet below, the rest of the command crew was in stasis.

Ouri and Priscilla were the only two humans present—and Priscilla was supposed to be taking R&R time on Tara, but this emergency had come up just as she was ready to disembark.

Still, Ouri counted herself more than lucky. With Amanda and Priscilla on hand there was little they couldn't do.

Her mind calmed, Ouri assessed the contingency plans and selected her next course of action.

"Priscilla, get the ship's C wing prepped and on their ladders. Also, find out if there is any elevated comm traffic between the groundside colony, the station and the platforms. If we're about to be hit from one of those locations, I want to know in advance."

"You got it," Priscilla replied.

<*Major Qhung,*> Ouri called down to the Marine command offices. <*I need a company of your finest on an assault transport, ready to launch in the next fifteen minutes.*>

<*Yes, sir, may I ask the nature of the engagement?*>

<*It would appear that our funeral attendees have come under attack and we've lost communication with them,*> Ouri supplied.

<*We'll be ready in ten!*>

<*Thank you.*>

The *Orkney* and *Dresden,* two of the ISF's new thousand-meter cruisers were in low Victorian orbit and Ouri raised their captains on the main holo tank.

"Colonel, We've been following the feed on the command net," Ophelia, captain of the Dresden, said the moment her image shimmered into view. "What do you need us to do?"

"We need to drop a platoon, but the clouds are too dense to provide cover from up there," Ouri said.

"We can drop below the clouds," Captain Peabody spoke in his gravelly voice. "I assume you're prepping a wing to come down as well?"

"They'll be on their ladders in under ten minutes," Ouri replied.

The two captains exchanged a look. "Then we better get moving," Ophelia said and cut the connection. Peabody was gone a second later.

"Colonel," Priscilla said. "There is no increased comm traffic from the platforms, or internally on them as far as I can tell, but there is an increase with the station. Nothing that seems suspicious, except that it's a higher volume than normal for this time of day—it's station night. Also—. Oh! President Tom for you."

Ouri brought the Victorian president up on the bridge's holo display.

"Colonel Ouri," the president was a clean-cut, well-spoken man in his fifties. He always had the right tone, and knew just what to say. That was one of the things that had always bothered her about him the most. Nothing ever seemed heartfelt.

She didn't let him start with whatever he had planned. "Mr. President, I understand that there's been some sort of shooting. I'm also having trouble contacting the *Intrepid's* away party."

"Yes, there was an attack by a group of citizens who are upset with the current state of affairs in the Kap system," President Tom replied evenly.

Ouri couldn't read any concern or alarm in his tone, nor did the Victorian president offer any gesture of concern or assurances of effort.

"You appear to have gotten free, why is it that my people have not?" Ouri asked frankly.

"I was protected by our security forces; I also was not the target—that appears to have been your people. My police have since have moved in and secured the area."

"Very well, are my crewmates safe?" Ouri asked, growing upset. This was the first piece of information the president should have provided.

The president appeared to pause and consider her question.

"It's pretty dangerous out there and I do not want to put any more Victorians at risk. I suppose that what I could do is offer to protect them from the angry citizens who are after them and return them to the *Intrepid*. But I think that a trade would be in order. Perhaps access to what you're building at your secret research site."

She wondered if he knew of the Gamma site, or if he just assumed there was secret research going on in the labs on Tara.

Either way, she wasn't surprised it had come to this. She was well aware that the Victorians wanted more of the *Intrepid's* tech. They didn't seem to understand that even in Sol—where advanced technology was not withheld from any group—it still wasn't free for the taking.

Tom's generation seemed to have no care that the deal struck with the *Hyperion* was for repair and resupply in exchange for specific technologies and the terraforming of Victoria.

As far as she was concerned the Victorians were making out like bandits. At best, the boost their mining platform and labor force provided only shaved a decade off what it would have taken the *Intrepid* to do on its own.

Despite her hard exterior, Tanis was really a bleeding heart.

"It sounds like you're detaining crew from the *Intrepid*. Is that the case?" Ouri asked. "If you are offering this trade, I want to see them."

President Tom paused again and Ouri felt certain he did not have anyone to present. It wasn't surprising, taking out Tanis, Joe and the rest would be no small task. Throw in a dozen Marines and Landfall would be a warzone before it was over.

"I'm calling your bluff, Mr. President. Not only am I not going to respond to your weak attempt at extortion, but I am invoking section 3.17 of the charter of Victoria. This grants the ranking officer aboard the *Intrepid* authority to take all and any means necessary to protect crew of the *Intrepid* from unlawful duress and detention on Victoria—unless you believe they are being lawfully detained..."

The president glanced outside the holo's view and scowled. "You told me they wouldn't do this," he muttered.

"I'm not sure who your advisor is, Mr. President, but they're wrong, I will do it."

Ouri cut the connection. Best to let him stew for a bit. Tom was the sort of man who only responded to threats and action. His smooth tone wouldn't help him when kilometer-long cruisers took position over his city.

Priscilla flicked accumulated scan data onto the main holo and Ouri looked it over. A heat signature bloomed near the park where the service had been held and she zoomed in, examining the terrain as best they could through the ES shield's glow.

A building was on fire across from the park, but there were no IR signatures matching the *Intrepid's* party.

Another satellite passed over Landfall and the resolution increased. She could see a number of Victorian's fleeing the building while others moved toward undercity access points.

"Bob, what do you think their plan is?"

<The spaceport is too far. I imagine that they know by now that they're not just up against a few malcontents. They are likely headed to one of these locations nearby, which can get them outside the ES shield.>

As Bob spoke he pivoted the city view and highlighted the possible egress locations the planetside crew would head for.

Ouri nodded. "That makes sense. We'll need to get them transport out from there."

<Major Qhung, where do you stand?>

<We're just finishing gearing up, the transport will be ready to drop in three minutes.>

<*Very good, we expect the planetside party to exit the ES dome from one of the locations I've sent to your command net,*> Ouri said.

<*Yes, Sir.*>

Ouri shook her head, having the conn of the *Intrepid* and being called sir by majors was not something she was used to—even after all these years.

"Looks like something is up, the pinnace at the spaceport appears to be prepping for takeoff," Priscilla said.

"Did they make it there?" Ouri was surprised, even for Tanis making it ten kilometers through hostile territory so fast was impossible.

"No, it's empty. I suspect that Tanis got a nano package to it and is sending it to her egress location."

"Handy. Make sure Major Qhung knows so he can follow it."

<*Planetside air support is lifting off in response,*> Bob provided.

"Faster than I thought," Ouri said.

<*Qhung is going to have a hot landing with those birds in the air,*> Amanda said. <*They must have already been prepped.*>

The Victorians claimed to have built the air force to deal with a possible incursion from Sirius, but Ouri had often suspected it was as much for their temporary neighbors as their Sirian oppressors. The atmospheric fighters were complemented by a respectable number of defense batteries.

"I guess the debate over who the planetary defenses are for is over," Ouri sighed.

<*That pinnace isn't going to make it past those fighters, but I pulled its destination and passed it to Qhung,*> Amanda said.

"C-wing's ETA?" Ouri asked.

<*Five minutes,*> Amanda supplied.

Ever since the incursion of the Sirian scout ships Joe had maintained three wings in a state of high readiness—shoot suits and all. This wasn't the planned action, but she was glad they were ready.

Ouri rose and paced across the *Intrepid's* bridge. The ships would be playing a dangerous game. The Victorian defenses had been constructed with the intention of destroying mid-size cruisers just like the two moving into position. Their tactics would require C wing to eliminate any enemy fighters and in-flight artillery so the cruisers could focus on the batteries.

The holo updated, showing the two ships just over fifty kilometers above the city—moving in random patterns to avoid laser fire. She could imagine what the ride was like. Jinking in atmosphere, even one as thin as Victoria's, was a gut twisting experience.

Ouri thanked the stars that the Victorians had not charged their batteries in advance—probably because the *Intrepid* would have detected the buildup. Instead the ground lasers were running off the city's main power grid, making for lower powered beams and longer recharge times.

"They're raising their reactor output to compensate," Priscilla said, also looking at the holo.

<C-Wing has dropped from their chutes, taking the hell ride down,> Amanda said.

Ouri admired their moxie. The fighters were boosting toward the planet at maximum thrust. The atmospheric entry was going to be brutal, but the maneuvers to avoid crashing into the ground would be worse.

The loyalty Tanis inspired was nothing short of amazing.

"Godspeed," she whispered aloud.

Observers in Landfall watched in mixed awe and horror as a pair of thousand meter cruisers broke through the clouds and rained laser fire on the city's defensive emplacements.

It was unlikely that any onlookers appreciated that the ships avoided launching missiles and made their strikes as surgical as possible, as the sky lit up with ionized particle streams.

Maneuvering thrusters held the ships in stationary positions, and ES fields directed the engine wash away from populated areas.

On the northern horizon a forest ignited under the intense heat and burned to cinders in minutes.

Ground batteries unleashed laser fire and missiles at the ships, which responded with point defense beams. Missiles exploded in the air over the city and no small number impacted the ship's shields.

The Victorian jets buzzed around the cruisers like angry gnats, peppering the ships with their beams and projectiles. The combined assault kept the cruisers more than busy.

Over the course of a long three minutes, hundreds of missiles spilled fire into the sky and thousands of lasers released their photon streams. The cruisers made only a few shots against the ground batteries, reserving most of their energy for defensive measures.

The Dresden suffered a shield failure on its port side, and an explosion bloomed on its hull as a missile made it through.

Below, most of the city appeared vacant, the citizenry huddled indoors or retreated to the undercity. A few Victorians were in the streets and on rooftops and those few let loose loud cheers at the sight above them.

An Edener retreat seemed imminent.

Yet the ISF ships did not move, and seconds later two dozen sonic thunderclaps tore through the air, flattening vegetation and shattering windows for miles.

C Wing had arrived.

The space fighters were less maneuverable in atmosphere than the Victorian jets, but what they lacked in finesse they made up for in raw power.

The ships slammed through the cloud cover at a thousand kilometers per hour, pivoted and braked mere hundreds of meters above the ground. Their pion engines screamed in the atmosphere and their engine wash tore craters in the earth beneath them.

Pools of molten rock filled the craters starting dozens of brush fires in the surrounding countryside.

The Victorian jets never knew what hit them.

C Wing unleashed withering beam fire from beneath, tearing the jets to pieces. Half the Victorian air force was gone in seconds, the remaining jets put up a brief fight, but a minute later the few survivors were in retreat.

Through the smoke and fire the Marine transport appeared. It angled toward the far side of the city and a pair of C Wing fighters moved in to provide escort.

With the Victorian jets gone, the cruisers directed their full energy against the surface to air batteries. Explosion after explosion shook the ground as one after another were destroyed.

The Victorians on the streets and rooftops of Landfall looked up in horror as the menacing warships of their once-saviors began a slow acceleration back into the clouds, leaving the land for dozens of kilometers around Landfall ruined and aflame.

Though the Edeners had won the battle, there would be no victor this day.

Tanis ducked behind a stone balustrade as shots rang out and the zip-ping of ballistic rounds echoed around her. She eased around the barrier and let fly with several suppressing rounds before ducking back.

Her nano had a perfect picture of the battlefield, but the tiny bots themselves were otherwise ineffective. All of the enemy's weapons were chemical ballistic and the Victorians they fought had no AI or internal systems to disrupt.

"So close," Tanis muttered.

"Yeah, one more building and we're out of this mess," Joe said from across the alleyway as he let fire with his own barrage.

It had been a slow, arduous battle to get this far. Andrews had taken a bullet in the leg, Lieutenant Smith was nursing an in-and-out shot in his shoulder and Tanis had been thrown across a hall at one point from a pulse blast.

The Victorians were putting everything they had into the fight. There was no doubt in Tanis's mind that President Tom was behind this. He must have thought he could make a quick grab for *Intrepid's* leadership and negotiate additional tech and concessions from Bob and Ouri.

Now that the initial attempt had failed miserably, his only option was to hit them as hard as he could and take whoever survived as the hostages.

"We have to get through that choke-point," Sergeant Lee said. "I just don't see a viable plan where we don't lose a lot of people."

"Too bad none of us brought grenades to the funeral," Trist grinned while changing the charge cylinder on her pistol.

"I'll remember that for next time," Brandt growled.

A low rumble shook the tunnel around them and Tanis glanced at the rock over her head.

"Things must be getting hot up there," Tanis said before glancing at Katrina—the woman's face a mask of worry.

"They'll be careful," Tanis said. "I crafted no contingencies that involve harming civilians."

Katrina cast a hard look in the direction of their attackers. "I hope they can tell who the civilians are. I don't know if I can… stupid kids, and that asshole Tom, you know he has to be behind this."

Tanis nodded. "I would be shocked if he wasn't."

"I just hope we can put this thing back together—I hope there's something left to put back together…"

Tanis considered her options and turned to one of the Marines.

"Lieutenant, send one/two back to that access we spotted a quarter-klick ago. Let's flank this mess here."

Lieutenant Smith nodded. "It seems like our best shot. Turin, you heard the lady, make it happen."

Sergeant Turin nodded his assent and huddled with Corporal Nair for a moment before one/two moved back down the corridor toward the access to the city above.

A moment later a new voice came over the combat net.

<Hey guys, I heard you needed some help.>

<Qhung! Where the hell are you? We're pinned down here,> Brandt responded.

In response, pulse blasts rang out from behind the Victorians. Several fell and moments later the rest surrendered.

"Right here," Qhung said, as he walked through the debris with a smile.

VICTORIA IN PERIL

STELLAR DATE: 3288931 / 09.08.4292 (Adjusted Gregorian)
LOCATION: Landfall, Victoria
REGION: Victorian Space Federation, Kapteyn's Star System

A Marine handed Tanis a rebreather and she stepped out of the warehouse's rear dock into a cluttered equipment yard. Even through the breathing apparatus the air reeked of carbon and ozone, it burned her eyes and she double-timed to the waiting shuttle.

Above, ISF fighters circled; beyond them lightening flashed through the clouds, striking the surrounding hills and the city's ES dome in an attempt to equalize static charge in the clouds. The volume and intensity of the strikes indicated that quite a battle had taken place over Landfall.

Tanis shook her head and shared a sorrowful look with Katrina. This was a sad enough day without witnessing the destruction of their work, the potential end to their people's friendships.

"We'll fix this," Tanis said.

"We have to," Katrina replied solemnly.

They boarded the assault transport and Tanis felt the team's combat net Link to the *Intrepid.*

<*Ouri, what's our status?*> Andrews beat her to the question.

<*Good to hear your voice, Captain,*> Ouri's reply conveyed genuine relief. <*The short version is that Tom tried to extort us in exchange for your safety and I called his bluff. He didn't have you, so I sent C-wing down with the* Dresden *and the* Orkney *as support. The Victorians launched their air force and…I…we did what we had to.*>

Ouri paused her report for a second and when she resumed her mental tone was steadier. <*We took quite the beating, but C Wing made it down in time and we took out the AA batteries and much of their air force. There were casualties on both sides.*>

Tanis glanced down the ramp of the transport at the smoking ruin of the Pinnace only a dozen meters away. She was genuinely surprised that Tom took things this far. His plan must have hinged on killing her quickly and seizing the rest as hostages. When that looked increasingly improbable, he had taken every effort to keep them in the city and bluff Ouri.

<*Seems like a weak plan,*> Jessica commented. <*They could never have mounted a credible threat. Their only advantage was an expectation of restraint from our military power.*>

<*I can't believe it came to this,*> Terrance said. <*We're a colony mission, not a military dictatorship. We sure look like one now.*>

Tanis shot him a cold look. She knew he didn't like the military buildup—neither did she—the trip to New Eden was supposed to be her way out of that life. But he was the one who built a colony ship with the sole purpose of secreting away the most valuable technology known to humanity.

<*Now is not the time, ignore it,*> Angela said quietly.

Tanis took her advice and responded to Jessica. <*It does seem like it, doesn't it? Even if they had us as hostages, we hold most of the cards.*>

<*Do we know who was involved? Other than Tom?*> Katrina asked.

<*From what we can tell it was largely a political movement, the population wasn't involved. The other cities are pretty quiet—Landfall is too, except for your neck of the woods. There were some riots on the station when the stationmaster tried to send assistance to the planet and the people stopped it. The mining platforms have been calling to the planet and us repeatedly; begging us both to stop and telling us they were not involved.*>

<*It's going to take some doing to sort this out,*> Terrance sighed. <*Just when we were so close.*>

<*Just a second,*> Ouri said before coming back a minute later. <*Shit, we have a bigger problem. We just got a report of enemy ships in-system. The stellar sensor array shows nothing, but an ore pusher saw them just over an AU out. It detected at least twenty-five vessels before it got out of Dodge.*>

Tanis banged on the hull behind her and called to the pilots. "Get us back up to the *Intrepid* now!"

The last few Marines pounded aboard and the transport's boosters came to life pulling it off the surface with a speed she would not have expected the bulky vessel to possess.

"How did the sensor net not pick them up?" Brandt asked. "It caught their last incursion."

Tanis was mentally narrowing down a suspect pool. The presence of the Sirius ships meant that Myrrdan knew about the incursion a decade ago. It also meant he had the means and the ability to tamper with the sensor net.

It was further confirmation that whoever he was, or whoever he was masquerading as, had to be high in the ISF command structure.

Tanis used her link through the *Intrepid* to reach out to the Victorian President's office.

It only took a moment for Tom's face to appear in her mind. His phony look of concern made Tanis wish she could punch him through the Link.

<Lieutenant Governor, I'm so glad to see that you are OK,> the president spoke with a grim smile. *<We're going to need to talk about reparations for your people's attack on our facilities.>*

<Tom, I don't give a damn about that, I want to know what you know about the fleet bearing down on us right now.>

The President's face drained of blood and he turned, looking outside of his virtual projection, *<What do you know about—wha—!>*

The Link was severed a moment later.

Tanis looked at the faces around her. "I believe the Victorian President has just been killed. I also think he was conspiring with someone and they saw the end of his usefulness. I saw him look at another person for guidance more than once."

<He did that when I talked with him too,> Ouri replied.

"You know who it must be," Jessica said to Tanis.

"Maybe. It could be another agent."

Jessica shook her head. "No, it's him. Drop me off at the spaceport with the Marines and we'll hit the parliament. It's time to run him down once and for all."

"What makes you so sure?" Andrews asked.

"After all this time I think he has finally come out into the open. It all makes sense. He learned about the picotech, and ensured that our layover would be longer here than we wanted, so that he could effect a plan. Sirius gave him the perfect opportunity. The timing is too pat; he is in league with them."

"I'll admit it fits," Terrance nodded.

"We're going to have one hell of a fight up there, we're likely not going to be able to give you any support," Andrews said to Jessica.

"What do you think I am?" Brandt asked.

"We need you upstairs," Tanis said.

Brandt sighed. "Then I'm going to send another platoon down to the spaceport. Two squads can't take on two million civilians. For that we'll need six."

She rose to discuss tactics with Lieutenant Smith and Jessica followed.

"I'm going with them," Katrina said, giving a deferential nod to Tanis and Andrews as she rose. "Keep us safe…again."

Tanis signaled the pilot to divert and put down at the spaceport while pouring over the scant data about the incoming fleet. It was a force intended to be overwhelming and Tanis felt real fear that there may be no easy way out of this situation.

The shuttle rocked as it touched down at the spaceport and all but two Marines too wounded to fight followed Jessica, Trist, and Katrina out of the bay.

Moments later they boosted into space.

BATTLE FOR VICTORIA

STELLAR DATE: 3288931 / 09.08.4292 (Adjusted Gregorian)
LOCATION: Landfall, Victoria
REGION: Victorian Space Federation, Kapteyn's Star System

"The rail platforms are coming online," Admiral Sanderson reported. "We are also launching picket fighters and planting RM's in strategic locations. We don't have a lot of them though—we never really expected to be in a fight this big."

"It looks like we can never have enough relativistic missiles," Andrews shook his head.

"The plant is pumping them out as fast as it can," Tanis said. "Just not fast enough it would seem—thank the stars at least some of the rail platforms got done."

A decade earlier, Tanis had ordered the building of a dozen automated railgun platforms to provide additional protection for the colony. To date only seven had been installed. Four were in synchronous orbits with Victoria around the Kap. The other three orbited Tara.

Though few railgun platforms protected capital world, each was capable of firing half-ton slugs at 0.2*c*. When the slugs impacted they would deliver forty-five exajoules of energy—a force equivalent to an eleven-giga-ton nuclear weapon.

They were just shy of world-killers.

Tanis took the XO's bridge station; Terrance sat near her, a look of deep concern on his face. Officers representing various ship sections filed in to coordinate with their departments and several ensigns sat at weapons and helm stations.

Priscilla winked at Tanis. "Glad you made it off the dirtball."

"You and me both," Tanis said with a smile.

"Bring us up to Anne's orbit, we need to establish a more easily defensible position," Andrews gave the order to helm, his voice calm; not a tremor of concern present.

Tanis brought up a display of all ship placements within 3AU on the main holo and rose to examine it.

The Intrepid Fleet was spread across the system on a combination of maneuvers, colonization assistance missions, and patrols.

Several were headed back to Victoria, already having been recalled by Ouri, a few would make it on time, most would be too late.

"The *Dresden* and *Orkney* are on station, holding at nine hundred kilometers starboard and port," one of the ensigns reported.

Tanis nodded pensively. "Have them switch places. The *Dresden* needs to keep that hole in its port side protected."

"Aye Ma'am."

<*You don't think I can take it?*> Sue, Trist's old AI asked.

<*I know you can take it. If I didn't, you wouldn't be running a Claymore-class starship,*> Tanis replied with a virtual wink.

<*I appreciate your vote of confidence. Sorry I got a hole blown in your fancy new ship,*> Sue replied.

<*You didn't put it there, just keep any more from getting made.*>

Sanderson stepped to her side. "The *Yosemite* will be here within the hour, but the *Terra* is too far out."

"We should keep it there. If they know of the Gamma site, they'll make an attempt to hit it. I think we should bring the *Peters* and *Starflyer* in from their patrol to bolster it. With the combined fighter compliment they should be able to hold off all but the most determined assault."

"I agree," Sanderson said.

Tanis nodded to Priscilla who relayed the order across the system.

Of the forty-seven capital ships in the Intrepid Fleet only eighteen would arrive before the Sirian ships were within firing range.

She organized the ships into three battlegroups, each with one of the new thousand-meter Claymore class cruisers as its anchor.

Each battlegroup had a seven hundred and twenty meter Trenton class cruiser and several of the fleet's new Pacific class destroyers.

She saw the *Andromeda* signal that Joe had arrived onboard and directed the ship into a polar orbit around Victoria. Since the last engagement with the Sirians, its stealth systems had seen further upgrades and the ship would be entirely invisible to the enemy.

The *Tromandy,* formerly known as the *Strident Arc,* reported ready as it passed Victoria's southern pole and Tanis assigned it to close station defense of the *Intrepid.* She gained a pyrrhic sense of satisfaction knowing that the ship which pursued the *Hyperion* to The Kap was now in the force arrayed against the Sirians.

<*I've found and corrected the data error in the sensor array. Stellar scan is updating,*> Bob said.

Tanis waited impatiently as the NSAI assembled a picture of the system from the thousands of sensors in the stellar array. When it did, true fear gripped her as the holo showed sixty-five Sirian ships.

"Ouri, I could have sworn you said something like twenty-five!"

<*You're not that good at math, are you?*> Angela asked.

Ouri's face was white. "That was the report…and they were way further out."

Tanis glanced around the bridge, the crew looked as scared as she felt. She had an ace up her sleeve, but it was a card she really did not want to play.

She turned to Captain Andrews and Admiral Sanderson.

<*I've had fleet conn for some years now, but would you like me to transfer it to either of you?*>

Captain Andrews shook his head.

<*I may be in charge on paper, Tanis, but you've been running the show, you know the personnel, and the fleet's strengths better than anyone. Sanderson?*>

Sanderson nodded. <*You have our absolute faith.*>

<*Good,*> Bob's voice boomed through their minds.

<*That was easier than it should have been,*> Tanis said privately to Angela.

<*The captain never signed up for this. It was supposed to be a milk run on the safest and fastest colony ship in the galaxy. Sanderson was a good officer in his day, but he never saw half the combat you have.*>

<*I appreciate the vote of confidence,*> Tanis said. <*I swear, sometimes I feel like a petty dictator holding all of these titles that I never really earned.*>

<*Trust me, you've earned them,*> Angela replied.

Tanis looked to Priscilla, "Give me all fleet."

The avatar nodded and a second later said, "you're Linked."

<*If you haven't heard already, we're in for a hell of a fight,*> Tanis said, feeling the presence of thousands of men and women just at the edge of her mind.

<We're outnumbered almost four to one and if you're worried, then that's good; means you're still alive. We know for a fact that the Sirians are overconfident, sloppy and their tech is centuries behind ours.

<We didn't make it this far, face down so many threats, and continually defy the odds to be defeated here and now. We have prepared well, we have powerful ships, strong defenses, and all of you. We've trained for this, prepared for this eventuality.>

Tanis paused a moment, a knot of emotion in her throat.

<You know your jobs, do them well as I know you can. Be diligent, proud, be fierce! Today our names are writ amongst the stars.>

Tanis nodded to Priscilla who cut the link.

The bridge crew erupted in cheers.

"Didn't know you had that much prose in you," Ouri said.

"I've read a lot of Keats recently."

<Keats wrote poetry, not prose,> Angela said.

<I do know that, did I just manage subtlety that you missed? That's an auspicious sign,> Tanis replied.

<Subtlety? Oh Keat's grave! Well done.>

Her speech was followed by a flurry of virtual meetings. Tanis refined the details of her plan with the fleet captains and when she was done, the holo updated with two countdowns.

One, at just shy of an hour showed the time until the Intrepid Fleet would be ready for combat.

The second, at only fifteen minutes, was the countdown until the Sirians were in range of the railgun platforms.

In front of her, the holo projection contained normalized numbers and a linear timeline, but the reality beneath that was far more complex.

Tanis re-checked all of the calculations herself. Not because she doubted the weapons and scan NSAI, but she preferred to internalize the math to understand the timings better. With distances over a light minute, and, with dozens of ships accelerating and breaking across the battlefield, no distance or time was what it appeared.

Local scan showed Victorian ships moving out of the area, and the platforms adjusting their orbits to be on the far side of Victoria when the battle was joined.

She hoped there would be a world for them to continue building when this was over.

Tanis's concentration was broken by a voice at her side.

"It's not going to be easy, is it?" Joe 's virtual presence stood beside her, brow furrowed as he studied the holo.

"Given the size of their force, they know everything…except maybe about Gamma—though we have to assume they do know about it. Still, they don't know where our rails are and when they'll hit. They have to be anticipating some heavy losses before their weapons get in range," Tanis said.

<I would bet that a lot of Victorians are thankful you forced those Rail Platforms down their throats,> Angela commented.

<I wouldn't count on it,> Tanis replied darkly.

"I prefer to think that what happened downworld today does not represent the majority of Victorians. Given that we know Tom was involved—maybe the perception we've had of the public has not been entirely true," Joe appeared to lean against the holo platform. "I certainly would like to think we have been better appreciated."

"Let's hope we get the opportunity to find out."

The time passed slowly and the *Andromeda* went silent, taking Joe's virtual presence with it, but not after a kiss that Tanis wished were real.

"General Richards," one of the lieutenants on weapons called out. "Based on scan we will have firing solutions for the rail platforms in three minutes, what are targeting priorities?"

Tanis's tactical guide called for the rails to tear the lead ships to shreds, turning them into clouds of deadly shrapnel for any other ships nearby. She examined the trajectories of the enemy ships and picked out the vessels which would do the most damage to their allies when destroyed. Once the four were marked she sent the decision to the weapons console.

The lieutenant nodded and—after Bob re-checked the work—approved the firing solution. Even traveling at one-fifth the speed of light, it would take the slugs over thirty minutes to reach their targets.

With such a large time delay they would only get one long-range shot each. Once the enemy ships realized that they were the targets of such powerful kinetic weapons they would add random shifts, colloquially known as jinks, to their movement, ensuring no further long-range shots could be made.

"I'm surprised they're not jinking already," Tanis said as she pulled up additional scan data from other posts.

"They're still a long way out of laser range. Maybe our friend didn't tell them about our rails," Andrews said. "Maybe he wanted us to wear them down."

<*It would fit the narrative,*> Angela commented.

"Using evasive maneuvers only after you take losses is how fools lose battles," Tanis shook her head. "It also means these guys may not behave the way we expect. Their cockiness will make them unpredictable."

"Let's hope they're predictably cocky," Sanderson scowled at the holo, as though he could will time to speed up and show the shots impacting.

Tanis signaled the platforms to take up new positions. With luck, once the enemy ships closed in, the platforms could make a few more shots.

She returned to her seat and checked the status of the fleet, stations, mining platforms, and the moon's batteries. The last few ships were nearly in position and the platforms had adjusted their orbits.

Everything that could be done was being done.

Tanis settled back to wait.

Jessica paced on the tarmac, pulling her jacket tight against a cold wind that was steadily picking up.

"Wimp, it's not that cold," Trist said from under the awning of a storage shed.

"Yes it is, you just don't have enough blood anymore to get cold."

Trist chuckled. "At least I have skin. I'm surprised that plastic stuff you have lets enough perspiration though for you to get cold at all."

Jessica rubbed her arms vigorously. "It breathes plenty well—as you should know." A snowflake drifted past and she pointed at it. "See! Snow! It's cold!"

"Whatever," Trist said with a grin, clearly enjoying riling her wife up.

<*ETA forty-five seconds,*> Lieutenant Smith updated them over the combat net.

"About time," Jessica groused and turned toward the landing cradle.

Marines pulled up in three equipment haulers and a bus which they had graciously requested from the spaceport staff. For their part, the Victorians they encountered were cautiously helpful.

None professed to have any knowledge about the attack on the funeral and even though the recent battle with the ISF cruisers didn't generate any love for the *Intrepid,* the news of the Sirian fleet put them in a tight position.

Tanis would never allow the Victorians to die at the hands of the Sirians, but Jessica didn't think it would hurt for the downworlders to wonder.

Katrina had helped keep things smooth and cordial. The spaceport workers may have distrusted the Edeners, but they weren't going to say no to one of the founders of their rebellion and subsequent colony.

The assault shuttle touched down and a platoon of Marines in powered armor rushed out and took positions around the landing field. Smoothly, and by the numbers, the Marines who had accompanied them to the funeral fell back and boarded the transport to don the spare armor brought down for them.

Jessica surveyed the deployment and once cover was well established, moved out from the lee of the building where she and Trist been sheltering.

As they approached the shuttle, Katrina stepped out of the bus to meet them.

"You know I'm coming with you," she said, her expression resolute, ready for a fight.

Jessica sighed. "I imagine I couldn't stop you if I wanted to."

"Heck, she couldn't stop me and I'm only two thirds your height," Trist said with a smirk.

"I'm going to put you with Smith's platoon," Jessica said. "Armor up and see where he wants you."

Katrina nodded and walked up the shuttle's ramp.

<*Seriously?*> Lieutenant Smith addressed Jessica privately. <*I know she's capable, hell, I saw her shoot at her own people not an hour ago, but we need to move fast.*>

<*She was combat trained before you were born, Lieutenant. You'll keep her safe and user her to your advantage,*> Jessica said in a tone that brooked no debate.

Smith was not given to complaints and Jessica knew he and his squads just wanted to get back into the fight. His eagerness was one of the reasons she placed Katrina with him. He wasn't going to go off half-cocked with the matriarch of this colony on his six.

And if he let anything happen to her they both knew Tanis would have his hide.

She reached the top of the shuttle's ramp to see Trist engaged in a rather comical scene—even Katrina was smiling.

"Damnit, this isn't going to fit," Trist said while looking up at a standard ISF Marine powered suit in its rack.

"I told them to send down our suits," Jessica said with a frown.

Her exaggerated physique was hard enough to fit in standard armor, but no Marine was anywhere close to Trist's one hundred-fifty centimeters.

"You're going to have to make do," Smith said to Jessica before turning to Trist. "We have procedure for you, the armor doesn't need *your* limbs in *its* limbs to work.

The lieutenant nodded to PFC Ramos who was already in his armor. The private pulled a suit out of its rack and gave it a deft twist, separating the torso from the legs.

"Forgive the intimacy. Kneel down," Smith said and walked behind Trist as she knelt. He slipped one arm under her ankles and another across her chest. In one swift move he picked her up like she weighed no more than a pillow. Her legs were folded back at the knee and he slid her into the armor's legs.

"Now fold your arms like they're chicken wings," he said to Trist. As she sat perched in the armor with her arms folded, he split the armor's torso into its front and back pieces and then placed them back around Trist.

The armor detected its inhabitant and slowly adjusted to her form, filling the empty lower leg and forearm spaces with gel.

"This…this is weird, Trist said as the armor's torso compressed, shortening to match her frame. Smith slipped the helmet over her head after a moment she raised her hand and wiggled her fingers.

<*Gah! This feels weird. The neural shunts are working. My actual hand isn't moving…at least I can't feel it moving,*> Trist said over the Link.

<*Good,*> Smith responded. <*Take a step, make sure your balance is ok.*>

Trist took a few tentative steps and gave a thumbs up.

The transport's systems selected the closest fit for Jessica and a powered suit lowered off the rack and split open in front of her. Her entry was much more graceful than Trist's and a moment later the protective shell closed around her.

Gel filled the spaces around her waist and the armor adjusted as much as possible to her lengthened legs and altered torso.

She Linked with the suit and a cool sensation washed over her skin as her outer touch senses transferred to the armor. The systems ran a quick check, and her visual HUD updated with data regarding the suit's systems.

<*No one shares this with anyone,*> Trist said over the 'toon Link.

Several of the Marine's avatars chuckled and Jessica was certain they'd remind Trist of this as frequently as possible.

The rest of the Marines were suited up and they moved off the transport, each grabbing a rifle at the top of the ramp.

Jessica selected a dual fire weapon which could switch between photon and proton streams. Behind her, Trist made the same selection.

<*Ready to kick some ass?*> Jessica asked her privately.

<*Hells yeah. This son of a bitch has hurt us all.*>

At the bottom of the ramp, Jessica addressed the Marines over the combat net.

<*It's a shit show down here, folks. We've pummeled their defenses and now there's an enemy fleet inbound. Most of your toons are from the same companies and there's no OIC. I'll fill that role, but Lieutenant Smith will have tactical authority.*

<*Upstairs things are grim, but we know our people, they'll take care of things. Keep your head down here, keep your eyes on scan, watch your brothers and sisters. We get our guy and all come back.*>

<*Thanks,*> Smith said to her privately before addressing the troops. <*You heard the colonel. We're Marines and we'll get the job done. Our*

company AI's aren't with us on this one, we'll be using the suit-networked NSAI. It's made transport assignments, so get moving.>

A round of muffled "oo-rahs" sounded through helmets and over the Link.

Moments later the Marines were bounding toward the ground transportation, their powered armor sending them meters into the air with each step.

Smith coordinated with the two other lieutenants and the platoon sergeants. They tweaked the approaches to the city and two force recon squads were dispatched ahead of the ground transports.

Jessica watched as the recon squads flashed rapid hand signals at one another before leaping into the air—their lighter armor and propulsion jets allowing them to fly hundreds of meters between touchdowns.

Smith's platoon would approach the city from the south, on the left flank. Their goal would be to take the parliament buildings and subdue any of the presidential guard who may remain.

They would also protect Katrina and ensure she could take control of the government while the other two platoons worked to keep Myrrdan from fleeing.

Jessica assigned herself to Lieutenant Usef's section of the net. He was headed straight up the center. She had no real idea where Myrrdan would be, but her gut told her to keep options open, and the center was best for that. The fact that Usef had a weapons platoon also played no small part in her decision.

On the right flank, circling around from the north, was Lieutenant Borden's platoon. They were lightly armored and would move fast, securing as much of the city's northern reaches before the enemy could reach them.

She hoped.

<*Readings coming in,*> the weapons group announced over the bridge net. <*Looks like three of the slugs impacted. One of the big boys got nailed and two of their half klickers. They're pretty spaced out, looks like only*

superficial—wait, no, a piece of hull just tore through another cruiser, several others have taken smaller impacts.>

"Yay for our side," Priscilla smirked. "I bet that'll give em some pause."

"They're jinking," scan reported. "They've ceased braking, I think they plan to churn and burn the colony."

"That's not going to happen," Captain Andrews replied. "Those dirtsiders may be a bunch of ungrateful asses, but they're our ungrateful asses."

"They must not have a lot of real combat experience in Sirius," Tanis said as she rotated the holo display. "I guess all the wars back in Sol were worth something after all."

<*Kicking ass across the galaxy?*> Angela asked privately. <*Seems like we'll never get away from this.*>

<*Only the dead…*> Tanis replied

"I assume there is a strategy for this?" Terrance asked

"Well, if you're blasting down on a world, then your trajectory is relatively fixed," Tanis replied and turned to the weapons team. "Take the two rails on the far side of Victoria and keep them peeking just above the poles."

"Grapeshot?" Asked one of the lieutenants.

"You got it. Calculate your spread to hit them at just over a hundred million klicks. Once the first ships get hit by the grapeshot, they'll likely disperse into one of these two patterns. Use the other two rails to fill those locations with grapeshot at that time." Tanis provided the patterns and coordinates over the bridge net and couldn't help feeling relief. The Sirians were not fighting smart, if they kept this up, it would be an even fight by the time their ships made it to Anne's orbit.

<*Don't get cocky,*> Angela commented. <*Even if we take out half of their ships, they still almost outnumber us two to one.*>

<*If the Antares can make it here from the Gamma site in time, we'll be free and clear.*>

Angela made a mental sound meant to indicate she didn't like the plan. <*That's a bell we can't un-ring. Once the human sphere realizes we have picotech, New Eden will be at war for centuries.*>

<*It's a last-ditch option, Andrews hasn't approved the option yet. It will certainly win this, though,*> Tanis replied.

Tanis knew she sounded certain, but she didn't want to unleash the pico tech either.

Centuries ago, when nano-tech was new and self-replication became possible en-masse, nanoweapons would unleash swarms of bots which would self-replicate by essentially eating whatever they were fired at. It was a dangerous tech, but because nano-bots could not disassemble all molecules, they could be blocked. Eventually technologies were developed to defeat nano-swarms and their use as offensive weapons waned.

Pico swarms were an entirely different story. The Sirian ships were wholly vulnerable to them. A strike from a pico bearing missile would cause their ships to be devoured in a matter of minutes.

Use of a pico weapon created two immediate dangers. The first was that none of the ships in the *Intrepid* fleet were immune to pico swarms either. The second was likely Angela's primary concern. Once it was known that the *Intrepid* possessed picotech, they would be chased to the ends of the galaxy.

Captain Andrews must have been reading her mind.

"ETA on the Antares puts it right when the battle is projected to occur," his tone didn't betray which way he was leaning in the decision.

"I've instructed them to maintain velocity. They'll fly past at 0.15*c*. Any missiles they launch will be all but undetectable," Tanis said

The captain nodded. "Don't expect a decision before that time. We won't fire those things unless there is no other choice."

"Agreed," Tanis rotated the holo again. "The grapeshot and the RM's will hit them pretty hard. Chances are that we'll break them before it comes to a fistfight."

"Who can say?" Sanderson shook his head. "Not a lot of space forces invade foreign systems. It's not like an insystem fight when there's somewhere to retreat. The fact that the Victorians chose to execute all of Yusuf's crew is not going to help either."

"You think they'll fight to the death?" Ouri asked from her station.

"I think we need to be prepared for it," Sanderson replied.

Scan updated with the latest projected trajectories for the Sirian ships. The vector confirmed a churn and burn on Victoria. It was imperative the battle be decided outside Anne's orbit.

"Are all of the RM's in position?" Tanis asked the weapons team.

"Yes, Sir, we've adjusted their locations per your latest projections."

"Good, I want them within three light minutes of the Sirian fleet when the grapeshot crossfire hits."

Tanis turned to look for Joe before remembering he wasn't on the *Intrepid.* So much for their pledge to not get separated again when things got crazy.

<*You knew that was a silly pledge when you made it,*> Angela said.

<*Hah! Don't give me that. I know you feel the same way.*>

<*I may, but pledging to stay cheek by jowl with someone for hundreds of years is still silly.*>

Tanis sighed, mentally acknowledging that Angela was right. But the fact that Joe had one of the most dangerous missions in the upcoming battle didn't help her nerves.

Dry leaves crunched underfoot as Jessica peered down an alley. Her nanoprobes told her it was clear, but minutes ago they had taken weapons fire from positions which scan also showed as clear.

It smarted to know that many of the people she was fighting had trained at her police academy. The fact that they used Edener weapons and armor smarted more. Especially when their aim proved true.

What didn't make sense was their armor being invisible to her nano—Tanis wasn't so trusting as to provide equipment their own forces couldn't counter.

Yet the Victorians were able to hide from scans that should have revealed them.

<*Anything?*> she called up to the assault transport overhead.

<*Negative, my sweeps show no one in that position. They could have gone into the undercity. My scan can't get through the city's ES dome and that much rock.*>

<*Not to mention two/three is almost right under that building. I can't imagine they're that blind.*>

<*Target acquired,*> Trist said. <*He's on the roof over there. I saw what looked like a flicker in an active camo field.*>

Jessica looked over squad positions on the platoon's combat net. Only one other fireteam was close to the sniper's position, but they were dealing with their own problems.

<*I'm not visible to that position, I'll circle around,*> Jessica replied.

<*Sergeant Amerson, secure whatever undercity access the flagged building has. You may get an unfriendly flushed down toward you,*> Jessica said to the leader of fireteam two/three.

<*On it, ma'am,*> came the reply.

She logged her approach on the combat net and began to slowly work her way toward a side entrance on the building the sniper was in.

She crept down the alley toward a parallel street. There was little cover for her, but likewise there was little for anyone else to hide in.

Her nano swept upward, watching windows and looking over the rooftops. No enemies appeared on their scans, though she saw a few scared families through some of the windows and felt a pang of regret.

She had never been part of a military action that caused families to huddle together in their homes. It wasn't a good feeling.

Jessica reached the end of the alley and her nano moved out onto the tree-lined boulevard.

A gust of wind rushed past her, blowing dry leaves through the air—momentarily blinding her motion tracking. She waited for a shot, but none came. If the sniper could see down this street, he wasn't paying attention.

Keeping under store-front awnings and the occasional tree, Jessica moved as quickly as she could. It had already been thirty minutes since they left the spaceport and she could feel anxiety growing at the thought of Myrrdan escaping their web.

She crossed another street and then angled away from the sniper's building to come at it from the side.

<*Is our friendly neighborhood sniper still there?*> Jessica asked.

<*Yeah, I'm working directly toward him and he's taking pot-shots at me,*> Trist replied.

<*Careful! One shot won't penetrate, but two or three could crack your armor.*>

A chuckle came over the link. <*You know, I read the same manual you did. He did clip my shoulder; he's getting a bit sloppy now…sheeeet. Ok, he's got a friend up there, you better hustle.*>

Jessica swore softly.

<*Enough skulking around, I'm going to the rooftops.*>

She looked over the area her nano had scouted. The roof to her left sported a lush garden that would provide perfect cover. She leapt up and landed behind a tool shed.

Her probes rushed through the plants, watching for movement in the air currents and errant heat signatures. Jessica followed them slowly, her own active camouflage shifting to hide her amongst the plant life.

At the edge of the garden she toggled her vision to a full spectrum blend. Just one building separated her from the sniper's position and she looked for any movement, or degradation of his active camo.

Her nano reached the edges of an enemy sensor cloud and she moved them around to the south. Once there she directed several of her probes to move into the enemy cloud.

Her feint worked and the density of the cloud near her decreased. She also saw some leaves on the rooftop move, as though a person laying on them had shifted.

"There's one," she said softly to herself.

<*Can you get them to take another shot at you?*> she asked Trist.

<*I have an holo-marine handy, what say I risk its neck instead?*>

<*Coward,*>

Trist's avatar stuck its tongue out at Jessica, and below, a very believable holographic representation of a person in powered armor dashed out into the street below.

Jessica wasn't watching the street; her eyes were on the rooftop, layers of nano augmenting her vision. At the moment Trist sent out her decoy, Jessica spotted the second sniper and was in the air, rifle taking aim.

A primal scream left her lips as her feet crashed down on the first sniper, the metric ton of her armor driving him half through the building's rooftop.

She dropped a sticky EM grenade on him and dashed toward the other sniper, firing proton beams as she went.

Behind her the grenade detonated while in front the second sniper's active camo flickered off as her shots scorched his armor.

He twisted on the ground, bringing his weapon to bear on her and Jessica dodged to the side, her vision showing the heated air where his beam had lanced out. She hit him two more times before a form in powered armor slammed down onto him from above.

<You think I was just going to hang out down there and wait?> Trist asked.

<Well, there was that coffee shop across the street, I bet they would have served you a cup.>

Trist dropped her own EM grenade on the enemy soldier before running out of its range.

<Two snipers down, incapacitated with EMs, we're moving on,> Jessica reported over the combat net.

The bridge crew busied themselves as best they could while the holo counted down to the grapeshot rounds. Stewards entered the bridge and provided food. Tanis grabbed two BLTs, the first disappearing in an instant.

"You'd think it was going to run off your plate," Captain Andrews said with a smile before taking a bite of his sandwich.

Tanis returned the smile. "You never know when you may get to eat again in situations like this."

The captain raised his eyebrow and Tanis got the message. If they missed their next meal it would likely be due to this one being their last.

A short time later the countdown on the holo reached zero and the first two rails fired their shots. Two minutes later the other rails slung their deadly payload into the black. Tanis sent new positions to all the railguns while intently watching the holo projection of the battlefield.

Tactical updated and showed the relativistic missiles also in the final minutes of their countdowns. The bridge net brought two more NSAI online as the myriad calculations required to predict all the possible battlefield configurations grew.

All eyes were either on the holo or personal VR representations of the same data. It looked like the tactic was going to work until, seconds before impact, one of the dreadnaughts jinked out of range.

The RMs had their own smart NSAI which would seek targets of opportunity as they came into range—better than the grapeshot which wasn't smart at all. If the enemy ships deviated even a hundred kilometers it would miss entirely.

"One ship out of the pocket. They'll miss the head-on grapeshot," Priscilla called out.

"They must have caught a reflection off it," Andrews mused.

Two other ships managed to shift out of range before the grapeshot met the rest of the Sirian fleet. Optical scopes on both the *Intrepid* and Anne's surface showed seven ships being torn to shreds by the hail of pellets.

"That's brutal," Ouri whispered as the ships all but disintegrated under the barrage.

The other Sirian vessels were lashing out with their forward beams, hoping to break apart any shot coming their way. ES scoops flashed on in an attempt to shift the pellets and shrapnel from their fellow ships away.

In some cases it appeared to be working, the scoops lit up sporadically as shot was deflected, but in two other cases ships didn't get their scoops up in time, or jink far enough.

"Nine ships down, eleven others have visible hull breaches," Priscilla reported.

"That puts their total at fifty-two," Andrews said. "Let's see if the crossfire hits any of them."

"It's going to require them to not change velocity for the calculations to work," Tanis said.

"One other ship just went dead," Priscilla added. "We're down to fifty-one with fifteen of those having suffered some sort of damage."

"Ten seconds to the grapeshot crossfire," weapons said. "It's hard to tell what our spread will look like at this range, but you appear to have predicted their dispersal pattern well," the officer said to Tanis.

They only had to wait a moment more before the holo updated with four more ships getting hit by the shot.

"Enemy ship count at forty-seven," Scan gave the update out loud. "They're breaking formation, looks like they're scattering into four separate groups."

"RMs have locked onto targets in three groups," weapons added. "We have fifteen missiles, six each on two of the groups and three on the other."

"Could finally even the odds," Sanderson said softly. "I've never rooted so hard for an RM before."

"I know what you mean," Tanis said.

<*We've hit some local police who don't want to give up,*> Lieutenant Borden said. <*They're dug in and anything we do to get them out will be lethal.*>

Jessica sighed. Wiping out a whole police squad was not the sort of thing that made long-term relations better. Especially when it was at the hands of armored Marines.

<*Can you skirt them?*> she asked.

<*I really don't like having armed folks at my back,*> Borden replied.

<*Have a shuttle foam them,*> Smith suggested.

<*Good call, I'll bring one down.*>

From her rooftop vantage point she saw one of the assault transports arc toward Borden's position. A self-guided missile unracked and lanced toward the ground. Moments before impact it exploded into a cloud of foam. Jessica knew from experience that once that foam hit it would solidify into a firm, yet breathable cocoon, and the enemy police force wouldn't be going anywhere.

The combat net showed the embattled squad on the move once more. Overall, the net was tightening. Two fireteams had also engaged presidential guard in powered armor, but otherwise all opposing forces had been police or civilian.

Several casualties had occurred—results of Jessica's orders to push forward quickly. She tried not to think about it too much. It was imperative that they pin Myrrdan down in the Parliament buildings.

Jessica saw that Smith's platoon was within a kilometer of the Parliament building and would reach its perimeter in minutes. Jessica was a half-kilometer ahead of Usef's platoon, but the scouts were a kilometer further. She leapt to the top of a building and signaled Trist to double-time it.

The pair bounded across rooftops, using sensor data from the scouts to pick the safest path. It was a risk exposing themselves like this, but Jessica couldn't allow Myrrdan to slip through her grasp.

Only a large plaza followed by a row of administrative buildings separated her from the Parliament when a call came over the Link from the scouts.

<*Drop! Enemy has heavy weapons!*>

Jessica turned on her down jets and saw Trist do the same. They slammed into a rooftop, crashing through to the building's top floor.

They rolled to cover against the wall and Jessica sent probes toward the windows and out onto the rooftop. Before she got a good look, artillery fire hit the roof and then the side of the building.

Fire raged around them and debris flew through the air. Trist dove out of the room and Jessica followed. They dashed down a long hall and then broke through a window and into another building.

Jessica was nearly out of nano, and Trist released a dampening cloud to mask their heat and radio signatures.

<*Aggressive, aren't they?*> Trist asked.

<*It would seem so,*> Jessica replied.

Usef acknowledged their situation on the combat net and his platoon moved to flank their position. The scouts pinpointed the locations of the artillery fire, but the mobile emplacements were too well shielded for their weapons.

<*Where did they get that shit anyway?*> Jessica asked. <*We didn't sell them any stuff like that.*>

<*I guess they're cleverer than we thought. Or there's a bigger black market than we thought.*>

<*More movement at the Parliament,*> the pilot of Assault 2 called down. <*Looks like a big force moving out.*>

<*Smith, are you facing opposition?*> Jessica asked.

<*Light, approaching the rear service entrance now,*> he replied.

Jessica shook her head. Why move troops out front when the Marines were kicking in the back door?

<*Assault 2, flush them toward us,*> Jessica called up to the transport overhead.

<Roger that. Permission to use LR2s?>

Jessica gave the approval and signed her auth code to the combat net's ledger. While much of the engagement had used non-lethal force, herding enemy troops in powered armor was going to take more serious firepower. LR2 missiles were like a shotgun of rail-delivered pellets in a short-range missile delivery system.

They were designed to tear through armored combatants while doing as little damage as possible to structures.

On the combat net she saw Assault 2 circle higher and launch four missiles at the enemy's west flank.

<Assault 1, I see you have a bunker buster in your arsenal, can you drop that on our friends with the big gun down here?>

<You call, we deliver,> came the pilot's response.

Assault 1 was covering the northern approach and Jessica saw the combat net update with seventy seconds to weapon deployment.

Thirty seconds later Assault 2 called in. *<Maneuver effective, the group is moving east toward you. I count twenty-three in armor and four without armor. Positions marked on the combat net.>*

Jessica sent an acknowledgement.

Fireteams from Usef's platoon began taking up positions in nearby buildings, ready to engage the approaching enemy once the artillery emplacement was dealt with.

<Projected engagement in fifty seconds,> Lieutenant Usef called out to the platoon. *<Fireteams, check updated assignments. We take them all, dead or alive.>*

The seconds ticked by at a snail's pace. Jessica glanced over at Trist and gave her a smile. Trist returned the expression and gripped her rifle tightly.

The building shook as a round from the artillery tore through the floor below them.

<What is Assault 1 doing, stopping to get lunch?> Trist asked.

<I did see a special at a little place across the street,> Jessica replied, praying to the stars that their position was masked well enough to buy them another fifteen seconds.

<Think he'd pick something up for me?>

<Only if you ask real nice.>

Jessica took several slow breaths, and then a long, relieved exhale as the deafening crack of the bunker buster tore through the air. The building shook and she prayed it would hold up after the punishment it had received.

Seconds later the Marines moved forward.

<*Engaging!*> Corporal Latham called out on the combat net.

Jessica peered through the window, checking for enemy positions with her eyes while layering combat net data over top. If Myrrdan was with the enemy, he wouldn't be one of the unarmored noncoms—they would be decoys. He would be armored. You didn't survive as long as he did by being vulnerable.

Trist was at another window taking a shot. <*Think he's down there?*>" she asked while moving across the room to another position.

Jessica sighed. <*Honestly? I don't know, but I hope so.*>

<*He better be, it sure would be nice to get some closure on this.*>

<*You're telling me!*> Jessica laughed ruefully.

The firefight had only been underway for a couple of minutes when Jessica heard a loud shot to her right. It didn't sound like any weapon Trist was carrying.

She turned to see Trist splayed on the floor, a large hole torn through her armor and torso.

A woman stood over her, a railgun cradled in her arms.

"Huh," the woman shook her head. "I wasn't sure that it would go completely through, her armor must have been weakened by that sniper fire earlier."

Jessica rolled onto her back, switched her rifle to the proton setting and leveled it at the woman.

"Drop the rail! Now!" she yelled, forcing fear for Trist from her mind.

The woman's mask cleared and Jessica recognized the person standing over her.

"What! Amy Lee?"

"Oh for stars' sake, Jessica, try to keep up. Would Amy Lee shoot Trist? She died back in Estrella de la Muerte. I've been using her…leftovers…since then."

Her mind reeled. Myrrdan had been amongst them, within their inner circle for over a century. She couldn't even count the times they had discussed plans and strategies with her present.

Jessica scoured her memories, trying to remember any instances where knowledge of the Gamma site may have been discussed with

Amy Lee present. The disaster was unimaginable, all their careful plans—.

Jessica's eyes flicked to Amy Lee's railgun, and time slowed down as she watched Amy—Myrrdan's finger curl around the trigger and twitch ever so slightly.

A moment later, everything went black.

Jessica gasped for air and her entire body arched as her armor shocked her heart back into motion. Her HUD flickered to life and showed an alarming amount of physical damage. She looked down at her torso to see compression gel oozing out of several cracks and a large hole just below her heart.

She took a deep breath and nearly screamed as agony lanced through her body. Jessica forced herself to calm, and took several shallow breaths as she scanned the room.

Myrrdan's body lay at her feet, completely missing its head. Beyond, Trist was slumped forward over her rifle.

Jessica pulled herself across the floor to Trist's side and gently flipped her over. A second hole was in her wife's chest, green silbio spilling out of both wounds.

She rushed her own nano into Trist's body, attempting to slow the bleeding, but it was too late, she had lost too much blood and the biological silicon which had supplanted her original organs. Without an internal AI, her body didn't have the direction to repair itself.

Jessica let out a gargled cry before remembering she could Link and get help. When she re-initialized her connection a message from Trist was waiting.

<I got him for you. I love you.>

Jessica bit back a sob as her own wounds sent pain searing through her body.

Trist was gone.

Squad three found her like that, sobbing uncontrollably beside the bodies of Trist and Amy Lee.

Tanis heard the gasp from the comm officer before she spotted the report on the planetside combat net.

"Oh gods," Ouri gasped. "She's dead!"

Tanis's first thought was of Katrina. She cursed herself for letting the woman go with Jessica, but Victoria was her world too.

"Who are you referring to?" she asked, her voice strained with suppressed emotion.

"Trist," Ouri said softly. "She was killed by…Amy Lee?"

Tanis's mind reeled. She pulled up the report, found the officer on the scene and grabbed his visual feed.

<*Lieutenant Usef, what the* ***fuck*** *happened here?*>

The few seconds of light-lag felt like an eternity before the lieutenant's reply came back.

<*Ma'am. It would appear that Amy Lee shot Trist and Jessica, but Trist managed to kill her. Jessica is badly injured, but she claims that Amy Lee was Myrrdan. We're…still piecing it together and securing the area. I'll keep you in the loop.*>

Tanis surveyed the room through Lieutenant Usef's eyes. The upper half of Trist's body was destroyed, likely hit at close range by the rail gun beside Amy Lee. Jessica was leant up against a low wall, a medic looking her over—taking stock of what would likely be a lot of internal damage.

<*Jessica,*> Tanis reached out to her friend over the Link. <*I'm so sorry.*>

<*She got him,*> Jessica replied. <*She got that sonofabitch...I just…I can't…still so much to do*>

<*Let the medic take care of you, we have things covered up here.*>

<*Ow! Careful!*> her admonition to the medic coming over the link as well. <*I saw the report, take those bastards out Tanis Richards style, but save some for me.*>

<*You got it,*> Tanis replied.

She shifted her attention back to her physical location to find tears streaming down her face. A sob threatened to erupt from her throat and she turned, taking deep breaths to calm herself.

Trist…She had become one of Tanis's closest friends over the years. She couldn't count the times they talked about their plans for retirement on New Eden, how nice it would be to finally kick back.

<*You and Jessica will keep her memory alive,*> Angela said softly. <*I…I'm sorry.*>

Tanis sensed real pain in Angela's voice.

<I know. We have to put this from our mind, time for mourning later.>

"One minute to RM impact," the weapons officer called out, wrenching Tanis back to reality.

She wiped her face and turned back to the bridge. All eyes were on her; even Andrews and Sanderson seemed to be waiting for her lead.

"I've had few friends as dear as Trist," her voice rasped as she spoke. "But we need to focus, we'll win this fight and mourn her properly when we blast these sons of bitches to pieces."

Nods and few soft statements of affirmation followed her words and then everyone turned in silence to watch the last seconds tick down before the RMs hit their targets.

Right on cue, nuclear fire bloomed in space, obscuring three of the enemy ship formations. The multiple detonations were so bright, that to observers on Victoria, it would be visible in full daylight.

"It'll take a moment to sift the ships from the debris," Priscilla reported. "It's a mess out there."

Scan updated and the holo showed a wide cloud of debris and radioactive dust heading toward the planet.

"Will it hit?" Terrance asked from Tanis's side.

"The Sirians were still accelerating toward the planet. Now that the debris is on a fixed vector it will miss. Though only by a hundred thousand kilometers or so," she replied.

"They lost nineteen ships," Priscilla announced and the bridge erupted in cheers. "Don't get too excited," she said. "Most of those were destroyer-class. We're still looking at two of their dreadnaughts, twenty-three cruisers and three destroyers."

Tanis looked over the holo and saw the remaining ships breaking into two widely dispersed formations. They were changing course, arcing stellar north and south to catch the *Intrepid* in a pincer.

"Incoming!" Priscilla shouted.

The holo lit up with the signatures of four RM's bearing down on the *Intrepid*. A second later distant explosions flared at the locations of two rail platforms.

The Sirians' hadn't been idly flying insystem.

"Thirty-two seconds until missile impact," Priscilla shouted, and Amanda sounded impact alarms audibly and over the Link.

The three cruisers protecting the *Intrepid* pivoted, firing lasers and rail batteries at the RM's. The *Intrepid's* weapons were also lancing out with every beam the ship had, and with a sudden lurch, the colony ship also rotated, attempting to present a smaller profile.

Countermeasure systems fired both refractive clouds and physical shrapnel out from the *Intrepid* in an attempt to confuse and obstruct the missiles.

The *Yosemite* got in a lucky shot; one of its .27-meter rail guns destroyed one of the RM's, while a beam from the *Intrepid* melted through another missile's casing, sending it spinning off course.

<*Bringing the scoop online,*> Bob said over the cries of the engineering representative that it hadn't even gone through test runs yet.

Tanis knew what Bob had in mind, he was calibrating the scoop to operate as an MDC, hoping to molecularly disassemble the other two missiles before impact. It was a tricky maneuver—it could destroy the friendly cruisers as easily as the approaching missiles.

"Will the RMs be in the field long enough to—?" Ouri asked as one of the approaching missiles spun off course moments after passing through the field.

The other made it through the field and Priscilla called four seconds to impact.

Time slowed to a crawl for Tanis. It seemed to take forever for the missile to cross the remaining distance to the *Intrepid.* She had time to read the incoming missile's data tag on the holo in its entirety. It predicted a twenty-megaton warhead—not that such a thing was necessary when you had so much relativistic kinetic energy to begin with.

Somewhere between seconds two and three Tanis saw three small objects—boosting in at over one hundred *g's*—converge on the RM. The scopes widened their view and the impact was caught on the visuals screens. It was a fantastic display as shrapnel and fire bloomed in every direction.

The impact pushed much of the debris over the *Intrepid,* but some stayed on course. Bob snapped a part of the scoop in closer to disintegrate as much debris as he could. Alerts went off as pieces of ship and missile got through, striking the *Intrepid* in over a dozen locations.

"Damage report," Andrews called out. "And what were those interceptors?"

"Three of our heavy lifters," Priscilla said softly. "The *Excelsior, Beirut,* and *Alexandra.*"

There was a moment of silence on the bridge. Tanis felt her heart clench at the thought of Troy and his fellows giving the ultimate sacrifice. He had proven himself a hero and savior of the *Intrepid* twice now.

"The enemy ships will be in range in five minutes," weapons announced. "It looks like they're going to engage us at high speed, bank around Victoria, and come back."

"We took out Victoria's defenses. The Sirians could nuke Landfall on their way by…" Tanis let the words hang.

"Is the Antares in range?" Andrews asked.

"It will be in range of the Sirians before the enemy is in range of the colony," Priscilla said, her tone somber.

"So we'll still have to engage," Andrews nodded and turned to Terrance. "If we can't stop them, the Antares will need to fire the missiles."

Terrance nodded slowly. "So be it."

Tanis reviewed the positions of the fleets fighters. Twelve of the wings were a light-second outsystem from Anne and were in position to engage the Sirians. They were already split into two groups, boosting hard to meet the two enemy formations.

<*Strike pattern C,*> Tanis relayed to the AI managing the fleet's fighters. The AI relayed affirmation of the order, and the holo showed their predicted paths meeting the enemy ships in seven minutes.

Given the fighter's *v* they would likely not get a second chance to be involved in the battle. Strike pattern C called for them to unload all of their ordinance on the highest value targets they could.

She saw Priscilla give the OK for two search and rescue rigs to depart from the support flotilla behind Anne. She nodded her appreciation to the avatar and returned her attention to the fleet.

Five more wings spread out in front of the four battlegroups, preparing to eliminate projectile weapons and any enemy fighters. However, given the enemy's plan to arc around Victoria after their initial pass-by she doubted they would deploy any fighters—unless they were on suicide runs.

Captains fleet-wide reported rails loaded and beam batteries charged. Tanis reviewed their targeting plans and firing solutions. She felt Bob passing over the calculations as well, likely concerned about his mortality as much as the rest of them.

The first waves of fighters engaged the two enemy formations and the skirmish was over three seconds.

One of the enemy destroyers lost its engines and the fighters disabled weapons and sensors across the enemy fleet. One fighter lobbed a parting missile into one of the dreadnaught's engines and that ship began to fall behind the rest of the enemy formation.

"Six minutes until our picket line makes contact," Priscilla announced.

Tanis slowly paced before the holo tank as the minutes passed by. The two enemy formations crept closer across the millions of kilometers, the holo's wide view of the battlefield making their progression seem agonizingly slow.

Around the bridge everyone checked and rechecked equipment, firing solutions, and Tanis wished she had another BLT

When the battle was finally joined it lasted less than two minutes.

The fighter shield was five hundred thousand kilometers out, with weapons capable of reaching ten thousand klicks. However, the enemy force was jinking, making targeting at that range tricky at best. The wings chose to get much closer before engaging, trusting their size and agility to make them impossible long range targets.

At the five-thousand kilometer mark, half the fighters spun and braked at maximum safe *g*. Weapons and engines spun around the ships and they laid down punishing fire on the enemy's forward shields and ablative plating. A destroyer exploded and several cruisers were holed, but not enough to slow them.

The other half of the fighters spun as they passed the enemy ships, targeting engines and rear defenses. A cruiser bloomed into eerie flame from this assault, and scan showed many of the enemy's weapons options going offline.

It was not a bloodless assault on the fighter's part. Eleven men and women would not be coming home—their ships destroyed by enemy point-defense systems. Another dozen ships were in varying states of incapacitation, left to wait for the search and rescue rigs to pick them up.

The surviving wings began a long loop to the far side of Victoria, preparing to engage the enemy again if the battle lasted that long.

<Here it comes,> Tanis said across the fleet command net. *<Stars and gods keep us all safe.>*

The Sirians had taken punishment beyond what any force could have expected before reaching their target. With well over half their ships destroyed or disabled, any regular force would have retreated. But the Sirians knew they had nowhere to go. If they didn't win here, they were likely dead anyway—though Tanis hoped to stop a full-scale execution this time. Many of the voices which called for the death of the crew of the *Strident Arc* were tempered, or no longer present.

Even still, she ensured that Amanda sent out a call for them to surrender—though she expected no response.

Seconds later the holo lit up, tracking hundreds of invisible energy beams lancing between the ships, highlighting penetrations, deflections, chaff clouds and missile strikes.

Tanis followed the flurry of activity with precision and clarity, giving direction to captains and their AI, orchestrating her fleet as though it were one instrument in her hand.

She was dimly aware that no one else was able to grasp the full scope of the battle like she could—like she and Angela could. Tanis felt her thoughts flowing between herself and her AI as though they truly did share just one mind.

In the first thirty seconds, explosions erupted from a dozen ships as beams penetrated shields and ablative plating on both sides. Coordinated firepower from a dozen ships at a time melting through any protections provided.

The *Intrepid* took only glancing blows, its point defense systems and refractive clouds from the fleet giving it ample cover.

Tanis had her eye on the enemy dreadnaughts. The second had fallen well behind its companions, but the first was in the midst of its own protective bubble, the vast majority of its weapons systems still active. If it made it within ten thousand kilometers of the *Intrepid* it would be able to burn through the glistening clouds and do serious damage.

<Com'on, Joe,> she said to herself.

<He'll be there. He knows what to do.>

Tanis prayed he was able to, the *Intrepid* was counting on it.

As if in answer to her prayers the enemy dreadnaught suddenly began to fire wildly in every direction, attempting to hit a target the *Intrepid's* sensors could not discern. She zoomed the holo until the dreadnaught nearly filled the entire bridge.

She signaled Priscilla to search for foreign objects on the enemy ship and sure enough, the mines were there. Fifteen limpet mines, containing nuclear shape charges, were attached to the hull. Escape pods were pouring out of the enemy vessel and Tanis found herself hoping as many got free as possible.

Seconds later the mines detonated and for a moment the dreadnaught appeared to crumple before it tore apart in a fantastic explosion of steel and fire.

<*You're welcome,*> Joe said.

The *Andromeda* had disgorged its deadly load and was joining the battle proper.

<*Thank you, we all thank you, and I love you.*>

<*Just doing my job,*> Joe said with a wink.

Seventy seconds later the battle was over. The enemy fleet was moving toward Victoria and the Intrepid Fleet converged on the straggling dreadnaught, incapacitating it with little resistance given.

No cheers sounded on the *Intrepid's* bridge. Two of the ISF cruisers and a dozen smaller ships were disabled or destroyed. No ship had come through the battle unscathed.

Tanis noticed several crew members cast sidelong glances her way, their expressions filled with awe at how she had pulled the *Intrepid's* fleet through the battle with such little damage.

She tried not to meet their gazes and instead confirmed that the support flotilla was moving out from behind Anne while she waited for confirmation of the enemy's trajectory.

When the confirmation came, there were several sharp intakes of breath as everyone saw what the enemy intended.

"They're going to ram them," Ouri whispered.

The remaining Sirian ships were altering their respective vectors, lining up with the elevator, Landfall and several other installations.

The destruction would kill nearly every Victorian in the system.

Captain Andrews glanced at Terrance and then at Tanis. Both nodded and Tanis made the call to the *Antares*

<Captain Fulsom, take them out.>

The *Antares* had boosted to over 0.1c as it raced from the Gamma site to the battlefield. There was no need for the ship to decelerate to join the conflict, it had only to drop its six tiny RMs.

Weapons which contained certain death for the crew of the Sirian ships.

Optical scopes zoomed in on the enemy warships, scan tracking the RM's, looking for signs of impact.

"There!" Priscilla called out.

The hull of an enemy cruiser began to crumple and dissolve. Moments later the other Sirian ships began to dissolve as well.

Tanis let out the breath she had been holding. Joe's presence appeared and he caught her eyes. They shared a moment of relief and fear for what the future would now hold.

Tanis could see the Sirian ships trying the standard defenses for nanoswarm attacks to no avail. She could only imagine the horror those crews must have felt in the last minutes, knowing that their bodies would be dissolved by tiny machines breaking them down to their component atoms.

Escape pods were pouring out of every ship as the crews escaped the wave of destruction. A moment later reactor containment on one of the cruisers was lost and the ship blossomed into a nuclear fireball.

That explosion was followed by the another cruiser losing antimatter containment and erupting in a violent explosion. The remaining ships blew several seconds later, the blasts indicating self-destruct charges—likely to save any remaining crew the horror of seeing their bodies dissolve before their eyes.

Escape pods and pieces of starship rained down on Victoria. Tanis prayed that the fixed lifespan programmed into the picoswarms would work. If that failsafe didn't function, they would watch the entire world below slowly dissolve.

She looked around the bridge and could see half the crew holding their breath—the same thought on everyone's minds. Did they just save the Victorians from one death only to deliver them to a far worse fate?

<I've confirmed the picotech died on schedule. Victoria is safe,> Bob said over the bridge net.

Several cheers erupted and congratulatory conversation sparked up. Tanis closed her eyes and leaned against a console. They had either saved the Victorians or doomed them for eternity.

Either way the *Intrepid* would be at war forever.

There were over two-thousand survivors of the Sirian's attack. Many of them, still aboard the drifting hulks, tried to fight the *Intrepid's* Marines instead of being taken prisoner. Tanis wasn't going to lose any more of her people. After the first ship fought back, she had it blown with a tactical warhead.

The rest of the Sirians surrendered peacefully.

Things on the Victoria's surface were simpler. Most of the world was so inhospitable that any escape pods which landed there saw their inhabitants die or gladly accept help when it arrived.

An emergency session of the Victorian parliament installed Katrina as president pro-tem. With the *Intrepid's* Marines backing her, the unrest in the city wound down quickly.

Four days later Tanis sat in a low chair on the beach, looking over the lake outside her cabin. Joe was beside her, half dozing in the artificial sunlight.

"It's going to take another decade to leave now," Tanis sighed.

"About that, yeah. We have to rebuild the rails, deal with all of the Sirian hulls, help the Victorians create prisons…it's a mess," Joe said in agreement.

"And Myrrdan…Amy Lee…she's finally gone," Tanis said with a catch in her throat as she also thought of Trist being gone.

Joe leaned over and placed a hand on her arm, knowing her thoughts were on Trist.

"I won't say she died honorably or had a good death," his voice was grim. "It was a shit death at the hands of a shitty person. But maybe she will rest a bit easier knowing that he's gone too."

Tanis sighed. "I still can't believe he—she—fooled us for so long."

Joe solemnly nodded his agreement. There were no words to express the sadness they felt for all those who had died on Victoria and in the blackness.

"Hullooo there!" A voice called out from down the path.

"Who could that be?" Tanis started.

Her question was answered a moment later as Ouri came into view, a smile on her face and a large basket in her hands.

"Hi, Ouri," Tanis said and propped herself up. "We weren't really expecting company…"

"Yes, I know, you had decided to wallow today, before the funerals tomorrow, but that's not going to happen."

"I don't know, Ouri…" Tanis began as Joe sat up with a smile.

"Com'on, hon, I think a celebration is just the thing we need."

Tanis turned a raised eyebrow on her husband. "You orchestrated this, didn't you?"

"Yes, he did, and boy am I glad for it," Jessica said as she approached behind Ouri. "I've had days of moping now. I know that if Trist were here she'd be partying. Maybe not a sedate picnic by the beach type of party, but you get the idea."

Tanis acquiesced and Ouri opened her basket, spreading a blanket on the sand and laying out sandwiches, wine and cheese.

Conversation was slow to pick up as everyone sampled the food and became lost in their thoughts.

"OK, even I can admit that this silence won't do," Tanis said. "I'll start." She took a deep breath, collected her thoughts and began.

"I sat in the quarters Trist used awhile back and cried for an hour last night. Maybe longer, I'm not sure. I'm going to miss her a hell of a lot—she really felt like a kindred spirit to me. We joked about growing old together on New Eden, sitting on our front porch in rocking chairs and gossiping about the good ole days. I'll still do that with you, Jessica," Tanis said with a smile to her friend.

"I know you will," Jessica said. "I plan to make it to that front porch, you know. We'll talk about how Trist would have been antsy and stealing the neighbor's silverware in a week.

"I'll always remember that time she and I ran the police academy on the Tara. Those were a crazy two years—I'm still sworn to secrecy about that time at the Blue Star night club."

"I'm going to miss Troy, too," Joe said. "He was a true hero, him and his hot tub."

"To the Victorians who Tom got killed, may they find their way through the stars," Ouri said, her expression sad as she likely thought of bringing the cruisers down over Landfall.

Tanis raised her glass. "To Trist, Troy and all our brothers and sisters—Victorian and Edeners alike—who lost their lives. May they always be remembered and may their names and deeds be remembered forever."

The others raised their glasses and gave the customary response. "We'll remember forever."

They finished their food and Ouri stood and peered down the path.

"Re-enforcements should be coming any minute now."

"What?" Tanis asked.

"For the party, of course."

"What party?" Tanis and Joe asked in unison.

"You told me that when things calmed down to hold a nice impromptu party, so I'm doing it."

"That was a hundred and fifty years ago!" Tanis blurted out.

"I took it as a standing order. It *is* actually my house after all," Ouri said with a wink.

The party lasted long into the night, eventually spilling across the lawns and into the house with hundreds of people in attendance. Tanis learned that celebrations were happening all across the *Intrepid* that night, as the crew gave thanks for their survival and the sacrifice of their comrades.

RECOMPENSE

STELLAR DATE: 3288936 / 09.13.4292 (A7djusted Gregorian)
LOCATION: Landfall, Victoria
REGION: Victorian Space Federation, Kapteyn's Star System

The long parties the night before threw the solemn services on the following day into stark contrast.

The morning had been filled with services on the *Intrepid* and several of the cruisers. Following those, Tanis took a pinnace to Landfall at Katrina's behest.

They had to mend the rift between their peoples and waiting would help nothing.

Tanis listened to Katrina's words, tears filling her eyes. It was the speech the still-grieving widow had planned to give at Markus's funeral. Katrina said as much as she started it and explained that even with all the events of the last week, Markus's vision was still her guiding light. The people of Victoria could achieve great things, but they could not be bound by their past, by their prejudices or petty jealousy.

If anything the speech resonated more now than it would have five days prior.

Katrina stepped down from the dais and Tanis stood, still rehearsing her lines. The words were carefully selected and she knew she had to get it just right in front of this mostly Victorian audience.

"I'm—." She hardly began before a scream interrupted her.

"You killed him! You! You evil bitch!"

The woman's screams broke echoed through the hall and Tanis looked up in surprise.

Sarah stood ten paces from her, the grieving mother's face streaked with tears, her eyes red and swollen.

"You brought all of this on us, if it wasn't for you, my Tom would still be alive! My Peter would still be alive! You're no different than they are, little gods who think they can take what they want!"

Tanis opened her mouth to speak, but no words would come out. The woman before her was old and stooped, in the final decades of her life.

A retort came to mind, but it was wrong and unfair. Tanis had nothing to give that this woman would accept. The fact that Sarah was always angry, always looking for someone to attack and blame, didn't make her words less true.

Any condolence Tanis could give—words from a woman who was in perfect health at over two-hundred years of age; with hundreds of years ahead of her; with the ability to carry dozens of children if she wished—those words would only cause more harm to Sarah.

Sarah, who had tried so hard to naturally carry a child to term, after what the years of exposure to hard radiation around Sirius had done to her body.

Tanis may well have killed Tom herself.

She didn't hear everything else Sarah screamed at her; she *did* feel the spit hit her face before Peter' brothers managed to drag Sarah out of the assembly.

Tanis turned her head and took a moment to clean the spittle off. It took a minute more for her own tears to cease.

No one spoke while she regained her composure, she thought maybe it was because no one knew she could cry. She always had to be strong, to put on a good face and inspire the people who depended on her, but somehow this event, this battle, it was the straw that broke the camel's back.

She just wanted peace.

<*We'll have it,*> Angela said.

<*I sure hope so…OK…I'm ready.*>

Tanis took a second deep breath and gave her speech.

She was told afterward that her words were eloquent and well delivered, but she barely remembered it. All she could recall was the sorrow in Sarah's eyes and the pain she felt at the loss of so many friends.

RELATIVITY

STELLAR DATE: 3293121 / 02.29.4304 (Adjusted Gregorian)
LOCATION: *ISS Intrepid*
REGION: Interstellar space near Kapteyn's Star

"We think it's some sort of undetectable gravity well."

Earnest stood at the head of the bridge conference room's table. Hovering above the table was a complex holographic display showing Kapteyn's Star at the bottom and an elongated tail streaming out from the star.

The *Intrepid* was only a month out from the Kapteyn's system and already a new calamity had befallen them.

For many, the departure from the system had been a bittersweet parting. Over the decades, many families had become intertwined between the two groups. In the end some Edeners stayed behind, while some Victorians joined new families on the colony ship.

They may have wished they hadn't.

"Our best models predict it to be a stream of dark matter. Something that has been hypothesized as stretching out from Kapteyn's in the past due to its extra-galactic orbit. It's currently all but impossible to gauge our vector, but we think we are a hairs-breadth under *c* and still on the correct vector…more or less."

Tanis burst out laughing so hard her body convulsed and tears streamed down her face. Everyone in the room was staring at her, aghast at her response. She took several gasping breaths, attempting to regain her composure.

"I don't see what's so funny," Terrance frowned.

"So…so much time spent being slowed down, held back…" Tanis gulped down a breath. "And now we're going too fast!"

She began laughing again. Beside her Abby started to chuckle and across the table Andrews let out a guffaw. Seconds later the entire group was laughing, slapping backs and generally looking like they'd lost their minds.

<*Should I call a medic?*> Bob asked Angela.

<*No, they need this, if they didn't finally have a reaction like this I'd worry more. Give them a few minutes,*> Angela replied.

As the laughter died down, Tanis managed to wheeze out, "can we…can we throw out an anchor?"

This brought about a new round of chuckles with several other suggestions for slowing the ship being called out. Eventually everyone regained control, and Earnest poured himself a glass of water, drinking it down before finally providing the answer.

"I don't think we'll have to slow down," he said. "I think that when we exit this dark matter accelerator we'll shed our velocity as quickly as we gained it. However, we'll likely shoot past our destination by a fair distance."

"How far?" Captain Andrews asked.

"It's hard to say… light-years at least, maybe hundreds."

Earnest's simple proclamation was met with stunned silence. It could be possible that the *Intrepid* would end up being the furthest ship from Sol, further than any of the FGT ships were known to be.

"Then again, it could be a lot less… or a lot more. It's really hard to tell how fast we're going. The difference between 0.9999*c* and 0.99999*c* is quite profound when it comes to time dilation."

"How can you not tell how fast we're going?" Admiral Sanderson asked.

"At this velocity, all light from the outside universe turns into a tiny pinprick fore and aft of the ship. We aren't even sure if we're in space controlled by special or general relativity or neither."

"So what is our plan?" Tanis asked.

"Go sideways," Earnest replied.

"That doesn't seem like much of a plan," Terrance said. "What if it tears the ship apart?"

Earnest shook his head. "I don't think that will happen. Because we're not *really* traveling this fast, there's no shearing force. Transitioning into regular space should be smooth and simple."

"We should test it," Sanderson said. "I imagine a probe could pop out."

"Indeed. We're actually prepared to do just that, we don't know if we'll be able to get any data from the test, but we should certainly try it first." Earnest waved his hand, and data readouts from a probe in a launch tube came up over the table.

"Bob, if you'd be so kind," he said.

The readout showed the probe launching from the ship's port side. External optics showed it moving into the blackness that surrounded the *Intrepid*. At three hundred kilometers out, the probe vanished.

<*Analyzing data,*> Bob said; everyone was silent for several moments before he continued. <*I believe the probe made it, I have data that showed it slipping outside this gravitational well gradually, not abruptly.*>

"That sure looked abrupt," Terrance shook his head. "I really don't like this; it seems too risky."

"More risky than anything else we've done?" Tanis asked.

"Those things were all calculated. We knew the math and the chances. Here we don't even know what science to use!" Terrance replied.

"I understand your concern," Captain Andrews nodded slowly. "To say there is no risk would be a lie, but there is also considerable risk in staying wherever we are. Is there an end to this special space? Will its properties change? We don't know."

Terrance leaned back in his chair and gave a wan smile. "Well then, what are we waiting for?"

Earnest began to rattle off a list of personnel he would need pulled out of stasis and other tasks which needed to be performed before the maneuver.

Terrance coughed. "That was rhetorical, Earnest."

The maneuver was planned and set to commence in one hour. Tanis decided to go for a walk before returning to the bridge for the event. Thirty minutes later she found herself in the forward lounge she and Joe had discovered all those years ago.

She wished he was here, but they had only brought key personnel out of stasis when the ship slipped into this dark layer. No need to ruin everyone's day with just another crisis.

Tanis leaned back on an acceleration couch and stared at the pinprick of light ahead of her. Somehow she thought all the light of the universe being condensed down to one tiny point would be brighter.

She contemplated watching the exit maneuver from the lounge. With its wide field of view, the stars would likely look amazing as they snapped from the single focal point back to their regular positions.

As she lay on the couch, imagining what the event would look like, a vibration began to build in the deck underneath her.

<Is there a problem?> She asked Bob.

<It seems that this region of space is less consistent than we thought, we may be exiting it now, not when we planned.>

<Should I get to the bridge?>

<I think you should not be up and about right now.>

Tanis calmed her fears and waited, listening to the chatter on the bridge net. She added her thoughts to a few decisions, but by and large there was little advice she could offer.

With no warning the vibrations turned into a lurch and the point of light exploded into a full starscape, bathing the lounge in its light.

It was as amazing as she thought it would be.

"Woohoo it wor—."

Tanis's jubilation was interrupted by a deafening rending sound followed by the scream of oxygen rushing from the room.

<Impact! Get to a pod!> Bob shouted in Tanis's mind.

Tanis leapt to her feet and clawed her way through the torrent of air rushing past her. Her HUD showed a bank of pods in the corridor outside the lounge and she couldn't help calculating the amount of oxygen she would need to make it.

<Don't, just GO!> Angela yelled in her mind.

Tanis pulled herself forward, grabbing anything she could to as she struggled step-by-step. It was becoming easier as less air rushed past her—a silver lining around the dark cloud of an oxygen deprived death.

The artificial gravity cut out—the particle accelerator must have gone offline—and with a final heave, Tanis reached the exit as the far side of the lounge tore away, revealing open space.

She gave the deep black a short glance before signaling the hatch to close behind her.

Now that the sound of rushing air and rending steel was gone, she had a moment to realize how much her entire body ached with cold.

Tanis shook herself back to full consciousness and forced herself to move through the shuddering ship toward the pods.

<What happened?> Tanis asked Angela while still gasping for breath.

Angela filled her mind with the knowledge that something the size of a small stone hit the ship in the moments before Bob could get the shielding back up. It had been traveling at near-relativistic speeds and impacted the bow like a bomb.

The sound of her heartbeat was pounding in her ears as she managed to pull herself into a pod and collapsed in its webbing.

Her internal monitoring showed burst blood vessels throughout her body, and her eyes felt like someone had tried to inflate them. She felt a final lurch and then the pod stilled beneath her.

<By the way, I don't know if you realized it, but you hit the eject when you closed the hatch on this thing,> Angela said. *<Now they're going to have to come find us.>*

"Sorry, I don't think so well with no oxygen in my brain, where did we pop back out?"

Angela didn't respond right away and Tanis activated a hard-console beside her seat.

"The computer must have been damaged, it can't tell where we are," she said after staring at the scan for a minute.

<I don't think the computer is damaged, I think we are lost. None of these stars look right…well some do, but I can't triangulate anywhere that matches where they would put us.>

Tanis brought up comm to hail the *Intrepid* for pickup and to see if the colony ship knew where they were.

"I'm not getting any response," Tanis said after a minute.

<I think I know why…I can't find them.>

Tanis felt panic creep in as she studied the meager scan the escape pod was able to provide.

"Well, we're close to a star, that's something, and I'm picking up radio signals from it."

<I see that too. Based on the star's spectra…no…>

"What is it, Angela?"

<I think this is 58 Eridani.>

"Well that's goo—. Wait, 58 not 82?" 58 Eridani was twenty-four light years further out than 82 Eridani, the star the colonists had named New Eden.

Twice as far from Sol as their original destination.

<Yes, it's definitely 58 Eridani, and there are radio signals, lots of them; the system is inhabited.>

"I see something on scan, it looks like it might be a ship," Tanis said, bringing up data and optical views. "Wait, this is wrong too, its ion trail shows antimatter and fusions drives, but the ship's too small."

<It just disappeared,> Angela interjected. *<I didn't see any acceleration.>*

"There it is, it came back…a lot closer, damn it's gone again."

Angela highlighted a point on the scan map. *<There it is, closer again.>*

"What the hell is going on?" Tanis almost yelled.

Her question was punctuated by a loud clang as something grappled the pod.

<It's here, it has us!>

It was not often that Angela's mental tone contained fear, but it certainly did now. Tanis was far from calm herself. Nothing made any sense, where was the *Intrepid,* how was 58 Eridani inhabited and how did a ship hop through space like this one had.

Optical cameras showed the pod being pulled into a small cargo bay and that was the last Tanis saw.

In the small bridge of the scout and salvage ship two men grinned at each other.

"Stasis field has the whole pod. This is going to be a good sell. That thing is from a colony ship, something called the *Intrepid,*" the first said. "I don't have anything on scan, but judging by the tech on the pod she's going to have some advanced tech."

"Thank god, we can finally cover what we owe Padre and get free and clear," replied the second.

"Well let's get a move on, then."

The pilot nodded before he activated his console and plotted a course.

"Engaging FTL drive."

THANK YOU

For more about your favorite characters and the world of Outsystem, visit www.aeon14.com for character bios, short stories and information about the Aeon 14 series.

If you've enjoyed reading Outsystem, a review on Amazon.com or goodreads.com would be greatly appreciated.

To get the latest news and access to free novellas and short stories, sign up on the Aeon 14 mailing list: http://eepurl.com/b2GQj9

M. D. Cooper

For more of the Aeon 14 universe, check out book 4 of the Intrepid Saga:

DESTINY LOST

Read on for the appendices and an excerpt from **Destiny Lost**

An excerpt from book 4, *Destiny Lost*…

AN UNEXPECTED CARGO

STELLAR DATE: 4981760 / 06.31.8927 (Adjusted Gregorian)
LOCATION: Trio Prime Station
REGION: Trio System, Silstrand Combine

4,623 years after the **Intrepid** *departed from the Kapteyn's system.*

Sera slammed the shooter down with a triumphant grin and watched with reddened eyes as the man from Thoria reached for his next glass. Around them, the crowd chanted their names as money changed hands.

Her opponent downed his drink and tossed the glass onto the table where it rolled against the two-dozen empty shooters between them. With a wave of his hand and an unappealing grin, he indicated that the floor was hers.

She took a deep breath to steady herself, chanting an internal mantra of *just one more, just one more.* The act of raising her arm caused Sera to sway in her seat, the smell of bodies pressed close around not helping her deepening nausea.

The Thorian saw her hesitation and his grin grew wider.

"Ready to give up?" he slurred, his putrid breath washing over her.

Sera didn't reply, only fixed him with a steely glare—at least she hoped it was a steely glare—and grasped the glass in her fist, throwing it back without further hesitation.

The alcohol washed down her throat like fire, and her tongue felt swollen in its wake. If she didn't know better, she'd assume the bartender had opened a bottle of stiffer drink.

She set the glass down and took slow, deep breaths, using all her concentration to keep the fire in her stomach and veins under control.

The Thorian grunted and stared at the row of shots before him—likely deciding which one to pick up. Finally selecting his drink, he grabbed it with a swift flourish and raised it high to throw it back.

In his current state, the gesture failed miserably and the drink splashed across his face. His features crumpled in confusion and his arms rotated slowly as he slid sideways out of his chair to the floor.

No one attempted to catch him and the man's head hit the deck plate with a solid crack.

Cheers and grumbles erupted around her as Sera was declared the winner. The victors were paid out, and the losers turned to the bar for another drink. In the midst of the post-contest exchange, one voice rose above the others.

A short, but well built man in a dirty shipsuit pushed to the front of the crowd.

"Cheater! She had to cheat, there's no way that waif could drink Greg under the table!" He slammed his hands on the table, bent over, his face inches from Sera's. "You used nano to clear the alcohol from your bloodstream."

Most people had some of the tiny nano-machines in their body, it was nearly impossible not to; they were almost as common as bacteria. A person's nano was controlled by their internal computer or AI—if you had the money or influence to hire one. Sera's nano could clear her bloodstream with ease—though that wasn't a fact she advertised. It took a lot of nano to filter that much booze over such a short period; a lot more than a simple freighter captain should possess.

Sera worked her mouth for a moment, making sure it would respond the way she wanted it to. "I did not. Have the bartender do a check." The words were slurred, but understandable.

Bartenders on Coburn Station were not allowed to let their patrons to get too drunk—an ordinance they rarely enforced. They had scanners on hand that could do a blood-alcohol level check and determine, based on that person's size and metabolic rate, if they were too inebriated to have another round.

The bartender had already stepped into the crowd, eager to do whatever it took to avoid a fight on his shift. He pressed the scanner against Sera's wrist and took samples of her blood for the reading.

"She's pissed," he said as he straightened. "Consistent with the amount and time she's been slugging them back." Smirking, he turned back to the bar. "Those shooters are only a third of what she's had tonight too."

The winners cheered all the louder and the losers ceased their grumbling. Everyone knew that bartenders altered their scanners, so they could give people more liquor than they should. If it said she was drunk, then she should be totally pissed.

<*One of these days, the losers aren't going to care what the scan says and take their satisfaction out of your hide,*> Helen admonished in Sera's mind.

Sera sent her internal AI a mental shrug. Helen didn't like it when Sera drank; she claimed it upset the chemical balance of Sera's body in a way that made the AI feel weird. Sera wasn't sure how that was possible, not that would change her behavior. She liked the feeling of chemical imbalance.

<*My hide's been through worse.*>

<*I know; I've been there each time. Doesn't mean I want a repeat. You know how disconcerting I find it when you get hurt that badly.*>

Helen could be annoying at times with her mothering, but Sera knew that her AI's concern was genuine. Pulling her thoughts from the familiar debate, Sera looked around the bar.

To smooth things over, the winners were buying the losers a round. Sera had put a hundred SIL credits down on herself and collected three hundred back. The odds had been stacked nicely against her.

Betting was illegal in Silstrand Alliance space, so money always changed hands in cash. The prohibition didn't seem to diminish the illegal activity; it just meant no one had to pay taxes on their winnings. Sera thought about that for a minute. Maybe that was why it was illegal; officials probably liked to gamble tax free too.

Stuffing the hard money into an inside pocket on her leather jacket she rose slowly; nearly teetering over at the last moment. A steady hand appeared under her elbow and Sera turned to see the dark smiling face of Cargo.

"Good haul on that, Captain," he guided her out of the bar and into the bustling main corridor of the station's promenade. "I made a couple hundred credits on your drinking skill."

"It's good to be useful," Sera slurred, as Cargo led her toward a small coffee shop which was renowned for its after-drunk-sober-up brew. Once inside, Sera ordered two of their strongest and let Cargo wait at the counter for the order. Her leather clothing squeaked nosily as she collapsed into a chair. Cursing the café's bright lights, she leaned back with a hand over her eyes, praying for a power outage.

<*You're not masking the squeak. What gives?*> Sera asked her AI.

<*It's what you get for drinking. I can't deal with two organic peculiarities at once. If you drink, I won't mask your clothing's noise. Take your pick.*> Helen was really on the warpath, determined to make Sera suffer. Thank god Cargo had shown up.

Her first mate knew she liked to get one last round in at a bar before they left a station—okay, maybe more than just *a* round. He often would find her and bring her back to the ship before she was too far gone.

Sera splayed her fingers and looked through them to see Cargo returning with an insufferable grin on his face. He had a coffee for himself and two of the sober-up drinks for her. He set them on the table and pushed them toward her, his smile widening.

"I bet those are going to taste horrible."

Sera stuck her tongue out as she leaned forward to pick one up. "Prolly."

"You should have let me know you were gonna get into another drinking contest," Cargo said and took a drink of his own beverage. "I would have had more cash on hand and made a larger wager."

"I'm sorry I didn't think to let you know so you could sate your gambling needs," Sera said while delivering another sour look.

"My gambling habit doesn't have the unpleasant side effects of your station drinking binges."

Sera eyed him blearily over the rim of her cup. "What side effects are those?"

"The first day of any trip. You're not exactly sunshine and roses the day after a binge."

"Am I ever?"

Cargo paused, appearing to ponder the statement with great cogitation.

Her mind echoed with the light watery sound of Helen laughing at Cargo's pause. Sera scowled and swatted at him. "Thanks!"

He gestured with a nonchalant wave toward the second cup, indicating she get to it. Sera had already used her nano to clear most of the alcohol from her bloodstream and contain it for the next time she visited the head. However, Cargo didn't know she could do that and she needed to keep up appearances.

Sera raised the cup to her lips and took a long pull of the vile liquid anyway. She didn't want to seem ungrateful. After downing it, she leaned back in her chair, feeling much steadier than when she first sat down.

"All things considered, it's not a bad bit of extra credit to finish the visit with," She said and patted her pocket.

Cargo grunted, "one day you'll run out of people who haven't seen you win a drinking contest and then what will you do for fun?"

"Dunno, I guess I'll have to find a new way to fleece the common man."

Cargo laughed heartily in response.

Several minutes later—with Sera moving under her own power—they made their way down the promenade and onto the commercial dock front. There was just as much traffic here, but of a different sort. Cargo transports trundled down the deck-plate and service trucks were everywhere, delivering supplies or repair equipment.

Sabrina was in berth seven twenty-four Station South. Long before she could see the ship around the curve of the docks, she could hear Thompson's voice berating some poor cargo handlers. The echoing shouts eventually resolved into words and Sera hid a smile behind her hand as they approached.

"You lazy dolts, can't you even lift a crate? I've seen hundred-year-old bots do a better job than you oafs. If you drop one more container, I'll take it out of your scrawny, mal-nourished hides. Now get to it, I don't have all day."

Thompson was a large blonde man who had been her supercargo for over six years. To avoid confusion with Cargo, they just called him the Super. He wasn't a very outgoing man, mostly taken to brooding and stumping about the ship, but his attention to detail made him a good crewmember. Combined with his size and skill with a pulse rifle, that made him the right sort of super for *Sabrina*.

"How's the last shipment?" Sera asked when she and Cargo reached the ship.

"Fine if these morons can manage to hold onto an effing handle." Thompson tossed the two dockworkers a contemptuous glare. "Don't know why they insist on using humans for this. Either way, we'll be loaded up with plenty of time to spare, don't worry, Captain."

"Good to hear," Cargo said. "Send the final docs up to me on the bridge when you're done."

Thompson nodded and turned back to the handlers as another crate slipped from their grasp. "God's great black space! What is *wrong* with you two, is this your first day on the job? I told you I was going to take it out of your hide and now I am. Which one of you wants to get your ear ripped off?"

"Somehow I don't think that is helping them with their work," Cargo laughed.

"Yeah, but I bet it makes him feel a lot better."

"I'll see you later, Captain; I've got to wash the smell of that bar you were in off me before my shift starts."

Sera took a deep breath. "Dunno, I kind of like that malty musk on you."

"In that case I'm gonna take an even longer shower," Cargo laughed and walked onto the ship. Sera stuck her tongue out at him and walked over to an inspection port to admire the sleek lines of her girl.

Sabrina was not a regular boxy freight hauler, having started her life as a pleasure yacht. Her previous owner had fallen on hard times lost possession of the ship in an outer system. *Sabrina* had needed repairs, and the local shipyard, where she had been in storage for owed taxes, didn't have the funds to make them. So she sat for forty years before Sera found her. With a hundred years of service before being impounded, she was getting on, but that didn't diminish the impact Sera felt when she first laid eyes on the ship.

There was an influential man who owed Sera a favor or two and she got him to give her the money to buy the ship and furnish it with the necessary repairs. The finer aspects of the yacht's interior had been stripped out long before Sera saw *Sabrina,* but it was the size of the vessel and the engines that mattered. This ship had the room to haul cargo and the power to do so quickly. There were some other modifications that had been made, but like her advanced nano, Sera didn't advertise those.

She noted with approval that the damage they had suffered on their last run had been repaired. They had been parked in a planetary ring, moving along with the flow of the rocks and ice, when a stray rock had damaged the port sensor array and left a long rent across a goodly portion of the ship. However, the profit from the questionable cargo, which had put them there in the first place, more than paid for the repairs.

Thompson let loose some final curses as the dockworkers finished loading the last crate. She turned to watch with a smile; the dockworkers were visibly trembling as they got on their cart and drove off.

Sera returned to viewing her ship. She enjoyed these final quiet moments alone before going on board and filling out departure docs; these last few minutes when it was just her, *Sabrina's* sleek hull, and the call of empty space. She could forget her past, previous failures. Here she was a good captain, *Sabrina* was prosperous, and she had a good crew.

Her reverie was interrupted by a stinging slap on her butt and Sera turned to see her pilot, Cheeky, standing behind her. She wore a coy smile and her hands were resting on tilted hips.

"One day I'll get you to give me some of that luvin' you lavish on *Sabrina,*" Cheeky said.

"One day I'll get you neutered and save us all a lot of hassle." Sera rubbed her stinging butt; Cheeky could really deliver a good slap. She found herself becoming aroused as she looked at her pilot.

Cheeky was an attractive woman who wore as little clothing as local law or custom would allow. On Coburn that meant she wore little more than three triangles of cloth, her shoes and a purse.

Sera shook her head to clear her mind. Cheeky also had altered glands that could put out much higher levels of pheromones than any human should be allowed to. "Make sure you shut that off and take a long shower, you know what happened last time your love smell filtered through the ship."

"We all had a good time." Cheeky wiggled her hips suggestively and blew her captain a kiss as she walked up the ramp. From behind, it was obvious why Cheeky had the name she did. Sera found herself wondering if it was a conscious effort to walk like that or if the woman had resorted to surgery.

Following her pilot onto the ship, Sera's internal AI flashed a notification that they had made a secure connection to the ship's private net. Sera checked the ship's general status and greeted its AI.

<*Good evening sweetie, how are you holding together?*> Sera asked *Sabrina.*

<*Well enough, though I take offense to the question. How else would I be holding together?*> The ship's mental tone conveyed annoyance.

Sabrina had been in a strange mood as of late. Sera chose to ignore the reply and smiled up at the nearest observation camera as Helen passed her authentication token to the bridge's net. Sera checked in, finding Cargo already working on departure paperwork; he must have decided to skip the shower.

<*Station given us our departure time yet?*>

<*0900 ship time tomorrow.*> His mental tone was relaxed. He enjoyed the little details of running the ship. Sera preferred to sit in her Captain's chair and give orders.

<*Everything delivered and stowed?*>

She could imagine him flipping through the plas sheets, checking them against the records logged in their databases, before he answered. Cargo hated making mistakes.

<*Just one package yet,*> there was a significant pause, Sera could feel his mental discomfort even over the net. <*It's from one of Kade's people here.*>

<*Kade? Why didn't I know about this?*> Sera asked Cargo and Helen.

<*It came on the list when we were out.*> Helen supplied.

Cargo muttered something rude and the bridge's net flashed with an image of Cargo's avatar doing something very unpleasant to a representation of Kade. <*At least we're delivering it at the regular drop point with the rest of his stuff; there's no extra trip.*>

The regular drop point was an out of the way FTL jump point that Kade's people used for trading with other ships. Kade's people being a pirate organization known as The Mark. Most of their people and ships were somewhat less than welcome at the more reputable stations, such as Coburn.

<*They never can schedule things ahead of time,*> Sera sighed.

<*They're not exactly an "ahead of time" sort of organization.*>

Sera told Cargo she'd be making the rounds and passed the active monitoring of the bridge's net to Helen.

When *Sabrina* had been a private yacht the main deck was where the owners presumably threw their parties and spent most of their time. Now it was the freight deck. The cargo hatch was on the port side, and from there Sera walked into the main corridor, which ran from the bow to the stern engine shielding. The various freight holds were located off this corridor. Some had normal air and gravity, some were refrigerated and some had low, or even no gravity.

Also along the corridor were the lifts and ladders to the other decks. Sera walked towards the bow of the ship and slid into one of the vertical ladder shafts, which ran through all the decks. From there she opened an access hatch to a maintenance tube. Inside the hatch were some knee and shoulder pads that she slipped on; it wouldn't do to scuff her leather.

The tube ended in a sealed inspection port. Sera opened it and peered out at the newly installed sensor equipment. The workmanship looked good. Everything was straight and attached firmly. The exterior indicators all showed green.

Beyond the array, Sera could see the space elevator that carried cargo and people between the surface and the station. Seeing it reminded her how far humanity had fallen from the glory it once held.

Millennia ago, when humanity had first set out to cross the stars, they had no faster than light technology. Interstellar travel was made possible only by utilizing massive fuel scoops. Ships had vast electrostatic funnels that spread for kilometers in front of them and allowed the gathering and compression of interstellar heavy hydrogen. The hydrogen, typically Deuterium and Tritium, was burned in nuclear fusion reactors to produce the thrust that pushed the ships between the stars.

Journeys between the stars took decades, or even centuries.

With the considerable effort and expense required to get to even the nearest stars, humanity strove to make the most of all available resources. Technology and engineering made impressive advances as societies demanded better use of raw materials.

The space elevator stretching from Coburn Station down to Trio was an example of the different sort of technology humans used to have. In present times, few worlds could afford to build elevators to their space stations. The materials were just too expensive and the process took too long. A ship's grav drive was more efficient in the short term. However, over centuries of use, the elevator would use much less power to achieve the same volume of transport. It was another example of the long-term approach that people used to take as opposed to the current mindset, which was decidedly shortsighted.

It was a shift created by the advent of FTL.

People had always suspected—at least once the significance of 299,792,458 meters per second was known—that some method of exceeding the speed of light was possible. Many theories of wormholes, space-time folding, alternate realities, and slipstreams were put forward and attempted. In the end, the workable form of faster than light travel encapsulated many of the ideas behind some of those theories, though it turned out to be much harder to harness than originally hoped.

Before FTL, each star system was isolated from the rest of humanity, but once a trip between two stars was reduced to a matter of weeks and not centuries, everything changed. Traveling to an uninhabited star to mine asteroids was something that could be easily achieved, and people's attitude toward conservation and efficiency disappeared within a century.

Helen injected a long yawn into Sera's thoughts. <*Enough already. We get it, you yearn for the good old days.*>

<*I don't really miss the days…just wish people could appreciate the way things used to be.*>

Helen didn't agree. <*You just miss your people. This isn't your world and you know it.*>

<*It is now; it has to be.*>

Helen didn't respond. It was an old conversation, one they performed out of habit more than a real expectation of change.

She walked through the freight deck's main corridor, poking her head into various holds, ensuring that everything was secure and ready for departure. The familiar smell of deck cleaner and oil wafted past and an unbidden memory of her first weeks on the ship came back.

She and Flaherty had spent many a day hauling equipment through these halls and shafts back when they were first refitting *Sabrina*. It had been long days and longer nights, but she was proud of what they had built.

Helen flashed the date of her memory over her vision and she was surprised to see that it had been just over ten years ago. Somewhere in the last few months, she had passed her ten-year anniversary with *Sabrina* without marking the occasion. No wonder the ship had been a bit snippy of late.

Sera chided Helen for not reminding her of the occasion, nor for clueing her in on the cause of *Sabrina's* poor temper.

<*I was unaware you were interested in marking anniversaries with AI.*> Helen was unrepentant.

<*What are you talking about?*> Sera replied. <*We always celebrate our anniversary.*>

Helen inserted the emotion of mild surprise, followed by a pout into Sera's mind. <*I thought that was just for me*>

Sera laughed and her avatar stuck her tongue out at Helen. <*Don't give me that, I'm not some little girl that you can twist around your ephemeral finger anymore.*>

Helen didn't respond, and Sera let out a long sigh. For being one of the most advanced AI in the Inner Stars, Helen could certainly be childish.

<*Sometimes I think Sabrina is rubbing off on you,*> Sera said to her one-time mentor and guardian.

<*I resent that,*> Helen retorted. <*Just because the ship's AI can't deal with the fact that I am her superior in every way doesn't mean I have to dumb it down.*>

<*You're superior to most planet administration AI we run into, but you don't go out of your way to make them feel inferior,*> Sera responded, mildly surprised to be the one to advocate maturity in their relationship.

<*Maybe I could be more accommodating for our dear Sabrina,*> Helen eventually responded.

<*Glad to hear it. Now I have to figure out how to make it up to her,*> Sera said.

<*Make what up?*> Helen asked innocently and Sera let out an audible scream.

She completed her review of the freight deck and took the aft ladder shaft up to the crew deck.

When she first bought *Sabrina,* the ship had lifts for reaching each deck, but Sera had removed all but one of the conveniences. Shafts were faster and still worked when the ship was under fire and conserving energy.

<Nothing to do with how you like to climb the ladders in front of the men on the ship,> Helen suggested.

<I do it to Cheeky too.> Sera smiled to herself as she stepped onto the crew deck.

<Funny, I thought you preferred it when she did it to you.>

The ladder was across from the galley and she stepped in to find Thompson and Flaherty eating their supper. She saw that it was nearing the end of second shift; most of the crew would be calling it a night soon.

"Evening Captain." Thompson said around a mouthful of his sandwich. Flaherty looked at her, nodded, and went back to his meal.

"Hey guys," Sera smiled at them as she poured a cup of coffee and hunted for fresh cream.

Thompson and Flaherty made an effective and efficient team when it came to managing the ship's cargo. Neither of them talked much and managed to communicate just about everything with grunts and gestures. They didn't even use the Link to talk—Sera had checked the logs.

Sera doctored her coffee up just the way she liked and bid them goodnight before taking the corridor to the bow, then climbing the ladder that led to the top deck. This was the smallest deck on the ship, containing only the bridge forward and a small observation lounge aft. The lounge had a magnificent view of the light flare from the engines when they were under heavy thrust and Sera had often sat back there, gazing out at it as the ship cruised through space.

Cargo was still on the bridge, readying the reports Sera had to sign before they could depart. Cheeky was also at her console, having added a tight halter top and tiny skirt to her ensemble. She yawned and stretched as she stood.

"You just had to make a final course alteration right before bed," She complained. "I had to plot it out and re-file with system traffic control."

"Sorry about that, I didn't think you'd already filed the report," Sera apologized.

"When else was I going to do it, when I was sleeping?"

Cargo laughed. "I thought you had gotten all of your 'sleeping' in on your shore leave.

Cheeky stuck her tongue out at the man. "Jealous."

Cargo couldn't help it as his eyes strayed down to the bold black print across Cheeky's chest. It read 'Got Milk?' He sighed wistfully. "I might be."

"Really?" Cheeky asked.

"No, not really," Cargo grinned.

"You're such a tease," Cheeky said as she turned and left the bridge.

"I'm a tease?" He murmured softly as she left.

"You are, you know," Sera said.

"How so? I don't flirt, I just do my job."

"Exactly!" Sera smiled as she shuffled the plas she had to sign into order. "You're totally unflappable. It's the ultimate come-on."

"I'm going to start the pre-warm-up checklist so things'll be ready in the morning."

"See! Always back to business with you."

"Do you want to do it?" Cargo turned, half rising out of his chair.

"Heck no, I've been up for thirty hours already."

Cargo nodded and sat back down.

Coburn, like many stations, required a full warm-up and test of all ship systems before undocking. The warm-up had to take place four hours before departure and Cargo was taking the third watch to run the sequence at oh five-hundred.

She turned to leave the bridge when Nance, the ship's bio, appeared in her mind.

<I just wanted to let you know, take short showers for the next while—I know how you like to luxuriate for an hour or more.>

Even though she was looking at Nance's mental avatar, the bio-engineer still wore a thick, tight hazsuit. Where Cheeky showed every inch of skin she could manage, Nance was the opposite, rarely showing any skin at all—even virtually.

<What's up?> Sera asked. *<I have the stink of a hundred drunks to wash off.>*

The bio scowled. *<Well, let's just say that you don't want to come down to environmental until I clean up. The regulator on tank nine malfunctioned and a line blew. Contaminated all sorts of shit with…well…shit.>*

<Was it that one you bought at Rattlescar?> Sera asked.

<Yeah, I knew I shouldn't have, but it was such a good deal,> the bio replied.

<Ripped off at Rattlescar again. You should know better.>

Nance's avatar nodded sullenly and Sera laughed. *<Well, I'll let you get to it. Can I at least have ten minutes?>*

Nance nodded. *<Yes, but a second over and I'm switching it to full cold.>*

<Is that any way to treat your captain?>

<Do ***you*** *want to come down here and clean up?>* Nance retorted.

<OK, OK, ten minutes, got it.>

Nance disappeared from her vision as Sera slid down the ladder to the third deck. She walked quietly past the crew cabin doors to her quarters at the end of the corridor. She palmed the door open with a yawn and entered her outer office where she handled the ship's business.

It was the standard utilitarian sort expected of a captain, her various certifications hung on the wall and a large oak desk dominated the small space. She laid the departure plas sheets on its surface and pulled up holo of each one. This was the part about captaining a starship she liked least. She was near finishing up and getting ready to peel off her leather when Cargo called her over the Link.

<Still up, Captain?>

<Barely>

<Hate to bother you with this, but you're the only other one awake, Kade's boys are down at the hatch with that last shipment.>

Despite his words, Cargo's tone didn't carry any apology.

Grumbling that she should have told Thompson to have himself or Flaherty wait up for it, she pulled her jacket back on and slid down the ladders to the freight deck. At the hold's opening to the station dock, two men were waiting with a four by four foot crate on a gravity pad. They were looking nervous and just a bit twitchy. Either they had some bad drugs in their systems or Kade was foisting something pretty damn dangerous on her.

One of the men spoke up as soon as he spotted her.

"Permission to come aboard?" he asked.

Sera granted it and the two men all but ran onto the ship, and moved out of direct sight from dock traffic, the cargo container following them on its float.

"So what does The Mark have for me today, boys?" Sera asked, none too pleased about the late hour or the obviously illegal contents of the crate. "What am I sticking my neck out for this time?"

Most cargo The Mark had her run was just semi-illegal. Either OK in the system she where was picking up or delivering to, just not both; or some stopping point along the way. There also had been the odd shipment that was illegal no matter where they were; this one had that feel.

The man who had asked permission to board grinned in what he probably thought was a winning fashion. It really wasn't. "S'nothing to worry about, just a little something that Kade wants."

"I don't care about that," Sera said as she reached over and snatched the bill of lading from him. "I care what *this* says it is." Scanning the pad, she found that the crate purported to contain a prize-racing hound in a holo sim. The dog thought he was in a regular kennel with other dogs for companionship and humans feeding him. The reality was just a crate with a feeding system, but he wouldn't know the difference and would be better for it.

"That really what's in there?" Sera didn't bother to hide her skepticism.

"Yeah, the dog's not as special as who used to own it." The man grinned again and Sera held up her hand.

"Yeah, sure. I really don't want to know more." She signed off on the delivery. "Any need to open it and check it out?"

The men went rigid and hastily assured her that the dog would be fine and there was no need to check it out. That clinched it for Sera, she would definitely have to check this cargo out once she was underway. If it had any type of tamper seal, she'd make up some excuse for it later.

Once it was secured in the fore port hold she informed Cargo that the delivery had been made and stowed. Then she closed the main cargo hatch and the auxiliary personnel port. Cargo confirmed the seal from the bridge and checked it off the pre-warm-up list.

<Get some rest, Captain, gonna be a long day tomorrow,> Cargo advised.

<Cargo! Now you've gone and jinxed it!>

APENDICES

This is not a complete glossary. For a more exhaustive list of people, places, terms, timeline, and encyclopedic entries, visit www.aeon14.com

TERMS & TECHNOLOGY

AI (SAI, NSAI) – AI is an acronym for Artificial Intelligence. AI are often also referred to as non-organic intelligence. They are broken up into two sub-groups: Sentient AI and Non-Sentient AI.

c – Represented as a lower case c in italics, this symbol stands for the speed of light and means constant. The speed of light in a vacuum is constant at 670,616,629 miles per hour. Ships rate their speed as a decimal value of c with c being 1. Thus a ship traveling at half the speed of light will be said to be traveling at 0.50 c.

CFT Shields – Carbon Fiber nano-Tube shields are created from carbon nano-tubes. These tubes are incredibly strong and can also be enhanced to absorb laser energy fire and disperse it.

ChoSec – The Callisto Orbital Habitat has a security force that is larger than the TSF in size due to the need to police over three trillion humans. It is quasi-military and provides both internal as well as external security to the Cho.

CO – This is an abbreviation meaning commanding officer. It is common in all branches of the military.

Cryostasis (cryogenics) – See also, 'stasis'.

Older methods of slowing down organic aging and decay involve cryogenically freezing the organism (usually a human) through a variety of methods. The person would then be thawed through a careful process when they were awakened.

Cryostasis is risky and has a higher failure rate, but one that makes few people consider it as an option. When true stasis was discovered, it became the de-facto method of slowing organic decay over long periods.

D2 (Deuterium) – D2 (2H) is an isotope of hydrogen where the nucleus of the atom is made up of one proton and one neutron as opposed to a single proton in regular hydrogen (protium). Deuterium is naturally occurring and is found in the oceans of planets with water and is also created by fusion in stars and brown dwarf sub stars. D2 is a stable isotope that does not decay.

Downworlder – Name the spacer Victorians use for colonists on Victoria and Tara.

Edener – Name the Victorians use for the crew and colony members of the *Intrepid.*

Electrostatic shields/fields – Not to be confused with a faraday cage, electrostatic shield's technical name is static electric stasis field. By running a conductive grid of electrons through the air and holding it in place with a stasis field the shield can be tuned to hold back oxygen, but allow solid objects to pass through, or to block solid objects. Fields are used in objects such as ramscoops and energy conduits.

Modified versions also see use as ship's shields where they are used to bleed off energy from beam weapons, or slow the impact of kinetic weapons.

EMF – Electro Magnetic Fields are given off by any device using electricity that is not heavily shielded. Using sensitive equipment, it is possible to tell what type of equipment is being used, and where it is by its EMF signature. In warfare it is one of the primary ways to locate an enemy's position.

EMP – Electro Magnetic Pulses are waves of electromagnetic energy that can disable or destroy electronic equipment. Because so many people have electronic components in their bodies, or share their minds with AI, they are susceptible to extreme damage from an EMP. Ensuring that human/machine interfaces are hardened against EMPs is of paramount importance.

FGT – The Future Generation Terraformers is a program started in 2352 with the purpose of terraforming worlds in advance of colony ships being sent to the worlds. Because terraforming of a world could take hundreds of years the FGT ships arrive and begin the process.

Once the world(s) being terraformed reached stage 3, a message was sent back to the Sol system with an 'open' date for the world(s) being terraformed. The GSS then handles the colony assignment.

A decade after the *Destiny Ascendant* left the Sol system in 3728 the FGT program was discontinued by the SolGov, making it the last FGT ship to leave. Because the FGT ships are all self-sustaining none of them came home after the program was discontinued—most of the ship's crews had spent generations in space and had no reason to return to Sol.

After the discontinuation FGT ships continued on their primary mission of terraforming worlds, but only communicated with the GSS and only when they had worlds completed.

Fireteam – Is the smallest combat grouping of soldiers. In the TSF Marines (like the USMC) it contains four soldiers; the team leader (often doubles as the grenadier), the rifleman (acts as a scout for the team), automatic rifleman (carries a larger, fully automatic weapon), the assistant automatic rifleman (carries additional ammo).

Fission – Fission is a nuclear reaction where an atom is split apart. Fission reactions are simple to achieve with heavier, unstable elements such as Uranium or Plutonium. In closed systems with extreme heat and pressure it is possible to split atoms of much more stable elements, such as Helium. Fission of heavier elements typically produces less power and far more waste matter and radiation than Fusion.

FTL (Faster Than Light) – Refers to any mode of travel where a ship or object is able to travel faster than the speed of light (c). According to Einstein's theory of Special Relativity nothing can travel faster than the speed of light. As of the year 4123 no technology has been devised to move a physical object faster than the speed of light.

Fusion – Fusion is a nuclear reaction where atoms of one type (Hydrogen for example) are fused into atoms of another type (Helium in the case of Hydrogen fusion). Fusion was first discovered and tested in the H-Bombs (Hydrogen bombs) of the twentieth century. Fusion reactors are also used as the most common source of ship power from roughly the twenty fourth century on.

g **(gee, gees, g-force)** – Represented as a lower case g in italics, this symbol stands for gravity. On earth, at sea-level, the human body experiences 1*g*. A human sitting in a wheeled dragster race-car will achieve 4.2*g*s of horizontal g-force. Arial fighter jets will impose g-forces of 7-12*g*s on their pilots. Humans will often lose consciousness around 10*g*s. Unmodified humans will suffer serious injury or death at over 50*g*s. Starships will often impose burns as high as 20*g*s and provide special couches or beds for their passengers during such maneuvers. Modified starfighter pilots can withstand g-forces as high as 70*g*s.

Graviton – These are small massless particles that are emitted from objects with large mass, or by special generators capable of creating them without large masses. There are also negatively charged gravitons which push instead of pull. These are used in shielding systems in the form of Gravitational Waves. The *GSS Intrepid* uses a new system of channeled gravitons to create the artificial gravity in the crew areas of the ship.

GSS – The Generational Space Service is a quasi-federal organization that handles the assignment of colony worlds. In some cases, it also handles the construction of the colony ships.

After the discontinuation of federal support and funding for the FGT project in 3738, the GSS became self-funded, by charging for the right to gain access to a colony world. While SolGov no longer funded the GSS the government supported the GSS's position and passed law ensuring that all colony assignment continued through the GSS.

Helium-3 – This is a stable, non-radioactive isotope of Helium, produced by T3 Hydrogen decay, and is used in nuclear fusion reactors. The nucleus of the Helium-3 atom contains two protons, but only one neutron as opposed to the two neutrons in regular Helium. Helium-3 Can also be created by nuclear reactions that create Lithium-4 which decays into Helium-3.

HUD – Stands for Heads Up Display. It refers to any type of display where information about surroundings and other data is directly overlaid on a person's vision.

Hyperion Accords – These accords were drafted by Tanis and signed by the *Intrepid* colony leaders and the *Hyperion* leadership. The accords outlined the cooperative governments, regions of ownership and slow transfer of technology and power that was to take place in the Kapteyn's Star system.

Link – Refers to an internal connection to computer networks. This connection is inside of a person and directly connects their brain to what is essentially the Internet in the fourth millennia. Methods of accessing the Link vary between retinal overlays to direct mental insertion of data.

Luminescent Society – The formal name of the aristocratic ruling class of the Sirius system. Members of the Luminescent Society are referred to as Luminescents or Lumins.

Maglev – A shorthand term for magnetic levitation. First used commercially in 1984, most modern public transportation uses maglev to move vehicles without the friction caused by axles, rails and wheels. The magnetic field is used to both support the vehicle and accelerate it. The acceleration and braking is provided by linear induction motors which act on the magnetic field provided by the maglev 'rail'. Maglev trains can achieve speeds of over one thousand kilometers per hour with very smooth and even acceleration.

MarSec (MSF) – The Marsian Security Force is a quasi-military organization that has its own small space force as well as ground forces and police-type security. They also make up the federal police force for the Mars Protectorate.

MBH – Miniature Black Holes are used to power artificial gravity systems. The black holes are spun to increase their mass which creates gravitational waves (not to be confused with gravity waves). GE is the main manufacturer of MBH's.

On the *Intrepid* MBHs are used in areas where the gravitational field of the main particle accelerator does not create artificial gravity. MBHs have the advantage of being able to be "spun down" so that their mass does not have to be taken into account when accelerating.

MDC (molecular decoupler) – These devices are uses to break molecules bonds to one another. This technology was first discovered in the early nineteenth century—by running electric current through water, William Nicholson was able to break water into its hydrogen and oxygen components. Over the following centuries this process was used to discover new elements such as potassium and sodium. When mankind began to terraform planets the technology behind electrostatic projectors was used to perform a type of electrolysis on the crust of a planet. The result was a device that could break apart solid objects. MDC's are massive, most over a hundred kilometers long and require tremendous energy to operate.

Mj – Refers to the mass of the planet Jupiter as of the year 2103. If something is said to have 9MJ that means it has nine times the mass of Jupiter.

MOS Sec – The MOS Security organization handles internal and external security around the MOS.

Nano, (nanoprobes, nanobots, etc…) – Refers to very small technology or robots. Something that is nanoscopic in size is one thousand times smaller than something that is microscopic in size.

Noctus – The name given for the lower caste of the Sirius system. The Noctus operate the mining platforms and refineries surrounding Sirius (Sirius A).

Pico, (picotech, picobots, etc…) – Refers to technology on a pico-scale—one thousand times smaller than nanotech.

After a series of accidents that nearly consumed an entire dwarf world, picotech research was banned in the Sol system.

Platoon – A military unit consisting of roughly 30 soldiers. In the TSF a standard Marine platoon has three squads, a staff sergeant (often a gunnery sergeant if it is a weapons platoon) and a second lieutenant as the platoon commander.

Railgun – Railguns fire physical rounds, usually small pellets at speeds up to 10 kilometers per second by pushing the round through the barrel via a magnetic field. The concept is similar to that of a maglev train, but to move a smaller object much faster. Railguns were first conceived of in 1918 and the first actual magnetic particle accelerator was built in 1950. Originally railguns were massive, sometimes kilometers in size. By the twenty-second century reliable versions as small as a conventional rifle had been created.

Larger versions take the form of orbital railgun platforms which can fire sabot rounds or grapeshot at speeds over a hundred-thousand kilometers per second.

Ramscoop – A type of starship fuel collection system and engine. They are sometimes also referred to as Bussard ramscoops or ramjets. Ramscoops were considered impractical due to the scarcity of interstellar hydrogen until electrostatic scoops were created that can capture atoms at a much more distant range and funnel them into a starship's engine.

Shorts – Because the Noctus live in lower gravity, they are quite tall. In contrast, the Lumins are a more standard human height (averaging just under two meters). As a result, the Noctus derogatively refer to them as Shorts.

SOC (Security Operations Center) – This is both the command organization for security on the *Intrepid* as well as the physical location on the ship where the offices of the SOC are located. The command organization has over two hundred humans and AIs working in the organization to oversee the security of the ship. Physical security departments, both internal and dockside do not operate directly out of the SOC, but have their own divisional locations within the ship.

Solar mass – A solar mass is an object with the mass of the Sol Star (Earth's sun) as of the year 2103.

SolGov – An abbreviation for Solar Government, SolGov was originally analogous to the early Earth U.N. It was the guiding governing body for the Sol system and interfaced with all of the many local governments across multiple worlds.

After the creation of the Sol Space Federation and the dissolution of the Solar Government, the term is still used to refer to the current government.

Sol Space Federation (SSF) – Formed in 3301, the Sol Space Federation became a true federal government for the entire Sol system. Unlike SolGov it has full legal authority over its constituent regional powers. The primary member states of the SSF are: The Terran Hegemony, the Mars Protectorate, the Jovian Combine, and the Scattered Worlds.

Squad – In the TSF Marines a squad consists of three fireteams. Headed up by a sergeant, the squad consist of 13 soldiers. Each squad within a platoon has a number, and each fireteam has a number. Thus, one/one refers to the first fireteam in the first squad in the platoon.

Stasis – Early stasis systems were invented in the year 2541 as a method of 'cryogenically' freezing organic matter without using extreme cold (or lack of energy) to do so. The effect is similar in that all atomic motion is ceased, but not by the removal of energy by gradual cooling, but by removing the ability of the surrounding space to accept that energy and motion. There are varying degrees of effectiveness of stasis systems. The FGT and other groups possess the ability to put entire planets in stasis, while other groups only have the technology to put small items, such as people, into stasis. Personal stasis is often still referred to as cryostasis, though there is no cryogenic process involved.

T3 (Tritium) – T3 (3H) is an isotope of hydrogen where the nucleus of the atom is made up of one proton and two neutrons as opposed to just a single proton and no neutrons in regular hydrogen (protium). T3 is radioactive and has a half-life of 12.32 years. It decays into Helium-3 through this process.

TSF – The Terran Space Force was originally the space force of the Terran Hegemony, but after the formation of the Sol Space Federation, the Terran Hegemony used its position of pre-eminence to make its military the federal military. Over the years, elements of different national and regional militaries merged into the TSF, bringing new elements and a mix of organizational structures to the military.

The space force is a mix of naval and army disciplines. It consists of sailors, Marines, pilots, and the regular army.

v – Represented as a lower case v in italics, this symbol stands for velocity. If a ship is increasing its speed it will be said that it is increasing *v*.

Vector – Vectors used are spatial vectors. Vector refers to both direction and rate of travel (speed or magnitude). Vector can be changed (direction) and increased (speed or magnitude).

PLACES

Alpha Centauri – A 3-star system, Alpha Centauri contains two yellow stars (originally known as simply A and B, but named Prima and Yogi after colonization) and a red dwarf known as Proxima which is the closet star to Sol.

Albion – The third planet in the Kapteyn's Star system, Albion is a terrestrial world that masses over that of seven Earths. It completes its orbit of Kapteyn's Star once every 121.5 days at an average orbital distance of 0.31AU. It has an orbital eccentricity of 0.23, which sometimes makes it the second planet in the Kapteyn's Star system.

The world spends much of its time outside the Kapteyn's Star system's habitable zone and does not have liquid water on its surface. Also, due to its mass, it is a high-*g* world with an average surface gravity of 2.1*g*.

Albion is orbited by twelve moons.

Anne – The solitary moon of Victoria. Anne is a carbon and silicate moon with no atmosphere or liquids. It is tidally locked to Victoria.

Brilliance Station – Orbital station over Incandus, the capital of the Sirius system.

Callisto – This moon is the 2nd largest orbiting Jupiter and is the third largest moon in the Sol system (following Ganymede and Triton). Its circumference is over 15,000 kilometers, compared to Luna's (Earth's moon) circumference of just under 11,000 kilometers, although before both moons were terraformed it was only half as dense as Luna.

In 3122 construction of the Callisto Orbital Habitat began around Callisto, a project which turned Callisto into the home of

3 trillion humans over the following millennia. By the year 3718 the mass of the orbital habitat greatly outweighed the mass of Callisto itself and the moon was anchored to the Cho. Because of this the Cho is now often referred to as a semi-orbital habitat.

During the construction of the Cho, there came a point where the multiple concentric rings obscured all view of space from the surface of Callisto. Ultimately the surface of the moon was reduced from a terraformed world to little more than a waste processing system for the orbital habitat. It is no longer considered a habitable world and no humans live there.

Cruithne (3735 Cruithne) – This asteroid, named after an early people of Ireland, was discovered in 1986. It is a unique asteroid which is in a 1:1 orbital resonance with Earth. This means, that with rare exception it is always on the same side of Sol as Earth and is spends half its time accelerating toward Earth, and the other half of its time accelerating away from earth.

From an Earth-bound perspective that makes Cruithne appear as though it is orbiting Earth, and when it was first discovered it was thought to be Earth's second moon.

Originally a 5 kilometer asteroid, Cruithne quickly became a significant trading hub because of its ability to function as a useful cargo slingshot platform to OuterSol. Cruithne is not a part of any planetary government, nor does it fall under the jurisdiction of the Terran Hegemony. It is, however, subject to the Sol Space Federation.

High Terra – As the second planetary ring created, (completed in 2519), High Terra is more elegant than the M1R, though Earth's planetary ring has slightly less habitable space than its Marsian counterpart. The ring also houses the city of Raleigh, which is the capital of both Earth and the Terran hegemony.

High Victoria – The station at the top of Victoria's space elevator is named High Victoria after Earth's ring. The initial station was completed only eleven years after the *Hyperion* accords.

Ignitus – Name of the innermost planet orbiting Sirius (Sirius A). This world was originally named Vishnu, but after the Luminescent Society gained control of the Sirius system, it was renamed.

InnerSol – This is the common name for the both the region of the inner solar system as well as the political groups that comprise that region. The boundary for InnerSol is nominally the main asteroid belt, but this is somewhat nebulous because some worlds within the belt are considered part of InnerSol (such as Ceres) while other sections, such as the Trojan asteroids are part of the Jovian Combine and thus in OuterSol.

Jovian Combine – The JC encapsulates all worlds in OuterSol—most notably Jupiter, Saturn, Neptune, and all their satellites. After the construction of the Cho, Jovian space began an upward rise toward not only housing the majority of all the humans in the galaxy, but also becoming the center or commerce and culture. In the year 4123 InnerSol and the Terran dominated SolGov was facing a regional government that was effectively more powerful than the federal government.

Jupiter – The largest planet in the Sol System, Jupiter has more mass than all the other planets combined.

In 2644 a process of heating up Jupiter was initiated. Targeted impacts of KBOs (Kuiper belt objects) caused pressure waves in the planet's hydrogen clouds. These waves triggered fusion in deuterium rich layers of Jupiter. This process has not made Jupiter a brown dwarf, or a star of any kind, it is just a much hotter planet, providing warmth and energy for the worlds nearby.

This process has been refined over the years and now the warming effect is generated by accumulating and igniting pools of Helium3 within Jupiter.

Kapteyn's Star – This star is 12.8 light-years from Sol and has the second highest relative motion to Sol of all the stars in the human sphere. Kapteyn's is estimated to be over ten billion years old and was formed in a dwarf galaxy outside the Milky Way. Unlike most stars it has a polar orbit around the galactic core and also orbits the galaxy retrograde. It spends most of its time above or below the disk of the galaxy.

Because of its age, Kapteyn's has fewer heavy elements and has a more bluish tint than most red dwarfs. It also has 32% of Sol's mass and 7% of its luminosity.

Kapteyn's is orbited by two major planets and seven larger dwarf worlds. It has also picked up hundreds of small worlds and asteroids during its journeys through the cosmos.

Its planets (in nominal order) are:

- Victoria (major planet)
- Alexandria
- Albion (major planet)
- Athens
- Sparta
- Knossos
- Perseus (location of the gamma site research facility)
- Troy
- Tarsis

Kap, The – The name the crew of the *Intrepid* calls "Kapteyn's Star". Similar to "the Sun".

Landfall – The capital of the Victoria colony. At the time of the Battle of Victoria the city had a population of two million.

LHS 1565 / GJ 1061 – Named “Estrella de la Muerte” by the crew of the *Intrepid* as it passed through the system, this star is a small red dwarf 12 light-years from Sol. With a diameter not much larger than Jupiter’s it has roughly 11% the mass of Sol and 1% its luminosity. No significant planetary objects exist in the system which only possesses a few asteroid belts.

Lucent (Sirius B) – The second star in the Sirius system, formerly known as Sirius B. This white-dwarf remnant has a strong magnetic shield which protects the worlds and habitats there from the harsh radiation of Sirius A.

Luminescent Space – The region of space surrounding Lucent, the second star in the Sirius system. This space is largely restricted only to members of Luminescent Society.

Mars Inner Shipyards (MIS) – After the MCEE was constructed, which made it possible to dock at a station further out from Mars and have materials transported down the gravity well, the Mars Inner Shipyards were constructed. Because high-tech manufacturing was occurring on the M1R as well, it became a better location for shipbuilding than the MOS and through the latter half of the fourth millennia and beginning of the fifth it overtook the MOS as InnerSol’s premier shipyard.

Mars 1 Ring (M1R or MIR) – The first planetary ring’s construction began in the year 2215 and through a massive effort was completed in 2391. The ring is just over 1600 kilometers wide and wraps around Mars at the planet’s geosynchronous orbital point making it 128,400 kilometers long.

The ring is not flat like a natural ring (such as Saturn’s) but faces the planet. It does not orbit at a speed to match the surface of Mars, but rotates at a slower speed to provide exactly 1*g* of gravity on the inside surface. Walls over 100 kilometers high line the inside of the ring and hold in atmosphere. The total surface area of the ring is 205 million kilometers. This is half the surface area of Earth and 72% more area than Earth’s landmass.

Considering that M1R has hundreds of levels it contains more than 100 times the surface area of planet Earth.

The completion of M1R definitively proved that mankind's future home was in space and not on the surface of worlds. In the year 4123 the population of the M1R had reached over seven hundred billion people.

Mars Protectorate – is the name for the political entity that encapsulates Mars, its moons, the Mars 1 Ring, and several asteroids in the main asteroid belt.

MCEE – The Mars Central Elevator Exchange is a secondary orbital ring around the planet Mars, which connects all of the outer habitats and shipyards to the Mars 1 Ring (M1R). Because of the need to keep gravity under 1*g*, all habitats and shipyards connected to the M1R must orbit Mars at a slower speed than the main ring. As a result, they must connect to it via elevators which can move along the surface of the MCEE. Maglev elevators can then travel from locations such as the Mars Outer Shipyards to the M1R without requiring passengers or cargo to transfer to other transports.

Mars Outer Shipyards (MOS) – This shipyard was once the premier shipyard in all of the Sol system. Built in 3229, the shipyard's main structure is over 1000 kilometers in length with thousands of cubic kilometers of equipment and detached service yards surrounding it. The shipyard's pre-eminence faded as the conditions which made the MIS more economical improved. In 4123 it was still one of the busiest shipyards in the Sol system, but until it won the *Intrepid*'s contract it had not done a high-profile build in decades.

New Eden – Known on charts as 82 Eridani, this stellar system was terraformed by the FGT in the late forty-first and early forty-second centuries. The stellar primary is a Sol-like star with two Earth-like planets in orbit.

"New Eden" also is the name the colonists gave to the first of the two Earth-like worlds in the system.

Noctilucent Space – This region of the Sirius system is the area around Sirius (Sirius A) where the Noctus people work the Lumin refineries and mining platforms. It is a harsh region filled with radiation from Sirius and navigational hazards from a millennia of mining.

OuterSol – Is the region of space between the main asteroid belt and the inside of the main Kuiper belt—though this has shifted as political entities shift.

Perseus – The seventh planet in the Kapteyn's Star system, Perseus is a cold, ice-world with an average orbital distance of 7AU from its host star. The world is small, but has a higher than average density for the system. Surface gravity is 0.36*g*.

Perseus is known as the Gamma site and is where Earnest's secret picotech research base is located.

Radius – The seventh moon of the gas giant, Nacreous, which orbits Sirius (Sirius A). This moon is a resort world for Luminescent Society.

Sol – This is the name of the star which in antiquity was simply referred to as 'The Sun'. Because humans call the star that lights up their daytime sky 'the sun' in every system it became common practice to refer to Sol by its proper name.

Sol system – The Sol system used to be referred to as the solar system. However, as humans began to first think about, and then actually colonize other stellar systems it became obvious that the term was very Sol-centric. The common usage became to call the systems simply by the name of the star. For example: Tau Ceti system, Alpha Centauri system, etc... Because humankind's home star is named Sol, the term Sol system came into use.

Scattered Worlds – is a political entity that contains many of the trans-Neptunian worlds. Its nominal inner border is the main Kuiper belt and its outer border is the Hills Oort cloud. The capital of the Scattered Worlds is Makemake.

Tara – Named for the stone of Tara in Ireland, Tara is the second moon of Albion. Tara is not originally from the Kapteyn's Star system and has a higher density and metalicity than other worlds in the system.

The moon has a diameter 0.9 times the size of Earth's, a mass of 0.8 Earths, and a density of 3.1g/cm3. As a result, the average surface gravity of Tara is 0.5*g*.

Though Tara's parent world, Albion, spends much of its time outside the Kapteyn's Star system's habitable zone, Tara has a molten core—largely due to its proximity to Albion, and a thick atmosphere due to volcanism. At the time of colonization, the world already had liquid water on its surface.

Tara is the location of the second colony in the Kapteyn's Star system and is often referred to as the "beta site."

Terra – While this is the Latin name for the Earth and—though there are some exceptions—the term is not commonly used to refer to the planet itself. Rather, *Terra* encompasses Earth, High Terra and Luna (as well as the assorted nations within the Terran sphere of influence).

Terran Hegemony – This is the official name for the InnerSol worlds either directly governed by Terra, or existing well within its geo-political influence. Notable worlds in the Terran Hegemony are Venus and Mercury.

Toro (1685 Toro) – Toro is an asteroid that has a resonant 5:8 orbit with Earth and a 5:13 resonant orbit with Venus. This means for every 5 of Earth's orbits and every 8 of Toro's, it orbits Sol in resonance with the Earth. During that period, it appears as though Toro orbits the Earth. It also makes for cost effective cargo transfer to Toro during that period. Toro, like Cruithne also is a useful slingshot accelerator for cargo being sent to OuterSol.

The original asteroid was roughly 3 kilometers in diameter, but subsequent construction expanded it irregularly by several more kilometers. It was made famous by what has been termed 'The Massacre of Toro', an event in which Tanis Richards played a key role.

Victoria – Victoria orbits Kapteyn's Star at an average distance of 0.17AU and completes its year every 48.6 days. Because of its proximity to Kapteyn's Star, the world is tidally locked with one side always facing its host star.

Victoria masses at 4.9 Earths with an average density of 1.1g/cm3. Given a diameter 3x that of Earth, it has a surface gravity of 0.6*g*.

The terraforming and colonization of Victoria began in 4253 and was completed one hundred and forty years later.

Victoria is the primary world of the Kapteyn's Star system with its capital being Landfall.

Vishnu – See Ignitus.

PEOPLE

Intrepid / ISF

Abby Redding – Engineer responsible for building the *Intrepid.*

Amanda – One of the two human AI interfaces for the *Intrepid.*

Amy Lee – First Lieutenant who works in the *Intrepid* Security Operations Center.

Angela – A military intelligence sentient AI embedded within Tanis.

Bob – Bob is the name Amanda gave to the *Intrepid's* primary AI after she was installed as its human avatar. She chose the name because she claims it suits him, though only she and Priscilla understand why. Bob is perhaps the most advanced AI ever created. He is the child of seventeen very unique and well regarded AIs. He also has portions of his neural network reflecting the minds of the Reddings. He is the first AI to be multi-nodal, to have each of those nodes be as powerful as the largest NSAI, and to remain sane and cogent.

Bourke – Chief of the main Victorian refinery outside Landfall.

Brandt – Initially the commander of the first Marine Battalion aboard the *Intrepid*, Brandt eventually became the commandant of the Marine forces in the ISF.

Carson – A fighter pilot from Sol, Carson is with the *Andromeda* when it battles the three Sirian scout ships.

Corsia – The AI operating the *ISF Andromeda*.

Earnest Redding – Engineer responsible for much of the *Intrepid's* design. Earnest is one of the leading scientific minds in the Sol system and was responsible for much of Terrance Enfield's success.

Erin – New Eden colony leader responsible for orbital space station construction.

Gerald – New Eden colony leader responsible for city planning and engineering.

Jason Andrews – An old spacer who has completed several interstellar journeys. Captain of the *Intrepid*.

Jessica Keller – A TBI (Terran Bureau of Investigations) officer who was chasing after Myrrdan, Jessica was found by Tanis in a stasis pod with no record of how she got there.

Jessica's experience with police procedure was useful in setting up the Victorian police force and academy. She also became an accomplished pilot in the ISF.

Joseph Evans – ISF Colonel, Joseph Evans is one of the ISF's top pilots and goes on to found the Victorian Space Academy.

Myrrdan – Often referred to as serial killer, murder, madman, and terrorist, Myrrdan was thought to be behind hundreds of atrocities in the Sol system. The command crew of the *Intrepid* believes him to be aboard their ship, attempting to gain access to the picotech.

Ouri – ISF Colonel responsible for the *Intrepid's* security.

Pearson – Commander of the *Andromeda's* fighter wings during the battle with the three Sirian scout ships.

Petrov – Pilot of the *Andromeda* during the battle with Yusuf's cruiser in the Kapteyn's Star system.

Phung – Marine Major who musters the assault transports during the operation to rescue the *Intrepid's* leadership from Landfall.

Priscilla – One of the two human AI interfaces for the *Intrepid.*

Dr. Rosenberg – Chief medical officer on the *Intrepid*.

Sergey – New Eden head of space-borne engineering.

Simon – Head of biology and organic terraforming and for New Eden colony.

Sue – Originally partnered with Trist, Sue went on to become the ship's AI on the Dresden.

Tanis Richards – Former TSF counterinsurgency officer, Tanis has held the ranks of major, lieutenant colonel, and general on the *Intrepid*. She was born on February 29th, 4052 on Mars.

Terrance Enfield – Financial backer for the *Intrepid*.

Tony – New Eden head of planetary engineering.

Trist – Former thief from the Callisto Orbital Habitat, Trist was left to die in a vat of silbio and ended up on the *Intrepid*. She was instrumental in getting Trent to reveal himself on Mars 1, and has since held a variety of roles assisting Tanis and the *Intrepid's* leadership.

Troy – AI pilot of the heavy tug, *Excelsior.*

Sirius / Victoria

Agnes – Markus's assistant as administrator of the SK87 mining platform.

Dmitry – Chief engineer of the *Hyperion* (SK87) mining platform.

Han – Major Han was the commander of the strike team on the Luminescent interceptor which was sent after the SK87 platform.

Huan – SK87 tug operator.

Irek – SK87 tug operator.

James – SK87 yard boss and close confidant of Markus.

Katrina – Daughter of Yusuf, Katrina is a former member of the Luminescent Society in Sirius. She was a spy for the Luminescents until she decided to switch sides and assisted Markus and the people of mining platform SK87 in their rebellion.

Luther – Luminescent Overseer of the SK87 mining platform.

Markus – Platform administrator of SK87, Markus ultimately formed a rebellion and exodus of his people on their mining platform from the Sirius system. Markus was the president of the Victorian colony for the first thirty years of its existence.

Sarah – A founding member of the *Hyperion's* rebellion, Sarah is a fiery woman who is often at odds with the Edeners and even her own people. She is the mother of the Victorian president at the time of the Battle for Victoria.

Simon – Markus's assistant who was killed by Yusuf on Brilliance Station.

Steven – Assistant to Luther, the Overseer of platform SK87.

Timmur – *Hyperion* (SK87) tug operator.

Tom – Son of Sarah and Peter, Tom went into politics early and served four terms as president of the Victorian colony before being killed by Myrrdan.

Yolanda – Noctus persona used by Katrina when undercover in Noctilucent space.

Intrepid Space Force Marine 1st Battalion

The ISF Bravo company was a part of the honor guard at Markus's funeral. In the following action they were re-enforced by the platoons from Alpha and X-Ray company.

Alpha Company

4th Platoon

Platoon Commander – Lieutenant Usef

Bravo Company

2nd Platoon

Platoon Commander – Lieutenant Smith

Squad 1

Squad leader – Sergeant Lee

Fireteam 1 (one/one)
Ready – PFC Lindsey
Team – Corporal Hill
Fire – PFC Bauer
Assist – PFC Timmins

Fireteam 2 (one/two)
Ready – PFC Sarin
Team – Lance Corporal Nair
Fire – PFC Ramos
Assist – PFC Sergey

X-Ray Company

1st Platoon

Platoon Commander – Lieutenant Borden

ABOUT THE AUTHOR

Michael Cooper likes to think of himself as a jack-of-all-trades (and hopes to become master of a few). When not writing, he can be found writing software, working in his shop on his latest carpentry project, or perhaps reading a book.

He shares his home with a precocious young girl, his wonderful wife (who also writes), a cat, a never-ending list of things he would like to build, and ideas...

Find out what's coming next at www.aeon14.com

87562857R00207

Made in the USA
Columbia, SC
15 January 2018